A FRIENDSHIP BEGINS

Killashandra watched as the stranger pressed a code then stepped before the screen. She politely moved back.

"Control? The shuttle that just landed can't be permitted to take off. Half the crystals in the drive must be overheating. Can't you tell from the ejection velocity monitor? . . . Well, now that's more reasonable," he continued after a moment. "I'm Carrik of the Heptite Guild, Ballybran—Yes, that's what I said. I could hear the secondary sonics right through the walls, so I damn well know there's overheating." Another pause. "Thanks, but I've paid my bill already. . . . Oh, as you will." He glanced at Killashandra. "Make that for two," he added, grinning at her as he turned from the console. He cupped his hand under Killashandra's elbow and steered her toward a secluded booth.

"But, I've a bottle of wine at my table—" she said, half protesting, half laughing at his peremptory escort.

"You'll have better shortly. I'm Carrik and you're . . . ?"

"Killashandra Ree."

He smiled, gray eyes lighting briefly with surprise. "That's a lovely name."

It looked as if her luck was about to change.

Also by Anne McCaffrey
Published by Ballantine Books:

DRAGONFLIGHT
DRAGONQUEST
THE WHITE DRAGON

ALCHEMY AND ACADEME

DINOSAUR PLANET

THE SHIP WHO SANG

TO RIDE PEGASUS

DECISION AT DOONA

CRYSTAL
SINGER

ANNE McCAFFREY

A DEL REY BOOK

BALLANTINE BOOKS • NEW YORK

A Del Rey Book
Published by Ballantine Books

Library of Congress Catalog Card Number: 82-4009

ISBN 0-345-28598-0

Manufactured in the United States of America

First Edition: August 1982

Cover art by Michael Whelan

To Kate and Alec and their children

Author's Note

Crystal Singer is based on four stories originally published in Roger Elwood's *Continuum* series. *Crystal Singer* is considerably expanded from these stories, thanks to the technical assistance of Ron Massey, Langshot Stables, Surrey. His long explanations and careful notes permitted me to venture daringly where no man had gone before.

CHAPTER 1

Killashandra listened as the words dropped with leaden fatality into her frozen belly. She stared at the maestro's famous profile as his lips opened and shut around the words that meant the death of all her hopes and ambitions and rendered ten years of hard work and study a waste.

The maestro finally turned to face her. The genuine regret in his expressive eyes made him look older. The heavy singer's muscles in his jaw relaxed sorrowfully into jowls.

One day, Killashandra might remember those details. Just then, she was too crushed by overwhelming defeat to be aware of more than her terrible personal failure.

"But . . . but . . . how *could* you?"

"How could I what?" the maestro asked in surprise.

"How *could* you lead me on?"

"Lead you on? But, my dear girl, I didn't."

"You did! You said—you said all I needed was hard work. Haven't I worked hard enough?"

"Of course you have worked hard." Valdi was affronted. "My students must apply themselves. It takes years of hard work to develop the voice, to learn even a segment of the outworld repertoire that must be performed."

"I've repertoire! I've worked hard and now—*now* you tell me I've no voice?"

1

Maestro Valdi sighed heavily, a mannerism that had always irritated Killashandra and was now insupportable. She opened her mouth to protest, but he raised a restraining hand. The habit of four years made her pause.

"You haven't the voice to be a *top-rank* singer, my dear Killashandra, but that does not preclude any of the many other responsible and fulfilling . . ."

"I won't be second rank. I want—I *wanted*"—and she had the satisfaction of seeing him wince at the bitterness in her voice—"to be a top-rank concert singer. You said I had—"

He held up his hand again. "You have the gift of perfect pitch, your musicality is faultless, your memory superb, your dramatic potential can't be criticized. But there is that burr in your voice which becomes intolerable in the higher register. While I *thought* it could be trained out, modified—" he shrugged his helplessness. He eyed her sternly. "Today's audition with completely impartial judges proved conclusively that the flaw is inherent in the voice. This moment is cruel for you and not particularly pleasant for me." He gave her another stern look, reacting to the rebellion in her stance. "I make few errors in judgment as to voice. I honestly thought I could help you. I cannot, and it would be doubly cruel of me to encourage you further as a soloist. No. You had best strengthen another facet of your potential."

"And what, in your judgment, would that be?"

He had the grace to blink at her caustic words, then looked her squarely in the eye. "You don't have the patience to teach, but you could do very well in one of the theater arts where your sympathy with the problems of a singer would stand you in good stead. No? You are a trained synthesizer? Hmmmm. Too bad, your musical education would be a real asset there." He paused. "Well, then, I'd recommend you leave the theater arts entirely. With your sense of pitch, you could be a crystal tuner or an aircraft and shuttle dispatcher or—"

"Thank you, maestro," she said, more from force of habit than any real gratitude. She gave him the half bow his rank required and withdrew.

Slamming the panel shut behind her, Killashandra stalked down the corridor, blinded by the tears she'd been too proud to shed in the maestro's presence. Though she half wanted and half feared meeting a fellow student who would question her tears and commiserate with her disaster, she was inordinately relieved to reach her study cubicle without having encountered anyone. There she gave herself up to her misery, bawling into hysteria, past choking, until she was too spent to do more than gasp for breath.

If her body protested the emotional excess, her mind reveled in it. For she had been abused, misused, misguided, misdirected—and who knows how many of her peers had been secretly laughing at her dreams of glorious triumphs on the concert and opera stage? Killashandra had a generous portion of the conceit and ego required for her chosen profession, with no leavening of humility; she'd felt success and stardom were only a matter of time. Now she cringed at the vivid memory of her self-assertiveness and arrogance. She had approached the morning's audition with such confidence, the requisite commendations to continue as a solo aspirant a foregone conclusion. She remembered the faces of the examiners, so pleasantly composed; one man nodding absent-mindedly to the pulse of the test arias and lieder. She'd been scrupulous in tempi; they'd marked her high on that. How could they have looked so—so impressed? So encouraging?

How could they record such verdicts against her?

"The voice is unsuited to the dynamics of opera. Unpleasant burr too audible." "A good instrument for singing with orchestra and chorus where grating overtone will not be noticeable." "Strong choral leader quality: student should be positively dissuaded from solo work."

Unfair! Unfair! How could she be allowed to come so far, be permitted to delude herself, only to be dashed down in the penultimate trial? And to be offered, as a sop, choral leadership! How degradingly ignominious!

From her excruciating memories wriggled up the faces of her brothers and sisters, taunting her for what they called "shrieking at the top of her lungs." Teasing her for the hours she spent on finger exercises and attempting to "understand" the harmonics of odd off-world music. Her parents had surrendered to Killashandra's choice of profession because it was, at the outset, financed by Fuerte's planetary educational system; second, it might accrue to their own standing in the community; and third, she had the encouragement of her early vocal and instrumental teachers. Them! Was it the ineptitude of one of those clods to which she owed the flaw in her voice? Killashandra rolled in an agony of self-pity.

What was it Valdi had had the temerity to suggest? An allied art? A synthesizer? Bah! Spending her life in mental institutions catering to flawed minds because she had a flawed voice? Or mending flawed crystals to keep interplanetary travel or someone's power plant flowing smoothly?

Then she realized her despondency was merely self-pity and sat upright, staring at herself in the mirror on the far wall, the mirror that had reflected all those long hours of study and self-perfection. Self-deception!

In an instant, Killashandra shook herself free of such wallowing self-indulgence. She looked around the study, a slice of a room dominated by the Vidifax, with its full address keyboard that interfaced with the Music Record Center, providing access to a galaxy's musical output. She glanced over the repros of training performances—she'd always had a lead role—and she knew that she would do best to forget the whole damned thing! If she couldn't be at the top, to hell with theater arts! She'd be top in whatever she did or die in the attempt.

She stood. There was nothing for her now in a room that three hours before had been the focal point of every waking minute and all her energies. Whatever personal items remained in the drawers or on the shelves, the merit awards on the wall, the signed holograms of singers she'd hoped to emulate or excel, no longer concerned her or belonged to her.

She reached for her cloak, ripped off the student badge, and flung the garment across one shoulder. As she wheeled around, she saw a note tacked on the door.

Party at Roare's to celebrate!

She snorted. They'd all know. Let them chortle over her downfall. She'd not play the bravely smiling, coura-geous-under-adversity role tonight. Or ever.

Exit Killashandra, quietly, stage center, she thought as she ran down the long shallow flight of steps to the mall in front of the Culture Center. Again, she experienced both satisfaction and regret that no one witnessed her departure.

Actually, she couldn't have asked for a more dramatic exit. Tonight, they'd wonder what had happened. Maybe someone would know. She knew that Valdi would never disclose their interview; he disliked failures; especially his own, so they'd never hear about it from him. As for the verdict of the examiners, at least the exact wording handed her would be computer sealed. But someone would know that Killashandra Ree had failed her vocal finals and the grounds for failure.

Meanwhile she would have effectively disappeared. They could speculate all they wanted—nothing would stop them from that—and they'd remember her when she rose to prominence in another field. Then they'd marvel that noth-ing so minor as failure could suppress her excellence.

Such reflections consoled Killashandra all the way to her lodgings. Subsidized students rated dwellings—no more the depressing bohemian semifilth and overcrowding of an-cient times—but her room was hardly palatial. When she failed to reregister at the Music Center, her landlady would be notified and the room locked to her. Subsistence living was abhorrent to Killashandra; it smacked of an inability to achieve. But she'd take the initiative on that, too, and leave the room now. And all the memories it held. Besides, it would spoil the mystery of her disappearance if she were to be discovered in her digs. So, with a brief nod to the landlady, who always checked comings and goings, Killa-shandra climbed the stairs to her floor, keyed open her room, and looked around. There was really nothing to take but clothing.

Despite that assessment, Killashandra packed the lute that she had handcrafted to satisfy that requirement of her profession. She might not care to play the thing, but she couldn't bear to abandon it. She packed it among the clothes in her carisak, which she looped over her back. She closed the door panel, skipped down the stairs, nodded to the landlady exactly as she always did, and left quietly.

Having fulfilled the dramatic requirement of her new role, she hadn't any idea what to do with herself. She slipped from walk-on to the fastbelt of the pedestrian way, heading into the center of the city. She ought to register with a work bureau; she ought to apply for subsistence. She ought to do many things, but suddenly Killashandra discovered that "ought to" no longer ruled her. No more tedious commitments to schedule—rehearsals, lessons, studies. She was free, utterly and completely free! With a lifetime ahead of her that ought to be filled. Ought to? With what?

The walkway was whipping her rapidly into the busier sections of the city. Pedestrian directions flashed at crosspoints: mercantile triangle purple crossed with social services' circle orange; green check manufactory and dormitory blue hatching, medical green-red stripes and then airport arrow red and spaceport star-spangled blue. Killashandra, paralyzed by indecision, toyed with the variety of things she ought to do, and was carried past the crosspoints that would take her where she ought to go.

Ought to, again, she thought, and stayed on the speedway. Half of Killashandra was amused that she, once so certain of her goal, could now be so irresolute. At that moment it did not occur to her that she was suffering an intense, traumatic shock or that she was reacting to that shock—first, in a somewhat immature fashion by her abrupt withdrawal from the center; second, in a more mature manner, as she divorced herself from the indulgence of self-pity and began a positive search for an alternate life.

She could not know that at that very moment Esmond Valdi was concerned, realizing that the girl would be reacting in some fashion to the demise of her ambition. Had she known, she might have thought more kindly of him, though he hadn't pursued her beyond her study nor done more than call the Personnel Section to report his concern. He'd come to the reassuring conclusion that she had sought refuge with a fellow student, probably having a good cry. Knowing her dedication to music, he'd incorrectly assumed that she'd continue in the study of music, accepting a choral leadership in due time. That's where he wanted her, and it simply did not occur to Valdi that Killashandra would discard ten years of her life in a second.

CHAPTER 2

Killashandra was halfway to the spaceport before she consciously decided that that was where she ought to go—"ought" this time not in an obligatory but in an investigative sense. Fuerte held nothing but distressing memories for her. She'd leave the planet and erase the painful associations. Good thing she had taken the lute. She had sufficient credentials to be taken on as a casual entertainer on some liner at the best or as a ship attendant at the worst. She might as well travel about a bit to see what else she *ought* to do with her life.

As the speedway slowed to curve into the spaceport terminal, Killashandra was aware of externals—people and things—for the first time since she'd left Maestro Valdi's studio. She had never been to the spaceport before and had never been on any of the welcoming committees for off-planet stellars. Just then, a shuttle launched from its bay, powerful engines making the port building tremble. There was, however, a very disconcerting whine of which she was almost subliminally aware, sensing it from the mastoid bone right down to her heel. She shook her head. The whine intensified—it had to be coming from the shuttle—until she was forced to clamp her hands over her ears. The sonics abated, and she forgot the incident as she wandered around the immense, domed reception hall of the port facility. Vidifax were ranked across the inner segment, each labeled with the name of a particular freight or passenger service, each with its own screen plate. Faraway places with strange sounding names—a fragment from an ancient song obtruded and was instantly suppressed. No more music.

She paused at a portal to watch a shuttle off-loading cargo, the loading attendants using pneumatic pallets to shift odd-sized packages that did not fit the automatic cargo-handling ramp. A supercargo was scurrying about, portentously examining strip codes, juggling weight units, and arguing with the stevedores. Killashandra snorted. She'd soon have more than such trivia to occupy her energies. Suddenly, she caught the scent of appetizing odors.

She realized she was hungry! Hungry? When her whole *life* had been shattered? How banal! But the odors made her mouth water. Well, her credit ought to be good for a meal, but she'd better check her balance rather than be embarrassed at the restaurant. At a public outlet, she inserted her digital wristunit and applied her right thumb to the print plate. She was agreeably surprised to note that a credit had been added that very day—a student credit, she read. Her last. That the total represented a bonus did not please her. A bonus to solemnize the fact that she could never be a soloist?

She walked quickly to the nearest restaurant, observing only that it was not the economy service. The old, dutiful Killashandra would have backed out hastily. The new Killashandra entered imperiously. So early in the day, the dining rooms were not crowded, so she chose a booth on the upper level for its unobstructed view of the flow of shuttles and small spacecraft. She had never realized how much traffic passed through the spaceport of her not very important planet, though she vaguely knew that Fuerte was a transfer point. The vidifax menu was long and varied, and she was tempted several times to indulge in the exotic foods temptingly described therein. But she settled for a casserole, purportedly composed of off-world fish, unusual but not too highly spiced for a student's untutored palate.

An off-world wine included in the selection pleased her so much that she ordered a second carafe just as dusk closed in.

She thought, at first, that it was the unfamiliar wine that made her nerves jangle so. But the discomfort increased so rapidly that she sensed it couldn't be just the effect of alcohol. Rubbing her neck and frowning, she looked around for the source of irritation. Finally, the appearance of a descending shuttle's retroblasts made her realize that her discomfort must be the result of a sonic disturbance, though how it could penetrate the shielded restaurant she didn't know. She covered her ears, pressing as hard as she could to ease that piercing pain. Suddenly, it ceased.

"I tell you, that shuttle's drive is about to explode. Now connect me to the control supervisor," a baritone voice cried in the ensuing silence.

Startled, Killashandra looked around.

"How do I know? I know!" At the screen of the restaurant's service console, a tall man was demanding: "Put me through to the control tower. Is everyone up there deaf? So you *want* a shuttle explosion the next time that one is used? Didn't you hear it?"

"I heard it," Killashandra said, rushing over to plant herself in the view of the console.

"You heard it?" The spaceport official seemed genuinely surprised.

"I certainly did. All but cracked my skull. My ears still hurt. What was it?" she asked the tall man, who had an air of command about him, frustrated though he was by officious stupidity. He carried his overlean body with an arrogance that suited the fine fabric of his clothes—obviously of off-world design and cloth.

"She heard it too, man. Now, get the control tower."

"Really, sir . . ."

"Don't be a complete subbie," Killashandra snapped.

That she was obviously a Fuertan like himself disturbed the official more than the insult. Then the stranger, ripping off an oath as colorful as it was descriptive of idiocy, flipped open a card case drawn from his belt. Whatever identification he showed made the official's eyes bulge.

"I'm sorry, sir. I didn't realize, sir."

Killashandra watched as the man pressed out a code, then his image dissolved into a view of the control tower. The off-worlder stepped squarely before the screen, and Killashandra politely moved back.

"Control? The shuttle that just landed can't be permitted to take off; it's resonating so badly half the crystals in the drive must be overheating. Didn't anyone up there hear the beat frequency? It's broadcasting secondary sonics. No, this is not a drunk and not a threat. This is a fact. Is your entire control staff tone deaf? Don't you take efficiency readings for your shuttles? Can't you tell from the ejection velocity monitor? What does a drive check cost in comparison to a new port facility? Is this shuttlestop world too poor to employ a crystal tuner or a stoker?

"Well, now that's a more reasonable attitude," said the stranger after a moment. "As to my credentials, I'm Carrik of the Heptite Guild, Ballybran. Yes, that's what I said. I could hear the secondary sonics right through the walls, so I damn well know there's overheating. I'm glad the uneven drive thrust has registered on your monitors, so get that shuttle decoked and retuned." Another pause. "Thanks, but I've paid my bill already. No, that's all right. Yes . . ." and Killashandra observed that the gratitude irritated Carrik. "Oh, as you will." He glanced at Killashandra. "Make that for two," he added, grinning at her as he turned from the console. "After all, you heard it as well." He cupped his hand under Killashandra's elbow and steered her toward a secluded booth.

"I've a bottle of wine over there," she said, half protesting, half laughing at his peremptory escort.

"You'll have better shortly. I'm Carrik and you're . . . ?"

"Killashandra Ree."

He smiled, gray eyes lighting briefly with surprise. "That's a lovely name."

"Oh, come now. You can do better than that?"

He laughed, absently blotting the sweat on his forehead and upper lip as he slid into his place.

"I can and I will, but it *is* a lovely name. A musical one."

She winced.

"What did I say wrong?"

"Nothing. Nothing."

He glanced at her skeptically just as a chilled bottle slid from the service panel.

Carrik peered at the label. "A '72—well, that's astonishing." He flipped the menu vidifax. "I wonder if they stock Forellan biscuits and Aldebaran paste?—Oh, they do! Well, I might revise my opinion of Fuerte."

"Really, I only just finished—"

"On the contrary, my dear Killashandra Ree, you've only just begun."

"Oh?" Any of Killashandra's associates would have modified his attitude instantly at that tone in her voice.

"Yes," Carrik continued blithely, a sparkling challenge in his eyes, "for this is a night for feasting and frolicking—on the management, as it were. Having just saved the port from being leveled, my wish, and yours, is their command. They'll be even more grateful when they take the drive down and see the cracks in the transducer crystals. Off the true by a hundred vibes at least."

Her half-formed intention of making a dignified exit died, and she stared at Carrik. It would take a highly trained ear to catch so small a variation in pitch.

"Off a hundred vibes? What do you mean? Are you a musician?"

Carrik stared at her as if she ought to know who or what he was. He looked around to see where the attendant had gone and then, leaning indolently back in the seat, smiled at her enigmatically.

"Yes, I'm a kind of musician. Are you?"

"Not anymore." Killashandra replied in her most caustic tone. Her desire to leave returned immediately. She had managed very briefly to forget why she was at a spaceport. Now he had reminded her, and she wanted no more such reminders.

As she began to rise, his hand, fingers gripping firmly the flesh of her arm, held her in her seat. Just then, an official bustled into the restaurant, his eyes searching for Carrik. His countenance simulated relief and delight as he hurried to the table. Carrik smiled at Killashandra, daring her to contest his restraint in front of the witness. Despite her inclination, Killashandra realized she couldn't start a scene. Besides, she had no real grounds yet for charging personal-liberty infringement. Carrik, fully aware of her dilemma, had the audacity to offer her a toast as he took the traditional sample sip of the wine.

"Yes, sir, the '72. A very good choice. Surely, you'll . . ."

The serving panel opened on a slightly smoking dish of biscuits and a platter of a reddish-brown substance.

"But, of course, Forellan biscuits and Aldebaran paste. Served with warmed biscuits, I see. Your caterers do know their trade," Carrik remarked with feigned surprise.

"We may be small at Fuerte in comparison to other ports you've seen," the official began obsequiously.

"Yes, yes, thank you." Carrik brusquely waved the man away.

Killashandra stared after the fellow, wondering that he hadn't claimed insult for such a careless dismissal.

"How do you get away with such behavior?"

Carrik smiled. "Try the wine, Killashandra." His smile suggested that the evening would be long, and a prelude to a more intimate association.

"Who are you?" she demanded, angry now.

"I'm Carrik of the Heptite Guild," he repeated cryptically.

"And that gives you the right to infringe on my personal freedom?"

"It does if you heard that crystal whine."

"And how do you figure that?"

"Your opinion of the wine, Killashandra Ree? Surely your throat must be dry, and I imagine you've a skull ache from that subsonic torture, which would account for your shrewish temper."

Actually, she did have a pain at the base of her neck. He was right, too, about the dryness of her throat—and about her shrewish temper. But he had modified his criticism by stroking her hand.

"I must apologize for my bad manners," he began with no display of genuine remorse but with a charming smile. "Those shuttle drive-harmonics can be unnerving. It brings out the worst in us."

She nodded agreement as she sipped the wine. It was a fine vintage. She looked up with delight and pleasure. He patted her arm and gestured her to drink up.

"Who are you, Carrik of the Heptite Guild, that port authorities listen and control towers order exorbitant delicacies in gratitude?"

"You really don't know?"

"I wouldn't ask if I did!"

"Where have you been all your life that you've never heard of the Heptite Guild?"

"I've been a music student on Fuerte," she replied, spitting out the words.

"You wouldn't, by any chance, have *perfect* pitch?" The question, unexpected and too casually put forth, caught her halfway into a foul temper.

"Yes, I do, but I don't—"

"What fantastic luck!" His face, which was not unattractive, became radiant. "I shall have to tip the agent who ticketed me here! Why, our meeting is unbelievable luck—"

"Luck? If you knew why I'm here—"

"I don't care *why*. You are here, and so am I." He took her hands and seemed to devour her face with his eyes, grinning with such intense joy she found herself smiling back with embarrassment.

"Oh, luck indeed, my dear girl. Fate. Destiny. Karma. Lequoal. Fidalkoram. Whatever you care to name the coincidence of our life lines, I should order magnums of this fine wine for that lousy shuttle pilot for endangering this port terminal, in general, and us, in particular."

"I don't understand what you're ranting about, Carrik of Heptite," Killashandra said, but she was not impervious to his compliments or the charm he exuded. She knew that her self-assurance tended to put off men, but here a well-traveled off-worlder, a man of obvious rank and position, was inexplicably taken with her.

"You don't?" He teased her for the banality of her protest, and she closed her mouth on the rest of her rebuff. "Seriously," he went on, stroking the palms of her hands with his fingers as if to soothe the anger from her, "have you never heard of Crystal Singers?"

"Crystal Singers? No. Crystal tuners, yes."

He dismissed the mention of tuners with a contemptuous flick of his fingers. "Imagine singing a note, a pure, clear middle C, and hearing it answered across an entire mountain range?"

She stared at him.

"Go up a third or down; it makes no difference. Sing out and hear the harmony return to you. A whole mountainside pitched to a C and another sheer wall of pink quartz echoing back in a dominant. Night brings out the minors, like an ache in your chest, the most beautiful pain in the world because the music of the crystal is in your bones, in your blood—"

"You're mad!" Killashandra dug her fingers into his hands to shut off his words. They conjured too many painful associations. She had to forget all that. "I hate music. I hate anything to do with music."

He regarded her with disbelief for a moment, but then, with an unexpected tenderness and concern reflected in his expression, he moved an arm around her shoulders and, despite her initial resistance, drew himself against her.

"My dear girl, what happened to you today?"

A moment before, she would have swallowed glass shards rather than confide in anyone. But the warmth in his voice, his solicitude, were so timely and unexpected that the whole of her personal disaster came tumbling out. He listened to every word, occasionally squeezing her hand in sympathy. But at the end of the recital, she was amazed to see the fullness in his eyes as tears threatened to embarrass her.

"My dear Killashandra, what can I say? There's no possible consolation for such a personal catastrophe as that! And there you were"—his eyes shone with what Killashandra chose to interpret as admiration—"having a bottle of wine as coolly as a queen. Or"—and he leaned over her, grinning maliciously—"were you just gathering enough courage to step under a shuttle?" He kept hold of her hand which, at his outrageous suggestion, she tried to free. "No, I can see that suicide was furthest from *your* mind." She subsided at the implicit compliment. "Although"—and his expression altered thoughtfully—"you might inadvertently have succeeded if that shuttle had been allowed to take off again. If I hadn't been here to stop it—" He flashed her his charmingly reprehensible smile.

"You're full of yourself, aren't you?" Her accusation was said in jest, for she found his autocratic manner an irresistible contrast to anyone of her previous acquaintance.

He grinned unrepentantly and nodded toward the remains of their exotic snack. "Not without justification, dear girl. But look, you're free of commitments right now, aren't you?" She hesitantly nodded. "Or is there someone you've been seeing?" He asked that question almost savagely, as if he'd eliminate any rival.

Later, Killashandra might remember how adroitly Carrik had handled her, preying on her unsettled state of mind, on her essential femininity, but that tinge of jealousy was highly complimentary, and the eagerness in his eyes, in his hands, was not feigned.

"No one to matter or miss me."

Carrik looked so skeptical that she reminded him that she'd devoted all her energies to singing.

"Surely not all?" He mocked her dedication.

"No one to matter," she repeated firmly.

"Then I will make an honest invitation to you. I'm an off-worlder on holiday. I don't have to be back to the Guild till —well"—and he have a nonchalant shrug—"when I wish. I've all the credits I need. Help me spend them. It'll purge you of the music college."

She looked squarely at him, for their acquaintanceship was so brief and hectic that she simply hadn't had time to consider him a possible companion. Nor did she quite trust him. She was both attracted to and repelled by his domineering, high-handed manner, and yet he represented a challenge to her. He was certainly the exact opposite of the young men she had thus far encountered on Fuerte.

"We don't have to stay on this mudball, either."

"Then why did you come?"

He laughed. "I'm told I haven't been on Fuerte before. I can't say that it lives up to its name, or maybe you'll live up to the name for it? Oh come now, Killashandra," he said when she bridled. "Surely you've been flirted with before? Or have music students changed so much since my day?"

"You studied music?"

An odd shadow flickered through his eyes. "Probably. I don't rightly remember. Another time, another life perhaps." Then his charming smile deepened, and a warmth entered his expression that she found rather unsettling. "Tell me, what's on this planet that's fun to do?"

Killashandra considered for a moment and then blinked. "You know, I haven't an earthly?"

"Then we'll find out together."

What with the wine, his adept cajolery, and her own recklessness, Killashandra could not withstand the temptation. She ought to do many things, she knew, but "ought" had been exiled someplace during the second bottle of that classic vintage. After spending the rest of the night nestled in Carrik's arms in the most expensive accommodation of the spaceport hostelry, Killashandra decided she would suspend duty for a few days and be kind to the charming visitor.

The vidifax printout chattered as it popped out dozens of cards on the resorts of Fuerte, more than she had ever suspected. She had never water skied, so Carrik decided they'd both try that. He ordered a private skimmer to be ready within the hour. As he sang cheerily at the top of a good, rich bass voice, floundering about in the elegant sunken bathtub of the suite, Killashandra recalled some vestige of self-preserving shrewdness and tapped out a few discreet inquiries on the console.

    1234/AZ . . .
    CRYSTAL SINGER . . . A COLLOQUIAL GALACTIC
    EUPHEMISM REFERRING TO MEMBERS OF THE HEPTITE
    GUILD, BALLYBRAN, WHO MINE CRYSTAL RANGES
    UNIQUE TO THAT PLANET. REF: BALLYBRAN, REGULUS
    SYSTEM, A-S-F/128/4. ALSO CRYSTAL MINING, CRYSTAL
    TECHNOLOGY, 'BLACK QUARTZ' COMMUNICATIONS.
    WARNING: UNAUTHORIZED LANDING ON BALLYBRAN
    INTERDICTED BY FEDERATED SENTIENT PLANETS, SEC-
    TION 907, CODE 4, PARAGRAPHS 78–90.

The landing prohibition surprised Killashandra. She tried to recall details from her obligatory secondary school course on FSP Rights and Responsibilities. The 900 Sec-

tion had to do with life forms, she thought, and the Code 4
suggested considerable danger.

She tapped out the section, code, and paragraphs and
was awarded a request for *Need to Know?* As she couldn't
think of one at the moment, she went to the planetary
reference, and the display rippled across the screen.

> BALLYBRAN: FIFTH PLANET OF THE SUN, SCORIA,
> REGULUS SECTOR: THREE SATELLITES; AUTHORIZED
> LANDING POINT, FIRST MOON, SHANKILL; STANDARD
> LIFE-SUPPORT BASE, COMMERCIAL AND TRANSIENT
> ACCOMMODATIONS. NO UNAUTHORIZED PLANETARY
> LANDINGS: SECTION 907, CODE 4, PARAGRAPHS 78–90.
> SOLE AUTHORITY: HEPTITE GUILD, MOON BASE,
> SHANKILL.

Then she followed dense lines of data on the spectral
analysis of Scoria and its satellites, Ballybran being the
only one that rated considerable print-out, which Killashandra could, in part, interpret. Ballybran had a gravity
slightly lower than galactic norm for human adaptability, a
breathable atmosphere, more oceans than land mass, tidal
complications caused by three moons, as well as an exotic
meteorology stimulated by sunspot activity on the primary.

> PRINCIPAL INDUSTRIES: (1) BALLYBRAN CRYSTALS
> (2) THERAPEUTIC WATERS.
> 1) BALLYBRAN LIVING CRYSTAL VARIES IN DENSITY,
> COLOR, AND LONGEVITY AND IS UNIQUE TO THE
> PLANET. VITAL TO THE PRODUCTION OF CONTROL ELE-
> MENTS IN LASERS; AS A MATERIAL FOR INTEGRATED-
> CIRCUIT SUBSTRATES (OF THE LADDER HIERARCHY);
> POSITRONIC ROBOTICS; AS TRANSDUCERS FOR ELECTRO-
> MAGNETIC RADIATION (FUNDAMENTALS OF 20 KHZ
> AND 500 KHZ WITH AUDIO SECONDARIES AND HAR-
> MONICS IN THE LOWER FREQUENCIES) AND HEAT
> TRANSDUCERS; AS OPTHERIAN SOUND RELAYS AND
> MUSICAL INSTRUMENTS; BLUE TETRAHEDRONS ARE A
> CRUCIAL PART IN TACHYON DRIVE SYSTEMS.
> "BLACK" QUARTZ, A PHENOMENON LIMITED TO
> BALLYBRAN, IS THE CRITICAL ELEMENT OF INSTANTA-

NEOUS INTERSTELLAR COMMUNICATION, HAVING THE
ABILITY TO FOLD SPACE, OVER ANY DISTANCE, SO THAT
MAGNETICALLY, ELECTRICALLY, AND, AS FAR AS IS
KNOWN, OPTICALLY, THERE IS NO EFFECTIVE SEPARA-
TION BETWEEN TWO COUPLED RESONATING SEGMENTS
REGARDLESS OF THE ACTUAL DISTANCE BETWEEN
THEM.

TIMING ACCURACY OVER A DISTANCE OF 500 LIGHT-
YEARS HAS PRODUCED CONSISTENT ACCURACY OF 1×10^{-8} OF THE CESIUM ATOM TIME STANDARD.

BLACK QUARTZ IS CAPABLE OF ACHIEVING SIMULTA-
NEOUS SYNCHRONIZATION WITH TWO OTHER SEGMENTS
AND SO PROVIDES A RING-LINK BACKUP SYSTEM. FOR
EXAMPLE, WITH SIX QUARTZ SEGMENTS, A TO F, A IS
LINKED TO C, D, & E; B IS LINKED TO C, E, & F . . .

That was more than she ever wanted to know about
black quartz communications, Killashandra thought as
diagrams and computations scrolled across the screen, so
she pressed on to more interesting data. She slowed the
display when she noticed the heading "Membership" and
reversed to the start of that entry.

CURRENT MEMBERSHIP OF THE HEPTITE GUILD ON
BALLYBRAN IS 4425, INCLUDING INACTIVE MEMBERS,
BUT THE NUMBER FLUCTUATES CONSIDERABLY DUE TO
OCCUPATIONAL HAZARDS. THE ANCILLARY STAFF AND
TECHNICIANS ARE LISTED CURRENTLY AT 20,007.
ASPIRANTS TO THE GUILD ARE ADVISED THAT THE
PROFESSION IS HIGHLY DANGEROUS, AND THE HEPTITE
GUILD IS REQUIRED BY FEDERATION LAW TO DISCLOSE
FULL PARTICULARS OF ALL DANGERS INVOLVED BE-
FORE CONTRACTING NEW MEMBERS.

Four thousand four hundred and twenty-five seemed an
absurdly small roster for a galaxy-wide Guild that supplied
essential elements to so many industries. Most galaxy-wide
guilds ran to the hundreds of millions. What were those
ancillary staff and technicians? The notation of "full particulars of dangers involved" didn't dissuade Killashandra
at all. Danger was relative.

THE CUTTING OF BALLYBRAN CRYSTAL IS A HIGHLY
SKILLED AND PHYSICALLY SELECTIVE CRAFT, WHICH,
AMONG ITS OTHER EXACTING DISCIPLINES, REQUIRES
THAT PRACTITIONERS HAVE PERFECT AND ABSOLUTE
PITCH BOTH IN PERCEPTION AND REPRODUCTION OF
THE TONAL QUALITY AND TIMBRE TO BE FOUND ONLY
IN TYPE IV THROUGH VIII BIPEDAL HUMANOIDS—
ORIGIN: SOL III.

CRYSTAL CUTTERS MUST BE MEMBERS OF THE
HEPTITE GUILD, WHICH TRAINS, EQUIPS, AND SUPPLIES
GUILD MEDICAL SERVICES FOR WHICH THE GUILD
EXACTS A 30 PERCENT TITHE FROM ALL ACTIVE
MEMBERS.

Killashandra whistled softly—30 percent was quite a
whack. Yet Carrik seemed to have no lack of credit, so 70
percent of his earnings as a Cutter must be very respectable.

Thinking of Carrik, she tapped out a query. Anyone
could pose as a member of a Guild; chancers often produced exquisitely forged documentation and talked a very
good line of their assumed profession, but a computer
check could not be forged. She got affirmation that Carrik
was indeed a member in good standing of the Heptite
Guild, currently on leave of absence. A hologram of Carrik, taken when he used his credit plate for spaceflight to
Fuerte five days before, flowed across the viewplate.

Well, the man was undeniably who he said he was and
doing what he said he was doing. His being a card-tuned
Guild member was a safeguard for her so she could relax
in his offer of an "honest" invitation to share his holiday.
He would not leave her to pay the charges if he decided to
skip off-world precipitously.

She smiled to herself, suddenly feeling sensuous. Carrik
thought himself lucky, did he? Well, so did she. The last
vestige of "ought" was the fleeting thought that she "ought
to" register herself with the Fuertan Central Computer as a
transient, but since she was by no means obligated to do so
as long as she didn't require subsistence, she did nothing.

As she was beginning to enjoy her new found freedom,
several of her classmates began to experience twinges of
anxiety about Killashandra. Everyone realized that Killa-

shandra must have been terribly upset by the examiners'
verdict. Though some felt she deserved the lesson, for her
overbearing conceit, the kinder of heart were disquieted
about her disappearance. So was Maestro Esmond Valdi.

They probably would not have recognized the Killashandra who was sluicing about on water skis on the
southern seas of the Western Hemisphere or swathed in
elegant gowns, escorted by a tall, distinguished-looking
man to whom even the most supercilious hoteliers deferred.

It was a glorious feeling to have unlimited funds. Carrik
encouraged Killashandra to spend, and practice permitted
her to suspend what few scruples remained from years of
eking necessities out of student allotments. She did have
the grace to protest his extravagance, at least at the outset.

"Not to worry, pet. I've credit to spend," Carrik reassured her. "I made a killing in dominant thirds in the Blue
Range about the time some idiot revolutionists blew half a
planet's communications out of existence." He paused; his
eyes narrowed as he recalled something not quite pleasant.
"I was lucky on shape, too. It's not enough, you see, to
catch the resonances on what you're cutting. You've got to
hope you remember which shape to cut, and that's where
you're made or broken as a Crystal Singer. You've *got* to
remember what's high on the market or remember something like that revolution on Hardesty." He pounded the
table in emphasis, pleased with that particular memory.
"I did remember that all right when it mattered."

"I don't understand."

He gave her a quick look. "Not to worry, pet." His
standard phrase of evasion. "Come, give me a kiss and get
the crystal out of my blood."

There was nothing crystalline about his lovemaking or
the enjoyment he derived from her body, so Killashandra
elected to forget how often he avoided answering her questions about crystal singing. At first, she felt that since the
man was on holiday, he probably wouldn't want to talk
about his work. Then she sensed that he resented her questions as if they were distasteful to him and that he wanted,
above all, to forget crystal singing, which did not forward
her plan. But Carrik was not a malleable adolescent, im-

ploring her grace and favor. So she helped him forget crystal singing, which he was patently able to do until the night he awakened her with his groans.

"Carrik, what's the matter? Those shellfish from dinner? Shall I get the medic?"

"No, no!" He twisted about frantically and took her hand from the communit. "Don't leave me. This'll pass."

She held him in her arms as he cried out, clenching his teeth against some internal agony. Sweat oozed from his pores, yet he refused to let her summon help. The spasms racked him for almost an hour before they passed, leaving him spent and weak. Somehow, in that hour, she realized how much he had come to mean to her, how much fun he was, how much she had missed by denying herself any intimate relationships before. After he had slept and rested, she asked what had possessed him.

"Crystal, my girl, crystal." His sullen manner and the haggard expression on his face made her drop the subject.

By the afternoon he was almost himself. But some of his spontaneity was gone. He went through the motions of enjoying himself, of encouraging her to more daring exercises on the waterskis while he only splashed about in the shallows. They were finishing a leisurely meal at a seaside restaurant when he finally mentioned that he must return to work.

"I can't say so soon?" Killashandra remarked with a light laugh. "But isn't the decision rather sudden?"

He gave her an odd smile. "Yes, but most of my decisions are, aren't they? Like showing you another side of fusty, fogey Fuerte."

"And now our idyll is over?" She tried to sound nonchalant, but an edge crept into her tone.

"I must return to Ballybran. Ha! That sounds like one of those fisherfolk songs, doesn't it?" He hummed a banal tune, the melody so predictable that she could join in firm harmony.

"We do make beautiful music together," he said, his eyes mocking her. "I suppose you'll return to your studies now."

"Studies? For what? Lead soprano in a chorus of annotated, orchestrated grunts and groans by Fififidipidi of the planet Grnch?"

"You could tune crystals. They obviously need a competent tuner at Fuerte spaceport."

She made a rude noise and looked at him expectantly. He smiled back, turning his head politely, awaiting a verbal answer.

"Or," she drawled, watching him obliquely, "I could apply to the Heptite Guild as a Crystal Singer."

His expression went blank. "You don't want to be a Crystal Singer."

The vehemence in his voice startled her for a moment.

"How do you know what I want?" She flared up in spite of herself, in spite of a gnawing uncertainty about his feelings for her. She might be the ideal partner for lolling about a sandy beach, but as a constant companion in a dangerous profession—that was different.

He smiled sadly. "You don't want to be a Crystal Singer."

"Oh, fardles with that 'highly dangerous' nonsense."

"It is true."

"If I've perfect pitch, I can apply."

"You don't know what you're letting yourself in for," he said in a toneless voice, his expression at once wary and forbidding. "Singing crystal is a terrible, lonely life. You can't always find someone to sing with you; the tones don't always strike the right vibes for the crystal faces you find. Of course, you can make terrific cuts singing duo." He seemed to vacillate.

"How do you find out?" She made her tone ingenuous.

He gave an amused snort. "The hard way, of course. But you don't want to be a Crystal Singer." An almost frightening sadness tinged his voice. "Once you sing crystal, you don't stop. That's why I'm telling you, don't even think about it."

"So . . . you've told me not to think about it."

He caught her hand and gazed steadily into her eyes. "You've never been in a mach storm in the Milekeys." His voice was rough with remembered anxiety. "They blow up out of nowhere and crash down on you like all hell let loose. That's what that phrase on Retrieval means, 'the Guild maintains its own.' A mach storm can reduce a man to a vegetable in one sonic crescendo."

"There are other—perhaps less violent—ways of reducing a man to a vegetable," she said, thinking of the spaceport official of the supercargo worrying over drone-pod weights—of teachers apathetically reviewing the scales of novice students. "Surely there are instruments that warn you of approaching storms in a crystal range."

He nodded absently, his gaze fixed above her head. "You get to cutting crystal and you're halfway through. You know the pitches will be changed once the storm has passed and you're losing your safety margin by the minute, but that last crystal might mean you'd get off-world . . ."

"You don't get off-world with every trip to the ranges?"

He shook his head, frowning irritably at her interruption. "You don't always clear the costs of the trip or past damages, or you might not have cut the right shape or tone. Sometimes the tone is more important than the shape, you know."

"And you have to remember what'll be needed, don't you?" If she had perfect pitch, and she knew she had an excellent memory, crystal singing seemed an ideal profession for her.

"You have to *remember* the news," he said, oddly emphasizing the verb.

Killashandra was contemptuous of the problem. Memory was only a matter of habit, of training, of mnemonic phrases that easily triggered vital information. She had plenty of practice in memorization.

"Is there any chance that I could accompany you back to Ballybran and apply—"

His hand had a vise grip on hers; even his breath seemed to halt for a moment. His eyes swept hers with an intense search. "You asked. Remember that!"

"Well, if my company—"

"Kiss me and don't say anything you'll regret," he said, abruptly pulling her into his arms and covering her mouth so completely she couldn't have spoken.

The second convulsion caught him so soon after the climax of their lovemaking that she thought, guiltily, that overstimulation was the cause. This time, the spasms were more severe, and he dropped into a fevered, exhausted sleep when they finally eased. He looked old and drawn when he woke fourteen hours later. And he moved like an advanced geriatric case.

"I've got to get back to Ballybran, Killa." His voice quavered, and he had lost his proud confidence.

"For treatment?"

He hesitated and then nodded. "Recharging, actually. Get the spaceport on the communit and book us."

"Us?"

"You may accompany me," he said with grave courtesy, though she was piqued at the phrasing of an invitation that was more plea than permission. "I don't care how often we have to reroute. Get us there as fast as possible."

She reached the spaceport and routeing, and after what seemed an age and considerable ineptitude on the part of the ticket clerk, they were passengers confirmed on a shuttle flight leaving Fuerte in four hours, with a four-hour satellite delay before the first liner in their direction.

He had an assortment of personal things to pack, but Killashandra was for just walking out and leaving everything.

"You can't get such goods on Ballybran, Killa," Carrik told her as he slowly began to fold the gaudy grallie-fiber shirts. The stimulus of confirmed passage had given him a surge of energy. But Killashandra had been rather unnerved by the transformation of a charming, vital man into a quivering invalid. "Sometimes, even something as inconsequential as a shirt helps you remember so much."

She was touched by the sentiment and his smile and vowed to be patient with his illness.

"There are hazards to every profession. And the hazards to crystal singing—"

"It depends what you're willing to consider a hazard," Killashandra replied soothingly. She was glad for the filmy, luminous wraparounds, which were a far cry from the coarse, durable student issue. Any hazard seemed a fair price for bouts of such high living and spending. And only 4,425 in the Guild. She was confident she'd make it to the top there.

"Do you have any comphrehension of what you'd be giving up, Killashandra?" His voice had a guilty edge.

She looked at his lined, aging face and experienced a twinge of honest apprehension. Anyone would look appalling after the convulsions that had wracked Carrik. She didn't much care for his philosophical mood and hoped that he wouldn't be so dreary all the way to Ballybran. Was that what he meant? A man on vacation often had a different personality than when working at his profession?

"What have I too look forward to on Fuerte?" she asked with a shrug of her shoulders. She wouldn't necessarily have to team up with Carrik when she got to Ballybran. "I'd rather take a chance, no matter what it entails, in preference to dragging about forever on Fuerte!"

He stroked her palm with his thumb, and for the first time his caress didn't send thrills up her spine. But then he was scarcely in a condition to make love, and his gesture reflected it.

"You've only seen the glamorous side of crystal singing—"

"You've told me the dangers, Carrik, as you're supposed to. The decision is mine, and I'm holding you to your offer."

He gripped her hand tightly, and the pleasure in his eyes reassured her more thoroughly than any glib protestation.

"It's also one of the smallest Guilds in the galaxy," she went on, freeing her hand to finish packing the remaining garments. "I prefer those odds."

He raised his eyebrows, giving her a sardonic look more like his former self. "A two-cell in a one-cell pond?"

"If you please, I won't be second-rate anything."

"A dead hero in preference to a live coward?" He was taunting her now.

"If you prefer. There! That's all our clothing. We'd better skim back to the spaceport. I've got to check with planetary regulations if I'm going off-world. I might even have some credit due me."

She took the skimmer controls, as Carrik was content to doze in the passenger seat. The rest did him some good, or he was mindful of his public image. Either way, Killashandra's doubts of his reliability as a partner faded as he ordered the port officials about imperiously, badgering the routeing agent to be certain that the man hadn't overlooked a more direct flight or a more advantageous connection.

Killashandra left him to make final arrangements and began to clear her records with the Fuerte Central Computer. The moment she placed her wrist-unit and thumb in place, the console began to chatter wildly, flashing red light. She was startled. She had only programmed a credit check, keyed in the fact that she was going off-world, and asked what immunization she might require for the systems they were to encounter, but the supervisor leaped down the ramp from his console, two port officials converged on her, and the exits of the reception hall flashed red and hold-locks were engaged, to the consternation of passersby. Killashandra, too stunned to react, instead stared blankly at the men who had each seized an arm.

"Killashandra Ree?" the supervisor asked, still panting from his exertions.

"Yes?"

"You are to be detained."

"Why?" Now she was angry. She had committed no crime, infringed no one's liberties. Failure to register change of status was not an offense so long as she had not used planetary resources without sufficient credit.

"Please come with us," the port officials said in chorus.

"Why?"

"Ahh, hmmmm," the supervisor mumbled as both officers turned to him. "There's a hold out for you."

"I've done nothing wrong."

"Here, what's going on?" Carrik was once more completely himself as he pushed through to place a protecting arm around Killashandra. "This young lady is under my protection."

At this announcement, the supervisor and officials exchanged stern and determined stares.

"This young lady is under the protection of her planet of origin," the supervisor announced. "There is some doubt as to her mental stability."

"Why? Because she accepted an honest invitation from a visitor? Do you know who I am?"

The supervisor flushed. "Indeed I do, sir," and though the man spoke more respectfully, he left no doubt that his immediate aim was to extract Killashandra from Carrik's patronage.

"Well, then, accept my assurances that Miss Ree is in excellent health, mental and physical." Carrik gestured for them to admire Killashandra's tanned and trim figure.

The supervisor was adamant. "If you'll *both* please come this way." His officers straightened resolutely.

As there was nothing for it but to comply, Carrik reminded this unexpected escort that they had booked shuttle flights due to lift off in one hour. He had every intention of keeping that schedule—and with Killashandra Ree. Rather than give rise to further speculation about her mental state, Killashandra remained uncharacteristically quiet.

"I suspect," she whispered to Carrik after they were shown into a small office, "that the music school may have thought me suicidal." She giggled, then attempted to mask the noise behind her hand when the supervisor glanced up at her nervously. "I just walked out of the center and disappeared. I saw no one who knew me on the way here. So they did miss me! Well, that's gratifying." She was inordinately pleased, but Carrik plainly did not agree. Well, she had only to reassure the authorities, and she was certain she could. "I think their reaction is rather complimentary, actually. And I'm going to make a dramatic exit from Fuerte, after all."

Carrik awarded her a look of pure disgust and folded his arms solidly across his chest, his expression fading to one of boredom. He kept his eyes fixed on the screen, which was scrolling through the departure information.

Killashandra half expected to see her father, though she found it difficult to imagine him bestirring himself on her behalf. But she did not expect Maestro Esmond Valdi to enter the small office, acting the outraged mentor, nor was she prepared for the attack he immediately launched on Carrik.

"You! You! I know what you are! A silicate spider paralyzing its prey, a crystal cuckoo pushing the promising fledglings from their nests."

As stunned as everyone else, Killashandra stared at the usually dignified and imperturbable maestro and wondered what role he thought he was playing. He had to be acting.

His dialogue was so—so extravagant. "Silicate spider!" "Crystal cuckoo!" If nothing else, his analogies were incorrect and uncalled for.

"Play on the emotions of an innocent young girl. Shower her with unaccustomed luxuries and pervert her until she's spoiled as a decent contributing citizen. Until she's so besotted, she has been brainwashed to enter that den of addled mentalities and shattered nerves!"

Carrik made no attempt to divert the flow of vituperation or to counter the accusations. He stood, head up, smiling tolerantly down at the jerky motions of Valdi.

"What lies has he been feeding you about crystal singing? What glamorous tales has he used to lure you there?" Valdi whirled toward Killashandra, his stocky figure trembling with outrage.

"I asked to go."

Valdi's wild expression hardened into disbelief at her calm answer.

"You *asked* to go?"

"Yes. *He* didn't ask *me*." She caught Carrik's smile.

"You heard her, Valdi," Carrik said, then glanced at the officials witnessing the admission.

The maestro's shoulders sagged. "So, he's done his recruiting with a master's skill." His tone registered resignation, he even managed to effect a slight break in his voice.

"I don't think so," Killashandra said.

Maestro Valdi inhaled deeply, obviously to support one last attempt to dissuade the misguided girl. "Did he tell you about . . . the mach storms?"

She nodded, hiding her amusement at his theatricality.

"The storms that scramble the brain and reduce the mind to a vegetable existence?"

She nodded dutifully.

"Did he fill your mind with garbage about mountains returning symphonies of sound? Crystalline choruses? Valleys that echo arpeggios?" His body rippled upward in an effort to express the desired effect of ridicule.

"No," she replied in a bored tone. "Nor did he feed me pap that all I needed was hard work and time."

Esmond Valdi, maestro, drew himself up, more than ever in an exaggeration of a classical operatic pose.

"Did he also tell you that once you start cutting crystal, you can never stop? And that staying too long away from Ballybran produces disastrous convulsions?"

"I know that."

"Do you also *know*"—Valdi rocked back on his heels—"that something in the water of Ballybran, in its very soil, in those crystals, affects your mind? That you don't *re-mem-ber*?" He separated the verb carefully into syllables.

"That could be a distinct advantage," Killashandra replied, staring back at the little man until he broke eye contact.

She was the first of the three to feel a peculiar itch behind her ears in the mastoid bone; an itch that rapidly became a wrenching nauseating pain. She grabbed Carrik by the arm just as the subsonic noise touched him and as Esmond Valdi lifted protecting hands to his ears.

"The fools!" Carrik cried as panic contorted his features. He threw aside the door panel, running as fast as he could for the control-tower entrance. Killashandra scurried after him.

Carrik vaulted the decorative barrier and landed in a restricted area, where he was deterred by a hastily engaged force curtain. "Stop it! Stop it!" he screamed, rocking in anguish and clawing at the curtain, oblivious to the sparks flying from his fingers.

Though the pain was no less bearable for Killashandra, she had presence of mind enough to bang on the nearest communit, to strike the fire buttons, press the battery of emergency signals. "The shuttle coming in—something's wrong—it's dangerous!" she yelled at the top of her oper-atically trained lungs. She was barely conscious of the panic in the vast reception hall resulting from her all too audible warning.

The possibility of a stampede by a hysterical mob was evident to those in the control tower, where someone, in reflex action, slapped on the abort signal to warn off all in-transit craft. Moments later, while the communit de-manded an explanation from Killashandra or from anyone who could make himself heard over the bedlam in the reception area, a nova blossomed in the sky and rained molten fragments on the spaceport below. The control tower was unable to contain the destruction within the grappling field, and soon parts of the shuttle were scattered over several kilometers of the Port Authority and the heavily populated business district.

Apart from bruises, lacerations, and a broken arm, there were only two serious casualties. A technician on the tarmac was killed, and Carrik would have been better off dead. The final sonic blast knocked him unconscious, and he never did fully recover his senses. After subspace consultation with Heptite Guild medics, it was decided to return him to Ballybran for treatment and care.

"He won't recover," the medic told Killashandra, whereupon Maestro Valdi instantly assumed the role of her comforter. His manner provided Killashandra with a fine counterirritant to her shock over Carrik's condition.

She chose to disbelieve the medic's verdict. Surely, Carrik could be restored to mental health once he was returned to Ballybran. He had been away from crystal too long; he was weakened by the seizures. There'd been no mach storm to scramble his mind. She'd escort him back to Ballybran. She owed him that in any reckoning for showing her how to live fully.

She took a good look at the posturing Valdi and thanked her luck that Carrik had been there to awaken her senses. How could she have believed that such an artificial life as found in the theater was suitable for her? Just look at Valdi! Present him with a situation, hand him the cue, and he was "on," in the appropriate role. None existed for these circumstances, so Valdi was endeavoring to come up with a suitable one.

"What will you do now, Killashandra?" he asked somberly, obviously settling for Dignified Elder Gentleman Consoling the Bereaved Innocent.

"I'll go with him to Ballybran, of course."

Valdi nodded solemnly. "I mean, after you return."

"I don't intend to return."

Valdi stared at her, dropping out of character, and then gestured theatrically as the air-cushion stretcher to which Carrik was strapped drifted past them to the shuttle gate.

"After that?" Valdi cried, full of dramatic plight.

"That won't happen to me," she said confidently.

"But it could! You, too, could be reduced to a thing with no mind and no memories."

"I think," Killashandra said slowly, regarding the posturing little man with thinly veiled contempt, "that everyone's brains get scrambled one way or another."

"You'll rue this day—" Valdi began, raising his left arm in a classical gesture of rejection, fingers gracefully spread.

"That is, if I *remember* it!" she said. Her mocking laughter cut him off midscene.

Still laughing, Killashandra made her exit, stage center, through the shuttle gate.

CHAPTER 3

Captain Andurs alerted Killashandra when the ship emerged from hyperspace and Ballybran was fully visible.

"Good view," he told her, pointing to the two inner moons, positioned at 10 and 5, but Killashandra only had eyes for the mysterious planet.

She had heard enough to expect just about anything from her first glimpse. Consequently she experienced an initial disappointment—until she caught sight of the first crystal flare: a piercing stab of light as the sun's rays reflected from an open crystal on one of the three visible continents. Cloud cover swirled across most of the ocean area, occluded two subcontinents in the Southern Hemisphere, but where the sun shone, occasional pinpoints of blinding light were visible—light that was all color, yet white and clear.

"How can they stand the intensity down there?" she demanded, squinting to reduce the keen glare.

"According to what I hear, you don't notice it on the surface."

"According to what I hear" had prefaced most of Captain Andurs' statements about Ballybran, a sour comment on the restriction against his landing on one of the richest planets in the galaxy.

From fellow passengers and garrulous crew members, Killashandra had gleaned additional information about Crystal Singers and Ballybran, a lot of which she discounted since most merely paraphrased Maestro Valdi's comments. Andurs, despite his limited first-hand knowledge, had proved to be the most informative. He had been on the space run from Regulus to Ballybran for nine standard years and was always listening, so he had heard more than anyone else—certainly more than she had been able to extract from the cryptic vidifax of the three ships she had traveled on during the voyage. There was something mysterious about Ballybran and the Heptite Guild and its members—a mystery that she deduced from what *wasn't* said about those three subjects. Individuals had privacy; so did certain aspects of any interstellar mercantile company, and one understood that references to certain planetary resources were understated or omitted. But the lack of routinely available printout on Ballybran, the Guild, and its select members doubled her suspicions.

Conversely, she had been tremendously impressed by the Guild's tacit power: high-rank medicorps men had awaited Carrik at the three intermediary ports. She herself had been accorded the most deferential treatment. She'd had very little to do other than check the life-support cradle that carried Carrik. The cradle was programmed for IV feedings, therapy, bathing, and the necessary drugs. The apparatus was checked by technicians at each port. Nothing, apparently, was too good for a Heptite Guild member. Or his escort. She'd had open credit in the ships' stores, was a member of the captain's private mess on all three ships. Except for the fact that she was left strictly alone, she thoroughly enjoyed the excitement of her first interstellar journey.

Possibly because the trip was nearly over, she had received most of her information from Andurs the previous night as he judiciously nursed a Sarvonian brandy through the evening.

"I hear it often enough to begin to believe it's possible . . . but they say crystal gets into your blood."

"That'd kill you," Killashandra replied though Carrik had used the same phrase.

"I can't tell whether they mean that the credits are so good," Andurs continued, ignoring her comment. "Crystal Singers really whoop it up—big spenders, fun people—until the shakes start. Funny about that, too, because Crystal Singers are supposed to heal faster than other humans, and they're not supposed to be as susceptible to the planetary goolies and fevers that catch you no matter what immunization you've got. And they stay younger." That capability annoyed Andurs. "I asked one of 'em about that. He was drunk at the time, and he said it's just part of singing crystal."

"Then there'd be a lot of people willing to sing crystal . . ."

"Yeah, but you also risk the shakes or . . ." Andurs jerked his thumb over his shoulder to indicate Carrik in his cabin, "I'd rather grow old."

"That doesn't happen often, does it?" Killashandra asked startled. She'd had the impression that Carrik's collapse was unusual.

"He's the first I've seen that bad," Andurs admitted. "Oh, they get the fevers, sometimes bad enough to be packed out in freezebags but not—" and he touched his forehead with one finger. "Not my business, but how did he get that way?"

His question, though an obvious one, startled Killashandra because no one else throughout the journey had asked, as if they were afraid of the answer.

"He was fine until we got to Fuerte Spaceport. Then a shuttle came in with a badly resonating drive. It exploded, and he got caught in the sonic backlash."

"Good of you to escort him back."

"I owed him that." Killashandra meant it. "You said the Guild maintains offices on the moon? Is that where you apply for membership as well?"

He looked at her in amazement. "Oh, you don't want to be a Singer."

"Why not?"

Andurs leaned toward her, staring hard into her eyes. "You weren't forced to come with him, were you? I mean, *he* didn't do anything to you?"

Killashandra didn't know whether to laugh or become

angry. "I don't know where you come from, Captain
Andurs, but on Fuerte privacy is respected."

"I didn't mean to imply that it wasn't . . ." Andurs
responded hastily, raising his hand to fend off her outrage.

"Do I look as if I've been conditioned?"

"No, actually you don't. It's just that you strike me as a
sensible woman, and crystal singing isn't sensible. Oh, I
know. I've heard all the fardling rumors, but that's spaceflot because all the Singers I've seen—and I've seen a lot in
nine years on this run—never bother anyone. They keep
to themselves, really. But there is something very peculiar
indeed about Ballybran and crystal singing. I do know"—
and he glanced over his shoulder, a needless caution since
they were alone in the lounge—"that not every one who
applies and gets accepted makes it as a Singer. Whoever
goes down to that planet"—he pointed toward the floor—
"stays there. Only Singers leave. And *they* always return."

"How many people apply for entry into the Guild?"
Killashandra was remembering the 20,007 technicians as
well as the 4,425 Singers, and she wondered what the gross
was if the net was so small.

"I can't answer that precisely." Andurs seemed perplexed as he scratched his head. "Never thought about it.
Oh, I get a few applicants almost every trip. Think we've
got eight, possibly nine on this flight. You get to know
who's commercial traveling, and who's hoping." Andurs
grinned at her. "We do have four Guild-vouched passages
besides yours. That means these people have been screened
at a Guild center somewhere. You know that tall, thin,
black-haired fellow?"

Killashandra nodded, remembering the man who had
boarded the ship at the last transfer point. He'd stared at
her inquisitively, and once she had found him standing
outside her cabin, a strange wild look on his face.

"He's come on his own. I wouldn't say he'd be accepted."

"Oh?"

Andurs twirled his brandy glass for a long moment before he answered. "Yeah, I don't think he's the type they
want."

"What is the type they want?"

"I don't really know," Andurs replied after a moment,

"but he's not it. The Guild will pay your way back to the nearest transfer point," he added as if this would be sufficient compensation for rejection. "I'll let you know when we emerge, Killa. Ballybran's one of the more interesting planets to see a moon's eye view of—especially if there's a storm in progress."

Killashandra remained at the view screen until Ballybran was eclipsed by the bulk of its largest moon, Shankill. If you've seen one moon installation, you've seen them all, she thought as she watched the domes and blackened landing pits swivel past. Her attention was briefly arrested by the sight of a second vessel swinging up over the horizon, a shuttle craft from the size of it, small enough to make no work of the landing. She thought she caught a flash of the Heptite Guild dodecahedron on the nose, but the shuttle moved into shadow too quickly for her to check.

Whatever reception she had subconsciously hoped for was vastly different from the one she received from Lanzecki, the Resident Master of the Heptite Guild. He was standing at the portal when the ship opened its airlock: a dour man, with a swarthy complexion and a squat figure, clothed in dull colors. The only things bright and active about him were his wide-set piercing brown eyes, which moved incessantly, seeming to catch more in one darting glance than they ought.

He gestured to the two men accompanying him who were dun garbed as well. They silently entered the ship and paced down the corridor, Killashandra in the lead. She had never felt more superfluous. In Carrik's stateroom, Lanzecki used that moment's hesitation to press the panel plate open. He glanced once at the still figure on the carrier, his face expressionless. He motioned the others to enter and take the carrier.

"Thank you, Killashandra Ree. You have an open ticket to whatever destination you desire and a credit of one thousand galactic units." He proferred two vouchers, each emblazoned with the Heptite Guild dodecahedron blackquartz crystal. He accorded her a deferential bow, and then, as the men guided Carrik past, he followed them down the corridor.

For a moment, Killashandra stared at the departing trio, the two metallic voucher slips clinging with static attraction to her fingers. "Guild Master? Lanzecki? Sir? Wait . . ." The stately progress continued without pause. "Of all the ungrateful—"

"I'd not call them ungrateful," said Captain Andurs, who had approached from the other end of the corridor. He craned his head to glance at the vouchers. "Not at all."

"I didn't expect praise," Killashandra exclaimed, though that indeed was what she had expected. "Just a word or two."

"You've got the important ones," Andurs reminded her with a wry smile. "One thousand. They're an odd lot at best," he went on as the Guildsmen turned toward the accordioned portal maw. "Like I said, there's all kinds of spaceflot about that Guild. I see strange things banging this old can from system to system, and I pretend not to see half of them." Suddenly, he slid his arm about her shoulders. "Now that the dead meat's gone, how about you and me—"

"Not now," Killashandra irritably pushed his arm away. "I want a word with that Guild Master first." She strode rapidly down the corridor toward the portal.

She never saw Carrik again, though he was listed among the inactive membership for a good many years. Not that she glanced at the lists, active or inactive, very often once the thrill of seeing her own name inscribed had passed.

She came to a halt at the opaque force screen of the debarkation arch, which blinked readiness to receive her credentials and reason for business on Shankill. She ignored it, watching in frustration as the Guild Master's figure disappeared through one of the five irised exits from the small lobby beyond the arch. She raced back to her cabin to jam her belongings into the carisak. By the time she had returned to debarkation, much to her disgust, she had to join the queue of passengers. As she waited, fighting her impatience, Captain Andurs emerged from the ship's forward section and made for the secondary gate by the debarkation arch. He caught a glimpse of her and turned back, a quizzical smile on his face.

"Going through with it, Killa?" he asked. He slid a hand up her arm to grip her elbow. Andurs' eyes had the sort of intensity she had begun to associate with desire, a pleasing response considering her abrupt manner with him earlier.

"Why not? I've been given no reason to stop and a very good one to try."

Andurs grinned. "Well, you'll find the process takes time. I'll be in the transients' hostel for at least five days." He made a grimace of resigned distaste and shrugged. "I'll be seeing you," he added with a half note of questioning, though his smile was inviting.

It irked Killashandra to see him jauntily present his wrist to the plate on the smaller arc and watch the entrance dilate immediately. When she finally submitted her wrist to the identity plate at debarkation control, she had become somewhat resigned to delay.

She was asked for her reason to land on Shankill.

"I wish to apply for membership in the Heptite Guild. I have perfect pitch," she added.

The display requested her credit rating, and Killashandra disdainfully slipped in the Guild voucher. It was instantly accepted, and the substantial credit balance displayed. The unit purred, clicked, and then, as a fax sheet rolled from the print slot, the arch dilated to permit access to the Shankill moon base. She was advised to read and conform to all rules and regulations of the Shankill Authority, which were included in the printout as were directions to transient accommodations, catering facilities, and the public areas of the installation.

She passed through the arch and into the lobby with the five exits. The third iris swirled open, and Killashandra, taking the hint, proceeded down that corridor to the hostel. She was surprised to emerge into a large open area, high-ceilinged and lined with holograms of trees lightly stirring in an absent breeze. A glow radiating from the plasglassed skylight simulated sunlight. She wondered, as she crossed the floor to the reception area if the mock light also followed Ballybran's rotational period.

Her second surprise was to find a human attendant behind the reception counter. "Killashandra Ree?" he asked politely, unsmiling.

She suppressed a desire to ask "Who else?" and nodded.

"You will not have had time to read the rules and regulations pertaining to Shankill Moon Base, therefore, it is my duty to request that you do so immediately upon settling in your accommodation. Failure to comply will result in restriction of personal liberty to prevent endangering the lives of others through ignorance. Please synch your digital to Ballybran's rotation with which all base times are synchronized. If you do not understand anything in the instructions, I am at your service to explain. Place your wrist unit on the plate. Thank you."

More accustomed to the monotone of machine-issued instructions, Killashandra could only stare at the man, wondering if he was some sort of android, though she'd never heard of such lifelike replicas of humans. Then he smiled slightly and tapped the plate.

"Been on a moon base before?" the man asked in a tone remarkably informal after his mechanical speech.

"No," she said as she placed her wrist to the plate and her thumb in the depression.

"This is my tenth. I'm an apprentice in satellite security. We get to do the routine work, you see. Not that anything's ever gone wrong here"—he pointed his forefinger firmly toward the floor to indicate the entire base— "though there's always a first time. Like our training programmer says, there's always a first time, and we're supposed to make sure that first times don't occur. That's why you'll find human specialists like me on moon bases. People get so used to machines and displays and automatic cautionary signs that they don't sink in"—he tapped his forehead—"and that's how accidents can happen."

"Seems like good psychology," Killashandra agreed absently, for she was noting with pleasure the winking green credit balance. A key poked above the flush counter. The man handed it to her.

"My name's Ford. You'll read that your room has its own life-support system that comes on-line automatically in case of failure of the base system. Only, by Brennan's

left ear, don't get caught in a hostel room during a leak-out
or a break—that's a sure way to go berk."

Killashandra wanted to tell him that his psychology had
a flaw if this was how he was supposed to reassure her. But
she refrained, smiled, and promised she'd read the instructions. Then she glanced about her.

"Your key's tuned to your room. It'll find you your way
back from any point in the base," Ford said jovially. "Just
go through that door," he added, leaning across his counter
and pointing to the left.

Killashandra felt the tug of the key in that direction, and
giving Ford another smile, she set off.

The key plate of the door frame was glowing in welcome
as she approached her assigned room. She inserted the key,
and the door panel retracted with a *whoosh*. As she walked
in, she could see why Ford didn't recommend a protracted
stay on the premises; the compact room would give anyone
claustrophobia. All the bodily comforts compacted into a
space 3½ meters long, 2 meters wide, and 3 high. A three-
drawer captain's bed occupied most of the space. Above it
was shelving, from the base of which projected the angled
audiovisual unit, obviously usable only to the occupant of
the bed. Any esthetics of space or decor had been waived
in considerations of safety and survival. To be sure, one
wasn't compelled to remain in this room. In fact, from the
authority's viewpoint, it was probably advisable that the
room be occupied only for sleep.

Killashandra flipped the carisak to the foot of the bed
and plopped down on it, noticing for the first time the row
of labled switches and buttons along the wall and the wall
slots from which, according to the labels, table, reading
lamp, and an individual catering unit would emerge. She
grimaced. Everything at finger-tip control. She wondered if
Ford's presence was to reassure the transients that they
were indeed human rather than extensions of some computer. Ford certainly exhibited humanity.

Sighing, she dutifully pulled the rules and regulations to
her. She had promised. Besides, forewarning herself
seemed wise even if, as Ford had averred, nothing had ever
happened on Shankill Station.

According to the fax sheet, he was correct. The Shankill
Moon Base had been functioning safely for 334 years,
Standard Galactic. The original installation had been considerably expanded when Federated Sentient Planets restricted habitation of Ballybran because of the planet's
dangers.

Killashandra had to reread that part twice. So the planet
itself was dangerous, though obviously that danger had
been overcome since people were now working and living
on the surface.

The following paragraphs blithely changed subject and
began enumerating safety hazards, regulations, and individual responsibilities. Killashandra dutifully read on, hearing an echo of Ford's warning: "There's always a first
time." As a transient, her main responsibilities were first
to seek the red-striped areas of whatever corridor or public
place she inhabited on hearing either rapid hoots (oxygen
leak) or sharp short whistles (penetration) or intermittent
siren (internal fire or emergency) and then to stay out of
everyone's way. Sustained hoots, whistles, or siren indicated the end of the emergency. If she was in her quarters,
she was to lie on the bed—not that there was anywhere
else in the room to be comfortable during enforced incar-
ceration. In all crises, helmeted personnel were authorized
to command unhelmeted individuals to any task required
to end the emergency.

She turned the sheet over and studied the map of the
base, which, comparing the total with the part she had
already seen, must be immense. Some units were composed
of nine sprawling levels, most subsurface; each one could
be sealed for all had backup life-support systems. The
largest areas were cargo and maintenance facilities, the
Guild and administration. Diagrams of the two smaller
bases on the moons, Shilmore and Shanganagh, decorated
the bottom of the sheet. These were both meteorological stations, and Shanganagh seemed to be completely automated.

Meteorology seemed to be the preoccupation of Ballybran, Killashandra thought—was that the danger on the
planet? Its weather? Carrik had mentioned the incredible
mach storms. That the winds of Ballybran were ferocious

enough to merit such a nickname was frightening enough.

She scanned the map again, noting the proximity of the Guild complex to the transients' quarters. Two tunnels/ corridors/avenues—whatever—over and the small unit between was the debarkation facility. She grinned at the convenient juxtaposition. Could it be completely fortuitous? Could she just walk over and present herself as an aspirant?

She suddenly experienced an unexpected diffidence and studied her digital. She was well within the normal working hours of most commercial establishments. She had read the important safety regulations, and she would certainly look for the red-striped area in any corridor and public place she entered. With a twitch of her shoulders, she strengthened her resolve and pressed the wall stud to activate the speech-recognition system.

"Request details for applying to Heptite Guild for membership."

The display rippled on.

APPLICATION FOR CONSIDERATION OF MEMBERSHIP IN HEPTITE GUILD REQUIRES PHYSICAL FITNESS TEST SG-1, PSYCHOLOGICAL PROFILE SG-1, EDUCATION LEVEL 3 PREFERRED BUT EXCEPTIONS CONSIDERED, PERFECT AND ABSOLUTE PITCH BOTH IN PERCEPTION AND REPRODUCTION OF THE TONAL QUALITY AND TIMBRE TO BE FOUND ONLY IN TYPE IV THROUGH VIII BIPEDAL HUMANOID, ORIGIN SOL III. MUTANTS NEED NOT APPLY.

APPLICATION MADE ONLY THROUGH HEPTITE GUILD OFFICES: SHANKILL MOON BASE, MAIN RECEPTION FACILITY.

FEDERATED SENTIENT PLANETS REQUIRE FULL DISCLOSURE OF ALL DANGERS INHERENT IN PROFESSION TO PROSPECTIVE CANDIDATES ONCE PHYSICAL, PSYCHOLOGICAL, AND APTITUDE TESTS HAVE BEEN PASSED TO THE SATISFACTION OF THE GUILD EXAMINING BOARD.

BALLYBRAN IS AN INTERDICTED WORLD, SECTION 907, CODE 4, PARAGRAPHS 78–90. FOR DETAILS, CONSULT HEPTITE GUILD.

"Well," Killashandra murmured, "information received by dribs and drabs. Heptite Guild, please."

The screen resolved around a woman's face.

"Heptite Guild, Shankill Moon base. May I assist you?"

"Killashandra Ree," she managed, mindful of courtesy, for she hadn't expected a personal answer. "I'd like to know if your member, Carrik, is all right?"

"He made the journey safely to the surface."

"I mean, will he recover?"

"That is possible but not predictable."

The woman's face was composed and obviously expectant.

"How do I get to be a Guild member?" Her query was blurted out. "I did tap data retrieval."

The woman smiled politely. "I am permitted to release additional information to interested persons. Your room designation?" Killashandra gave her the information. "You will have access to the relevant data until 0800 tomorrow. If you desire the preliminary examinations, you may present yourself to the Guild during normal working hours."

The image faded, which was just as well because Killashandra was consumed with curiosity as to what more of Ballybran's mysteries would be revealed by the promised additional data. Not all, she was certain.

The display began with a historical summary of the planet. Furious, she was about to cancel the program when it occurred to her that the wise performer studied the role and the composer, to understand his intent, before any audition. If the Guild had released this data to her, they would also know if she had availed herself of the courtesy. Joining the Heptite Guild might not depend alone on perfect pitch, good physical condition, and the right psychological adjustment—or why were there so few members?

She settled herself to study the material, though the preliminary paragraphs on "man's ever-pressing need for material resources in his search of the galaxies" reminded her depressingly of secondary school's orientation propaganda. She didn't have to wade through much of that but got quickly to the section on Spican quartz.

In a routine explore and evaluate search, Scoria's planets were probed. Ballybran, the only one with suitable atmosphere and gravity, gave happy evidence of crystal and quartz formations in its inverted ranges. A team was dispatched, Barry Milekey of Trace its leader. The initial findings of the geologists indicated a planet of immense potential, and samples were rushed back to Sector Research Division. The E and E of Ballybran had lucked out. The first crystal sample to be analyzed properly, a blue porphyry type, proved, due to peculiarities of its composition, a marvelous optical storage device, allowing computers virtually instantaneous access to improbably large volumes of data stored in matrixes of exceptionally small dimensions. The crystal's fine-grain synapse structure enabled even a smallish (1 cm³) segment to serve as a gigaword memory.

However, it was Milekey's discovery of the so-called black quartz—under normal conditions neither black nor quartz—that led to the complete revolution of interstellar communications. Owing to its thermal characteristics, Black Ballybran is a pigmented rock crystal, translucent in natural light.

Under certain types of magnetic stress, Black Ballybran, for lack of any better description, absorbs all light and seems to become *matte* black. Milekey had observed this phenomenon when he chipped the first lump from the black crystal face.

Again by accident, while being examined by the crystalographers, the substance's true properties were discovered. If two identical segments of black quartz were subjected to synchronized magnetic induction, a two-way communication link was established between the crystal segments. When investigators increased the distance between the samples, it was discovered that, unlike other electromagnetic phenomena, black quartz eliminated the time lag.

Concurrent with the laboratory discoveries and proposed applications of the new crystals came the first of several problems to be solved in the mining of this rich source. The first E and E team had only gathered up loose chips of the various types of crystal, or such larger chunks as had already been fractured from the mother lode. In attempts to cut with ordinary carbon-10 blades, the crystal had shattered. Laser cutters were tried, but they shattered, melted, or damaged the crystal.

The habit of one of the crystallographers of singing as he worked led to an unexpected solution. The man noticed that some crystal faces would resonate to his voice, and he suggested the use of a subsonic cutter. Though not completely successful, experiments along this line finally produced the sophisticated audio pickup that resonated, amplified, and reduced the required note to set the subsonic diamond blade.

Once the problem of wresting unblemished crystals from the face was solved, Ballybran was opened to private miners. During the next spate of storms, those miners who heeded the warnings promptly and reached the sheltered valley sustained no injury. The imprudent were discovered in the storm's wake, dead or mad. Storm winds blowing across the resonant crystal range coaxed enough sonics from the sensitive rock to shatter unprotected minds.

Keenly aware of the unexplained deaths of the nine miners, everyone became conscious of previously ignored physical discomforts. The meditechs began filing reports of disorientation, hypo- and hyperthermic spells, erratic sense perceptions, muscular spasm and weakness. No one in the several base camps escaped the minor ailments. Most symptoms passed, but some victims found one sense or another—in most cases hearing—to be affected. The medical team was hastily augmented, and everyone was put through exhaustive tests. At first, crystal was suspected of inducing the symptoms. However, those handling the crystal off-planet appeared unharmed by contact, while meteorologists and support technicians who never touched the stuff on Ballybran, were also affected. Crystal was absolved. The planet's ecology then became the prime target for intensive examination, and this area of investigation proved positive. The spore producing the symptoms was soon isolated, and the planet Ballybran was placed on Code 4 as a preventive measure.

Killashandra turned off the display to ponder that. Anything below Code 15 was a stern prohibition against landing. Ballybran's spore produced complicated reactions—

sometimes fatal—in the human body. Yet the culprit had been isolated, but the planet was *still* on a Code 4!

Evasion! Killashandra thought, irritated. She started the display again, but the text now cited the formation of the Heptite Guild. She halted it.

What was it Andurs had said? "Only Singers leave the planet?" Obviously, the handicapped remained on Bally-bran. Twenty-thousand-odd staff and technicians as opposed to Singers. Killashandra snorted. Those were better odds, actually, than the ones against achieving stellar rank in the performing arts. She rather liked that. Yes, but what happened if you weren't one of the one-in-five? What sort of technical workers were employed?

She queried the vidifax.

"Technicians: Ballybran crystal workers, tuners, artificers of crystal drive components and interstellar resonating units, meditechs, programmers, mechanics, therapists, agronomists, caterers . . ." the list continued down to menial functions.

So, once committed to Ballybran, only Singers left. Well, she'd be a Singer. Killashandra pushed aside the console and, knitting her fingers behind her head, leaned back on the narrow bolster.

What contributed to that subtle difference between Singer and support staff? Particularly if perfect pitch was a prerequisite to leaving the planet. If infrasonic cutters were used to extract the crystal from the rock face, sheer strength wasn't the second requisite. Attitude? Aptitude?

The spore disease? Killashandra drew the console back to her and tapped out a recall.

"This area of investigation proved positive, and the spore producing the illness was isolated . . ."

"Isolated," Killashandra muttered under her breath. "Isolated but not negated, or cured, and the planet Code 4."

So it had to be immunity to the spore itself that determined who sang crystal?

Nothing ventured, nothing gained, she thought, and tapped out a query on the spore. She chuckled as the display announced a restricted subject. Only so much in-

formation then was vouchsafed the candidate. Fair enough.
Privacy was as much the right of a Guild as an individual, and the FSP required full disclosure before a candidate took the final irrevocable plunge.

She pushed back the console and swung off the bed.
Pausing just long enough to brush her hair and check the
fall of her tunic, she slid aside the door panel. It closed
quietly behind her.

When she reached the ramp connecting levels, she studied the wall map mounted there. She was two levels below
and to one side of the Guild, and there was but one access
to that part of the base. She hurried up the ramp with an
aggressive stride. It felt good to walk about. After confinement for nine days in shuttles and spaceships, even a moon
base seemed spacious. The amenities of Shankill reflected
its use as a commercial as well as resident scientific facility.
Considerable thought and care had been taken to approxi-
mate planetary surroundings, to make residents and transients forget the hostile conditions outside. Holograms on
the outside of the rampway depicted a pleasant mountain
scene that, Killashandra was sure, would change in lighting
to coincide with the base's diurnal pattern. It was close to
midday "outside," but she ignored the faint complaints
from her stomach.

Through a lock, past the red-hatched area she had promised herself to seek out, the corridor widened into a broad
foyer. Set around the wall were holograms of trees and
flowers, nodding and dipping among the banked bright-
leaved shrubs. She thought the decorator had mixed the
flora of several planets in the display, but with holograms
that scarcely caused botanical problems. Besides, the
effect was colorful.

The catering facility below her was set out on several
levels, the first one a wide corridor between two beverage
areas, one with a human attendant. She bore left, entering
another short corridor that bridged the catering and Guild
areas.

Though it crossed her mind that the Guild offices were
closed for midday meals, she was surprised to gain instant
admission to the reception area. There, she stopped in
wonder.

Moon base or not, the twelve-sided hall was immense, the ceiling at least 5, possibly 6 meters high. An immense crystal artform, multicolored and faintly luminous, hung from the center of the arches that supported the ceiling. A curved console was the only furnishing in the open chamber, but Killashandra noted the lights of display niches set at random levels on the sidewalls.

"Well," she uttered in soft amazement, then heard the chandelier chime in response. It was not, as she'd initially thought, a lighting fixture. It also seemed to incorporate a variety of crystal forms and colors: some masterpieces of crystal artifice. Surely a waste. Suddenly she realized the mass was slowly rotating, its luminous ends sending motes of light about the room, changing patterns as it turned and always accompanied by the soft, almost subliminal chiming.

If the noise didn't twist you, thought Killashandra, the light would mesmerize. She declined the subtle hypnosis and began to prowl about the enormous reception hall. The first niche held a fan of minute shards of a pale-pink crystal, the sort probably utilized as computer chips or transducers. She wondered how sharp their edges might be. The next display provided magnification to show crystalline threads of various hues and diameters. Surely, one didn't "cut" those. Perhaps the yellowish crystal fractured into such strands.

The porcupine of a crystal drive unit dominated the next showcase, but the largest area was devoted to the black crystal, which, indeed, was neither black nor, apparently, a crystal. When she moved on to the next wall of the dodecahedron and squinted through one of the eyeholes, she saw another piece, very definitely black in the special lighting.

Suddenly, the chandelier chimed, and, startled, Killashandra turned to find the tall, thin, nervous man from the spaceship standing at the entrance. He had cleared his throat noisily, and the chandelier was responding to the harsh sound. He now looked as if he were going to dash from the hall in terror.

"Yes?" she asked, forestalling his flight. She might as well find out what was haunting him.

"No mean to break privacy," he blurted out in a hoarse whisper. He obviously had encountered the peculiar reaction of the chandelier before. "But the man with you on the ship? He was a Singer?"

"Yes."

"What happened to him? That spore get him?"

"No," Killashandra replied. The poor man's eyes threatened to pop out of his head he was so worried. "He was caught in the sonic backlash when a shuttle blew up. Sensory overload."

The relief brightened his face, and he mopped at his forehead and cheeks with a film.

"They tell you only so much and not enough. So when I saw him—"

"You want to become a Crystal Singer?"

He gulped, his larynx cartilage bobbing up and down in his nervousness.

"Are you a Singer?" There was awe in his voice. "I thought you must be from the way the captain was treating you." He wasn't so certain of that now, obviously.

"No, I'm not."

His attitude changed instantly as he straightened up and thrust his shoulders back.

"Well, I'm going to be," he stated firmly, and the chandelier echoed him. He glanced nervously above and seemed to draw his head protectively into his shoulders.

"If that's what you want," Killashandra said equably, and then strode past him. She'd seen all of the hall she wanted and could do with some food.

"You mean, you won't try to argue me out of it?" he asked, following her.

"Why should I?"

"Everyone else does."

"I'm not everyone else."

"It's supposed to be very dangerous."

"I'm not worried."

"Are you going to apply, too?"

She stopped and turned on him so swiftly that he nearly walked into her.

"You're invading my privacy—"

"Oh, no, no." He fended off such an accusation with

raised arms and a startled expression. "But why else would you be in the Heptite Hall?"

"To buy crystal."

"You're not a buyer—"

"You're invading my privacy!" She stalked off as fast as she could, half tempted to press the close button on the panel that separated the linking corridor with the catering foyer.

"I just wanted to talk . . ." His voice followed her but he at least had remained behind.

The energy generated by her irritation carried her past the bar area to a T-junction of aisles leading to business stalls and cubicles, some closed by privacy screens. Broad-leafed plants lined a short flight of steps into the dining area. Service slots and bright-orange menu panels were positioned against the walls, and she was making her way to the nearest when she heard herself called.

"Over here, Killashandra Ree." Captain Andurs rose from a group of spacemen to beckon her. "C'mon. Join us."

Well, he'd at least be protection against that imbecile if he followed her, so she waved back and stepped up to scan the menufax. She was overwhelmed by the selections scrolling on display. When she spotted the seafood casserole she'd eaten that momentous evening at Fuerte, she ordered it.

"Brew's good, too," Andurs said, coming to assist her. He deftly punched a sequence, paused and tapped again. "Goes down better with some of these."

She was about to protest his abruptness, all too familiar with the vagaries of overprogrammed and stubborn student hall catering units, when the service panel slid open to reveal all three orders. Efficiency was a pleasure.

"Here, have a sip of the brew and see if you like it," Andurs suggested, offering her the liter glass. "No sense making unnecessary trips. Spoils conversations. See, I told you it was good. It's not processed: allowed to age normally, and that means a good brew. They know how here." Then he dialed up not only a liter glass for her but a large beaker as well. "I'd stick to the brews here or your own planet's ferment or distillations if they stock 'em—and I'd be surprised if they didn't. You could really turn off on some drinks if you have the wrong metabolism, you know."

"I appreciate the advice," she said as they made their way back to the others.

"Do you?" Andurs sounded cynical. "We've been rescheduled. We'll be on our way tomorrow, 1000 base time. Rush cargo. Bound for Regulus Exchange. You can use that Guild voucher and cross the Milky Way if you've a mind to."

"I've a mind to stay here and see how it goes."

"Done any checking?" he asked, lowering his voice, for they were nearly to the table now.

"Enough."

"No matter what prints out, it wouldn't be enough or all the truth." Andurs' tone was dourly repressive.

"By FSP law, they have to make full disclosure of the dangers."

Andurs snorted, but they had reached the table by then and he was disinclined to continue that discussion.

She had only just been introduced to the flight engineer, whom she hadn't met during the journey, when she noticed tension on the faces of the supercargo and the second officer. Curious, she glanced over her shoulder to see what caused their dislike and then half turned in her chair to get a clear look.

Two men and a woman stood there observing the seated diners. It was not their rough, stained garments, the scarred boots, or unkempt hair that caught Killashandra's eye—though these were unusual enough in a society that respected cleanliness—but the trio's imperious bearing, a sort of lofty disdain that excluded everyone else, and the brilliance of their eyes. The tableau, briefly held during the trio's survey, broke up as the three moved purposefully toward a corner table where, as Killashandra followed their progress, two other similarly attired people sat.

"And who do they think they are?" Killashandra asked, as annoyed by their manner as the second officer and supercargo. Even as she spoke, she knew the answer, for she had seen that hauteur, that inner luminosity before—in Carrik. "Singers, are they?"

"Yes," said the super flatly.

"Are they always like that?"

"Wasn't your friend Carrik?" Andurs countered.

"Not exactly like that."

"Then he was most unusual," the super replied in a daunting tone. "They're at their worst just in from the ranges—as those are. Lucky for us, Andurs, there are two Monasterian ships in. They'll ship out on those."

Andurs nodded curtly and then, as if to make certain Killashandra did not continue the sore subject of Singers, began a volley of questions about supplies and cargo way-bills. Taking the hint, she applied herself to her food but did cast surreptitious glances toward the fascinating group of Singers. Killashandra was all the more surprised that they seemed not to have much to say to each other, though the trio had deliberately sought out the pair. Nor did they leave their table longer than it took one of them to dial and collect several wine beakers at a time. They paid no attention to others in the now-crowded dining area.

Since there was considerable traffic, greeting of friends, and good-natured teasing from table to table, Killashandra could make some discreet evaluations. A good relationship seemed to exist between base residents—Guild members or not—and transients. She recognized the various professions and skills by the distinctive uniform colors and hatchings of calling and rate. The travelers were garbed in whatever suited their fancies, the styles and fashions of two or three dozen cultures and disciplines. Ship personnel always wore the space-dark uniforms, sober counterpoint to the riot of civilian dress. Several life-supported aliens appeared briefly in the main foyer but they quickly retired to the catering level that accommodated their exotic requirements.

Having leisurely finished their meal, the supercargo and engineer excused themselves, claiming duties before liftoff. Andurs waved them a genial go-ahead and then turned to Killashandra.

"D'you see what would happen if you become a Singer?"

"What?" she asked guilelessly.

Andurs flicked his fingers impatiently at the aloof quintet. "You'd be alone. Wherever you went."

"I wasn't alone with Carrik. He was very good company."

"For a specific reason, I've no doubt, and don't spout Privacy at me."

Killashandra laughed at his sour reply. "The reason was mutual, my friend. And I still don't see why the Crystal Singers are at fault."

" 'And who do they think they are?' " he mimicked in a fair imitation of her instinctive reaction to the Singers.

"Well, I also didn't notice anyone making them welcome the way everyone else—"

"Nor will you. Disagreeable bastards, that's what they are. And they always act that superior."

"Carrik—" she began, remembering how much fun he had been.

"He might have been halfway gone by the time you met him. They change—and not for the better."

"They would have to, wouldn't they?" she said, somewhat abruptly, for Andurs' irrational insistence on generalities annoyed her. "The fax said they take rigorous physical, psychological, and aptitude tests. Only the best are taken, so they would be above the ploddies you have to put up with everywhere else in the galaxy."

"You don't understand. They are *very* different!" Andurs was becoming agitated in his effort to explain.

"I'll never understand if you won't be specific."

"Well, I can." Andurs almost leaped at her offer. "The Singer in the brown tunic—how old would you say he is? And don't stare at them too hard. They can be offensive if irritated. Especially when they're just off the Ranges like that set."

Killashandra had noticed the brown-clad man; he was the tallest one and exuded some of the same magnetic quality that had distinguished Carrik.

"I'd say about second half of his third decade, perhaps beginning of his fourth."

"I'm in my fourth and have been making this run for nine years standard. I know he's been a Singer for at least nine decades because his name's appeared on the passenger lists for my ship for that long."

Killashandra glanced discreetly over at the subject in question. It was hard to believe the man was well over his first hundred years. Modern science delayed the worst ravages of physical degeneration but—

"So eternal youth is your gripe?"

"No, not mine. Frankly I wouldn't want to have more than ten or twelve decades. It's not just that Singers look young longer, though that does get at some, it's—it's other differences . . ."

"Psychological? Professional? Physical? Or financial?"

"Look, the point is, there are differences that the rest of us note, sense, feel, and resent in Singers!" Andurs was vehement now, pounding one fist into the other palm to emphasize his points. "Whatever it is separates you forever from the rest of mankind. Is that what you want?"

Killashandra gave the question due consideration before she looked Andurs in the eye and said, "Yes. Crystal Singers are a rigidly selected, highly trained professional minority. And I want to be a member of that sort of group. I've had some training in that direction already," she added with a sour smile.

"Then your bringing Carrik back . . ." Andurs' nostrils flared with suspicion, and he leaned away from her.

"Was what I owed the man," she added hastily, for she didn't like that expression to appear so soon, and for no cause, on Andurs' face. She honestly had been motivated by regret for Carrik's condition. "Who knows? I may not pass the requirements. It harms no one for me to try, does it?" She gave Andurs a sweet, somewhat tremulous smile. "I was not motivated toward any goal when I encountered Carrik, you see—"

"Then ship out with me—or on any of the other ships. This"—Andurs' forefinger pointed at the floor—"is a dead end."

Killashandra sneaked one more look at the Cyrstal Singers—proud, aloof, and curiously radiant. She contrived a thoughtful frown for Andurs' benefit, but the group, remote and inaccessible, were indeed people apart, clearly marked by a subtle difference that set them above humans otherwise no less physically attractive or intelligent. This distinction would cause Singers to be singled out no matter where they were. Forever, Killashandra thought, as Stellar performers when basking in the applause of ador-

ing audiences. Since she was deprived of the one, she
would try for this.

"There is something about them . . ." she said aloud with
a diffident lift of her shoulders and a wry smile. "You
know, you're right about the brew—" and she turned a
more winning smile at Andurs.

"I'll get more."

She spent a pleasant evening with the captain, though
she was glad that it was just an evening, for his limitations
soon became apparent. Carrik had had many revelations
for her. But when Andurs left for his ship at date change,
it was only with expressions of regret and additional urg-
ings for her to be on board. Though he was only going as
far as Regulus Exchange, Killashandra could pick up a
ship bound anywhere in the galaxy with her Guild voucher.

She thanked him, affecting more drowsiness than she
felt, and left him with the notion that she had been swayed
by his persuasions and person.

She didn't learn until much later that his ship, the *Rag
Blue Swan Delta*, had delayed departure until peremptorily
forced to leave by an aggravated landing officer. By that
time she was already in the Guild block of the base.

CHAPTER 4

Arriving punctually at the beginning of business hours, Killashandra was not the only one so prompt. Some of the dozen or so milling about the large reception area were quite obviously buyers, peering at the displays and jotting entries on their wrist units. The tall, thin young man was there. He looked startled to see Killashandra and swerved away from her. Just as Killashandra noted two men and a woman emerge from a panel in the far side of the dodecahedron, someone stamped in from the base entrance. Killashandra glimpsed a set, hard, angry face and the close-cropped hair of a space worker as the bone-thin figure of a female swept past her.

The chandelier responded to the vibrations of her passage and picked up the tone of her voice. From the resonance of the chiming artform, Killashandra knew the woman was making demands. What surprised Killashandra more was that the Guild woman did not pay any attention, her head remaining bent over the module. The angry space worker repeated her question, sharp enough now for Killashandra to hear that the woman was demanding to be taken immediately for testing as a Guild candidate.

Suddenly, one of the Guildsmen, excusing himself from his conversation with a buyer, touched the programmer on her arm, directing her gaze to the now irate space worker.

Another angry spate of words jarred the crystal drops,
although the Guild programmer seemed not the least disturbed either by her discourtesy or the space worker's ire.
In the next moment, the panel at the back of the room
opened again, and the space worker moved toward it, her
head set at an aggressive angle, her stride jarring her slender frame. The panel closed behind her.

A sigh attracted Killashandra's attention, and she turned
to find a young man standing beside her. He would have
deserved a second look anywhere, for he possessed close-
curled red hair, a recessive trait rarer now than the true
blond. He had evidently watched the interchange between
the space worker and the Guild programmer as if he had
anticipated such a confrontation. His sigh had been one
of relief.

"She made it," he murmured under his breath, and then,
noticing Killashandra, smiled at her. His unusually light-
green eyes twinkled in mischief. The antipathy Killashandra had instinctively felt for the space worker was replaced
by an instant affinity to the young man. "She's been in a
snit, that one, the whole journey here. Thought she'd go
through the debarkation arch like a projectile when it
started laying on the formality. And after all that . . ." He
spread his hands wide to express his astonishment at her
ease.

"There's more to it than going through a doorway,"
Killashandra said.

"Don't I just know it, but there was no telling Carigana.
For starters, she was annoyed that I got to do the prelim at
Yarro on Beta VI. As if it were a personal affront to her
that she had to come all the way here." He stepped closer
to Killashandra as a knot of people, buyers from their
varied manner of dress, entered. "Have you taken the
plunge yet?" And then he held up his hand, grinning so
winningly when Killashandra stiffened at such a flagrant
breach of privacy that she couldn't, after all, take offense.
"I'm from Scartine, you know, and I keep forgetting manners. Besides, you don't look like a buyer"—his comment
was complimentary for he gestured with good-humored
contempt at the finery of most of the other occupants of
the hall—"and transients would never venture further than

the catering area, so you must be interested in crystal singing . . ." He raised his eyebrows as well as the tone of his voice in question.

It would have taken a far more punctilious person than Killashandra to depress his ingenuous manner, but she answered with the briefest of smiles and a nod.

"Well, because I've been through the prelim, I've only to report my presence, but if I were you, though I'm not, and it's certainly not my wish to invade your privacy, I'd give Carigana a chance to get organized before I followed her in." Then he cocked his head, grinning with a sparkle at odds with his guilelessness. "Unless you're hanging back with second thoughts."

"I've thoughts but none of them seconds," Killashandra said. "You did the prelim at Yarro?"

"Yes, you know the tests."

"SG-1's, I hear."

He shrugged diffidently. "Medigear feels the same for all levels, and if you're adjusted, the psych is nothing. Aptitude's aptitude and a fast one, but you look like you've done tertiary studies, so what's to knot your hair over?" His expression was sharp as his eyes flicked to the wall through which Carigana had passed. "If you've got hair!"

"Those tests—they're not complicated, or painful, or anything?. . ." The tall nervous young man had sidled up to them without either noticing his approach.

Killashandra frowned slightly with displeasure, but the other young man grinned encouragingly.

"No sweat, no stress, no strength exerted, man. A breeze," and he planed his hand in a smooth gesture indicating ease. "All I got to do now is go up to the panel, knock on the door, and I'm in." He snapped the shoulder strap of his carisak.

"You've been given the full disclosure?" the dark-haired man asked.

"Not yet." The red-head grinned again. "That's the next step and only done here."

"Shillawn Agus Vartry," the other said formally, raising his right hand, fingers spread in the galactic gesture that indicated cooperation without weapon.

"Rimbol C-hen-stal-az" was the red-head's rejoinder.

Killashandra wasn't in the mood to be drawn into further conversation about applying for Guild membership, not with this Shillawn swallowing and stammering his way to a decision. She accorded Rimbol a smile and the salute as she backed away courteously before veering toward the module with more assurance than she felt. Once there, she spread her fingers wide where the movement would catch the woman's eye.

"I'd like to apply for membership to the Heptite Guild," she said when the woman raised her head. Killashandra had meant to say she wanted to become a Crystal Singer, but the words had shifted in her mind and mouth with uncharacteristic discretion. Perhaps Carigana's very bad example had tempered her approach.

The programmer inclined her head in acknowledgment of the request, her fingers flashing across the terminal keys. "If you will proceed through that entrance." She motioned toward the opening panel in the wall.

Killashandra could just imagine how anticlimactic that mild phrase must have been for the storming Carigana. She smiled to herself as the panel closed behind her without so much as a sigh. Exit Killashandra Reé softly and with no fanfare.

She found herself in a short corridor, with a series of color-coded and design-patched doors on either side, and made for one that opened quietly. Just as she entered the room from one door, a man with an odd crook to one shoulder entered from another. He gave her such a quick searching look that she felt certain he had had to greet Carigana.

"You agree to submit to SG-1 examinations of physical, psychological, and aptitudinal readiness? Please state your name, planet of origin, and whatever rank you hold. This information is being processed under the Federated Sentient Planets' conditions regarding admission into the Heptite Guild of Ballybran." He ran through the speech in two breaths, staring expectantly at her while her mind caught up with his rote comments.

"Yes, I, Killashandra Ree of Fuerte, agree to the examinations. Rank, tertiary student in performing arts, released."

"This way, please, Killashandra Ree." She followed him into an anteroom, the usual examination facility. The panel on one door blazed red, and Killashandra supposed that Carigana was within, being subjected to the same tests she was about to undergo.

She was shown to the next cubicle, which held the couch and hood that were standard physical diagnostic equipment for her species. Without a word, she settled herself on the couch as comfortably as possible, inured since childhood to the procedures, to the slightly claustrophobic sensation as the upper half of the diagnostic unit swung down over her. She didn't mind the almost comforting pressure of the torso unit or the tight grip across one thigh and the hard weight on her left shin, but she never could get used to the constricting headpiece and the pressures against eyes, temple, and jaw. But cerebral and retinal scanning were painless, and one never felt the acupuncture that deadened the leg for the blood, bone marrow, and tissue samples. The other pressures for organ readings, muscle tone, heat and cold tolerances, sound sensitivity, were as nothing to the final pain-threshold jolt. She had heard about but never experienced the pain-threshold gamut—and hoped never to have to do so again.

Just as she was about to scream from the stimuli applied to her nerve centers the apparatus abruptly retracted. As her nervous system tingled with the aftereffect, she did groan and massaged the back of her neck to ease muscles that had tensed in that split second of measurable agony.

"Take this restorative now, please," the meditech said, entering the room. He gave her a glass of carbonated green liquid. "Set you right. And if you'll just sit here," he added as a comfortable padded chair rolled to the center of the room while the medigear slid to the left. "When you are recovered, press the button on the right chair arm, and the psychological test will begin. A verbal address system is used. Responses are, of course, recorded, but I'm sure you're familiar with the procedures by now."

The drink did clear the last miasma of the threshold test from her senses, making her feel incredibly alert. All the better preparation for psychological testing.

Killashandra had always had mixed feelings about that

sort of evaluation—so much might depend on one's frame of mind at that particular hour, day, and year. She experienced her usual halfhearted desire to give all the wrong answers, but this was coupled with the keen awareness of self-competition. Too much depended on the exams. She had no need to play any of the games she might have risked at other levels and times. She could not, however, comprehend the purpose of some questions that had never been asked during any other evaluation session. Of course, she'd never applied to the Heptite Guild before, so their criteria were bound to be different. Nor had she undergone a computerized verbal address psych test before, which was generally conducted face to face with a human examiner.

Toward the last few moments of the session, the speed of questioning increased to the point where she was actually sweating to produce answers to the displayed questions in an effort to keep up the pace.

She could still feel her heart racing when the Guild man returned, this time bearing a tray with steaming food packs.

"Your aptitude tests will be presented after you've eaten and rested. You may request entertainment from the fax or sleep." At his words, a contour couch appeared from a storage area. "When you are ready, inform the computer and the final examination will begin."

Killashandra was ravenous and found the nutritious meal delicious. She sipped the hot beverage slowly and asked for soothing Optherian "balances" to clear her mind of the tensions caused by the last portion of the psych tests.

In her previous evaluation sessions, the manner of the human attendants had often indicated the level of her performance—and she was accustomed to scoring high. But the Guild tech had been so impersonal, she couldn't guess how she was doing.

After she'd finished her meal, she elected to continue and signaled her readiness. Whereupon she was tested for pitch, the severest evaluation of that faculty she'd ever endured, including estimates of vibrational errors and unnerving subliminal noises below 50 and above 18,000 cycles. That recorded, the testing moved on to deceptively

complex hand-eye coordinations that again left her
drenched with sweat. She was run through a series of depth-
perception exams and spatial relationships. The latter had
always been one of her strong points, but by the time the
session was over, she was wrung out with fatigue and was
shaking.

Maybe it was wishful thinking on her part, but when the
meditech returned, she fancied something of respect in his
glance.

"Killashandra Ree, since you have completed the first
day's examinations up to standard, you are now the guest
of the Guild. We have taken the liberty of transferring
your personal effects to more comfortable quarters in the
Guild block. If you will follow me . . ."

Ordinarily, such an action, taken without her consent,
would have constituted an invasion of privacy, but her energies were too depleted for her to summon up a protest.
She was led deeper into the Guild block, down three levels
from the main and the only entrance, or exit, to the rest of
Shankill Base. Her easy penetration of the hallowed pre-
cinct amused rather than alarmed her. There was really no
need for her to be isolated from the rest of the base population after what were very standard examinations. Except
for the pain-threshold test, she had nothing to warn any
other prospective applicant about. Unsuccessful applicants
would be more dangerous to the Guild because of their
disappointment. What happened to them, she wondered?
What, for instance, had become of the angry Carigana?
She'd be glad to be out of that one's vicinity in the event of
her failure. And where were Rimbol and that irritating,
twitchy young man, that Shillawn something?

How far into the Guild did she have to go to get this free
room and board, she wondered, fatigue irritating her. She
desired nothing more than to stretch out and sleep. She felt
as drained as she had the night of the final student concert.
How long ago was that now? In terms of distance or time?
She had no patience with her own conundrums. How
much farther now?

The Guild man had paused at a door, which slid open.

"If you'll put your print on file, you will find your belongings within. At the end of this corridor is a common

lounge, although you will also find catering facilities in your room. Tomorrow you will be summoned for the final phase."

A bleep from the man's wrist-unit curtailed any questions she might have asked; for he acknowledged the reminder, inclined his head politely to her and retraced his steps.

She placed her thumb in the depression for the print lock and entered her new accommodation. It was not only larger—spacious in comparison to the hostel room—it was also more luxuriously appointed. A chair was drawn up to a small table, already set with a beaker of brew from the catering panel, which was lit. Killashandra gratefully sampled the drink, noting that the menufax was set to fish selections. She wondered just how much information the Guild had already had programmed about her since she had given her name, planet of origin, and rank. Deliberately, she spun the display to other proteins and ordered what was described as a hearty casserole of assorted legumes and a light wine.

She had just finished her meal when the door announced a visitor. She hesitated a long moment, unable to imagine who would be calling; then the door added that the visitor's name was Rimbol, who required a word with her. She pressed the door release.

Rimbol leaned in, grinning. "C'mon out for bit. Just for a drink. It's free." Then he winked. "Neither Carigana nor Shillawn are present. Just some others who've already passed their prelims. C'mon."

The amusement in his wheedling voice was the deciding factor. Killashandra knew herself well enough to realize that even if she tried to sleep, she'd only play back the tests and become so depressed over omissions and commissions that she'd never achieve a true rest. A few drinks and a bit of relaxation in Rimbol's infectious company would do her much more good, especially if both Carigana and that nervous Shillawn were absent.

She was a bit taken aback, however, when 'just some others' numbered twenty-nine. Rimbol, sensing her surprise, grinned and gestured at the catering area.

"A brew's what you need. This is Killashandra," he announced in a slightly raised voice to the room in general. Her presence was acknowledged by slight nods or smiles or a brief hand gesture. A certain degree of informal companionship was already enjoyed by the others. The group, involved in some sort of four-player card game, didn't even look up as she and Rimbol collected their drinks.

"You make thirty, you know," Rimbol said as he guided her to a seat on the one unoccupied lounger. "Shillawn and Carigana thirty-two, and there's supposed to be one more going through prelim today. If that's a pass, it means we'll all go down to Ballybran tomorrow."

"That is, if no one gets scared after disclosure," said a girl who wandered over to join them. "I'm Jezerey, late of Salonika in the Antares group."

"I didn't think they canceled after disclosure," Rimbol said, frowning in surprise.

"You may well be right, but I do know that thirty is the smallest group they'll train," Jezerey went on, settling herself on the couch with a long sigh. "I've been waiting seven weeks standard." She sounded disgusted. "But Borton"— and she gestured toward the card players—"has been here nine. He'd just missed a class. Nothing will make him decline. I'm not so sure about one or two of the others— and we've got a few to spare. Rimbol says that nothing would unpersuade that Carigana, and from the look on her face when old Crookback brought her in, I'm as glad she decided she didn't like us either and stayed in her room. Space workers are odd lots, but she's—she's—"

"She's just intense," Rimbol noted when Jezerey faltered. "I don't think she trusts space stations any more than spaceships. She was tranked to her brows on the trip here. Shillawn"—and Rimbol favored Killashandra with a wry expression—"was knackered out of his bones, so *I* invaded Privacy and put a knockout in his brew. Got him to bed."

"Why would someone like him want to be a Crystal Singer?" Killashandra asked.

"Why do any of us?" Rimbol answered, amused.

"All right, why would you?" Killashandra fired the question right back at him.

"Wasn't allowed to continue as an instrumentalist. Not enough openings on my mudball for a string player. Crystal singing's the next best thing."

Killashandra nodded, looking to Jezerey.

"Curiously enough," the girl said with a bemused expression, "I was redundant in my profession, too. Limb-replacement therapist. And the Dear knows there're enough accidents on Salonika." She wrinkled her nose and then caught the puzzled expressions of Rimbol and Killashandra. "Mining world, asteroid belts around us and the next planet out. Next to mining, you might say replacement was our biggest industry."

"Space workers aren't apt to be redundant, either," Killashandra commented, looking at Rimbol.

"Carigana wasn't. Psyched out when her safety cable snapped—I get the impression she was deep-spaced a long time before they found her. She didn't say"—and Rimbol emphasized the last word—"but she's probably unstable for such employment."

Jezerey nodded sympathetically.

"Shillawn?" Killashandra asked.

"Told me he was a chemotech," Rimbol replied. "His project was finished up, and he was given an assignment he didn't like. Underground. He's a touch claustro! I think that's what makes him so nervous."

"And we all have perfect pitch," Killashandra said more to herself than the others because the phrases Maestro Valdi had spat accusingly, particularly the one about a 'silicate spider,' came appropriately to mind. She dismissed the niggling suspicion as invalid.

An explosive curse burst from one of the card players, and his earnest request for arbitration from any and all in the room interrupted their private conversation.

Although Killashandra took no part in the intense discussion that followed, she deemed it good sense to lend her presence to a group with whom she might be spending considerable time. She also saw them as a group with no other common factor—aside from the invisible prerequisite of perfect pitch—than age. All seemed to be within their third decade; most apparently just finished with tertiary education; no two from the same system or planet.

Killashandra remained on the fringes of the good-humored but volatile game discussion until she had finished another glass of the very good brew. Then she quietly retired, wondering as she prepared for sleep just how thirty-plus people from so many different planets had all heard of the Crystal Singers.

She had just finished her morning meal when a soft, deep chime brought her attention to the screen. She was requested to go to the lounge room.

"You sneaked away nice and early," a cheerful tenor said behind her. She turned to find Rimbol approaching, the awkward figure of Shillawn just behind him. "Missed the fun, you did."

"Who won the argument?" she asked after a courteous nod to Shillawn.

"No one and everyone. It was the arguing that was fun!" The red-headed lad grinned.

They had reached the lounge by then, and from the other corridors the rest of the successful filed, some re-forming the groups she'd noticed the previous evening. Only Carigana seemed apart; she sat on the back of one of the loungers glowering at everyone. Something about the angry girl was familiar to Killashandra, but she couldn't place what.

Just then, from the fourth entrance, limped a tall woman holding the left side of her long gown slightly away from her thigh. Her gaze swiftly scanned the room, counting, Killashandra thought, and made her own tally. Thirty-three. Out of what gross number of applicants, she wondered again, over the nine weeks Jezerey had said Borton had waited?

"I am Borella Seal," the woman announced in the clear, rich voice of a trained contralto. Killashandra regarded her with closer interest. "I am a miner of crystal, a Crystal Singer. Since I am recovering from an injury sustained in the ranges, I have been asked to disclose to you the dangers of this profession." She pulled aside the long gown and revealed wounds so ugly and vividly contused that several people recoiled. As if this was the very reaction she had wanted, Borella smiled slightly. "I will expose the wound again for a specific purpose other than arousing nausea or sympathy. Take a good look now."

Shillawn's elbow nudged Killashandra, and she was about to give him a severe reprimand for such a private insult when she realized he was drawing her attention to Carigana. The girl was the only one who approached Borella Seal and bent for the close inspection of the long gashes scoring the upper leg.

"They appear to be healing properly, though you ought to have had them bonded. How'd you get 'em?" Carigana was clinically impersonal.

"Two days ago, I slipped on crystal shale and fell fifteen meters down an old worked face."

"*Two* days?" Anger colored Carigana's voice. "I don't believe you. I've seen enough lacerations to know ones as deep as these don't heal that much in two days. Why the color of the bruising and the state of the tissue already healed show you were injured weeks ago."

"Two days. Singers heal quickly."

"Not that quick." Carigana would have said more, but Borella Seal gestured dismissal and turned to the others.

"By order of the Federated Sentient Planets, full disclosure of the dangers peculiar to and inherent in this profession must be revealed to all applicants who have satisfactorily completed the initial examinations." She accorded them a slight nod of approval. "However, as is also permissible by FSP law, professional—problems—may be protected by erasure. Those to whom this practice is unacceptable may withdraw."

"How much is erased?" Carigana asked.

"Precisely one hour and twenty minutes, replaced by a recollection of oversleeping and a leisurely breakfast."

"On record?"

"If requested, the Guild supplies the information that a minor but inadmissible physical defect has been discovered. Few question the Heptite Guild." For some reason Killashandra thought that fact amused Borella. Carigana's frown had deepened. "Any objectors?" Borella asked, looking straight at the space worker.

When no other voice was raised, she asked them to file

before the screen she then activated, giving their name and
stating their willingness to comply with erasure. The process didn't take long, but Killashandra felt that she had
taken an irrevocable step as her acceptance was officially
and indisputably recorded.

Borella then led them down a short hall to a door,
Carigana the first to follow. Her gasp and half halt as she
passed the entrance forewarned the others but in no way
prepared anyone for the display in that short corridor. On
either side were bodies in clear fluid—all but one glinted as
if coated with a silicon. The planes of the faces looked
rock hard; limbs, fingers, and toes were extended as if
solidified, and not by the rigor of death. The crystalline
sheen couldn't be some trick of the light, Killashandra
thought, for her own skin showed no change. What roiled
her stomach were the facial expressions: three looked as if
death had overtaken them in a state of insanity; two appeared mildly surprised, and the sixth angry, her hands
raised toward some object she had been trying to grasp.
The last was the most grisly: a charred body forever in
the position of a runner, consumed by a conflagration that
had melted flesh from bone.

"This is what happens to the unprotected on Ballybran.
It could also happen to you, though every effort is made to
reduce such risks to a minimum. If you wish to retire now,
you are completely at liberty to do so."

"External danger does not constitute a Code 4 classification," Carigana said, her tone accusatory.

"No, it doesn't. But these are representative of two of
the dangers of Ballybran which the Heptite Guild is required by Federated Sentient Planets to reveal to you."

"Is that the worst that can happen?" Carigana asked
scornfully.

"Isn't being dead enough?" someone asked from the
group.

"Dead's dead—crystal, char, or carrion," Carigana replied, shrugging her shoulders, her tone so subtly offensive
that Killashandra was not the only one who frowned with
irritation.

"Yes, but it is the manner of dying that can be the

worst," said Borella in such a thoughtful way that she had everyone's attention. She accorded them the slightest smile. "Follow me."

The grim corridor opened on to a small semicircular lecture hall. Borella proceeded to a small raised platform, gesturing for the group to take the seats, which would have accommodated three times their number. As she turned to face them, a large hologram lit behind her, a view of the Scorian system, homing quickly on Ballybran and its three moons. The planet and its satellites moved with sufficient velocity to demonstrate the peculiar Passover of the moons, when all three briefly synchronized orbits—a synchronization that evidently took place over different parts of the parent world.

"The crystallization displayed in the corridor is the most prevalent danger on Ballybran. It occurs when the spore symbiont, a carbon silicate occurring in an unorthodox environment peculiar to Ballybran, does not form a proper bridge between our own carbon-based biological system and the silicon-based ecology of this planet. Such a bridge is essential for working on Ballybran. If the human host adapts properly to the spore symbiont, and I assure you it is not the other way round, the human experiences a significant improvement in visual acuity, tactile perceptions, nerve conduction, and cellular adaptation. The first adaptations are of immense importance to those who become miners of crystal, the Crystal Singers. Yes, Carigana?"

"What part of the body does the symbiont invade? Is it crystalline or biological?"

"Neither, and the symbiont invades cellular nuclei in successful adaptations—"

"What happens to the unsuccessful ones?"

"I shall discuss that shortly if you will be patient. As part of the cell nucleus, the symbiont affects the DNA/ RNA pattern of the body, extending the lifespan considerably. The rumor that Crystal Singers are immortal is exaggerated, but functional longevity is definitely increased by fifty or more *decades* beyond actuarial norms. The adaptation provides an immunization to ordinary biological disease, enormously increasing the recuperative ability. Broken bones and wounds such as mine are, I warn you, part of the daily work of a Crystal Singer. Tolerance to extremes of heat and cold are also increased."

And pain, no doubt, Killashandra thought, remembering not only the test but Borella's lack of discomfort with her deep wounds.

Behind the Singer, the holograms were now views of Ballybran's rugged terrain, quickly replaced by a time-lapse overview from one of the moons, so that the planet's twelve continents were visible in seconds.

"On the negative side, once acclimated to Ballybran and adapted to the symbiont, the Singer is irreversibly sterile. The genetic code is altered by the intrusion of the symbiont into the nuclei, and those parts of the DNA spiral dealing with heredity and propagation are chemically altered, increasing personal survival traits as opposed to racial survival—a chemical alteration of instinct, if you will."

Carigana gave a pleased sound like a feline expression of enjoyment.

"The other, and basically the most important negative factor, is that a Singer cannot remain too long away from Ballybran's peculiar ecology. The symbiont must recharge itself from its native place. *Its* death means the death of the host—a rather unpleasant one, for death from extreme old age occurs within a period inversely related to the host's elapsed lifespan."

"How long can a Singer stay away from Ballybran without ill effect?" Killashandra asked, thinking of Carrik and his reluctance to return.

"Depending on the strength of the initial adaptation, and that varies, for periods of up to four hundred days. A Singer is not required to be absent for longer than two hundred days on assignment off-planet. Two hundred and fifty days is suitable for leisure. Sufficient, I assure you, for most purposes."

Killashandra, seated behind the space worker, saw Carigana draw breath for another question, but Borella had changed the hologram to show a human writhing in the grip of a shaking fever, all too reminiscent of the hypothermia that had affected Carrik. The man was seized by massive convulsions. As the focus tightened first to his hands, then his chest and face, he aged from an athletic

person in his third, possibly fourth decade, to a wrinkled
and dehydrated, hairless, shrunken corpse in the time it
took viewers to gasp.

"He was one of the first Singers to make a successful
symbiotic adaptation. He died, regrettably, at Weasust
while setting up the black quartz relay station for that
sector of the FSP. It was the first time a Singer had been
absent for a prolonged period, but that particular danger
had not yet been recognized."

"Did you know him?" Shillawn asked with a perception
that surprised Killashandra, for she had wondered the
same thing.

"Yes, I did. He trained me in the field," Borella replied,
dispassionately.

Killashandra made some mental calculations and regarded the flawless complexion and erect figure of their
mentor with surprise.

"Is that Milekey man still alive?" Carigana asked.

"No. He died during a major fault in the range which
bears his name."

"I thought this symbiont kept you from broken bones
and wounds?"

"The symbiont provides increased recuperative ability
but cannot replace a severed head on a body whose
wounds have resulted in complete blood loss. For less dras-
tic injuries—"and she pulled the gown aside from her left
leg.

Rimbol's soft whistle of astonishment summed up Killashandra's amazement, too. They had all seen the purple
bruising and lacerations: now the contusions were faintly
yellow splotches, and the wounds were visibly closing.

"What about those for whom the symbiont doesn't
work?" asked the undaunted Carigana.

"The main purpose of the intensive physical examination
was to evaluate rejection and blood factors, tissue health,
and chromosome patterns against those of the known successful adaptations." A graph appeared on the screen, the
line indicating success rising triumphantly over the past
three decades where it had hovered in minor peaks over a
span of three hundred or more years. "Your tests indicate
no undesirable factors evaluated against records now dat-

ing back over three hundred twenty-seven standard years. You all have as good a chance as possible of achieving complete acceptance by the symbiont—"

"The odds are five to one against."

Killashandra wondered if Carigana gave even the time of day in that same hostile tone.

"No longer," Borella replied, and a light appeared on the upward swing of the graph line. "It's now better than one out of three. There are still factors not yet computed which cause only partial adaptation. I am compelled by FSP law to emphasize that."

"And then?"

"That person obviously becomes one of the 20,007 technicians," Shillawn said.

"I asked *her*." Carigana gave Shillawn a scathing glance.

"The young man is, however, right."

"And technicians never leave Ballybran." Carigana's glance slid from Borella to Shillawn, and it was obvious what her assessment of Shillawn's chances were.

"Not without severe risk of further impairment. The facilities on Ballybran, however, are as complete as—"

"Except you can't ever leave."

"As you are not yet there," Borella continued imperturbably, though Killashandra had the notion the Singer enjoyed sparring with the space worker, "the problem is academic and can remain so." She turned to the others. "As I was about to point out, the odds have been reduced to three out of five. And improving constantly. The last class produced thirty-three Singers from thirty-five candidates.

"Besides the problem of symbiont adaptation required for existence on Ballybran, there is an additional danger, of the more conventional type." She went on less briskly, allowing her comments on the odds to be absorbed. "Ballybran's weather." The screen erupted into scenes of seas lashed into titanic waves, landscapes where ground cover had been pulped. "Each of the three moons contains weather stations, and sixteen permanent satellites scan the surface constantly.

"Scoria, our primary, has a high incidence of sun-spot activity." A view of the sun in eclipse supported that statement as flares leaped dramatically from behind the eclipsing moon's disk. A second occluded view showed the primary's dark blotches. "This high activity, plus the frequent conjunction of the moons' orbits, a triple conjunction being the most dangerous obviously, ensure that Ballybran has interesting weather."

A bark of laughter for such understatement briefly interrupted Borella, but her patient smile suggested that the reaction was expected. Then the screen showed breathtaking conjunction of the moons' orbits.

"When the meteorological situation becomes unstable, even in terms of Ballybran's norms, the planet is subjected to storms which have rated the euphemism, mach storm. As the crystal ranges of Ballybran extend downward rather than up,"—the screen obediently provided a view from a surface vehicle traversing the down ranges at speed—"one might assume that one need only descend far enough below the planet's surface to avoid the full brunt of wind and weather. A fatal assumption. The ranges constitute the worst danger." The view changed to a rapid series of photographs of people, their expressions ranging from passive imbecility to wild-eyed violence. "The winds of the mach storm stroke the crystal to such sonic violence that a human, even one perfectly adapted to his symbiont, can be driven insane by sound.

"The vehicles provided by the Guild for Singers' use have every known warning device, although the most effective one is lodged in the bodies of the Singers themselves; the symbiont, which is more sensitive to the meteorological changes than any instrument man can create. Sometimes the human element overcomes the keen senses of the symbiont, and a Singer is impervious to warnings.

"Such injury is the main reason for the tithe levied by the Guild on all active members. You may be certain of the best possible care should such an accident befall you."

"You said the symbiont increased recuperative ability for structural damage." the irrepressible Carigana began.

"A broken mind is scarcely a physiological problem. Within its scope, the symbiont is a powerful protector. It is not in itself sentient, so though it could restore damaged brain tissue, it cannot affect what man chooses to designate 'soul'."

Somehow Borella's tone managed to convey the notion that Carigana might not possess that commodity. Killashandra was not the only one to catch that nuance, which apparently eluded its intended target.

"How was the symbiont first discovered?" Killashandra asked, determined that Carigana was not going to dominate the session.

"By the first prospector, Milekey. He made a successful adaptation with the spore, considering the transition illness to be only some irritating infection."

"He wasn't the only one on that mission, according to the fax," Shillawn said.

"No, he wasn't, though the deaths of the other members of his geology team were not at first linked to Ballybran. Milekey made several excursions into the ranges to examine crystal faces and cut new types for evaluation. He also helped develop the first effective cutter. His personal tapes indicate that he felt a strong compulsion to return to Ballybran frequently, but, at the time, it was thought that this was merely due to his interest in the crystal and the increasing uses to which it could be put. He also did not connect his ability to avoid the storms to the presence of the symbiont.

"This aspect was discovered when the transition disease struck Cutter after Cutter, leaving crystalized bodies similar to those in the hall."

"There's one that was charred," Rimbol said, swallowing against nausea.

"And that is the third danger of Ballybran. Fortunately not as prevalent these days since common sense and education in the use of equipment decrease the probability. The crystal ranges can build up localized high-voltage and sonic charges near which ordinary communits do not operate properly, nor do other types of electrical equipment, some of which are necessary to the operation of sleds and conveniences. Fireballs can occur. And, despite all the precautions, a Singer can be volatilized. It is a danger we must mention."

"You say that those who do not make a good adaptation to the symbiont specialize in technical work—but what constitutes a poor adaptation?" Jezerey asked, leaning forward, elbows on her knees.

"Some impairment of one or more of the normal physical senses. But this is often coupled with an extension to the other senses not impaired."

"What senses?" Shillawn asked, his thin throat muscles working as if he had trouble getting the words out.

"Generally hearing is impaired." Borella gave a slight smile. "That's considered a blessing. No shielding has ever been invented to silence the full fury of a mach storm. Often eyesight increases into the ultraviolet or infrared spectra, with an ability in some to sense magnetic fields. Increased tactile sensitivity has enabled artistically inclined guildsmen to produce some of the most treasured art of modern times. There is, however, no way of predicting what form the impairment will take, nor what compensation will be effected."

"Have you pretty pictures of the victims?"

"The handicaps are rarely visible, Carigana."

"The handicap plus sterility plus immolation on a storm-lashed planet in exchange for a greatly increased lifespan? That constitutes the Code 4?"

"It does. You have thus been duly informed of the risks and the permanent alteration to your chemistry and physical abilities. Any further pertinent questions?"

"Yes. If you say there are more Singers these days, how does that affect individual profit with so many cutting in the ranges?" asked Carigana.

"It doesn't," Borella replied, "not with the expanding galactic need for the communications link provided only by black quartz from Ballybran; not when Singers are capable, quick and cautious; not when there are people, like yourself, motivated to succeed in joining our select band."

Attuned as her ear was to nuances in vocal tone, Killashandra did not quite perceive how Borella could deliver such a scathing reprimand with no variation in the pitch or timbre of her voice. Yet a sudden flush of humiliation colored Carigana's space-tan skin.

"How often are there injuries like yours?" a girl asked from the back of the theater.

"Frequently," Borella replied with cheerful unconcern. "But I'll be back in the ranges"—Killashandra caught the note of longing, for it was the first time emotion had shown in the Singer's contained voice—"in a day or two."

"Singing crystal is worth such risks, then?" Killashandra heard herself ask.

Borella's eyes sought hers and held them as a slow smile crossed her lips.

"Yes, singing crystal is worth any risk." The force of that quiet statement caused a silence. "I shall leave you to discuss the matter among yourselves. When you have made your decision, just follow me." She moved toward the door at the side of the platform. It opened and closed with a soft *whoosh* behind her.

Killashandra looked over at Shillawn and Rimbol, noticed that the others were seeking emotional support from their nearest neighbors. Carigana, deep in a sullen mood, was pointedly ignored. Killashandra rose to her feet with an energy that attracted all eyes.

"I made up my mind before I ever arrived," she said. "And I don't scare easily, anyhow!"

She strode down the steps toward the exit, hearing the movement of others behind her, though she didn't turn her head. A curious elation, tinged with apprehension and a certain fearfulness, seized her as she passed the portal. Then it was too late.

Killashandra wasn't sure what she had expected to find on the other side of the door panel. She half thought Borella might be present to see how many had not been deterred. Instead, she was surprised to find uniformed members of the FSP Civil Service, their faces and attitudes as grave as if they were at a disintegration or interment. The senior officer motioned her to follow the first person in line, a male who, in turn, gestured Killashandra toward another of the cubicles that seemed to infest all levels of the moon base. Behind her, she heard the surprised intake of breath of whichever candidate had directly followed her.

A slab table and two chairs occupied the small room. She moved toward one seat, but the officer's gesture stopped her.

"Bontel Aba Gray, Rank 10, FSP Civil Service, Shankill Moon Base, Ballybran, date 23/4/3308: applicant will present identity to the outlet, stating aloud name, rank, and planet of origin."

Only after Killashandra had disgustedly complied with the formality was she allowed to seat herself opposite Bontel Gray.

"Is it true that you have received physical, psychological, and aptitude tests under the auspices of the Heptite Guild?"

"Yes."

"You have been informed of the hazards involved in the Code 4 classification of the planet Ballybran?"

"Yes." She wondered how Carigana was accepting the additional aggravation. That is, if Carigana had passed through the door.

Gray then questioned her in depth on Borella's lecture. Each of Killashandra's answers was recorded—but for *whose* protection, Killashandra wondered. She was reaching her aggravation point when he stopped.

"Do you swear, aver, and affirm that you are here of your own free will, without let or hindrance, conditioning or bribery, by any person or persons connected with the Heptite Guild?"

"I certainly do so swear, aver, and affirm."

He glanced at the ident slot, which suddenly glowed green. Placing both hands on the table as if wearied by this duty, Gray pushed himself to his feet. "The formalities are now concluded," he said with a tight smile. "May you sing well and profitably."

The man remained standing as she rose and left. She had the impression, a sideways glance, that he unfastened his tunic collar, his expression sliding into regret as he watched her leave.

Borella was in the main hall, her eyes focused on each cubicle door as it opened and a recruit appeared. Killashandra noticed that just the faintest hint of satisfaction appeared on the woman's face as her entire "class" reassembled.

"A shuttle waits," she said, once more leading the way.

"When do we get this spore business done?" Carigana asked, striding ahead of two others to reach Borella.

"On Ballybran. We did, at one point, use an artificial exposure, but the effects were no less successful than the natural process. Generally, infection occurs within ten days of reaching the surface," she added before Carigana could inquire. "The adaptation process can vary—from no more than mildly uncomfortable all the way to dangerously febrile. You will all be monitored, naturally."

"But haven't you discovered which physical types are more apt to react severely?" Carigana seemed annoyed.

"No," Borella replied mildly.

Further questions from Carigana were forestalled by their arrival at the shuttle lock. Nor were they the only passengers—in fact, the applicants were apparently the least important, a fact that obviously caused Carigana to seethe. Borella casually motioned them all to seating in the rear of the vessel and slipped in beside a striking man whose garb of violently colored, loosely sewn patches suggested he might be a Singer returned from holiday.

"Much of a catch?" His drawled question caught Killashandra's ear as she passed. It was almost as much of an insult as the expression in his eyes as he observed the recruits filing to seats.

"The usual," Borella replied. "One can never tell at this stage, you know."

The tone of Borella's voice made Killashandra stare over her shoulder at the woman. The depth and resonance was gone, replaced by a sharper, shrewish, yet smug note. So the impressing and impressive detachment of the successful Singer, condescending to interpret the hazards of her profession to the eager but uninformed, was a role played very well by Borella. Killashandra shook her head against that assumption. The terrible lacerations on Borella's leg had been no sham.

"Crystal cuckoo?" "Silicate spider?" Had Maestro Valdi some measure of truth in his accusations?

Well, too late now—having sworn, averred, and affirmed, every opportunity to renege was behind her. Killashandra fixed her seat buckle for the weightless disengagement of the shuttle from moonlock.

CHAPTER 5

The journey was not long, and it was smooth, allowing Killashandra time for reflection. Was the shuttlecraft pilot a failed Singer recruit? How poor an adaptation still allowed rank and status within the Guild structure? She suppressed the nagging fear of failure by remembering the graph, indicating the recent upswing of the incidence of success in symbiosis. She distracted her grim thoughts by cataloging the other candidates, determining in advance to stay well away from Carigana, as if the irascible woman would welcome a friendly overture. Rimbol, on the other hand, reminded her pleasantly of one of the tenors at her Music Center, a lad who had always accepted the fact that his physical and vocal gifts would keep him a secondary singer and player. At one point, Killashandra had despised the boy for that acceptance: now she wished she had bothered to explore how he had achieved that mental attitude, one she might be forced to adopt. She wondered if the tenor might not have done better, attempting to become a Crystal Singer. Why had so little been said at the Music Center about this alternative application of perfect and absolute pitch? Maestro Valdi must have known, but his only suggestion had been to tune crystal, not sing it.

She wished for the distraction of views of nearing Ballybran, but the passenger section had no port, and the view-screen set over the forward bulkhead remained opaque. She felt the entry into the atmosphere. The familiar shuddering shook all the passengers, and Killashandra felt the drag nausea and disorientation and the impression of exterior sound. She tried to recall the screen printout of the planet. The image that was brightest in her memory was of the conjunction of the three moons, not the continental masses of Ballybran and the disposition of the crystal ranges.

Concentrate, concentrate, she told herself fiercely in an effort to overcome entry side effects. She had memorized complicated music scores, which obediently rolled past her mind, but not the geography of her new home.

At this point, she could feel the retro blasts as the shuttle began to slow. Gravity increased, shoving her flesh against her bones, face, chest, abdomen, thighs:—more a comforting pressure, like a heal suit. The shuttle continued to maneuver and decelerate.

The final portion of any journey always seems the longest, Killashandra thought as she grew impatient for the shuttle vibration to cease, signaling arrival. Suddenly, she realized that her journey had begun a long time before, with her passive trip on the walkway to the Fuertan space facility. Or had it begun the moment she had heard Maestro Valdi confirm the auditors' judgment of her career potential?

Forward motion ceased, and she felt the pressure pop in her ears as the entry was unsealed. She inhaled deeply, welcoming the fresher air of the planet.

"D'you think that's wise?" Shillawn asked from across the aisle. He had his hand over his nose.

"Whyever not? I've been on spacecraft and stations for too long not to appreciate fresh, planet-made air."

"He means, about the symbiont and its natural acquisition," Rimbol said, nudging her ribs with his elbow. He grinned with mischief.

Killashandra shrugged. "Now or later, we've got to get it over with. Me? I prefer to breathe deeply." And she did, as a singer would, from deep in her belly—her back muscles tightening, her diaphragm thickening until her throat, too, showed the distension of breath support.

"Singer?" Rimbol asked, his eyes widening.

Killashandra nodded, exhaling slowly.

"No openings for you, either." He made a sound of disgust. Killashandra did not bother to contradict him. "You'd think," Rimbol went on, "that with all the computer analysis and forecasting, they'd know up front instead of wasting your time. When I think of what—"

"We can leave now," Shillawn said, interrupting them with the peculiar tracheal gulp that characterized his speech.

"I wonder how many musicians make their way into this Guild by default," Killashandra muttered over her shoulder to Rimbol as they made their way out.

"Default? Or deliberately?" he asked, and prodded her to move forward when she faltered.

She had no time to think about "deliberately" then, for she had reached the disembarkation ramp and had her first glimpse of Ballybran's green-purple hills on one side and the uncompromising cubes of buildings on the other. Then she was inside the reception area where personal effects were being wafted up on a null-grav column.

"After recruits have collected their baggage, they will please follow the—ah—dark gray stripe." A voice issued from speaker grills. "Room assignments will be given at the reception lounge. You are now designated as Class 895 and will answer to any announcements prefaced by that number. Again, recruits now arriving by shuttle from Shankill Moon Base are designated Class 895. Proceed, Class 895, along the corridor marked with the dark gray stripe for room assignments."

"Couldn't care less, could he?" Rimbol said to Killashandra as he slung a battered carisak over one shoulder.

"There's the guide line." Killashandra pointed at the wall of the far lefthand corridor. "And Carigana's ahead by half a light-year." She watched as the girl's figure marched purposefully out of sight up the ascending rampway.

"Surprised?" Rimbol asked. "Hope we don't have to share accommodations."

Killashandra shot him a startled look. Even as a lowly

student on Fuerte, she had had privacy. What sort of a world was his Yarro?

The other shuttle passengers had quickly dispersed, Borella and her companion taking the far right ramp, while the center two received the bulk of the arrivals.

"You'd think with all the color available in the galaxy, they'd find brighter markers," Shillawn remarked gloomily when he caught up with Rimbol and Killashandra.

"Distinctive, if not colorful," Killashandra remarked, reaching the ramp. "Though there's a quality about this gray . . ." and she passed her hand across the painted line. "Textured, too. Hatch pattern."

"Really?" Rimbol touched the stripe. "Strange."

Carigana had already disappeared around the first curve of the ramp, but the three were otherwise the vanguard of Class 895. How dull to be designated by a number, Killashandra thought, having considered herself out of classrooms forever a scant few weeks before. And if they were 895, and the Guild had been operating for 400 standard years, how many classes did that make a year? Just over two? And thirty-three in this one?

Now that the first excitement of landing on Ballybran had waned, Killashandra began to notice other details. The light, for instance, was subdued on the rampway but had a clarity she hadn't encountered before. Rimbol's sturdy boots and Shillawn's shoes made no sound on the thick springy material that carpeted the hallway, but her slippers produced a quiet shuffling. She felt the textured band again, curious.

They passed several levels, each color coded in one of the dull chromatics, and Killashandra assumed there must be some reason for the use of such drab shades. Suddenly, the ramp ended in a large room, obviously the reception lounge for recruits—but it also held comfortable seating units, an entertainment complex, and across one end, audio-visual booths.

A dun-garbed man, of middle years with a sort of easily forgettable face rose from one of the seating units and walked toward them. "Class 895? Your adviser am I, Tukolom. With me you will remain until adaptation and training have ceased. To me your problems and complaints you will bring. All members of the Guild are we, but senior in rank to you am I, to be obeyed, thought harsh or unjust am I not."

His smile, meant to be reassuring, Killashandra knew, barely lighted his eyes and did not rouse any friendliness in her, though she saw Shillawn return the grin.

"Small class though this be, your quarters are here. Kindly to leave what you have brought in any room of your choosing and join in food and drink. To begin the work tomorrow. To orient yourselves in this facility today."

He gestured to the left-hand corridor leading off the lounge where open doors left patches of light on the textured carpet.

"Is only to put thumb print in door lock to receive privacy."

Others had arrived as Tukolom spoke, and while Killashandra gestured to her companions to proceed to the private rooms, he began his little speech all over again to the next batch. Rimbol pointed at the first door on the left, closed and red lighted to indicate the occupant did not wish to be disturbed. Carigana!

With a snort, Killashandra marched down the hall, almost to its end, before she indicated to Rimbol and Shillawn which room she intended to take. She saw them move for the rooms on either side of her. She pressed her thumb into the plate, felt the vibration as the print was recorded, and then entered the room, the door panel sliding soundlessly behind her.

"This facility has been programmed to responded to any change in your life signals," announced a pleasant voice, rather more human than mechanical. "You may program the catering units and audiovisual units and change any furnishing not to your liking."

"My liking is for privacy," Killashandra said.

"Programmed," the voice dispassionately replied. "Should your physical health alter on the monitors, you will be informed."

"I'll probably inform you," Killashandra muttered under her breath, and was pleased to hear no reply. Just as well, she thought. She tossed her carisak to the bed. Some people preferred to have a voice responding to their idle remarks: she preferred the sanctity of quiet.

Her quarters were as good as the guest facility in the Shankill Base, nothing gaudy but certainly substantial: bed, table, chairs, writing surface, tri-d screen, the customary audiovisual terminals, a catering slot convenient to the table, a storage closet. The hygienic unit was larger than expected, and it included a deep bath. She flipped on the small fax dispenser and watched as all varieties of bathing lotions, salts, fragrances, and oils were named as available.

More than pleased, Killashandra dialed for a foaming fragrant bath, at 35° C, and the tub obediently began to fill itself.

You never feel completely clean, Killashandra thought as she undressed, using the spray cabinets on ship and station. You really needed to soak in the hot water of a full-immersion bath.

She was drying off in warm air jets when Tukolom announced it was his pleasure to meet Class 895 in the lounge for the evening meal.

Tukolom's curious syntax appeared to function only in spontaneous remarks. It was totally absent from the flood of information he imparted to them during that meal. He also refused to be deflected from his set passages by questions or to be diverted by Carigana when she anticipated his points.

Since it was obvious to everyone except Carigana that it was useless to interrupt Tukolom and since the food presented a variety of hot and cold dishes, protein, vegetable and fruit, the Class 895 listened and ate.

Tukolom discoursed first on the sequence of events to befall them. He stated the symptoms common to the onset of the symbiotic illness, occurring between ten and thirty days after exposure, beginning with headache, general muscular soreness, irritability, blurred vision, and impaired hearing. Such symptoms were to be reported to him immediately and the person afflicted to return to the room assigned, where the progress of the adaptation could be monitored. Any discomfort would be alleviated without affecting the course of the symbiotic intrusion.

"When rape is inevitable, huh?" whispered the irrepressible Rimbol in Killashandra's ear.

Meanwhile, Class 895 would have orientation courses on the history and geography of Ballybran, instruction in the piloting of ground-effects craft, meteorology lectures, and survival techniques. The class would also be requested to perform duties within the Guild relevant to the preservation of cut crystal and restoration of facilities after any storm. Normal work hours and days were in effect, which would allow ample time for recreation. Members were encouraged to continue any hobbies or avocations that they had previously enjoyed. Once members had been cleared for use of surface vehicles, they might take whatever trips they wished as long as they filed and had had approved a flight plan with control center. Special clearance and a proficiency test were required for the use of water vessels.

As abruptly as he had started his lecture, Tukolom concluded. He looked expectantly around.

"Is this the main Guild installation?" Carigana asked, caught by surprise at the opening.

"The main training area, yes, this is. Situated on the largest continental mass which bears the largest of the productive crystal ranges, Milekey and Brerrerton. The facility is located on the Joslin plateau, sheltered by the Mansord upthrust on the north, the Joslin discontinuity on the south, to the west by the White Sea and the east by the Long Plain. Thus, the installation is generally sheltered from the worst of the mach storms by its felicitous situation."

Tukolom had perfect recall, Killashandra decided: a walking data retrieval unit. Rimbol must have reached a similar conclusion, for as her eyes slid past his, she saw amusement twinkling. Shillawn, however, continued to look impressed by the man's encyclopedic manner.

"How many other settlements are there?" Borton asked.

"Learning tomorrow's lesson today a good idea is not," Tukolom pronounced solemnly. He then neatly avoided further questions by leaving the lounge.

"Aurigans are impossible," Carigana announced, frowning blackly at the departing figure. "Always dogmatic, authoritarian. Could they find no one else suitable as a mentor?"

"He's perfect," Rimbol replied, cocking his head as he regarded Carigana. "He's got total recall. What more could you ask of a teacher?"

"I wonder . . ." began Shillawn, stammering slightly, "if he had it before he . . . got here."

"Didn't you hear that Borella woman?" demanded Carigana. "Most handicaps are sensory . . ."

"At least his syntax improves when he recalls."

"Every other human species in the galaxy, and some not so human," Carigana continued undeterred, "can manage interlingual except the Aurigan group. It's a delusion on their part. *Anyone* can learn interlingual properly." She was swinging one leg violently; all the while the corners of her mouth twitched with irritation, and her eyes blinked continually.

"Where are you from?" Rimbol asked guilelessly.

"Privacy." She snapped the qualification curtly.

"As you will, citizen," Rimbol replied, and turned his back on her.

That was also an insult but not an invasion of Privacy, so Carigana had to be content with glaring about her. Class 895 averted its eyes, and with a noise of disgust, Carigana took her leave. The space worker had had a dampening effect on the entire group because suddenly everyone began to talk. It was Rimbol who dialed the first drink, letting out a whoop.

"They've got Yarran beer! Hey, come try a real drink!" He exhorted all to join him and before long had everyone served, if not with the Yarran beer he touted, at least with some mild intoxicant. "We may never get off this planet again," he said to Killashandra as he joined her, "but they sure make it comfortably homelike."

"A restriction is only restricting because you know it exists," Killashandra said. " 'Nor iron bars a prison make,' " she added, dredging up an old quote unexpectedly.

"Prison? That's archaic," said Rimbol with a snort. "To-night let's enjoy!"

Rimbol's exuberance was hard to resist, and Killashandra didn't care to. She wanted to abandon her skeptical mood, as much because she didn't want to echo Carigana as to purge her mind of its depressions. There had been some small truth in the space worker's complaints, but blunt though Killashandra knew herself to be, even she could have made points more tactfully. Of course, the girl was probably on a psych-twist, from what Rimbol had learned of her. How had she passed that part of the Guild preliminary exams? More importantly, if Carigana was so contemptuous of the Guild, why had she applied for admission?

Conversations swirled pleasantly all around her, and she began to listen. The recruits came from varied backgrounds and training disciplines, but each and every one of them, geared to succeed in highly skilled work, had been denied their goals at the last moment. Was it not highly coincidental that all of them had hit upon the Heptite Guild as an alternative career?

Killashandra found that conclusion invalid. There were hundreds of human planets, moon bases, and space facilities offering alternative employment to everyone, that is, except herself and Rimbol. In fact, the two musicians could probably have taken on temporary assignments in their original fields. A second objection was that, thirty-three people were an infinitesimal factor among the vast multitudes who might not have jobs waiting for them in their immediate vicinities. Colonial quotas were always absorbing specialists, and one could always work a ship one-way to get to a better employment market. She found the reflections a trifle unsettling, yet how could such a subtle recruitment be accomplished? Certainly no probability curve could have anticipated her crossing Carrik's path in the Fuertan space port. His decision had been whimsical, and there could have been no way of knowing that her aimless wandering would take her to the space port. No, the coincidence factor was just too enormous.

She sat for a few moments longer, finishing the Yarran beer that Rimbol had talked her into trying. He was telling some involved joke to half a dozen listeners. By no means as shy with drink in him and lacking his stammer, Shillawn was talking earnestly to one of the girls. Jezerey was half asleep, though trying to keep her eyes open as Borton argued some point with the oldest recruit, a swarthy faced man from Amodeus VII. He had his second mate's deep space ticket as well as radiology qualifications. Maybe the Guild needed another shuttle pilot more than they needed crystal miners.

Killashandra wished she could gracefully retire. She did not intend making the same mistakes with this group that she had in the Music Center. Carigana had already provoked dislike by her unacceptable behavior, so Killashandra had a prime example she was not going to emulate. Then she caught Jezerey's eyes as the girl yawned broadly. Killashandra grinned and jerked her head in the direction of the rooms.

"You can talk all night if you want to," the girl said, rising, "but I'm going to bed, and so is Killashandra. See you in the morning." Then she added as the two reached the corridor, "Shards, was I glad of an excuse. G'night."

Killashandra repeated the salute and, once in her room, gratefully gave the verbal order to secure her privacy until morning.

A curious glow at the window attracted her attention, and she darkened the room light that had come on at her entrance. She caught her breath then at the sight of the two moons: golden Shankill, large and appearing far nearer than it actually was; just above it, hanging as if from a different radius altogether, the tiny, faintly green luminescence of Shilmore, the innermost and smallest moon. She was accustomed to night skies with several satellites, but somehow these were unusual. Though Killashandra had never been off Fuerte before she met Carrik, she had had every intention of traveling extensively throughout the galaxy, as a performing soloist of any rank would have done. Perhaps it was because she might be seeing only these moons for the rest of her life that they now had a special radiance for her. She sat on the edge of her bed, watching their graceful ascent until Shilmore had outrun her larger companion and disappeared beyond Killashandra's view.

Then she went to bed and slept.

The next morning, she and the other recruits learned the

organization of the Guild Complex and were obliquely informed that the higher the level, the lower the status. They were introduced rapidly to the geology of Ballybran and made a beginning with its complex meteorology.

Trouble started about midafternoon as the students were viewing the details of the Charter of the Heptite Guild as a diversion after meta-maths. Rimbol muttered that the Guild was damned autocratic for a member of the Federated Planets. Shillawn, swallowing first, mumbled about data retrieval and briefing.

It took a few moments before the import of the section dealing with tithes, fee, and charges was fully understood. With a growing sense of indignation, Killashandra learned that from the moment she had been sworn in at the moon base as a recruit, the Guild could charge her for any and all services rendered, including a fee of transfer from the satellite to the planet.

"Do they charge, too, for the damn spores in the air we're breathing?" Carigana demanded, characteristically the first to find voice after the initial shock. For once, she had the total support of the others. With a fine display of vituperation, she vented her anger on Tukolom, the visible representative of the Guild that she vehemently declared had exploited the unsuspecting.

"Told you were," Tukolom replied, unexpectedly raising his voice to top hers. "Available to you was that data at Shankill. The charter in the data is."

"How would we have known to ask?" Carigana retorted, her anger fueled by his answer. "This narding Guild keeps its secrets so well, you're not led to expect a straight answer to a direct question!"

"Thinking surely you would," Tukolom said, unruffled and with an irony that surprised Killashandra. "Maintenance charges only at cost are—"

"No where else in the galaxy do students have to pay for subsistence—"

"Students you are not." Tukolom was firm. "Guild members are you!"

Not even Carigana could find a quick answer to that. She glared around her, her flashing eyes begging someone to have a rejoinder.

"Trapped us, haven't you?" She spat the words at the man. "Good and truly trapped. And we walked so obligingly into it." She flung herself down on the seating unit, her hands flopping uselessly about her thighs.

"Once trained, salary far above galactic average," Tukolom announced diplomatically into the silence. "Most indebtedness cleared by second year. Then—every wish satisfy. Order any thing from any place in galaxy." He tendered a thin smile of encouragement. "Guild credit good anywhere for anything."

"That's not much consolation for being stuck on this planet for the rest of your life," Carigana replied with a snarl.

Once she had absorbed the initial shock, Killashandra was willing to admit that the Guild method was fair. Its members must be furnished with private quarters, food, clothing, personal necessities, and medical care. Some of the specialists, the Singers especially, had a further initial outlay for equipment. The cost of the flitter craft used by Crystal Singers in the ranges was staggering; the sonic cutting gear that had to be tuned to the user was also expensive and a variety of other items whose purpose was not yet known to her were basic Singer's tools.

Obviously, the best job to have on Ballybran was that of a Crystal Singer even if the Guild did "tithe" 30 percent of the crystal cut and brought in. She duly noted the phrase, *brought in*, and wondered if she could find a vocabulary section in the data bank that would define words in precisely the nuance meant on Ballybran. Interlingual was accurate enough, but every profession has terms that sound familiar, seem innocuous, and are dangerous to the incompletely initiated.

A wide variety of supporting skills put the Singers into the ranges, maintained the vehicles, buildings, space station, research, medical facilities, and the administration of it all. Twenty thousand technicians, essential to keep the four thousand or so Singers working, and this very elite group was somehow recruited from the galaxy.

The argument over entrapment, as Carigana vehemently insisted on calling it, continued long after Tukolom left. Killashandra noticed him as he gradually worked his way

from the center of the explosion, almost encouraging
Carigana to become the focus, then adroitly slipped down a
corridor. He's pulled the fade-away act before, Killashandra
thought. Perversely, she then became annoyed because she
and her group were reacting predictably; it was one thing
to have a stage director prescribe your moves on stage, quite
another to be manipulated in one's living. She had thought
to be free of overt management, so she experienced a surge
of anger. To rant as Carigana was doing solved nothing except the immediate release of an energy and purpose that
could be used to better advantage.

Ignoring Carigana's continuing harangue, Killashandra
quietly moved to a small terminal and asked for a review
of the Charter. After a few moment's study, she left the
machine. There was no legal way in which one could relinquish membership in the Heptite Guild except by dying.
Even in sickness, mental or physical, the Guild had complete protective authority over every member so sworn,
averred, and affirmed. Now she appreciated the FSP officials and the elaborate rigmarole. On the other hand, she
had been *told*; she could have withdrawn after full disclosure if she hadn't been so eager to flaunt Maestro Valdi
and prove to Andurs that she'd be right as a Crystal Singer.
The section on the Guild's responsibilities to the individual
member was clear. Killashandra could see definite advantages, including the ones that had lured her to Ballybran. If
she became a Crystal Singer . . . She preferred "Singer" to
the Guild's dull job description, "Cutter."

"Ever the optimist, Killa?" Rimbol asked. He must have
been standing behind her a while.

"Well, I prefer that role to hers." She inclined her head
sharply in Carigana's direction. "She's beating her gums
over ways to break a contract that we were warned was
irrevocable."

"D'you suppose they count on our being obstinate by
nature?"

"Obviously, they have psychologists among the membership." Killashandra laughed. "You want what you can't or
shouldn't have or are denied. Human nature."

"Will we still be human after symbiosis?" Rimbol wondered aloud, cocking his head to one side, his eyes narrow with speculation.

"I can't say as I'd like Borella for an intimate friend," Killashandra began.

"Nor I." Rimbol's laugh was infectious.

"I did hear her come out with a very human, snide comment on the shuttle."

"About us?"

"In general. But I *liked* Carrik. He knew how to enjoy things, even silly things, and—"

Rimbol touched her arm, and the glint of his blue eyes reminded her of the look in Carrik's when they'd first met.

"Comparisons are invidious but . . . join me?"

Killashandra gave him a longer, speculative look. His gaiety and ingenuous appearance, his gregariousness, were carefully cultivated to counterbalance his unusual coloring. The expression on his face, the warmth of his eyes and smile, and the gentle stroking of his hand on her arm effected a distinct change in her attitude toward him.

"Guaranteed Privacy between members of equal rank." His voice was teasing and she had no desire to resist his temptation.

With Carigana's strident voice in their ears, they slipped down the corridor to her room and enjoyed complete Privacy.

The next morning Tukolom marshaled Class 895, some of whom were decidedly the worse for a night's drinking.

"Borton, Jezerey, also Falanog, qualified are you already on surface and shuttle craft. To take your pilot cards to Flight Control on first level. Follow gray strip down, turn right twice, Guild Member Danin see. All others of this class with me are coming."

Tukolom led without turning to discover if he was being followed, but the class, sullen or just resigned, obeyed. Shillawn stepped in behind Killashandra and Rimbol.

"I figured it out," he said with his characteristic gulp. His anxiety to please was so intense that Killashandra asked him what had he figured out. "How much it will all cost until we start earning credits. And . . . and what the lowest credit rating is. It's not too bad, really. Guild charges at cost and doesn't add a tariff for transport or special orders."

"Having done us to get us here, they're not out to do us further, huh?"

"Well"—and Shillawn had to shuffle awkwardly to keep a position where his words would be audible only to Rimbol and Killashandra—"it *is* fair."

Rimbol shrugged. "So, what is the lowest Guild wage? And how long will it take to pay off what we're racking up just by breathing?"

"Well"—Shillawn held up his jotter—"the lowest wage is for a caterer's assistant and that brings in three thousand five hundred credits plus Class three accommodations, clothing allowance and two hundred luxury units per standard year. We're charged at the base-level accommodations, shuttle passage was only fifteen cr, but any unusual item from catering—except two beakers of beverages up to Grade four—is charged against the individual's account. So, if you don't eat exotic, or drink heavy, you'd clear off the initial levies at a c.a.'s pay in"— Shillawn had to skip after them as he glanced down at his jotter and lost his stride—"in seven months, two weeks and five days' standard."

Rimbol caught Killashandra's eye, and she could see that the young Yarran was hard put to suppress his laughter.

"Why did you only consider the lowest-paid member, Shillawn?" she asked, managing to keep her voice level.

"Well, that was practical."

"You mean, you didn't compute any of the higher grades?"

"The highest-paid position is that of the Guild Master, and such information is not available."

"You did try?" Now it was Killashandra's turn to have to skip ahead or be overrun by Shillawn's long legs.

"I wanted to see just what areas are open to the average member . . ."

"How high could you retrieve data?"

"That's the good part," Shillawn beamed down at them.

"The next rank after Guild Master is Crystal Cutter—
Singer, I mean. Only the credit varies too erratically, depending as it does on how much usable crystal a Cutter
brings in."

"If Crystal Singers are second, who's third in rank?"

"Chief of Research, Chief of Control, and Chief of
Marketing. All on equal rating."

"Credit per year?"

"Their base pay is 300,000 pgy, plus living, entertainment, travel, and personal allowances 'to be determined'."

The base figure was sufficient to draw an appreciative
whistle from Rimbol.

"And, of course, you're going to be Chief of Control, I
expect," a new voice said and the three friends realized that
Carigana had been listening.

Shillawn flushed at her sarcasm.

"And you'll be chief rant-and-raver," Rimbol said, unexpectedly acerbic, his blue eyes signaling dislike.

Carigana flipped her thumbnail at him and strode on,
head high, shoulders and back stiffly straight.

"Any sympathy I had for that woman is fast giving place
to total antipathy," Rimbol said, making an even more
insulting gesture at the space worker's back.

With her head start on the rest of Class 895, Carigana
was first to reach the ground-craft depot, but she had to
wait until the flight officer checked in all thirty. They were
taken to a large section inside a gigantic hangar that
housed three vehicles on simulation stands: a skimmer, the
general workcraft, which could be adapted for variations
of atmosphere and gravity and could be driven by children.
A single bar controlled forward, reverse, and side movement. The skimmer had no great speed but plowed its air
cushion with equal efficiency over land, water, snow, mud,
ice, sand, or rock. Its drive could be adapted to a variety of
fuels and power sources.

The second stand simulated an airsled, not as clumsy as
its name implied and capable of considerable speed and
maneuverability. It was the long-haul craft, the Crystal Cutter's official vehicle, capable of delivering cargo and passengers to any point on Ballybran.

The third simulator was a satellite shuttle, it caused

Rimbol's eyes to widen appreciatively, but Killashandra sincerely hoped she would not be asked to pilot it.

Though all were bored by waiting their turn, Killashandra had no trouble with the skimmer simulation. The sled was more complex, but she felt she acquitted herself fairly well, though she'd certainly want a lot more practice in the vehicle before flying any distance.

"You know who failed the skimmer test?" Rimbol asked, joining her as she emerged from the airsled.

"Shillawn?" But then she saw the gangly man still waiting on line.

"No. Carigana!"

"How could anyone not be able to fly a skimmer?"

"A skimmer needs a light hand." Rimbol's smile was malicious. "Carigana's used to a spacesuit. Ever noticed how she always turns her entire body around to face you? That's from wearing a servomech for so long. That's why her movements are so jerky—overcorrected. She over-reacts, too. As we all know. Hey, we'd better scurry. Instructor Tukolom"—and Rimbol grinned at the title with which the flight officer had pointedly addressed their tutor —"says we're due back at the training lounge for the afternoon's entrancing lectures."

Carigana might well have been floating in deep space in a servomech suit for all the notice she gave to Tukolom's recitations on the care and packing of crystal cuttings. He informed Class 895 that they must pay strict attention to these procedures, as one of their first official tasks for their Guild would be to prepare crystal for export. As he spoke —he reminded them—Crystal Cutters were in the ranges, making the most of the mild spring weather and the favorable aspects of the moons. When the Cutters returned, Class 895 would be privileged to have its first experience with handling crystal, in all its infinite variety . . . and value.

The reverence with which Tukolom made the announcement showed Killashandra a new and unexpected facet of the humorless instructor. Did crystal affect even those who did not sing it? How long had Tukolom been a Guild member? Not that she really wanted to know. She was just intrigued by his uncharacteristic radiance when discussing, of *all* the dull subjects, the packing of crystal.

As soon as Tukolom released the class from the lecture, she murmured something about returning in a moment to Rimbol and slipped away to her room. She drew out the console and tapped the Flight Office, requesting the use of a skimmer for personal relaxation. The display spilled out a confirmation that she could use vehicle registry VZD7780 for two hours, confined to overland flight.

As she slipped from her room, she was relieved to see Rimbol's door open. He was still in the lounge, so she suppressed the vague disquiet she felt about sneaking off without him. Her first visit to the crystal ranges was better experienced as a solo. Besides, if Rimbol and Shillawn couldn't figure out how to obtain a clearance, they didn't deserve one.

The vast hangar complex was eerily empty. A light breeze sighed through the vacant racks for Singers' airsleds as Killashandra hurried to the skimmer section. An airsled engine revved unexpectedly and caused her to leap inches off the plascrete surface; then she saw the cluster of mechanics on the far side of the building, where lights exposed the sled's drive section.

Killashandra finally located the VZD rack and her assigned craft at the top of the skimmer section. The vehicle was sand-scraped, although the plasglas bubble was relatively unscathed. She climbed in, backed the skimmer carefully clear of the rack, and proceeded from the hangar at a sedate pace.

"Pilot may fly only in area designated on master chart," a mechanical voice announced; to her left, an opaque square lit to display an overlay of the Joslin plateau, the Guild complex out of which a small flashing dot, herself, was moving.

"Pilot complies."

"Weather alert must be obeyed by immediate return to hangar. Weather holding clear and mild: no storm warning presently in effect." As she cleared the hangar, she noticed three figures emerge from the ramp. She chuckled—she'd got her skimmer first.

She didn't want to be followed, so she pushed the con-

trol bar forward for maximum speed. The master chart cut
off just at the fringe of the Milekey Range to the northeast
but close enough for her to see exactly what she had mortgaged her life for. It was suddenly very necessary to Killashandra to stand on the edge of this possible future of
hers; to be close to it; to make it more vivid than Tukolom's carefully recited lessons; to make her understand why
Borella had smiled in longing.

The old skimmer didn't like being pushed to maximum
speed and vibrated unpleasantly. None of the function
dials were in the red, so Killashandra ignored the shaking,
keeping on the northeasterly course. The Brerrerton Range
would have been closer, almost directly south, but Milekey
had been the range Carrik frequently mentioned, and her
choice had been subconsciously affected by him. Well, the
others were certain to head to the nearer range, which was
fine by her.

Once she had bounced over the first hill, Killashandra saw
the smudge of the range, occasionally reflecting the wester-
ing sun. Beneath her, the dull gray-green shrub and ground
cover of Ballybran passed without change. Dull exteriors
so often hid treasures. Who could ever have thought Ballybran worth half credit? She recalled the model of the
planet that Borella had shown them on Shankill. It was as
if cosmic hands had taken the world and twisted it so that
the softer interior material had been forced through the
crust, forming the jagged ranges that bore crystal, and then
capriciously the same hands had yanked the misshapen
spheres out, the ridges falling inward.

The plain gave way to a series of deep gullies that in a
wetter season, might have become streams. The first of the
jagged upthrusts coincided with the edge of her chart, so
she settled the skimmer on the largest promontory and
got out.

To either side and before her, the planet's folds stretched,
each cline peering through a gap or a few meters higher
than the one before. Shading her eyes, she strained to see
any evidence of the shining crystal that was the hidden and
unique wealth of such an uninviting planet.

The silence was all but complete, the merest whisper of
sound, not wind, and transmitted not through the atmo-

sphere but through the rock under her feet. A strange sound to be experienced so, as if her heel were responding to a vibration to which her keen ears, expectant, were not attuned. Not precisely comprehending the urge to test the curious unsilence, Killashandra drew a deep breath and expelled it on a fine clear E.

The single note echoed back to her ears and through her heels, the resonance coursing to her nerve ends, leaving behind, as the sound died away, a pleasurable sensation that caressed her nervous system. She stood entranced but hesitated to repeat the experience, so she scanned the dirty, unpretentious mounds. Now she was willing to believe what Carrik had said and, equally, was credulous of the hazards attached. The two facets of singing crystal were linked: the good and bad, the difficult, the ecstatic.

She quickly discarded a notion to fly deeper into the range. Common sense told her that any crystal in the immediate vicinity would long since have been removed. A more practical restraint was Killashandra's recognition that it would be easy to lose oneself beyond the curiously reassuring flatness of the plain and the sight of the White Sea. However, she did skim along the first ridges, always keeping the plain in sight and at the edge of her flight chart. The undulating hills fascinated her as the sharper, young thrusts and anticlines of Fuerte had not. Ballybran's ranges tempted, taunted, tantalized, hiding wealth produced by titanic forces boiling from the molten core of the planet: a wealth created by the technical needs of an ever-expanding galactic population and found on an ancient world with no other resources to commend it. That was ever the way of technology: to take the worthless and convert it into wealth.

Eventually, Killashandra turned the skimmer back toward the Guild Complex. She had renewed her determination to become a Singer, which had been dampened somewhat by Tukolom and an instructional mode that subtly ignored the main objective of the recruits—becoming a Crystal Singer. She could understand why their initiation took the form it had—until the symbiosis occurred, no lasting assignments could be made, but other worthwhile skills and ranks could be examined. She sighed, wondering if she could sustain another defeat. Then she laughed, remembering how facilely she had shrugged off ten-years' hard work when Carrik had dangled his lure. Yet, to be perfectly honest, he hadn't dangled: he'd argued against her taking such a step, argued vehemently.

What had Rimbol said about being denied making an object more desirable? And it was true that the maestro's histrionic condemnation of Carrik and Crystal Singers had done much to increase her desire. She had, of course, been so elated by her interlude with Carrik that the luxurious standard of living—and playing—to which he had introduced her had been a lure to one who had had no more than student credit. Carrik's fascinating personality had bemused her and given her the recklessness to throw off the restraints of a decade of unrewarded discipline.

Now that she had stood close to crystal source, felt that phenomenal vibration through bone and nerve, a call to the core of her that her involvement with music had never touched, she was strengthened in her purpose.

A lone figure was climbing about the skimmer racks when Killashandra returned. She noticed eight other empty slots as she parked her vehicle. The figure waved urgently for her to remain by her skimmer and quickly climbed up to her. Killashandra waited politely, but the man checked the registry of the skimmer first, then ran his hands along the sides, frowning. He began a tactile examination of the canopy without so much as glancing at her in the seat. He muttered as he made notations on his jotter. The display alarmed him, and for the first time he noticed her, opening the canopy.

"You weren't out long. Has something happened to one of the others? Nine of you went out!"

"No, nothing's wrong."

Relieved, he gave a pull to the visored cap he wore.

"Only have so many skimmers, and I shouldn't ought to've given out nine to recruits, but no one else requested."

Killashandra stepped from the skimmer, and the hangar man was instantly inside, running fingers over the control surface, the steering rod, as if her mere physical presence might have caused damage.

"I'm not careless with equipment," she said, but he gave
no indication he had heard.

"You're Killashandra?" He finished his inspection and
looked around at her as he closed the canopy.

"Yes."

He grunted and made another entry on his jotter, watching the display.

"Do you always inspect each vehicle as it's used?" she
asked, trying to be pleasant.

He made no comment. Was it because of her lowly rank
as a recruit? A sudden resentment flared past the serenity
she had achieved in the range. She touched his arm and
repeated her question.

"Always. My job. Some of you lot are damned careless
and give me more work than necessary. Don't mind doing
my proper job, but unnecessary work is not on. Just not
on."

A loud whine from the service bays startled Killashandra, but the hangar man didn't flinch. It was then that she
realized the man was deaf. A second ear-piercing whine
erupted, and she winced, but it elicited no reaction from
the man. Deafness must be a blessing in his occupation.

Giving the returned skimmer one last sweep of his hand,
the hangar man began to climb to check another vehicle,
unconscious of Killashandra's presence. She stared after
him. Had his job, his dedication to the preservation of his
skimmers, supplanted interest in people? If she received
deafness from the symbiont, would she detach herself from
people so completely?

She made her way down to the hangar floor, startled
each time the engine being repaired blasted out its un-
baffled noise. She might have renounced music as a career,
but never to hear it again? She shuddered convulsively.

She had been so positive on Fuerte that hers was to be a
brilliant career as a solo performer, maybe she'd better not
be so bloody certain of becoming a Crystal Singer and
explore the alternatives within the Guild.

Suddenly, she didn't want to return to the recruits'
lounge, nor did she wish to hear the accounts of the other
eight who had skimmed away from the Guild Complex.
She wanted to be private. Getting out by herself, to the

edge of the range, had been beneficial, the encounter with the hangar man an instructive countertheme.

She walked quickly from the hangar, caught by the stiff breeze and bending into it. The eastern sky was darkening; glancing over her shoulder, she saw banks of western clouds tinged purple by the setting sun. She paused, savoring the display, and then hurried on. She didn't wish to be sighted by the returning skimmers. Finally past the long side of the Complex, she struck out up a low hill, her boots scuffling in the dirt. A warm spicy smell rose when she trod on the low ground cover. She listened to the rising wind, not merely with her ears but with her entire body, planting her boot heels firmly in the soil, hoping to experience again that coil of body-felt sound. The wind bore the taint of brine and chill but no sound as it eddied past her and away east.

There the sky was dark now, and the first faint stars were appearing. She must study the astronomy of Ballybran. Strange that this had not been mentioned in the lectures on meteorology; or was it a deliberate exclusion since the knowledge would have no immediate bearing on the recruits' training?

Shanganagh, the middle moon, rose, honey-colored, in the northeast. She seemed almost to creep out, much as Killashandra was doing, to be away from the more powerful personality of Shankill and the erratic infringements of Shilmore. Killashandra grinned—if Rimbol were symbolized by Shankill, that would make Shillawn, Shilmore. Shanganagh was the odd one out, avoiding the other two until inexorable forces pulled her between their paths at passover.

Shanganagh paled to silver, rising higher and lighting Killashandra's way until she reached the crest of a rolling hill and realized that she could walk all night, possibly getting lost, to no purpose. Student pranks had been tolerated, in their place, on Fuerte in the Music Center, but it would be quite another matter here where an old deaf hangar man cared more for his vehicles than the people who used them.

She turned and surveyed the crouching hulk of the Guild, its upper stories lit by the rising moon, the remainder sharp black thrusts of shadow. She sat down on the hillside, twisting her buttocks to find some comfort. She hadn't realized how huge the Complex was and what a small portion of it was above the surface. She had been told that the best quarters were deep underground. Killashandra picked up a handful of gravel and cast the bits in a thin arc, listening to the rattle as bush and leaf were struck.

The sense of isolation, of total solitude and utter privacy, pleased her as much as the odors on the wind and the roughness of the dirt in her hand. Always on Fuerte, there had been the knowledge that people were close by, people were seeing, if not intently observing her, impinging on her consciousness, infringing on her desire to be alone and private.

Suddenly, Killashandra could appreciate Carigana's fury. If the woman had been a space worker, she had enjoyed the same sense of privacy. She'd never needed to learn the subtle techniques of cutting oneself from contact. Well, if Killashandra understood something of Carigana's antisocial manner, she still had no wish to make friends with her. She spun off another handful of dirt.

It was comforting, too, to know that on Ballybran, at least, one could take a nighttime stroll in perfect safety— one of the few worlds in the Federated Sentient Planets where that was possible. She rose, dusted off her pants, and continued her walk around the great Guild installation.

She almost stumbled as she reached the front of the building, for a turf so dense that it felt like a woven fabric had been encouraged to grow there. The imposing entrance hall bore the shield of the Heptite Guild in a luminous crystal. The tall, narrow windows facing south gave off no light on the first level, and most were dark on the upper stories. She wondered which ratings were so low as to live above ground. Caterers' assistants?

Killashandra was beginning to regret her whimsical night tour as she passed the long side of the building, the very long side. Ramps, up and down, pierced the flat wall at intervals, but she knew from Tukolom's lecture that these led into storage areas without access to the living quarters, so she trudged onward until she was back at the vast hangar maw.

She was very weary when she finally reached the ramp to the class's quarters. All else was quiet, the lounge empty and dark. Though Rimbol's door light was green, she hurried past to her own. Tomorrow would be soon enough for companionship. She went to sleep, comforted by the irrevocable advantage of privacy available to a member of the Heptite Guild.

Killashandra wasn't as positive of that the next afternoon as she struggled to retain her balance in the gusts of wind and, more importantly, tried not to drop the precious crate of crystal. The recruits had been aroused by the computer at a false dawn they had to take on faith. The sky was a deep, sullen gray, with storm clouds that were sucked across the Complex so low they threatened to envelop the upper level. The recruits had been told to eat quickly but heartily and to report to the cargo officer on the hangar floor. They were to be under her supervision until she released them. Wind precautions were already evident; the 12-meter-high screen across the hangar maw was lowered only to admit approaching airsleds; evidently the device was to prevent workers' being sucked from the hangar by fierce counterdraughts.

Cargo Officer Malaine took no chances that instructions would be misunderstood or unheard. She carried a bullhorn, but her orders were also displayed on screens positioned around the hangar. If they had any doubts as they assisted the regular personnel in unloading, the recruits were to touch and/or otherwise get the attention of anyone in a green-checked uniform. Basic instructions remained on the screen; updates blinked orange on the green displays.

"Your main assignments will be to unload, very, very carefully, the cartons of cut crystals. One at a time. Don't be misled by the fact that the cartons have strong hand grips. The wind out there will shortly make you wish you had prehensile tails." Cargo Officer Malaine gave the recruits a smile. "You'll know when to put on your head gear," and she tapped a closefitting skull cap with its padded ears and eyescreen. "Now"—and she gestured to the plasglas wall of the ready-room facing the hangar— "the sleds are coming in. Watch the procedure of the hangar personnel. First, the Crystal Singer is checked, then the cargo is off-loaded. You will concentrate on off-loading. Your responsibility is to transfer the crystal cartons safely inside. Any carton that comes in is worth more than you are! No offense, recruits, just basic Guild economics. I also caution you that Crystal Singers just in off the ranges are highly unpredictable. You're lucky. All in this group have been out a good while, so they'll probably have good cuttings. Don't drop a carton! You'll have the Singer, me, and Guild Master Lanzecki on your neck—the Singer being first and worst.

"Fair does not apply," Malaine said in a hard voice. "Those plasfoam boxes"—and she pointed at the line of hangar personnel hurrying to the cargo bay, white cartons clutched firmly to their chests—"are what pay for this planet, its satellites, and everything on them. No one gets a credit till that cargo is safely in this building, weighed in, and graded—Okay, here's a new flight coming in. I'll count you off in threes. Line up and be ready to go when called. Just remember: the crystal is important! When the klaxon sounds—that means a sled is out of control! Duck but don't drop!"

She counted the recruits off, and Killashandra was teamed with Borton and a man she didn't know by name. The recruits formed loose trios in front of the window, watching the routine.

"Doesn't seem hard," the man commented to Borton. "Those cartons can't be heavy," and he gestured at a slim person walking rapidly carrying his burden.

"Maybe not now, Celee," Borton replied, "but when the wind picks up—"

"Well, we're both sturdy enough to give our teammate a hand if she needs one," Celee said, grinning with some condescension at Killashandra.

"I'm closer to the ground," she said, looking up at him with a warning glint in her eyes. "Center of gravity is lower and not so far to fall."

"You tell him, Killa." Borton nudged Celee and winked at her.

Suddenly Celee pointed urgently to the hangar. The recruits saw a sled career in, barely missing the vaulted roof, then plunge toward the ground, only to be pulled up at the last second, skid sideways, and barely miss a broadside against the interior wall. A klaxon had sounded, its clamor causing everyone to clap hands over his ears at the piercing noise. When the trio looked again, the airsled had slid to a stop, nose against the wall. To their surprise, the Singer, orange overalls streaked with black, emerged unscathed from the front hatch, gave the sled an admonitory kick, gestured obscenely at the wind, and then stalked into the shelter of the cargo bay. Then she, Borton, and Celee were being beckoned out to the hangar floor.

As Killashandra grabbed her first carton from a Singer's ship, she clutched it firmly to her chest because it was light and could easily have been flipped from a casual grip by the strong wind gusting about the hangar. She got to the cargo bay with a sigh of relief, only to be stunned by the sight of the Crystal Singer, who was slumped against a wall while snarling at the medic who was daubing at the blood running down the Singer's left cheek. Until the last carton from his sled was unloaded, the Crystal Singer remained at his observation point.

"By the horny toes of a swamp bear," Celee remarked to Killashandra as they hurried back for more cartons, "that man knows every nardling *one* of his cargo, and he sure to bones knows we're doing the unloading. And the bloody wind's rising. Watch it, Killashandra."

"Only two more in that ship," Borton yelled as he passed them on his way in. "They want to hoist it out of the way!"

Celee and Killashandra trotted faster, wary of the hoist now descending over the disabled ship. No sooner had they lifted the last two cartons from the sled than the hoist clanked tight on its top. At that instant, Killashandra glanced around her and counted five more sleds wheeling in, fortunately in more control. Seven unloaded vehicles were heading to the top of the sled storage racks.

As the hangar became crowded, unloading took longer, and keeping upright during the passage between sled and cargo bay became increasingly more difficult. Killashandra saw three people flung against sleds, and one skidded against the outer wind baffle. An incoming sled was caught

in a side gust and flipped onto its back. Killashandra shook
her head against the loud keening that followed, unsure
whether it was the sound of the gale or the injured Singer's
screaming. She forced her mind to the business of unloading and maintaining her balance.

She was wheeling back from the bay for yet another
load when someone caught her by the hair. Startled, she
looked up to see Cargo Officer Malaine, who jerked the
helmet from Killashandra's belt and jammed it atop her
head. Abashed at her lapse of memory, Killashandra
hastily straightened the protective gear. Malaine gave her
a grin and an encouraging thumbs up.

The relief from the wind's noise and the subsidence of
air pressure in her ears was enormous. Killashandra, accustomed to full chorus and electronically augmented
orchestral instruments, had not previously thought of
"noise" as a hazard. But to be deaf on Ballybran might not
be an intolerable prospect. She could still hear the gale's
shrieks, but the cacophony was blessedly muffled, and the
relief from the sound pressure gave her fresh energy. She
needed it, for the physical strength of the gale hadn't
abated at all.

In the course of her next wind-battered trip, a wholesale
clearance of sleds took place behind her back. The emptied
sleds were cleared, and the newer arrivals slipped into the
vacant positions. Some relief from the wind could be had
by darting from the wind shadow of one sled to that of the
next. The danger lay in the gap, for there the gale would
whip around to catch the unwary.

Why no one was killed, why so few ships were damaged
inside the hangar, and why not a single plasfoam container
was dropped, Killashandra would never know. She was at
one point certain, however, that she had probably bumped
into most of the nine thousand Guild members stationed in
the Joslin Plateau Headquarters. She later learned her assumption was faulty: anyone who could have, had carefully contrived to remain inside.

The cartons were not always heavy, though the weight
was unevenly distributed, and the heavy end always ended
up dragging at Killashandra's left arm. That side was certainly the sorest the next day. Only once did she come

close to losing a container: she hefted it from the ship and nearly lost the whole to a gust of wind. After that, she learned to protect her burden with her body to the wind.

Aside from the intense struggle with the gale-force winds, two other observations were indelibly marked in her mind that day. A different side of Crystal Singers, their least glamorous, as they jumped from their sleds. Few looked as if they had washed in days: some had fresh wounds, and others showed evidence of old ones. When she had to enter a sled's cargo hold to get the last few cartons, she was aware of an overripe aroma exuding from the main compartment of the sled and was just as glad that there was a fierce supply of fresh air at her back.

Still the sleds hurled themselves in over the wind baffle and managed to land in the little space available: the gale was audible even through her ear mufflers, and the force of the wind smacked at the body as brutally as any physical fist.

"RECRUITS! RECRUITS! All recruits will regroup in the sorting area. All recruits to the sorting area!"

Dazed, Killashandra swung around to check the message on the display screens, and then someone linked arms with her, and they both cantered into the gale to reach the sorting area.

Once inside the building, Killashandra nearly fell, as much from exhaustion as from pushing her body against a wind no longer felt. She was handed from one person to another and then deposited on a seat. A heavy beaker was put into her hands, and the noise-abatement helmet was removed from her head. Nor was there much noise beyond weary sighs, an occasional noisy exhalation that was not quite a groan, or the sound of boots scraping against plas-crete.

Killashandra managed to stop the trembling in her hands to take a judicious sip of the hot, clear broth. She sighed softly with relief. The restorative was richly tasty, and its warmth immediately crept to her cold extremities, which Killashandra had not recognized as being wind sore. The lower part of her face, her jaw and chin, which had been exposed to the scouring wind, were also stiff and painful. Taking another sip, she raised her eyes above the cup and noticed the row opposite her: noticed and recognized the faces of Rimbol and Borton, and farther down, Celee. Half a dozen had black eyes, torn or scratched cheeks. Four recruits looked as if they'd been dragged face down over gravel. When she touched her own skin, she realized she, too, had suffered unfelt abrasions, for her numb fingers were pricked with dots of blood.

A loud hiss of indrawn breath made her look to the left. A medic was daubing Jezerey's face. Another medic was working down the row toward Rimbol, Celee, and Borton.

"Any damage?" Killashandra, despite her exhausted stupor, recognized the voice as that of Guild Master Lanzecki's.

Surprised, she turned to find him standing in an open door, his black-garbed figure stark against the white of piled crystal cartons.

"Superficial, sir," one of the medics said after a respectful nod in the Guild Master's direction.

"Class 895 has been of invaluable assistance today," Lanzecki said, his eyes taking in every one of the thirty-three. "I, your Guild Master, thank you. So does Cargo Officer Malaine. No one else will." There wasn't even a trace of a smile on the man's face to suggest he was being humorously ironic. "Order what you will for your evening meal: it will not be debited from your account. Tomorrow you will report to this sorting area where you will learn what you can from the crystals brought in today. You are dismissed."

He withdraws, Killashandra thought. *He fades from the scene. How unusual. But then, he's not a Singer. So no sweeping entrances like Carrik or the three Singers at Shankill, nor exits like Borella's.* She took another sip of her broth, needing its sustenance to get her weary body up the ramp for that good free meal. Come to remember, the last good free meal she'd had had also been indirectly charged to the Guild. She was, as it happened, one of the last of the recruits to leave the sorting area. A door opened somewhere behind her.

"How many not yet in, Malaine?" she heard Lanzecki ask.

"Five more just hit the hangar floor, one literally. And Flight says there are two more possible light-sights."

"That makes twenty-two unaccounted—"

"If we could only get Singers to register cuts, we'd have some way of tracking the missing and retrieve at least the cargo . . ."

The door swooshed tight, and the last of the sentence was inaudible. The exchange, the tone of it, worried her.

"Retrieve the cargo." Was that the concern of Malaine and Lanzecki? The *cargo*? Malaine certainly had stressed the cargo's being more valuable than the recruits handling it. But surely the Crystal Singers themselves were valuable, too. Sleds could be replaced—another debit to clear off one's Guild account—but surely Singers were a valuable commodity in their own peculiar way.

Killashandra's mind simply could not cope with such anomalies. She made it to the top of the ramp. She had to put one hand on the door frame to steady herself as she thumbed her door open. A moan of weariness escaped her lips. Rimbol's door whisked open.

"You all right, Killa?" Rimbol's face was flecked with fine lines and tiny beads of fresh blood. He wore only a towel.

"Barely."

"The herbal bath does wonders. And eat."

"I will. It's on the management, after all." She couldn't move her painful face to smile.

After a long soak absorbed the worst fatigue from her muscles she did force herself to eat.

An insistent burp from the computer roused her the next morning. She peered into the dark beyond her bed and only then realized that the windows were shuttered and the gale still furious outside.

The digital told her that it was 0830 and her belly that it was empty. As she started to throw back the thermal covering, every muscle in her body announced its unreadiness for such activity. Cursing under her breath, Killashandra struggled up on one elbow. No sooner had she put her fingers on the catering dial than a small beaker with an effervescent pale-yellow liquid appeared in the slot.

"The medication is a muscle relaxant combined with a mild analgesic to relieve symptoms of muscular discomfort. This condition is transitory."

Killashandra cursed fluently at what she felt was the computer's embarrassingly well timed invasion of Privacy, but she drained the medicine, grimacing at its oversweet taste. In a few moments, she began to feel less stiff. She took a quick shower, alternating hot and cold, for unaccountably her skin still prickled from yesterday's severe buffeting. As she was eating a high-protein breakfast, she hoped that time would be allowed for meals today. She doubted that the rows of crystal containers could all be sorted and repacked in one day. And such a job oughtn't need the pace of yesterday.

Sorting took four days of labor as intense as fighting the storm wind, though presenting less physical danger. The recruits, each working with a qualified sorter, learned a great deal about how not to cut crystal and pack it and which forms were currently profitable. These were in the majority, and most of the experienced sorters directed a constant flow of abuse at Singers who had cut quantities of the commodity then most overstocked.

"We've got three ruddy storage rooms of these," muttered Enthor, with whom Killashandra was sorting. "It's blues what we need and want. And blacks, of course. No, no, wrong side. You've got to learn," he said, grabbing the carton Killashandra had just lifted to the sorting table. "First, present the Singer's ident code." He turned the box so that the strip, ineradicably etched on the side, would register. "Didn't have that little bit of help and there'd be war unloading, with cartons getting mixed up every which way and murder going on."

Once the ident number went up on the display, the carton was unpacked and each crystal form carefully put on the scale, which computed color, size, weight, form, and perfection. Some crystals Enthor immediately placed on the moving belts, which shunted them to the appropriate level for shipment or storage. Others he himself cocooned in the plastic webbing with meticulous care.

The sorting process seemed boringly simple. Sometimes it was not easy to retrieve the small crystals that had been thrust at any angle into the protective foam. Killashandra almost missed a small blue octagon before Enthor grabbed the carton she was about to assign to replacement.

"Lucky for you," the sorter said darkly, glancing about him, brows wrinkled over his eyes, "that the Singer who cut this wasn't watching. I've seen them try to kill a person for negligence."

"For this?" Killashandra held up the octagon, which couldn't have been more than 8 centimeters in length.

"For that. It's unflawed." Enthor's quick movement had placed the crystal on the scale and checked its perfection. "Listen!" He set the piece carefully between her thumb and forefinger and flicked it lightly.

Even above the rustling and stamping and low-voiced instructions, Killashandra heard the delicate, pure sound of the crystal. The note seemed to catch in her throat and travel down her bones to her heels.

"It's not easy to cut small, and right now this piece's worth a couple of hundred credits."

Killashandra was properly awed and far more painstaking, risking her fingers to search a plasfoam carton that seemed heavier than empty. Enthor scolded her for that, slapping her gloves across her cheek before he tugged one of his off and showed her fingers laced by faint white scars.

"Crystal does it. Even through gloves and with symbiosis. Yours would fester. I'd get docked for being careless."

"Docked?"

"Loss of work time due to inadequate safety measures is considered deductible. You, too, despite your being a recruit."

"We get paid for this?"

"Certainly." Enthor was indignant at her ignorance. "And you got danger money for unloading yesterday. Didn't you know?"

Killashandra stared at him in surprise.

"Just like all new recruits." Enthor chuckled amiably at her discomfort. "Not got over the shock, huh? Get a beaker of juice this morning? Thought so. Everyone does who's worked in a gale. Does the trick. And no charge for it, either." He chuckled again at her. "All medical treatment's free, you know."

"But you said you got docked—"

"For stupidity in not taking safety precautions." He wiggled his fingers, now encased in their tough skin-tight gloves, at her. "No, don't take that carton. I will. Get the next. Fugastri just came in. We don't want him breathing down your neck. He's a devil, but he's never faulted me!"

"You're being extremely helpful—"

"You're helping me, and we're both being paid by the same source, this crystal. You might as well know *this* job properly," and Enthor's tone implied that she might not have as good an instructor in any other sector. "You might end up here as a sorter, and we sorters like to have a good time. What'd you say your name was?"

"Killashandra."

"Oh, the person who brought Carrik back?" Enthor's tone was neither pleased nor approving: he just identified her.

Obscurely, Killashandra felt better: she wasn't just an identity lost in the Guild's memory banks. People besides Class 895 had heard of her.

"Did you know Carrik?"

"I know them all, m'dear. And wish I didn't.—However, it's not a bad life." He gave another of his friendly chuckles. "A fair day's wage for a fair day's work and then the best possible domestic conditions." His grin turned to a knowing leer, and he gave her a nudge. "Yes, you might remember my name while you can, for you won't if you become a Singer. Enthor, I am, level 4, accommodation 895. That ought to be easy for you to remember, as it's your class number."

"What was yours?" Quickly, Killashandra sought a way to turn the conversation away from his offer.

"Class number? 502," he said. "Nothing wrong with my memory."

"And you're not deaf."

"Couldn't sort crystal if I were!"

"Then what did the symbiont do to you?" She blurted it out before she realized she might be invading his privacy.

"Eyes, m'dear. Eyes." He turned and, for the first time, faced her directly. He blinked once, and she gasped. A protective lens retracted at his blink. She saw how huge his irises were, obscuring the original shade of the pupil. He blinked again, and some reddish substance covered the entire eyeball. "That's why I'm a sorter and why I know which crystals are flawless at a glance. I'm one of the best sorters they've ever had. Lanzecki keeps remarking on my ability. Ah, you'll shortly see what I mean . . ."

Another sorter, a disgruntled look on his face, was walking toward them with a carton and escorted by an angry Singer.

"Your opinion on these blues?" The Singer, his face still bearing the ravages of a long period in the ranges, curtly took the container from the sorter and thrust it at Enthor. Then the Singer, with the rudeness that Killashandra was beginning to observe was the mark of a profession rather than a personality, blocked the view of the sorter whose judgment he had questioned.

Enthor carefully deposited the carton on his work space and extracted the crystals, one by one, holding them up to his supersensitive eyes for inspection, laying them down in a precise row. There were seven green-blue pyramids, each broader in the base by 2 or 3 centimeters.

"No flaws perceived. A fine shear edge and good point," Enthor rendered his opinion in a flat tone markedly different from his conversational style with Killashandra. With an almost finicky precision, he wiped and polished a tiny crystal hammer and tapped each pyramid delicately. The fourth one was a half note, instead of a whole, above the third, and thus a scale was not achieved.

"Market them in trios and save the imperfect one for a show piece. I recommend that you check your cutter for worn gaskets or fittings. You're too good a Singer to make such an obvious mistake. Probably the oncoming storm put you off the note."

The attempt at diplomacy did not mollify the Singer, whose eyes bulged as he gathered himself to bellow. Enthor appeared not to notice, but the other sorter had stepped backward hastily.

"Lanzecki!"

The angry shout produced more than the swift arrival of Lanzecki. A hush fell over the sorting room, and the Singer seemed unaware of it, his savage glance resting on Enthor, who blithely tapped figures into his terminal.

Killashandra felt a hand on her shoulder and stepped obediently aside to allow Lanzecki to take her place by Enthor. As if aware of the Guild Master's presence, Enthor again tapped the crystals, the soft tones falling into respectful silence.

Lanzecki was not listening: he was watching the dials on the scales. One eyebrow twitched as the half tone sounded and the corresponding digits appeared on the display.

"Not a large problem, Uyad," Lanzecki said, turning calmly to the flushed Singer. "You've been cutting that face long enough to fill in half tones. I'd suggest you store this set and fill it to octave. Always a good price for pyramids in scale."

"Lanzecki . . . I've *got* to get off-planet this time. I have got to get away! I won't survive another trip to the ranges . . . not until I've had time off this bloody planet!"

"This is but one carton, one set, Uyad-vuic-Holm. Your cargo has been very good according to the input here," for Lanzecki had made use of the terminal even as Uyad's manner changed from ire to entreaty. "Yes, I think it'll be sufficient to take you off-planet for a decent interval. Come, I'll supervise the sort myself."

Simultaneously, several things happened: working noises recommenced in the room; Lanzecki was guiding the distressed Singer to another sorting slide, his manner encouraging rather than condescending, which Killashandra could not help but admire in the Guild Master; the other sorter had returned to his position. Enthor swiftly packed the offending pyramids, marked their container, and dealt it to a little-used slide above his head, then, seeing her bemused, gave her a friendly dig in the ribs.

"An even pace makes light of the biggest load. Another box, m'dear."

Even pace or not, they didn't seem to be making much of an impression on the mound of containers waiting to be sorted. What made a repetitive day interesting was the tremendous input of information Enthor divulged on crystal, grading, sound, and disposition. When he noticed she was taking a keen interest in the valuations, he chided her.

"Don't sweat your head remembering prices, m'dear. Change every day. Value's computed by the Marketing Office before we start sorting, but tomorrow, values might be totally different. One aspect of crystal's enough for me to cope with: I leave the merchandising to others. Ah, now here's beauty in rose quartz! Just look at the shading, the cut. Dooth's work, or I miss my guess," and Enthor peered at the carton, blinking his eyes for a lens change. "I don't. I'd know his cut among the whole roster's."

"Why?" Killashandra leaned closer to inspect the octagon. It was beautiful, a deep pale pink with a purple tinge, but she couldn't understand Enthor's enthusiasm.

The sorter took a deep breath as if to explain and then exhaled sharply.

"Ah, but if you *knew*, you'd have my rating, wouldn't you?" He blinked again and regarded her with a shrewd narrowing of his eyes.

"Not necessarily," she replied. "*I'd* prefer to sing crystal . . ."

Enthor looked from her to the rose octagon. "Yes, perhaps *you* would at that. However, I recognize Dooth's cut when I see it. When—if—you cut crystal, you will know crystal that is so fine, so rare."

With both hands, he laid the heavy jewel on the scale plate, running two fingers over his lips as he watched the configurations change and settle.

"I thought you said there was a surplus of rose crystal . . ."

"Not of this weight, color, or octagonal," he said, his fingers tapping out a sequence. "I happen to have heard"— and Enthor lowered his voice—"that someone very highly placed in the Federated Planets is looking for large pieces this hue." He lifted the octagon to the coating rack where the deep pink was swiftly cocooned from sight with plastic webbing, and at a touch of his finger on the terminal, an identifying code was stippled along the hardening surface.

At the close of the first day of sorting, Killashandra felt as tired as she had after unloading in the gale. She said as

much as Shillawn and Rimbol joined her in a weary trudge
to their lounge.

"We're getting paid for our efforts," Shillawn said by
way of cheering them.

"Yesterday we got a danger bonus as well," Killashandra
said, not to be outdone.

"Making use of the data banks, are you?" Rimbol asked,
grinning at her with some malice. Killashandra hadn't admitted to him that she'd taken a skimmer out the evening
before the storm, but he'd known.

"Told we were. Available to us is the data." Killashandra
so aptly mimicked Tukolom's ponderous tones that she had
the other two laughing. "I'm going for a shower. See you in
the lounge later?"

Rimbol nodded, and so did Shillawn.

In the catering slot by her bed was another beaker of the
lemon liquid. She drank it and had her shower, by the end
of which she felt sufficiently revived to enjoy a quiet evening at dice with Rimbol and Shillawn.

Though no more peevish crystal cutters added excitement to the sorting routine during the next three days,
Killashandra did have an unusual slice of luck. Halfway
through the second day, Lanzecki and the handsome
woman Killashandra guessed must be the chief marketing
officer walked swiftly into the sorting room and marched
right up to Enthor.

"Gorren's conscious. Muttering about black crystal.
Have any of his cartons been released to you yet?"

"By my bones, no!" Enthor was shocked and amazed.
Shocked, he later confided to Killashandra, that Gorren's
cuttings had been stored separately and amazed because he
hadn't known that Gorren had returned. He'd half expected to hear, Enthor continued solemnly, that Gorren
had been one of the Singers trapped in the ranges by the
storm. Gorren's black crystals were always entrusted to
Enthor for evaluation.

A work force was hastily assembled in the sorting room,
checking the labels of the many boxes still waiting evaluation. The group that had unloaded Gorren's ship—his had
been the one to overturn—were identified and summoned.
Fortunately, the handlers were regular hangar personnel,

and since they had known the cartons were Gorren's and valuable, they had placed them on a top layer, fifth stack, with buffering layers on either side.

Reverently, the eleven valuable cartons were handed down. Since it had been impressed constantly on Killashandra that very little could damage these specially constructed boxes or their contents, and she'd seen some of these same men indifferently lobbing cartons through the air to one another, she reflected that the presence of Lanzecki and Chief Marketing Officer Heglana had a salutary effect.

She was more surprised to see the two officials each take up a carton and was delighted when Enthor, his expression severe, pressed one firmly into her body, waiting until she had grasped the handles tightly.

Killashandra was elated by Enthor's confidence in her and walked the short distance back to the sorting room with the black crystal crammed against her breasts. Unaccountably, she was trembling with tension when she deposited her burden safely beside the others.

Later, she remembered that Enthor had moved with his normal dispatch to unpack: it was probably just because so many important people were watching and she herself caught their suppressed excitement that Enthor appeared to be dawdling. Tension can be transferred, and the sorting room was certainly crackling despite the hush. Those at nearby sorting tables had managed to be in positions to observe the unpacking, while those not directly in the Guild Master's view had suspended work completely, watching.

As Enthor lifted the first black crystal from its protecting foam, a sigh rippled through the watchers.

"Flipped right over, didn't he?" Heglana remarked, and made a clicking sound in her throat. Lanzecki nodded, his eyes on Enthor's hands.

The second black was larger, and to Killashandra's surprise, Enthor did not place it safely apart from the first but against the first where it seemed to fit securely. She felt a tingle at the very base of her head that spread upward across her skull. She shook her head, and the sensation dissipated. Not for long. A third, the largest crystal, fit against the second, a fourth and a fifth. The tingle in her head became a tightening of the scalp. Or was it her head bones pressing outward against her skin, stretching it?

"Five matched crystals. Gorren hadn't imagined it." Lanzecki's voice was level, but Killashandra sensed his satisfaction with such a cut. "Quality?"

"High, Lanzecki," Enthor replied calmly. "Not his best cut, but I dare say the flaws, minute as they are, will not impair the function if the units are not too far separated."

"Five is a respectable link," Heglana said, "for an interplanetary network."

"Where are the flaws? In the king crystal?"

"No, Lanzecki"—Enthor's fingers caressed the largest of the five as if reassuring it—"in the first and fifth of the cut." He gestured to either side. "Marginal." He deftly transferred the interlocking quintet to the scales and ordered his sequence. The display rested at a figure that would have made Killashandra exclaim aloud had she not been in such company.

Whoever Gorren was, he had just made a fortune. She mentally deducted the requisite 30 percent tithe. So Gorren had a small fortune, and there were ten more cartons to unpack.

Enthor removed the contents of three containers while Lanzecki and Heglana observed. Killashandra was somewhat disappointed by these, though the two watching nodded in satisfaction. The smaller units were not as impressive, though one set contained twelve interlocking pieces, the "king" crystal no longer than her hand at octave stretch and no thicker than her finger.

"He may be down to the base of this cutting," Lanzecki said as the fourth container was emptied. "Proceed, Enthor, but transfer the total to my office for immediate display, will you?" With an inclination of his head to Enthor, he and Heglana swiftly left the sorting room.

A universal sigh ran about the room and activity picked up on all the other tables.

"I don't think we've come to the prize yet, Killashandra," Enthor said, frowning. "The hairs on the crest of m'neckio . . ."

"The what?" Killashandra stared at him, for he was describing exactly her sensation.

Enthor shot her a surprised glance. "Scalp itch? Spasm at the back of your head?"

"Am I coming down with symbiont fever?"

"How long have you been here?"

"Five days."

He shook his head. "No! No! Too soon for fever." He narrowed his eyes again, turning his head to one side as he squinted at her. Then he pointed to the seven remaining containers.

"Pick the next one."

"Me?"

"Why not? You might as well get used to handling"—he paused, scrubbed at his close cropped hair—"crystal. Myself, I don't agree with Master Lanzecki. I don't think Gorren has come to the end of the black face he's been cutting. Gorren's clever. Just enough substantial stuff to get off-planet, and slivers now and then. That way he's got Lanzecki in a bind and a route off-planet any time he chooses. Pick a carton, girl."

Startled by the command, Killashandra reached for the nearest box, hesitated, and drawn by a curious compulsion, settled her hands on its neighbor. She picked it up and would have given it over to Enthor, but he gestured for her to place it on the table, its ident facing the scanner.

"So open it!"

"Me? Black crystal?"

"You chose it, didn't you? You must learn to handle it."

"If I should drop—"

"You won't. Your hands are very strong for a girl's, fingers short and supple. You won't drop things you want to hold."

Tension, like a frigid extra skin about her torso, crept down her thighs. She had felt this way, standing in the wings before an entrance in the Music Center, so she took three deep breaths, clearing her lungs and diaphragm as she would if she were about to sing a long musical phrase.

Indeed, when her questing fingers closed on the large soapy-soft object in the center of the plasfoam, she exhaled a long, low "ah" of surprise.

"NO!" Enthor turned to her in outrage. "No, no," and he darted forward, clapping his hand to her mouth. "Never sing around raw crystal! Especially"—and his tone intense with anger—"near black crystal!" He was so agitated that he blinked his lens on and off, and the red of his unprotected eyes effectively cowed Killashandra. Enthor looked about him in a frenzied survey to see if any one at the nearer tables had heard her. "Never!"

She didn't dare tell him at that juncture that the black crystal had vibrated in her hands at her spontaneous note and her finger bones had echoed the response of other segments still unpacked.

With an effort, Enthor regained his composure, but his nostrils flared, and his lips worked as he struggled for calm.

"Never sing or whistle or hum around raw crystal no matter what the color. I can only hope you haven't inhibited the magnetic induction of a whole ring linkage with that ill-advised—ah—exclamation. I'll say it was an exclamation if I should be asked." He let out one more unaspirated breath and then nodded for her to take out the crystal.

Killashandra closed her eyes as she freed the heavy block. Enthor was not going to like this if she had indeed blurred raw crystal. Told she had been and at some length and with considerable emphasis by Tukolom all about the subtle and delicate process by which segments of the black quartz crystal were subjected to synchronized magnetic induction, which resulted in the instantaneous resonance between segments as far apart as five hundred light years. The resonance provided the most effective and accurate communications network known in the galaxy. That she might have inadvertently damaged the thick block she now exposed to Enthor's startled gaze weighed heavily in her mind.

With an intake of breath for which she might have returned him his caution on sound, Enthor reverently took the dodecahedron from her.

"How many more are with it?" he asked in an uneven voice.

Killashandra already knew how many there should be.

Twelve, and there were. She retrieved them from their webbing, handing them carefully to Enthor, though they were not as massive or tall as the king crystal. They fit as snugly to the central block as they had lived with it until Gorren had cut the crystals from the quartz face.

"Well!" Enthor regarded the matched set on the scale.

"Are—are they all right?" Killashandra finally found a contrite voice for the urgent question.

Enthor's little hammer evoked a clear tone that rippled from her ear bones to her heels, like an absolving benison. Even without Enthor's verbal reassurance, she knew the crystal had forgiven her.

"Luck, m'dear. You seem to have used the note on which they were cut. Fortunate for me."

Killashandra leaned against the sorting table to balance her shaky self.

"A set like this will provide a multiple linkage with thirty or forty other systems. Magnificent!" By this time, Enthor was examining the thirteen crystals with his augmented vision. "He cut just under the flaw," he murmured, more to himself, then remembered the presence of Killashandra. "As one would expect Gorren to do."

Brusquely but with precise movements, he put the crystals on the scale. Killashandra allowed herself an unaspirated sigh at the size of the huge fortune in credits Gorren had just acquired.

"Magnificent!" Enthor said. Then he gave a chuckle, his glance back at Killashandra sly. "Only Lanzecki will have the devil's own time persuading Gorren to cut anything for the next two galactic years. There's not that much black being cut. Being found. Still in all, that's Lanzecki's problem, not mine. Not yours. Bring another carton, m'dear. You've the knack of picking them, it seems."

"Luck," Killashandra said, regarding the remaining boxes, none of which seemed to draw her as that other had done.

She would rather have been wrong but the rest of Gorren's cut was unexciting. The small clusters were unexciting. The small clusters, absolutely flawless, would be quite sufficient for the larger public entertainment units that provided realistic sensual effects, Enthor told her.

That night, most of the recruits insisted on her telling them about the black crystal, and Lanzecki and the chief marketing officer, for they had been unable to hear much and not permitted to stare. She obliged them, including a slightly exaggerated version of Enthor's dressing down that she felt would be salutary. Besides, the telling relieved the tension she still felt at how close she had come to buggering up enough credit to ransom a planet.

"What could they do to you if you had?" Shillawn asked, swallowing nervously as if he envisioned himself muffing it in a similar instance.

"I don't know."

"Something bizarre, I'm sure," Borton said. "Those Singers don't spare anyone if their cuttings are mishandled. I was lucky enough to be the sorter who did Uyad's cut." Borton grinned. "I hid in the storage behind enough cartons, so I didn't get much of the back blast."

"So that's where you were," Jezerey asked, teasing.

"Bloody well told. I'm not here to bucket someone else's bilge."

Conversation continued about the variety of cuts and sizes and colors of the crystals from the Brerrerton and Milekey Ranges. Killashandra added nothing else, considering it more discreet to remain silent. When she could do so without attracting attention, she rose and went to her room. She wanted to think and recall the sensation of handling that massive black crystal. It hadn't been really black, not black at all, nor clear the way the rose or indeed any of the other crystals had been. She had accepted the designation at the time, for surely Enthor knew his crystals, and certainly the black quartz was different.

She tapped data retrieval for all information on black quartz crystal and specimens thereof. The data included black crystal in segmented units, none quite like the dodecahedron. Another display showed an octagon in its luminous, unchanged state, then the same form shading gradually to a matte black as it responded to thermal changes artificially induced. The data began to take up the lecture Tukolom had given, and she switched it off, lying back and recalling the sensation of her first contact with black crystal.

The next day, recovery teams brought in the cargo from sleds that had not reached the safety of the Guild Complex, and depression settled over the sorting room when the cartons, dinged, scarred, and discolored, were deposited on sorting tables. The mood was partially lightened when two containers disgorged some good triple and quadruple black crystal.

"What happens to them?" Killashandra asked Enthor in a low voice.

"To what?"

"The crystal of the Singer who didn't make it."

"Guild." Enthor's terse reply seemed to imply that this was only fair.

"But doesn't a Guild member have the right to dispose of the . . . things of which he dies possessed?"

Enthor paused before opening the carton before him.

"I suppose so," he finally answered. "Problem is most Singers outlive their families by hundreds of years; they tend to get very greedy; don't make many friends off-world and are unlikely to remember them if they have. I suppose some do. Not many."

Halfway through the next day, the backlog of crystal cartons having been substantially reduced, the recruits were assigned to help the hangar crew clean and resupply the Singers' sleds, for the storm was blowing itself out. There was some disgruntlement, but the hangar officer hadn't the look of someone to antagonize. It seemed to Killashandra that discretion was necessary.

"I'm not going to clean out someone else's filth for the nardy day's credits that gives," Carigana said. "No one ever cleaned up for me in space, and I'm not doing it on the ground. Pack of vermin, that's all they are, for all their airs and arrogance." She glared at the others, daring them to follow her example. Her contempt as she walked off was palpable.

Remembering the state of some of the sleds, Killashandra would have been sorely tempted to follow—if anyone other than Carigana had set the example.

"We do get paid. And it's better than twiddling your fingers!" Shillawn caught at Killashandra's arm as if he had divined her thoughts.

"Doesn't matter to me," the hangar officer went on, forgetting Carigana the instant she was out of sight, "but there is a bonus for every rank finished. The first eight are already done. Singers can make life intolerable for those who don't assist them. This storm is nearly blown out, and there'll be Singers frothing to get into the ranges. Met'll give 'em clearance by midday tomorrow. Get on with it. Get 'em cleaned and stocked and the Singers out where they belong."

He resumed his seat at the control console, peering out at the vast orderly ranks of airsleds where the regular suppliers were already at work. He frowned as his gaze rested briefly on the undecided recruits; the grimace deepened as he saw a damaged sled being hoisted for repair.

"There must be some way the Guild handles dossers like Carigana," Borton said, squinting after the space worker. "She can't get away with it!"

"We don't have to clean up after a bunch of shitty Singers," said Jezerey, her eyes flashing her personal rebellion. "I remember some of those sleds. Faugh!" and she pinched her nose shut with two fingers.

"I want a closer look at some of the equipment inside the sleds," Rimbol said, turning on his heel toward the sled racks.

"Closer smell, too?" asked Jezerey.

"You get used to any stinks in time," Rimbol said, waving off that argument. " 'Sides, it keeps my mind off other things."

"Those sleds will keep your mind off many things," Jezerey snapped back.

They were all silent a moment, knowing exactly what Rimbol meant. They were near the earliest day of onset of the symbiotic fever.

"We do get paid. And the hangar officer mentioned a bonus . . ." Shillawn let his sentence fall off, swallowing nervously.

"Hey, you, there. You recruits. I could use some help."

A supplier, by the shade of his uniform, leaned out of an upper level. Jezerey continued to grumble, but she followed the others toward the array of cleaning equipment.

Not since Killashandra had left her family's small tree

farm on Fuerte had she had to muck out on this scale. By
the fifth sled, as Rimbol had suggested, she had become
inured to the various stenches. It was also, as he had said,
worth the chance to examine a Crystal Singer's airsled first-
hand: at its worst and, after proper restoration, at its best.

The sled's control console took up the bow section,
complete with pilot safety couch. Built into the couch's
armrests were an assortment of manual override buttons.
Alongside the main hatch were the empty brackets for the
crystal cutter; the instruments were serviced after each trip
to the ranges. The main compartment was the Singer's in-
range living accommodations, adequate if compact. A
thick webbing separated the forward sections from cargo
storage and the drive section.

Her supplier, to give the ancient man his proper title,
was so deaf that Killashandra had to shake him violently to
get his attention. However, once she had asked a question
(for his lipreading was good), she received an encyclopedic answer and a history of the particular sled and its
Singer. The fellow might be elderly, but he worked so
swiftly that Killashandra was hard-pressed to do her share
in the same time.

The supplier, for he admitted no name to Killashandra's
polite inquiry, seemed to have a passion for orderly, gleam-
ing, well-stocked vehicles. Killashandra wondered at his
dedication since the order he cherished would so soon deteriorate to slime and shit.

"One can always get at crystal," the old man said. He
invariably pointed out the five hatches: the one into the
main compartment, the bottom through the drive area, and
the two on either side and the top of the storage compartment. "Strongest part of the sled as well. On purpose, of
course, since it's crystal is important. If a Singer gets injured, or worse"—and he paused reverently—"especially if
Singer's injured, the crystal can be salvaged, and he isn't
out of credit. Singers get very incensed, they do, if they're
done on crystal, you know. Maybe you will. You be a
recruit, don't you? So this is all new to you. Might be the
only time you see a sled. Then again, it might not—no,
safety net is always fastened." He did the catches himself,

a mild reproof to her quickness in stowing the empty crystal containers. "Can't have these, full or empty, bouncing about in flight or in a storm."

He consulted his wrist-unit, peering around at the hatch to confirm the sled number.

"Oh, yes, special orders for this one. Never eats animal protein. Prefers nonacid beverages." He beckoned to Killashandra to follow him to Stores. He took her past the sections from which they had been restocking, and into a blandly pink section. She rather hoped the food wasn't the same color. It'd be enough to put her off eating entirely.

The sled's catering unit did not allow much diversity, but the supplier assured her that the quality was always the best that was obtainable even if the Singers sometimes didn't realize what they were eating in the frenzy of their work.

Frenzy, Killashandra decided, was an inadequate description of the state in which most sleds had been left, though the supplier reminded her time and again that the storm that had forced all the Singers in had caused some of the internal spillage.

After another wearying day, she had helped clean and stock ten sleds, three more, her supplier noted, than he would have been able to do himself.

Technically, the next day was a rest day, but the hangar officer told the recruits that any who cared to continue would get double credit.

Shillawn shoved his hand up first; Rimbol, grimacing at Killashandra, followed with his; and she, perforce, volunteered as well. The hangar officer, however, was surprised when all present signaled their willingness. He grunted and then went back into his office.

"Why did we volunteer?" asked Jezerey, shaking her head.

"Thoughts of double credits to be earned, staving off the pangs and uncertainties of debt!" Rimbol rolled his eyes. "My supplier had a thing about debt."

"Mine did, too," Killashandra replied.

"At this rate"—and Borton pulled across his shoulders at aching muscles—"we'll be ahead of the Guild even before we get the fever."

"They'll charge us for time off then without due cause," said Jezerey sourly.

"No," Shilawn corrected her. "All medical treatment is free."

"Except you don't get paid for work you can't do."

"May you never stand outside during a full Passover," said Rimbol, intoning his blessing in a fruity voice.

"I don't think I've worked this hard since I was a kid on my father's fishing trawler," Borton continued. "And fishing on Argma is done in the oooold-fashioned way."

"Which is why you studied spaceflight?" asked Killashandra.

"Too right."

"Well, you're slaving again," said Jezerey, fatigue making her sullen.

"But we're Guild members," Rimbol mocked her.

"Reducing our initial debt," Shillawn added with a sigh of relief.

"All green and go!"

At Rimbol's quip, they reached the top of the ramp and the lounge. Rimbol made drinking motions to Killashandra, smiling wistfully.

"Not until I'm clean, really clean!"

"Me, too," Jezerey said, her whole body giving way to a shudder.

They all made for their private quarters. Carigana's red-lit door caught Killashandra's gaze as she passed it.

"Don't worry about her, Killa. She's trapped by more than just the Guild," Rimbol said, taking her elbow to move her on.

"I'm not sorry for her," Killashandra replied, obscurely annoyed by herself and Rimbol's remark.

"No one's ever sorry about anything here," Shillawn commented almost sadly. "No one thanks anyone. No one has good manners at all."

This was very true, Killashandra thought as she wallowed in steaming-hot, scented water, scouring the stench of the day's labors from body and breath.

The matter of debt stuck in her mind, and the old supplier's obsession with it. She pulled the console before her as she lay languidly on her bed after her bath.

Suppliers earned more than caterer's assistants. And bonuses for speedy completion of their duty. She tapped for her own account and discovered that her labors were covering her living expenses and eating away at the shuttle fare. If she got double time for the next day and perhaps a speed bonus, she'd be clear of debt. It was only then that she remembered the two Guild vouchers. If she submitted them, she might even be able to pay for whatever equipment her postsymbiosis rank required. A soothing thought. To be one step ahead of the Guild. Was that what prompted the supplier?

Out of curiosity, she asked for a roster of the Guild in rank order. It began with Lanzecki, Guild Master, then the chiefs of Control, Marketing, and Research, and the names of active Singers followed. That information wasn't in the form Killashandra wanted. She thought a moment and then asked for enlistment order. Barry Milekey was the first member of the Guild. The names, with the planet of origin, rolled past on the display. They must all be dead, she thought, and wondered that no such notation was made. Once a Crystal Singer, always a Crystal Singer? No, some of these must have been support personnel. *If* Borella's statistics were to be believed since the rate of adaptability to the symbiont spore had been low in the early days of the Guild. What did surprise her was that nearly every planet of the Federated Sentient Planets inhabited by her life form was represented on the Guild roster. Several planets had more than a fair share, but they were heavily populated worlds. There were even two Fuertans. That was an eye opener. What the listing did not show was when they had joined the Guild. The names must be listed in order of membership, for it was certainly not alphabetical. Borella's name flashed by, then Malaine's and Carrik's. She wondered if Enthor's had passed already but, on cue, his appeared. He originated from Hyperion, one of the first planets settled in Alpha Proxima in the Great Surge of exploration and evaluation that forced the organization of the Federated Sentient Planets. Was he younger than Borella, Malaine, or Carrik? Or had he joined as an older man? And the supplier, who wouldn't admit to a name—when had he joined? She shuddered.

Sorter aptly fitted Enthor's skill, whereas supplier was a
glamorous title for a job that could have been done mechanically and wasn't. Cutter, applied to a Crystal Singer,
certainly didn't imply the rank the designation commanded.

She flipped off the console. Computers hadn't changed
all that much since their invention; one still had to know
what question to ask even the most sophisticated system.
The Guild's tremendous data banks, using Ballybran crystals with their naturally structured synapselike formation,
stored data nonvolatilely for indefinite retention, but Killashandra was far more adept at finding obscure composers
and performers than galactic conundrums.

Later, she joined the others in the lounge for a few
drinks, wondering if Shillawn had fathomed any startling
interpretations from his time with the data banks. He was
far too involved in figuring out a mechanical means of
cleansing the sleds, and Killashandra was glad when Rimbol tapped her arm and winked.

"I think I'm too tired for much, Killa," he said as they
reached his room, "but I'd like my arms around something
warm, friendly, and in my decade."

Killashandra grinned at him. "My sentiments entirely.
Can your account stand a Yarran beer?"

"And one for you, too," he replied, deliberately misin-
terpreting her.

They slept soundly and in harmony as if, indeed, the
company kept was mutually beneficial. When the computer
woke them, they ate heartily, without much conversation
but still in accord, and then reported to the hangar officer.
As they were the first to arrive, the man looked with some
anxiety back up the ramp.

"They'll be along," Rimbol told him.

"I've got sleds that must be ready by midday. You two
start with these. Other numbers will come up on the display boards when I find out which flaming Singers will lift
their asses out of the racks today."

Killashandra and Rimbol hurried off, hoping to be out
of his range if the other volunteers didn't arrive. They had
cleaned and stocked eight sleds by midday. Numbers had
disappeared periodically from the display, so Killashandra
and Rimbol knew that other recruits had gone to work.

Almost at the stroke of 1200 hours, raised voices, echoing in the vastness of the hangar, warned Killashandra and Rimbol of the influx.

"I don't like the tone of that," she said, giving a final swipe to the cutter brackets on the sled they had just readied.

"Sound of angry mob in the distance," Rimbol said, and pulling her arm, urged her into the stock rooms and behind a half-empty section where they had a view of the rack beyond them as well as the hangar entrance.

Bangs, curses, metallic slammings, and the thud of plastic resounded. Drive motors started, too fast for such an enclosed space, Rimbol told Killashandra. She plugged her fingers in her ears. Rimbol grimaced at one particularly loud screech and followed her example. The exodus didn't take long, but Killashandra was wide-eyed at the piloting and wondered that the Singers didn't collide with such antics. As abruptly as the commotion had started, it ended. The final sled had veered off to the Brerrerton Ranges.

"We did eight sleds?" Rimbol asked Killashandra. "That's enough at double time. Let's go. I've had enough!"

When they reached the lounge, it was empty. Carigana's door was red-lit and closed. Rimbol still held Killashandra's hand. Now he pulled her toward him, and she swayed against his lean body.

"I'm not tired now. Are you?"

Killashandra was not. Rimbol had a way about him, for all his ingenuousness and deceivingly innocent appearance, that was charmingly irresistible. She knew that he counted on this appeal, but as he didn't disappoint and gave no evidence of possessiveness, she complied willingly. He was like his Yarran beer, cool, with a good mouth and a pleasant aftertaste: satisfying without filling.

They joined the others as they straggled back to the lounge, consoling themselves for their scraped and solution-withered fingers with thoughts of the double credits accruing to their accounts.

"You know what the Guild can do, though?" Shillawn began, seating himself opposite Rimbol and Killashandra. He swallowed and then sipped at his own drink in quick gulps.

"Guild do what?" Borton and Jezerey asked, joining the others.

"About dossers like her." Shillawn nodded his head in Carigana's direction.

"What?" Jezerey asked, sliding into a lounger, her eyes bright with anticipation.

"Well, they can reduce her rations."

Jezerey didn't think much of that discipline.

"And other amenities can be discontinued at random."

"Such as?" Jezerey realized that Shillawn's face was contorted more by amusement than the effort to speak.

"Well, such as cold water instead of hot: the same with food. You know, the cold hot and the hot cold. Then the computer takes to making noises and shuffling the sleeping unit. Other furniture collapses when least expected, and, of course, the door doesn't always respond to your print. And," Shillawn was warming to the delighted response of his audience—"and since you have to print in for any meals, and it wouldn't be accepted"—he spread both arms wide and smirked again—"all sorts of insidious, uncomfortable, miserable things can happen."

"How in the name of any holy did you get the computer to tell you that?" Killashandra demanded. Her request was seconded by the others.

"Didn't ask the computer," Shillawn admitted, casting his eyes away from them. "I asked the supplier I worked with yesterday."

Rimbol burst out laughing, slapping his thighs. "The best computer is still the human brain."

"That's about all my supplier has left that's human," Shillawn said in a disgusted tone of voice.

"And that's happening to Carigana?" Jezerey asked, her expression hopeful.

"Not yet, but it could if she keeps up. Meanwhile, she's two days in debt for bed and biscuits, and we're four ahead."

"Yet Guild rules state—" Borton began.

"Sure"—and Rimbol chortled again—"but they haven't deprived someone of shelter or sustenance, just made them bloody hard to acquire or uncomfortable."

"I dread the thought of a future as a stockist or a supplier," Jezerey said, echoing the unspoken anxiety in everyone, judging by the gloom that settled over the quintet.

"Think positively," Shillawn suggested with a slight stammer that impeded the advice. "We've been here eight days now."

"Well, we ought to know fairly soon," Rimbol said. "We've been here eight days now."

"Almost nine." Shillawn's correction was automatic.

"Tomorrow?" Jezerey's voice held a tinge of horror.

"Could be much longer than ten days if I remember what Borella said about the incubation period," Shillawn reassured her in a mock cheerful tone.

"That's enough, friend," Killashandra said firmly, and drained her beaker. "Let us eat, drink, and be merry—"

"For tomorrow we die?" Rimbol's eyebrows shot upward.

"I don't intend to die," Killashandra replied, and ordered a double beaker of Yarran beer for herself and Rimbol.

They had quite a few refills before they went to bed together. As Killashandra woke in her own room, she assumed they'd ended up there, but Rimbol was gone. The light was far too brilliant for her eyes, and she dimmed the plasglas on the unshuttered windows. After the storm and its attendant hard labor, it was pleasant to look out on the hills. She scoffed at herself for missing 'a view.' The rain must have encouraged growth, for vivid reddish-purple blooms tinged the slopes, and the gray-green vegetation was brighter. Doubtless she would grow to love the seasonal changes of Ballybran. Until she'd gone with Carrik to see the sights of Fuerte, she hadn't quite appreciated natural scenery, too accustomed to the holograms used in performances.

Carigana was the first person she saw as she entered the lounge. Killashandra hoped the day would improve from that point. The space worker had an ability to ignore people, so that Killashandra was not obliged to acknowledge her presence. The woman's obstinancy annoyed her. No one had forced her to apply to the Heptite Guild.

The recruits were laggard, and by the time all had assembled, Tukolom was clearly impatient.

"Much to be done is this day," he said. "Basic lessons delayed have been—"

"Well, it will be a relief to sit and relax," someone said from the center of the group.

"Relax is not thinking, and thought must earnest be," Tukolom replied, his eyes trying to find the irreverent. "Geography today's study is. All of Ballybran. When adjusted you are, another continent may you be sent to."

Carigana's exaggerated sigh of resignation was echoed by others, though Tukolom stared only at her for such a public display of insolence. Carigana's vocabulary of monosyllables punctuated Tukolom's fluid explanations throughout the morning until someone hissed at her to stop it.

Whoever had organized the lecture material had had a sense of humor, and though Killashandra wagered with herself that Tukolom could not have been aware of the amusing portions of his rote discourse, she, and others, waited for these leavening phrases. The humor often emphasized the more important aspects of the lessons. Tukolom might be reciting what he had patiently learned or switching mental frames in an eidetic review, but he had also learned to pace his delivery. Knowing the strain of uninterrupted speaking, Killashandra was also impressed by his endurance.

"I wouldn't mind farming in North Ballinteer," Rimbol confided in her as they ate lunch during the midday break. "Nice productive life, snow sports in the winter . . ."

Killashandra stared at him. "Farmer?"

"Sure, why not? That'd be meters ahead of being a supplier! Or a sorter. Out in the open . . ."

"In mach storms?"

"You heard your geography lesson. The produce areas are 'carefully situated at the edge of the general storm belts or can be shielded at need'." Rimbol imitated Tukolom's voice and delivery well, and Killashandra had to laugh.

That was when she saw a group moving together with a menacing deliberation, closing off one corner and its lone occupant. Noting her preoccupation, Rimbol swiveled and cursed under his breath.

"I knew it." He swung out of his chair.

"Why bother, Rimbol? She deserves it."

"She can't help being the way she is. And I thought you

were so big on Privacy on your world. On mine, we don't permit those odds."

Killashandra had to accede to the merit of that reply and joined him.

"What do I care about that?" Carigana's strident voice rose above the discreet murmur addressed to her by the group's leader. "And why should you? Any of you? They're only biding their time until we get sick. Nothing matters until then, not all your cooperation or attention or good manners or volunteering"—and her scorn intensified —"to clean up messes in sleds. Not me! I had a pleasant day—What?" She snapped her head about to the questioner. "Debit?" She tossed her head back and laughed raucously. "They can take it out of my hide—later. Right now, I can get anything I want from stores. If you had any intelligence, you'd do the same thing and forget that stuffed mudhead—"

"You helped unload crystal . . ." Killashandra heard Jezerey's voice.

"Sure I did. I wanted to see this crystal, just like everyone else . . . Only "—and her tone taunted them—"I also got wise. They'll work you at every mean, disagreeable, dirty grind they've got until the spore gets you. Nothing will matter after that except what you're good for."

"And what do you expect to be good for?" Jezerey demanded.

"Crystal Singer, like everyone else!" Carigana's expression mocked them for the ambition. "One thing sure. I won't be sorting or supplying or mucking in mud or . . . You play along like good cooperative contributing citizens. I'll do what I choose while I still have eyes and ears and a mind that functions properly."

She rose quickly, pushing herself through the unsympathetic crowd, then pounded down the corridor to her room. The red light flashed on.

"You said something about Privacy?" Killashandra couldn't refrain from asking Rimbol as they turned desultorily away from the silent group.

"She does prove the exception," he replied, unruffled.

"What did she mean about a mind that functions properly?" Jezerey asked, joining them. She was no longer as confident as she had been when confronting Carigana.

"I told you not to worry about it, Jez," Borton said, coming behind her. "Carigana's got space rot, anyhow. And I told you that the first time I saw her."

"She's right about one thing," Shillawn added, almost unable to pronounce the 'th'. "Nothing really does matter until the symbiont spore works."

"I wish she hadn't said 'sick'," and Jezerey emphasized her distaste with a shudder. "That's one thing they haven't shown us . . . the medical facilities . . ."

"You saw Borella's scar," Shillawn said.

"True, but she's got full adaptation, hasn't she?"

"Anyone got headache, bellyache, chills, fever?" Rimbol asked with brightly false curiosity.

"Not time yet." Jezerey pouted.

"Soon. Soon." Rimbol's tone became sepulchral. Then he waved his hand in a silencing gesture and jerked his thumb to indicate Tukolom's return. He gave a heavy sigh and then grinned because he inadvertently echoed Carigana. "I'd rather pass time doing *something* . . ."

That was the unanimous mood as the recruits turned to their instructor. The ordeal of symbiotic adaptation was no longer an explanation delivered in a remote and antiseptic hall on a moon base: it was imminent and palpable. The spore was in the air they breathed, the food they ate, possibly in the contact of everyone they'd worked with over the past ten days.

Ten days, was it? Killashandra thought. *Who would be first?* She looked about her, shrugged, and forced her mind to follow Tukolom's words.

Who would be first? The question was in everyone's eyes the following morning when the recruits, with the exception of the obdurate Carigana, assembled for the morning meal. They sought each other's company for reassurance as well as curiosity. It was a bright clear day, the colors of the hills mellower, deeper, and no one raised any objection when Tukolom announced that they would visit the succession houses on the Joslin plateau where delicacies were grown.

When they arrived in the hangar for transport, they

witnessed the return of a heavy-duty wrecker, a twisted knot of sled dangling from its hoist. The only portion of the airsled that resembled the original shape was the storage area, though the under and right hatch were buckled.

"Do they plan all this?" Rimbol quietly asked Killashandra in a troubled voice.

"The recovered sled? Perhaps. But the storm—C'mon now, Rimbol. Besides, what function would such a display serve? We're stuck here, and we'll be Singers . . . or whatever." Killashandra spoke severely, as much to reassure herself as Rimbol.

He grunted as if he had divined her anxiety; then jauntily he swung up the ramp to their transport vehicle without another glance at the wreck.

They sat together, but neither spoke on the trip, although Killashandra began several times to point out beautiful clusters of flowering shrubs with vivid, often clashing, shades of red and pink. The gray had completely disappeared from the ground cover, and its rich deep green was now tinged with brown. Rimbol was remote, in thought, and she felt that fancies about flora would be an invasion of his privacy.

The moist humidity and lush aromas of the huge hothouses reminded Killashandra of Fuerte's tropical area, and Carrik. The agronomist demonstrated the baffles that deflected the mach winds from the plasroofs as well as the hydroponics system that could be continued without human assistance. He also lectured on the variety and diversity of fruits, vegetables, grasses, lichens, fungi and exotics available to the Guild caterers. When he went on to explain that research was a part of the Agronomy Department, improving on nature wherever possible in sweetness, texture, or size, he led them outside the controlled-climate units.

"We must also improve on nature's whimsy," he added just as the recruits noticed the work crews and the damage to the next building.

Killashandra exchanged glances with Rimbol, who was grinning. They both shrugged and joined the agronomists in finishing the storm repairs.

"At least, it's only finishing," Rimbol muttered as he

pressed a trigger on a screw gun. "What do they do when they haven't got three decades of recruits to fill up work gangs?"

"Probably draft suppliers and sorters and anyone else unoccupied. At least, here everyone takes a turn," she added, noticing that both Tukolom and the chief agronomist were heaving plastic as willingly as Borton and Jezerey.

"There, now, you can let go, Killa." He stood back to survey the panel they had just secured. "That ought to hold . . . until another boulder gets casually bounced off the corner."

Shielding her eyes from the glare of the sun to her left, Killashandra peered northerly, toward the crystal ranges.

"Don't even think about it," Rimbol said, taking her hand down and turning her. He gathered up his tools. "I wonder what's in store for us tomorrow?"

He had no banter on the return trip, nor had anyone else. Killashandra wished she'd thought to ask the agronomist about the ground-cover plants and shrubs. And amused herself by wondering if he bothered with such common varieties.

Tension put an effective damper on recruit spirits that evening, a damper unrelieved even by some moderate drinking. Rimbol, who had been the class wit, was not disposed to resume that mantle.

"Are you all right?" Killashandra asked him as he stared into his half-empty beer.

"Me?" He raised his eyebrows in affected surprise at her question. "Sure. I'm tired. No more than the accumulation of more hard work in the past . . . few days than I've had to do in years. Student living softens the muscles."

He patted her arm, grinning reassuringly, and finished his beer, politely ending that subject. When she returned with a refill of her own beaker, he was gone. *Well*, she thought sadly, he has as much right to Privacy as I, and neither of us is good company tonight.

Sleep did not come easily that night for Killashandra. She doubted she was alone in her insomnia, though that was no consolation. Her mind continually reviewed the symptoms Borella had described for the onset of the adaptation. Fever? Would she recognize one, for she'd never had a severe systemic illness. Nausea? Well, she had had bad food now and again or drunk too much. Diarrhea? She'd experienced that from overeating the first sweet yellow melons as a girl. The thought of being completely helpless, weak in the thrall of an alien invasion—yes, that was an appropriate description of the process—was abhorrent to Killashandra. Cold swept across her body, the chill of fear and tension.

It had all seemed so easy to contemplate on Shankill: symbiosis with an alien spore would enrich her innate abilities, endow her with miraculous recuperative powers, a much increased lifespan, the credit to travel luxuriously, the prestige of being a member of a truly elite Guild. The attractive parts of a felicitous outcome of her adaptation to the spore had, until this dark and lengthy night, far outweighed the unemphasized alternatives. Deafness? She wouldn't have sung professionally anyhow, not after what the judges had said about her voice, but the choice not to sing had to be hers, not because she couldn't hear herself. To be a sorter, like Enthor, with his augmented vision? Could she endure that? She'd bloody have to, wouldn't she? Yet Enthor seemed content, even jealous of his ability to value crystal.

Had she not desired to be highly placed? To be first sorter of the exclusive Heptite Guild qualified. How long would it take to become first sorter? With lives as long as those the inhabitants of Ballybran could lead?

How long would it have taken her to become a Singer of stellar rank, much less solo performer anywhere, had her voice passed the jury? The thoughts mocked her, and Killashandra twisted into yet another position in which to find sleep.

She was well and truly caught and had no one to blame but herself. Caught? What was it the older Singer had asked Borella on the shuttle? "How was the catch?" No, "Much of a catch?" "The usual," Borella had replied. "One can never tell at this time."

Catch? Fools like herself, warned by Carrik and Maestro Valdi, not to mention the FSP officials, were the catch, those who would trade solid reality for illusion—the illu-

sion of being wealthy and powerful, feared, and set apart
by the tremendous burden that came with crystal singing.

And no guarantee that one would become a Singer!
Carigana had been right. Nothing would matter until adaptation, for none of the lectures and work had been specifically oriented toward the role of the Singer: nothing had been explained about the art of cutting crystal from the face, or how to tune a cutter, or where in the ranges to go.

Tossing, Killashandra recalled the contorted features of Uyad, arguing for credit to take him off-planet: the stained Singers stumbling from their sleds across the wind-battered hangar—and the condition of those sleds that gave an all too brutal picture of the conditions that Singers endured to cut enough crystal to get off the planet.

Yet Borella's voice had held longing when she spoke of returning to the crystal ranges . . . as if she couldn't wait.

Would singing crystal be analogous to having the lead role in a top-rank interstellar company?

Killashandra flailed her arms, shaking her head from side to side. Anything was better than being classed as an anonymous chorus leader. Wasn't it?

She rearranged her limbs and body into the classic position for meditation, concentrated on breathing deeply and pushing back all extraneous and insidious conjectures.

Her head was heavy the next morning, and her eyes felt scratchy in their sockets. She'd no idea how long she had slept finally, but the brightness of the morning was an affront to her mental attitude; with a groan, she darkened the window. She was in no mood to admire hillsides.

Nor was anyone else in a much better state, ordering their breakfasts quietly and eating alone. Nonetheless, Killashandra was disgusted not to have noticed the absences. Especially Rimbol's. Later, in a wallow of private guilt, she rationalized that she had been groggy with lack of sleep and certainly not as observant as usual. People were straggling into the lounge. It was Shillawn, stammering badly, who first noticed.

"Killashandra, have you seen Rimbol yet? Or Mistra?" Mistra was the slender dark girl with whom Shillawn had been pairing.

"Overslept?" was her immediate irritated reaction.

"Who can sleep through the waking buzz? He's not in his room. It's—too empty."

"Empty?"

"His gear. He had things when he came. Nothing's there now."

Killashandra half ran to Rimbol's room. It was, as Shillawn had said, very empty, without the hint of a recent occupation, antiseptically clean.

"Where is Rimbol, former occupant of this room?" Killashandra asked.

"Infirmary," a detached voice said after a negligible pause.

"Condition?"

"Satisfactory."

"Mistra?" Shillawn managed to ask.

"Infirmary."

"Condition?"

"Satisfactory!"

"Hey, look, you two"—and Borton diverted the attention of the group waiting in the corridor—"Carigana's gone, too."

The forbidding red light on that door was off.

Shillawn gulped, glanced apologetically at Killashandra. Carigana's condition, too, was satisfactory.

"I wonder if dying is considered satisfactory," Killashandra said, seething with frustration.

"Negative," replied the computer.

"So we get whisked away in the night and never seen again?" Jezerey asked, clinging to Borton's hand, her eyes dark and scared.

"Distress being noted by sensitive monitors, proper treatment immediately initiated," Tukolom said. He had arrived without being noticed. "All proceeds properly." He accorded them an almost paternal smile that faded quickly to an intense scrutiny of the faces before him. Apparently satisfied, he beckoned them to follow him to the lounge.

"He makes me feel as if I ought to have come down sick, too," Jezerey murmured so that just Killashandra and Borton heard.

"I wish the hell I had," Killashandra assured her. She tried not to imagine Rimbol, tossing feverishly, or convulsed.

"Today concerns weather," Tukolom announced portentously and frowned at the groans from his audience.

Killashandra hid her face and gripped her fingers into fists until her nails dug painfully into her palms. *And he has to pick today to talk about weather.*

Some of what he said on the subject of meteorology as that science applied to Ballybran and its moons penetrated her depression. In spite of herself, she learned of all the safety devices, warnings, visual evidences of imminent turbulence, and the storm duties of Guild members—*all* available personnel were marshaled to unload Singers' airsleds, not just unclassified recruits.

Tukolom then guided his meek students to the met section of the Guild control rooms, and there they were able to watch other people watching satellite pictures, moon relays, and the printout of the diverse and sensitive instrumentation recording temperatures, suspended particles, wind speed and direction from the sensor network on the planet.

Killashandra didn't think much of herself as a met worker. The swirling clouds mesmerized her, and she found it difficult to remember which moon view she was supposed to observe. The computer translated the data into forecasts, constantly updated, compared, overseen by both human and machine. Another sort of symbiosis. One she didn't particularly care to achieve.

Tukolom shepherded them down to the hangar again, to accompany a maintenance crew to one of the nearby sensor units. They were filing aboard the transport when Jezerey went into a spasm, dropping to the plascrete, her face flushed. She moaned as a convulsion seized her.

Borton was on his knees beside her, but two strangers appeared as if teleported, inserted her into a padded cocoon, and bore her off.

"Entirely normal are such manifestations of the adaptation," Tukolom said, peering into Borton's face as the man stared anxiously after his friend. "Delay these technicians longer we may not."

"They don't bloody care," Borton said in a savage tone, bouncing into the hard seat next to Killashandra. "She was a package to them. They're glad to see us get sick."

"I'd rather come down than watch others," Killashandra replied, softening her voice out of compassion for his distress. She already missed Rimbol's irreverent comments and his sustaining good humor. Borton had been paired with Jezerey all during their long wait on Shankill.

"Not knowing 'when' gets to you."

Borton stared out at the hills passing under the transport, immersed in his concern, and she did not invade his privacy.

Jezerey's collapse cast a further pall over the remaining travel. Shillawn, sitting across the aisle from Killashandra, swallowed with such rhythmic nervousness that she couldn't look in his direction. The habit had always irritated her: now it was a major aggravation. She looked in the other direction past Borton, to the swiftly changing view. The colors of the brush, the stunted trees, even the glancing lights the sun struck from exposed rock formations formed a delightful visual display. Though she had always been acutely aware of stage motion, rhythm, and flow, Killashandra had not had much opportunity to view the natural state. The surface of this rugged, unkempt, ancient planet emphasized the artificiality of the performing arts world and its continual emphasis on the "newest" form of expression. She had once considered the performing arts the be-all and end-all of ambition. Ballybran, in its eternal struggle for survival against gigantic natural forces, appealed to another instinct in her.

The recruits examined the weather station, its sensors fully extended and the thick trunk of the unit completely extruded from the installation into which it retreated like a burrowing animal during "inclement weather." Their guide's phrase occasioned wry laughter. He even smiled at their response. Ballybraners had struck Killashandra as a humorless crew, and she wondered if the fever would wrest her sense of the ridiculous from her. Rimbol wouldn't be the same person without his funning.

Tukolom then announced that they would assist the technician by applying to the weather station a protective

film against gale-flung particles. The recruits had first to
scrape off the previous application, not an arduous job
since the gale had removed most of the substance, which
was not a jelly, a lubricant or a true paint.

Killashandra found the scraping and painting soothing
occupations, for she had to concentrate on keeping her
brush strokes even. Overlapping was better than skimping.
She could see where the alloy of the arm she worked on
had been scored in thin lines that argued other workers had
not been as conscientious. Concentration kept her from
disturbing reflections such as Rimbol's being "satisfactory"
and Jezerey's convulsions.

Borton demonstrated his anxieties by being loud in complaint on the return journey, nagging at Tukolom for more
details than the "satisfactory" prognosis. Although Killashandra sympathized with the former shuttle pilot's concern for his friend, his harangues began to irritate. She was
sorely tempted to tell him to turn it off, but the scraping
and painting had tired her, and she couldn't summon the
energy to speak.

When the transport settled back at the hangar, she made
sure she was the last to descend. She wanted nothing more
than a hot bath and quiet.

Nor was she refreshed at all by the bathing. She dialed
for a Yarran beer and for information on Rimbol. He was
continuing "satisfactory," and the beer tasted off. A different batch, she thought, not up to the standard of the Guild
at all. But she sipped it, watching the dying day color her
hillside with rapid shifts into the deepest purples and
browns of shadow. She left the half-finished beer and
stretched out on her bed, wondering if the fatigue she felt
was cumulative or the onset of the symbiotic fever. Her
pulse was normal, and she was not flushed. She pulled the
thermal cover over her, turned on her side, and fell asleep
wondering what would be found for the remainder of the
recruits to do on the morrow.

The waking buzz brought her bolt upright in the bed.

"Lower that narding noise!" she cried, hands to her ears
to muffle the incredible din.

Then she stared about her in surprise. The walls of her

quarters were no longer a neutral shade but sparkled with many in the all-too-brilliant morning sun. She turned up the window opacity to cut the blinding glare. She felt extraordinarily rested, clearer of mind than she had since the morning she realized she didn't owe Fuerte or the Music Center any further allegiance. As she made for the toilet, the carpeting under her bare feet felt strangely harsh. She was aware of subtle odors in the facility, acrid, pungent, overlaid by the scent she used. She couldn't remember spilling the container last night. The water as she washed her face and hands had a softness to it she had not previously noticed.

When she shrugged into her coverall, its texture was oddly coarse on her hands. She scrubbed them together and then decided that perhaps there'd been something abrasive in the paint she had used the day before. But her feet hadn't painted anything!

Noise struck her the moment the door panel opened. She flinched, reluctant to enter the corridor, which she was startled to find empty. The commotion was coming from the lounge. She could identify every voice, separating one conversation from another by turning her head. Then she noticed the guide stripe at the far end of the corridor, a stripe that was no longer dull gray but a vivid bluish purple.

She stepped back into her room and closed the panel, unable to comprehend the immense personal alteration that had apparently transformed her overnight.

"Am I satisfactory?" she cried out, a wild exultation seizing her. She threw her arms about her shoulders. "Is MY condition satisfactory?"

A tap on her door panel answered her.

"Come in."

Tukolom stood there with two Guild medics. That did not surprise her. The expression on Tukolom's face did. The mentor drew back in astonishment, expressions of incredulity, dismay, and indignation replacing his customary diffidence. It struck Killashandra as peculiar that this man, who had undoubtedly witnessed the transformation of thousands of recruits, should appear displeased at hers.

"You will be conducted to the infirmary to complete

the symbiosis." Tukolom took refuge in a rote formula. His hand left his side just enough to indicate that she should leave with the medics.

Thoroughly amused at his reaction and quite delighted with herself, Killashandra stepped forward eagerly, then turned with the intention of picking up the lute. Now that she knew she'd have her hearing the rest of her life, she wanted the instrument.

"Your possessions to you will be later brought. Go!" Tukolom's anger and frustration were not overt. His face was suffused with red.

There was not the least physical or philosophical resemblance between Tukolom and Maestro Valdi, yet at the moment Killashandra was reminded of her former teacher. She turned her back on Tukolom and followed her guides to the ramp. Just as she emerged from the corridor, she heard Tukolom peremptorily calling for attention. Glancing back over her shoulder, she saw that every head was turned in his direction. Once again, she had made a major exit without an audience.

CHAPTER 6

It was bad enough to be whisked away as if she'd committed a crime, but the meditechs kept asking if she felt faint or hot or cold, as if she was negligent when she denied any physical discomfort. Therefore, she could scarcely admit to a sense of vitality she had never previously experienced, to the fact that everything about her, even their plain green tunics, had taken on a new luster, that her fingers twitched to touch, her ears vibrated to minute sounds. Most of all, she wanted to shout her exultation in octaves previously impossible for the human voice.

The extreme anticlimax came when the chief meditech, a graceful woman with dark hair braided into an elaborate crown, wanted Killashandra to submit to the physical scanner.

"I don't need a scanner. I have never felt so well!"

"The symbiont can be devious, my dear Killashandra, and only the scanner can tell us that. Do please lie down. You know it doesn't take long, and we really need an accurate picture of your present physical well-being."

Killashandra stifled her sudden wish to scream and submitted. She was in such euphoria that the claustrophobic feel of the helmet didn't bother her, nor did the pain-threshold nerve jab do more than make her giggle.

"Well, Killashandra Ree," Antona said, absently smoothing a strand into her coronet, "you are the lucky one." Her smile as she assisted Killashandra to her feet was the warmest the young woman had seen from a full Guild member. "We'll just make certain this progress has no setbacks. Come with me and I'll show you your room."

"I'm all right? I thought there'd be some fever."

"There may be fever in your future," Antona said, smiling encouragingly as she guided Killashandra down a wide hall.

Killashandra hesitated, wrinkling her nose against the odors that assailed her now: dank sweat, urine, feces, vomit, and as palpable as the other stenches, fear.

"Yes," Antona said, observing her pause, "I expect it'll take time for you to become accustomed to augmented olfactory senses. Fortunately, that's not been one of my adaptations. I can still smell, would have to in my profession, but odors don't overwhelm me. I've put you at the back, away from the others, Killashandra. You can program the air conditioner to mask all this."

Noises, too, assaulted Killashandra. Despite thick sound-deadening walls, she recognized one voice.

"Rimbol!" She twisted to the right and was opening the door before Antona could stop her.

The young Scartine, his back arched in a convulsion, was being held to the bed by two strong meditechs. A third was administering a spray to Rimbol's chest. In the two days since she had seen him, he had lost weight, turned an odd shade of soft yellow, and his face was contorted by the frenzy that gripped his body.

"Not all have an easy time," Antona said, taking her by the arm.

"Easy time!" Killashandra resisted Antona's attempt to draw her from the room. "The fax said satisfactory. Is *this* condition considered satisfactory?"

Antona regarded Killashandra. "Yes, in one respect, his condition is satisfactory—he's maintaining his own integrity with the symbiont. A massive change is occurring physically: an instinctive rejection on his part, a mutation on the symbiont's. The computer prognosis gives Rimbol an excellent chance of making a satisfactory adjustment."

"But . . ." Killashandra couldn't drag her eyes from Rimbol's writhing body. "Will I go like that, too?"

Antona ducked her head, hiding her expression, an evasion that irritated Killashandra.

"I don't think that you will, Killashandra, so don't fret. The results of the latest scan must be analyzed, but my initial reading indicates a smooth adaptation. You'll be the first to know otherwise. Scant consolation, perhaps, but you *would* barge in here."

Killashandra ignored the rebuke. "Have you computed how long he'll be like that?"

"Yes, another day should see him over the worst of the penetration."

"And Jezerey?"

Antona looked blankly at Killashandra. "Oh, the girl who collapsed in the hangar yesterday? She's fine—I amend that." Antona smiled conciliatorily. "She is suffering from a predictable bout of hyperthermia at the moment and is as comfortable as we can make her."

"Satisfactory, in fact?" Killashandra was consumed by bitterness for that misleading category but allowed Antona to lead her out of Rimbol's room.

"Satisfactory in our terms and experience, yes. There are degrees, you must understand, of severity with which the symbiont affects the host and with which the host rejects the symbiont." Antona shrugged. "If we knew all the ramifications and deviations, it would be simple to recruit only those candidates with the requisite chromosomes. It isn't that simple, though our continuous research gets closer and closer to defining exact parameters." She gave Killashandra another of her warm smiles. "We're much better at selection than we used to be."

"How long have you been here?"

"Long enough to know how lucky you are. And to hope that you'll continue so fortunate. I work generally with self-treating patients, since I find the helpless depress me. Here we are."

Antona opened a door at the end of the corridor and started to retrace her steps. Killashandra caught her arm.

"But Rimbol? I could see him?"

Another expressive shrug. "If you wish. Your belongings

will be along shortly. Go settle in," she said more kindly. "Program the air conditioner and rest. There's nothing more to be done now. I'll inform you of the analysis as soon as I have the results."

"Or I'll inform you," Killashandra said with wry humor.

"Don't dwell on the possibility," Antona advised her.

Killashandra didn't. The room, the third she'd had in as many weeks, was designed for ease in dealing with patients, though all paraphernalia was absent. The lingering odors of illness seeped in from the hall, and the room seemed to generate antiseptic maskers. It took Killashandra nearly an hour to find a pleasant counterodor with which to refresh her room. In the process, she learned how to intercept fax updates on the conditions of the other patients. Never having been ill or had occasion to visit a sick friend, she didn't have much idea of what the printout meant, but as the patients were designated by room number, she could isolate Rimbol's. His monitor showed more activity than the person in the next room, but she couldn't bring herself to find out who his neighbor was.

That evening, Antona visited her room, head at a jaunty angle, the warm smile on her face.

"The prognosis is excellent. There'll be no fever. We are keeping you on a few days just to be on the safe side. An easy transition is not always a safe one." A chime wiped the smile from her face. "Ah, another patient. Excuse me."

As soon as the door closed, Killashandra turned on the medical display. At the bottom, a winking green line warned of a new admission. That was how Killashandra came to see Borton being wheeled into the facility. The following day, Shillawn was admitted. The fax continued to display "satisfactory" after everyone's condition. She supposed she agreed, having become fascinated with the life-signal graphs until the one on Rimbol's neighbor unexpectedly registered nothing at all.

Killashandra ran down the hall. The door of the room was open, and half a dozen technicians could be seen bent over the bed. Antona wasn't among them, but Killashandra caught a glimpse of Carigana's wide-eyed face.

Whirling, she stormed into the chief medic's office. Antona was hunching over an elaborate console, her hands graceful even in rapid motion on the keys.

"Why did Carigana die?" Killashandra demanded.

Without looking up from the shifting lights of the display, Antona spoke. "You have privileges in this Guild, Killashandra Ree, but not one gives you the right to disturb a chief of any rank. Nor me at this time. I want to know why she died more than you possibly could!"

Rightly abashed, Killashandra left the office. She hurried back to her room, averting her eyes as she passed the open door to Carigana's. She was ashamed of herself, for she didn't genuinely care that Carigana was dead, only that she had died. The space worker had really been an irritant, Killashandra thought candidly. Death had been a concept dealt with dramatically in the Music Center, but Carigana was Killashandra's first contact with that reality. Death could also happen to her, to Rimbol, and she would be very upset if he died. Even if Shillawn died.

How long Killashandra sat watching the life-signs' graphs, trying to ignore the discontinued one, she did not know. A courteous rap on the door was immediately followed by Antona's entrance, and her weary expression told Killashandra that quite a few hours must have passed. Antona leaned against the door frame, expelling a long sigh.

"To answer your question—"

"I apologize for my behavior—"

"We don't know why Carigana died," Antona went on, inclining her head to accept the apology. "I have a private theory with no fact to support it. An intuition, if you will, that the desire to be acceptable, to surrender to the symbiont is as necessary to the process of adjustment as the physical stamina, which Carigana had, and those chromosomes which we have established as most liable to produce a favorable adaptation. You did want to become a Crystal Singer very much, didn't you?"

"Yes, but so do the others."

"Do they? Do they really?" Antona's tone was curiously wistful.

Killashandra hesitated, only too aware of the inception

of her own desire to become a Crystal Singer. If Antona's theory held any merit, Killashandra should also be dead, certainly not so blatantly healthy.

"Carigana didn't like anything. She questioned everything," Killashandra said, drawn to give Antona what comfort she could. "She didn't have to become a Crystal Singer."

"No, she could have stayed in space." Antona smiled thinly, pushed herself away from the wall, and then saw the graphs on the display. "So that's how you knew. Well" —and she tapped the active graph in the left-hand corner —"that's your friend, Rimbol. He's more than just satisfactory now. The others are proceeding nicely. You can pack your things. I've no medical reason to keep you here longer. You'll be far better off learning the techniques of staying alive in your profession, my dear, than sitting deathwatch here. Officially, you're Lanzecki's problem now. Someone's coming for you."

"I'm not going to get sick?"

"Not you. You've had what's known as a Milekey transition. Practically no physical discomfort and the maximum adjustment. I wish you luck, Killashandra Ree. You'll need it." Antona was not smiling. Just then, the door opened wider. "Trag?" The chief meditech was surprised, but her affability returned, that moment of severity so brief that Killashandra wondered if she had imagined it. "I shall undoubtedly be seeing you again, Killashandra."

She slipped out of the room as an unsmiling man of medium build entered. His first look at her was intent, but she'd survived the scrutiny of too many conductors to be daunted.

"I don't have much to pack," she said, unsmiling. She slid off the bed and swiftly gathered her belongings. He saw the lute before she picked it up, and something flickered across his face. Had he once played one?

She stood before him, carisak over her shoulder, aware that her heart was thumping. She glanced at the screen, her eyes going to Rimbol's graph. How much longer before he was released? She nodded to Trag and followed him from the room.

Killashandra was soon to learn that Trag was reticent by nature, but as they made their way down the infirmary corridors, she was relieved to be conducted in silence. Too much had happened to her too fast. She realized now that she had feared her own life-signs would suddenly appear on the medical display. The sudden reprieve from that worry and her promotion out of the infirmary dazed her. She did not appreciate until later that Trag, chief assistant to the Guild Master in charge of training Crystal Singers, did not normally escort them.

As the lift panel closed on the infirmary level, Trag took her right hand and fastened a thin metal band around her wrist.

"You must wear this to identify you until you've been in the ranges."

"Identify me?" The band fitted without hindering wrist movement, but the alloy felt oddly harsh on her skin. The sensation disappeared in seconds, so that Killashandra wondered if she had imagined the roughness.

"Identify you to your colleagues. And admit you to Singer privacies."

Some inflection in his voice made the blood run hot to her cheeks but his expression was diffident. At that point, the lift panels opened.

"And it permits you to enter the Singer levels. There are three. This is the main one with all the general facilities." She stepped with him into the vast, vaulted, subtly lit lobby. She felt nerves that had been strung taut in the infirmary begin to relax in moments. Massive pillars separated the level into sections and hallways. "The lift shaft," Trag continued, "is the center of these levels of the complex. Catering, large-screen viewing, private dining, and assembly rooms are immediately about the shaft. Individual apartments are arranged in color quadrants, with additional smaller lifts to all other levels at convenient points on the outer arc. Your rooms are in the blue quadrant. This way." He turned to the left and she followed.

"Are these my permanent quarters?" she asked, thinking how many she had had since meeting Carrik.

"With the Guild, yes."

Once again, she caught the odd inflection in his voice. She supposed it must have something to do with her being out of the infirmary before any of the others of her class. She was curiously disjointed. She had experienced that phenomenon before, at the Music Center, on days when no one could remember lines or entrances or sing in correct tempi. One simply got through such times as best one could. And on this, certainly a momentous one in *her* life, acquiescence was difficult to achieve.

She nearly ran into Trag, who had halted before a door on the right-hand side of the hall. She was belatedly aware that they had passed recesses at intervals.

"This apartment is assigned to you." Trag pointed to the lock plate.

Killashandra pressed her thumb to the sensitized area. The panel slid back.

"Use what is left of the morning to settle in and initiate your personal program. Use whatever code you wish: personal data is always voice coded. At 1400 hours, Concera will escort you to the cutter technician. He'll have no excuse not to outfit you quickly."

Killashandra noted the cryptic remark and wondered if everyone would address her comments she couldn't understand yet apparently ought to. As she mused on what "ought to" had accomplished for her, Trag was striding back down the hall.

She closed the panel, flicked on the privacy light, and surveyed her permanent Guild quarters. Size might denote rank here as on other worlds. The main room here was twice the size of her ample recruit accommodation. To one side was a sleeping chamber that was apparently all bed. A door on one wall was open to a mirrored dressing area that, in turn, led into a hygiene unit with a sunken tank sprouting an unusual number of taps and dials. On the other side of the main room was a storage closet larger than her student room on Fuerte and a compact dining and self-catering area.

"Yarran beer, please." She spoke more to make noise in the sterile and ringingly quiet place. The catering slot opened to present a beaker of the distinctive ruddy beer.

She took the drink to the main room, sipping as she

frowned at the utilitarian furnishings. Laying her lute carefully on a chair, she let her carisak slip off her shoulder and onto the floor, seized by an urge to throw her possessions around the stark apartment, just to make it look lived in.

Here she was, Killashandra Ree, installed in spacious grandeur, achieving status as a Crystal Singer, that fearsome and awful being, a silicate spider, a crystal cuckoo with a luxurious nest. This very afternoon, she was to be tuned to a Cutter that would permit her to slice Ballybran crystal, earn stunning totals of galactic credits, and she would cheerfully have traded the whole mess for the sound of a friendly voice.

"Not that I'm certain I have a friend anywhere," she said.

"Recording?"

The impersonal voice, neither tenor nor contralto, startled her. The full beaker of beer trembled in her hand.

"Personal program." That was what Trag had meant. She was to record those facts of her life that she wished to remember in those future times when singing crystal would have scrambled her memory circuits.

"Recording?"

"Yes, record and store to voice print only."

As she gave such facts as her date and place of birth, the names of her parents, grandparents, sisters, and brothers, the extent and scope of her education, she stalked about the main room, trying to find exactly the right spot in which to display her lute.

"On being awarded a grant, I entered the Music Center." She paused to laugh. How soon did one begin to forget what one wished to forget?

"Right now!"

"Recording?"

"End of recording. Store." And that was that. She knew she could reconsider, but she didn't want to remember those ten years. She could now wipe them out. She would. As far as she would be ever after, henceforth, and forevermore concerned, nothing of moment happened after the grant award until she encountered Carrik. Those ten years of unremitting labor and dedication to ambition had never occurred to Killashandra Ree, Cutter in the Heptite Guild.

To celebrate her emancipation from an inglorious past, Killashandra dialed another beer. The digital indicated an hour remained before Concera was to take her to the appointment. She ordered what was described as a hearty, nourishing soup of assorted legumes. She checked her credit, something she must not forget to do regularly, and found herself still in the black. If she were to enter the rest of the Guild voucher and her open ticket, she would have quite a healthy balance. To be consumed by the equipment of a Crystal Singer. She'd keep those credits free.

That reminded her of Shillawn, and of other credit-debit discussions. She keyed the Guild's commissary, ordered additional furnishings, rugs of the Ghni weavers, and by 1400, when Concera touched her door chime, Killashandra had wall-screens that mixed the most unlikely elements from an ice-world to the raving flora of the voracious Eobaron planets. Startling, but a complete change from sterility.

Concera, a woman of medium height and slender build, glided into the main room, exclaimed at the sight of the wall-screens, and looked questioningly at Killashandra.

"Oh, aren't you clever? I would never have thought of combining different worlds! Do come right along. *He* has such a temper at the best of times, but without his skill, we, the Singers I mean, would be in a terrible way. He *is* a superior craftsman, which is why one humors his odd temper. This way."

Concera covered quite a bit of ground with her gliding gait, and Killashandra had to stretch her legs to keep pace.

"You'll get to know where everything is very soon. It's nice to be by oneself, I feel, instead of in a pack, but then different people have different tastes," and Concera peered sideways at Killashandra to see if she agreed. "Of course, we come from all over the galaxy, so one is bound to find someone compatible. This is the eighth level where most of the technical work is done—naturally the cutters are made here, as they are the most technical of all. Here we are."

Concera paused at the open entrance and, with what seemed unexpected courtesy, pushed Killashandra ahead of her into a small office with a counter across the back third and a door leading into a workshop. Her entry must have triggered an alarm in the workroom, for a man, his sun-reddened face set in sour lines, appeared in the doorway.

"You're this Killashandra?" he demanded. He beckoned to her and then saw Concera following. "You? I told you you'd have to wait, Concera. There's no point, no point at all, in making you a handle for three fingers. You'll only outgrow it, and there's all that work could be put to better use."

"I thought it might be a challenge for you—"

"I've all the challenges I need, Concera." He replied with such vehemence that when he returned his stare to Killashandra, she wondered if his disagreement with the woman would spill over on to her. "Let me see your hands."

Killashandra held them, palm up, over the counter. He raised his eyebrows as he felt with strong impersonal fingers across the palm, spread her fingers to see the lack of webbing from constant practice, the hard muscle along the flat of the hand and thumb pad.

"Used your hands right, you have." He shot another glance at Concera.

It was only then that Killashandra noticed that the first two fingers on Concera's left hand had been sheared off. The stumps were pinkish white, healed flesh but oddly shaped. It occurred to Killashandra in a rush that made her stomach queasy that the two missing digits were regenerating.

"If you stay, you be quiet. If you go, you won't be tempted. This'll take two–three hours."

Concera elected to leave, which had no positive effect on the morose technician. Killashandra had naively assumed that tuning a cutter would be a simple matter, but it was a tedious process, taking several days. She had to read aloud for a voice print from boring printout on the history and development of the cutting devices. She learned more than she needed to know—some of the more complicated mechanisms proved unreliable in extremes of weather; a once-popular model was blamed for the high-voltage discharge which had carbonized the corpse Killashandra saw on Shankill. The most effective and reliable cutter, refined from Barry Milekey's crude original, required that the user have perfect pitch. It was a piezoelectric device that converted the Crystal Singer's vocal note and rhythm into high-frequency shock waves on an infrasonic carrier. The cutting edge of the shock wave was pitched by the Singer to the dominant tone of the "struck" crystal face.

Once set to a voice pattern, the infrasonic device could not be altered. Manufacture of such cutters was restricted to the Guild and safeguarded yet again by computer assembly, the program coding known only by the Guild Master and his executive assistant.

As Concera had mentioned, the technician was a temperamental man. When Killashandra was reading aloud, he was complaining about various grievances with the Guild and its members. Concera and her request for a three-fingered handle was currently his favorite gripe—"Concera is cack-handed, anyway, and always splitting her grips." Another was that he ought to have had another three weeks fishing before returning to work. The fish had just started to bite, and would she now sing an octave in C.

She sang quite a few octaves in various keys and decided that there were worse audiences than apparently receptive audition judges. She hadn't used her voice since the day she met Carrik; she was sore in the gut from supporting tone and aware the sound was harsh.

When Concera glided into the room, Killashandra was overwhelmingly relieved.

"Back tomorrow, same time. I'll do casts of your good ten fingers." And the man sent an arch glance at Concera.

Concera hurried Killashandra out of the workshop and the office.

"He does like his little jokes," she said, leading the way down one corridor and left at the next. "I only wanted a *little* favor so I could go back into the ranges without wasting so much time." She entered a room labeled "Training," sighing as she closed the door and flicked on the privacy light. "Still"—and she gave Killashandra a bright smile, her eyes sliding from a direct contact—"we have your training to take in hand." She waved Killashandra to one of the half-dozen chairs in the room facing a large hologram projector. She picked up a remote control unit from a shelf, darkening the room and activating the projector. The outsized lettering of the Guild's rules, regulations, and precepts hovered before them. "You may have had a Milekey transition, but there's no easy way to get over this."

"Tukolom—"

"Tukolom handles only basic information, suitable for anyone joining the Guild in any capacity." Concera's voice had a note of rancor. "Now you must specialize and repeat and repeat." Concera sighed. "We all have to," she added, her voice expressing patient resignation. "If it's any consolation to you, I'd be doing this by myself and I've always found it much easier to *explain* than memorize." Her voice lightened. "You'll hear even the oldest singers muttering regs and restricts any night in the Commons Hall. Of course, you'll never appreciate this drill until it's *vital!* When you reach that point, you won't remember how you know what you do. Because that's when you really *know* nothing else."

Despite Concera's persuasive tone, Killashandra found the reasoning specious. Having no choice in study program or teacher, Killashandra set herself to memorize regulations about working claims, claiming faces, interference with claims, reparations and retributions, fines and a clutter of other rules for which she could see no need since they were obvious to anyone with any sense.

When she returned to the privacy of her quarters and the anomalies of her wall-screens, she checked with the infirmary and was told that Rimbol was weak but had retained all his senses. Shillawn, Borton, and Jezerey were satisfactory, in the proper use of that word. Killashandra also managed to extract from data retrieval the fact that injured Singers like Concera and Borella undertook the role of preceptor because of the bonus involved. That explained the spiteful remarks and ambivalent poses.

The next morning, when Concera drilled her on her understanding of each section of the previous day's subjects, Killashandra had the notion that Concera silently recited paragraph and section just one step ahead of her pupil.

The afternoon was spent uncomfortably, in the workshop of the Fisherman, where casts were made of her hands. The Fisher maundered on about having to make hundreds of casts during a Singer's lifetime. He told her she wasn't to complain to him about blisters from hand grips, an affliction that he alleged was really caused by a muscling up that wasn't *any* fault of his.

Killashandra spent that evening redecorating her room.

She had a morning drill with Concera, spent a half hour with the Fisher, who grumbled incessantly about a bad morning's fishing, the inferiority of the plastic he had to work with, and the privileges of rank. Killashandra decided that if she were to ruffle at every cryptic remark tossed her way, she'd be in a state of constant agitation. The remainder of the afternoon, Concera reviewed her on crystal shapes, tones, and the combinations that were marketable at the moment: black crystals in any form always having the highest value. Killashandra was to review the catalog, commit to memory which shape was used for what end product, the range in price, and the parameters of value variation in each color. She was taken through the research departments, which sought new uses for Ballybran crystal. There she noticed several people with the eye-adjustment of Enthor.

In the days that followed, she was given instruction in the sled-simulator, "flying" against mach storm winds. By the end of the first lesson, she was as battered, sweaty, and trembling as if the flight had been genuine.

"You'll have to do better than that," the instructor commented unsympathetically as she reeled out of the simulator. "Take a half hour in the tank and come back this afternoon."

"Tank?"

"Yeah, the tank. The radiant fluid. Left-hand taps. Go on! I'll expect you back at 1500."

Killashandra muttered the terse instructions all the way back to her rooms, shedding her clothes as she made her way to the tank. She turned on the left-hand taps, and a viscous liquid oozed out. She got the temperature she wanted and dubiously lowered herself into the tank. In minutes, tension and stress left her muscles, and she lay, buoyed by the radiant bath, until the stuff cooled. That afternoon, her instructor grudgingly admitted that she had improved.

A few days later, half a morning through a solo training flight across the White Sea where thermal patterns made good practice, every visual warning device on the controls turned red, and a variety of sirens, claxons, bells, and nerve-tinglers was activated. Killashandra immediately veered northeast to the Guild Complex and was relieved when half the monitors desisted. The rest blared or blinked until she had landed the sled on its rack and turned off the power. When she complained to her instructor about the warning overload, he gave her a long, scathing look.

"You can't be warned too often about the approach of turbulence," he said. "You Singers might be as deaf as some of us no matter how we rig cautions. While you remember advice, remember this: a mach storm won't give you a second chance. We do our fardling best to insure that you have at least one. Now change your gear for cargo handling. A blow's on the way!"

He strode off, waving to attract attention from a cluster of hangar personnel.

The storm was not rated Severe and only the southeast section of the continent had been alerted. Forty Singers had logged out in that general area, and thirty-nine straggled in. The flight and hangar officers were conferring together as Killashandra passed them.

"Keborgen's missing. He'll get himself killed!"

"He's been bragging he was out for black. *If* he managed to remember where the claim is . . ."

Killashandra had no excuse to linger near the two at that point, but when the other ships had been cleared and racked, she stayed on after the rest of the unloaders had been dismissed.

The wind was not strong enough at the complex to require the erection of the baffles, so Killashandra stationed herself where she could watch the southern quadrant. She also kept an eye on the two officers and saw them abandon their watch with a shrug of shoulders and shakes of the head.

If Keborgen had actually cut black crystal, she would've liked to have unloaded it. She wasn't needed on the sorting floor. She consoled herself with the knowledge that she had racked up some danger credit already, and wasn't much in

the red for decorating her room and days of uncredited
instruction. Being a recruit had had advantages.

She was crossing the hangar to return to her quarters
when she heard the sound, or rather felt it, like a thread
dragged across exposed nerve ends. She wasn't yet accustomed to her improved vision, so she shook her head and
blinked, expecting to clear the spot on the right retina. It
stayed in position in the lower right-hand quadrant, dipping and swaying. Not a shadow in her own eye but a sled,
obviously on course for the complex. She was wondering if
she should inform anyone when wrecker personnel began
to scramble for the heavy hoist sled. In the hustle, no one
noticed that Killashandra had joined the team.

The wrecker didn't have far to go for the sled plowed
into the hills forty klicks from the complex. The comtech
could get no response from the sled's pilot.

"Bloody fool waited too long," the flight officer said,
nervously slapping his fingers against his thigh. "Warned
him when he went out, not to wait too long. But they never
listen." He repeated variations of those sentiments, becoming more agitated as the wrecker neared the sled and
the damage was visible.

The wrecker pilot set his craft down four long strides
from the Singer's sled.

"You others get the crystal," the flight officer shouted as
he plunged toward the crumbled bow of the sled, which
was half buried in loose dirt.

As Killashandra obeyed his order, she glanced back on
the sled's path. She could see, in the distance, two other
slide marks before the crashing sled had bounced to a
stop.

The storage compartment had withstood impact. Killashandra watched with interest as the three men released the
nearest hatch. As soon as they emerged with cartons, she
darted in. Then she heard the moans of the injured Crystal
Singer and the drone of curses from the flight officer and
medic attending him.

The moment she touched the nearest carton, she forgot
the injured man, for a shock, mild but definite, ran along
her bones from hand to heel to head. She gripped the
carrier firmly, but the sensation dissipated.

"Move along. Gotta get that guy back to the infirmary," she was told by returning crewmen.

She picked the carton up, minding her steps, ignoring the exhortation of the crewmen who passed her out. She crouched by the carton as the cocoon of the injured Singer was deftly angled into the wrecker.

During the short trip back to the complex, she wondered why there was such a fuss. Surely the symbiont would repair the man's injuries, given the time to do so. She supposed that the symbiont relieved pain. Borella hadn't appeared uncomfortable with her awful thigh wound, and Concera, given to complaints, had said nothing about pain in her regenerating fingers.

As soon as the wrecker landed, the Singer was hurried to waiting meditechs. Hugging the carton that she devoutly hoped contained black crystal, Killashandra walked straight through the storage area into the sorting room. She had no problem finding Enthor, for the man almost bumped into her.

"Enthor," she said, planting herself and pushing the carton at him, "I think this has black crystal."

"Black crystal?" Enthor was startled; he blinked and peered frowningly at her. "Oh, it's you. You?" His lensed eyes widened in surprise. "You? What are you doing here?" He half turned in the direction of the infirmary and then up to the recruits' level. "No one's been cutting black crystal—"

"Keborgen might have been. He crashed. This is from his sled." She gave the carton an urgent shove against his chest. "The flight officer said he had been out to cut blacks."

Out of habit, Enthor took hold of the carton, quite unable to assimilate either her explanation or her sudden appearance. Killashandra was impatient with Enthor's hesitation. She did not want to admit to the contact shock she had felt in Keborgen's sled. Deftly, she propelled Enthor at his table, and though still perplexed, he presented the ident to the scan. His hands hovered briefly but dropped away as he twisted toward Killashandra.

"Go on," she said, annoyed by his dithering. "Look at them."

"I know what they are. How did you?" Enthor's indecision was gone, and he stared, almost accusingly, into her eyes.

"I felt them. Open it. What did Keborgen cut?"

His unearthly eyes still on hers, Enthor opened the box and lifted out a crystal. Killashandra caught her breath at the sight of the dull, irregular 15 centimeter segment. Consciously, she had to make her lungs expel air as Enthor reverently unpacked two additional pieces that fit against the first.

"He cut well," Enthor said, scrutinizing the trio keenly. "He cut very well. Just missing flaw. That would account for the shapes."

"He has cut his last," the deep voice of the Guild Master said.

Startled, Killashandra whirled and realized that Lanzecki must have arrived moments before. He nodded to her and then beckoned to someone in the storage area.

"Bring the rest of Keborgen's cut."

"Is there more black in it?" Enthor asked Killashandra as he felt carefully about in the plaspacking.

Killashandra was vibrantly aware of Lanzecki's intense gaze.

"In that box or the cargo?"

"Either," Lanzecki said, his eyes flickering at her attempt to temporize.

"Not in the box," she said even as she ran her hand along the plasfoam side. She swallowed nervously, glancing sideways at Lanzecki's imposing figure. His clothing, which she had once thought dull, glinted in a richness of thread and subtle design very much in keeping with his rank. She swallowed a second time as he gave a brief nod of his head and the six cartons from Keborgen's sled were deposited on Enthor's table.

"Any more black crystal?" Enthor asked.

She swallowed a third time, remembered that the habit had irritated her in Shillawn, and ran her hands over the cartons. She frowned, for a curious prickle rippled across her palms.

"Nothing like the first one," she said, puzzled.

Enthor raised his eyebrows, and she could only have

imagined his eyes twinkling. He opened a box at random and removed, carefully, a handful of cloudy slivers, displaying them to Lanzecki and Killashandra. The other boxes held similar slivers.

"Did he cut the triad first or last?" Lanzecki spoke softly as he picked up a finger-long splinter, examining its irregularities.

"He didn't say?" Enthor ventured quietly.

Lanzecki's sigh and the brief movement of his head answered that question.

"I thought the precious symbiont healed—" Killashandra blurted out before she knew she was going to speak.

Lanzecki's eyes halted her outburst.

"The symbiont has few limitations: deliberate and constant abuse is one. The age of its host is another. Add the third factor—Keborgen stayed too long in the ranges despite storm warnings." He turned back to look at the three pieces of black crystal on the weighplate and at the credit valuation blinking on the display.

If Keborgen was dead, who inherited the credit? She jumped as Lanzecki spoke again.

"So, Killashandra Ree, you are sensitive to the blacks, and you have enjoyed a Milekey transition."

Killashandra could not avoid the Guild Master's disconcerting appraisal. He seemed neither as remote nor detached as he had the day she had arrived at Shankill with Carrik. His eyes, especially, were intensely alive. A nearly imperceptible upward movement of his lips brought her restless gaze to his mouth. Wide, well-shaped lips evidently reflected his thoughts more than eye, face, or body. Did she amuse him? No, probably not. The Guild Master was not known for his humor; he was held in great respect and some awe by men and women who were awed by little and respected nothing but credit. She felt her shoulders and back stiffen in automatic reaction to the flick of amusement.

"Thank you, Killashandra Ree, for your prompt discovery of that triad," Lanzecki said with a slight inclination of his head that reinforced his gratitude. Then he turned and was gone, as quickly as he had arrived.

Exhaling, Killashandra leaned against Enthor's table.

"Always good to know black when it's near you." Enthor paused as he gingerly unpacked shards. He blinked his eyes to focus on the weight display. "Trouble is finding it in the first place."

"What's the second place?" she asked impudently.

Enthor blinked his lens into place and gave her a shrewd look. "Remembering where the first place was!"

She left him, walking back through Sorting to Storage and out onto the hangar deck, the shortest way back to an arc lift down to her quarters. Hangar personnel were busy dismantling Keborgen's wreck. She grimaced. So a damaged ship was repaired as long and as often as necessary during its owner's lifetime—and then stripped. Had Carrik's sled been dismembered?

She halted at a sudden notion, wheeled and stared out at the hills in the direction of Keborgen's erratic last flight. She half ran to the Hangar Ready Room for a look at the met printout, continuously displayed and updated by the minute.

"That storm to the southeast? It's dissipating?"

The weather officer glanced up, a frown on his face. Forestalling rejection, Killashandra held up her wrist-band. He immediately tapped out a replay of the satellite recording, which showed the formation of the storm and its turbulent progress along the coast of the main continent and the Milekey Ranges. The gale had blown up quickly and, as unpredictably as most Ballybran storms, caressed one large sector of the range and then roiled seaward across the edge of the Long Plain where warm air had met its colder mass.

"I was on the wrecker which brought Keborgen in, but I must have dropped my wrist-unit there. Can I use a skimmer?"

The met officer shrugged. "For all of me you can have a skimmer. No weather to speak of in our zone. Check with Flight."

Flight thought her cack-handed to have dropped equipment and assigned her a battered vehicle. She paused long enough to note that the recovery pattern of the wrecker was still displayed on the emergency screen. Once she left the office, she made notes on her wrist unit.

She unracked the skimmer and left the hangar at a sedate pace entirely consistent with a routine errand, then flew to the crash site. She was increasingly possessed by the thought that Keborgen, trying to outrun the storm, surely must have come back to the complex by the most direct route. Though Concera had maundered on and on about how careful Singers were to protect their claims by using devious routes to and from, Keborgen might just as easily have flown straight in the hope of reaching safety. His sled had come in well behind the others from the same area.

Given that possibility, she could establish from data retrieval the exact second when the storm warning had been broadcast, compute the maximum speed of his sled, the direction of flight at the time of his crash, and deduce in what general area he had cut black crystal. She might even do a probability computation on the length of time Keborgen had delayed at his claim by the span of time it had taken the other thirty-nine Singers to return.

She hovered the skimmer over the crash site. The sharp mounds were beginning to soften as a brisk breeze shifted the soil. Skewing the skimmer, she located the next skid mark and two more before she spotted the raw scrape across the bare rock of a higher slope. She landed to examine the marks closely. The scar was deeper on the north side, as if the sled had been deflected by the contact. She stood in the mark and took bearings through her wrist unit. Then she returned to the skimmer and quartered the sector, looking for any other evidence of Keborgen's faltering, bumping last flight.

Shadows and sunset made it inadvisable for her to continue her search. Killashandra checked her bearings and then returned to the complex.

CHAPTER 7

Killashandra leaned back from the terminal in her room, noted that the time display marked an early-morning hour. She was tired, her eyes hot with fatigue, and she was ravenous. But she had every bit of data she could extract from the Guild's banks that might be useful in narrowing her search for Keborgen's black-crystal claim. She keyed the program into the privacy of her personal record, then stood and walked stiffly, arching against the ache in her back, to the catering unit where she dialed for a hot soup. Though she had stored the data, she couldn't stop thinking about her plan. And all the obstacles to its implementation.

Keborgen was dead. His claims, wherever they had been, were now open according to the vast paragraphs on "Claims, the making and marking thereof, penalties for misappropriation, fines and restrictions," and all subparagraphs. However, the claim first had to be found. As Enthor had said, that was the first problem. Killashandra might have theories about its location, but she had neither sled to get there and look nor cutter to take crystal from the "open" face. Her research revealed that Keborgen had worked the claim for at least four decades and analysis proved that twelve black-crystal cuttings had come from the same face, the next to last one some nine years previously. The second problem, as Enthor had so pithily stated, was remembering.

To relieve the tedium of drill, Killashandra had asked Concera how Singers found their way back to claims after an absence, especially if memory was so unreliable.

"Oh," Concera had replied airily, "I always remember to tell my sled what landmarks to look for. Sleds have voice print recorders so they're dead safe." She hesitated, looking in an unfocused way that was habitual with her. "Of course, storms do sometimes alter landmarks, so it's wiser to record contour levels and valleys or gorges, things that aren't as apt to be rearranged by a *bad* blow. Then, too," she continued in a brighter voice, "when you've cut at a particular face a few times, *it* resonates. So if you can recall even the general direction and get there, finding the exact spot is much easier."

"It isn't so much singing crystal then, as being sung to by crystal," Killashandra had noted.

"Oh, yes, very well put," Concera said with the false cheerfulness of someone who hadn't understood.

Killashandra finished the soup and wearily shuffled to the bedroom, shedding her coverall. She wasn't unsatisfied with the information she'd accumulated. She could narrow the search to older claim markings in the geographical area dictated by the top speed of Keborgen's elderly sled, the time the storm warning was issued, and the registered storm wind speed.

She fretted about one point. Keborgen's sled recorder. She had seen the sled being dismantled, but would the Guild technicians have rescued the record for the data that might be retrieved? She wasn't certain if anyone had ever broken a voice code. It hadn't been so much as whispered that it was possible. Though the rules did not state the Guild was able to take such an action, a terrible breach of privacy under FSP rights, the Charter didn't specifically deny the Guild that right, either, once the member was dead. On the other hand, Trag had said that private personal records were irretrievable.

The darkness and absolute silence of her bedroom compounded her sudden doubt. The Guild could and occasionally did exhibit a certain ruthlessness. For sanity's sake, she had better decide here and now whether or not the Guild adhered faithfully to its stated and endlessly cited principles. She took a sudden comfort in the very length of the Charter. Its voluminous paragraphs and sections obviously reflected contingencies and emergencies that had been dealt with over four hundred years of usage and abuse.

With a sigh, Killashandra turned over. Avoiding restrictions and defying laws were completely in the human condition. As the Guild prohibited, it also protected or the bloody planet would have been abandoned to the spores and crystal.

She woke later in the morning to the insistent buzz of her terminal. She was informed that her cutter was now ready and she was to collect it and report to training room 47. Groggy from insufficient sleep, Killashandra took a quick shower and ate a good meal. She found herself directing glances to the computer console, almost as if she expected last night's data to spring from the cover and expose itself.

Computers had to deal with fact, and she had one advantage that wouldn't compute: a sensitivity to black crystal—Keborgen's black crystal. Computers did not volunteer information, either, but she had few doubts that with the news of Keborgen's death, the opening of his rich claim would be widely known. Only 39 Singers had come in from that same storm. She couldn't know how many other Singers had returned from leave and were available to search. She knew that the odds against her finding the claim were good on the one hand and unlikely on the other. The delivery of her cutter she took as propitious.

She was waiting for the lift when she heard her name called in an incredulous shout.

"Killashandra! I'm recovered. I'm a Singer, too."

Herself astonished, she turned to find Rimbol striding toward her.

"Rimbol!" She returned his enthusiastic embrace, acutely aware that she hadn't given him any thought at all in several days.

"I was told you'd got through the transition satisfactorily, but no one else's seen you! Are you all right?" Rimbol held her from him, his green eyes searching her face and figure. "Was it just the fever, or did you come see me at one point?"

"I did at several points," she replied with perfect truth and instinctive diplomacy. "Then I was told that I was interfering with your recovery. Who else is through?"

Rimbol's expression changed to sorrow. "Carigana didn't make it. Shillawn is deaf and has been assigned to research. Mistra, Borton, Jezerey, bless the pair; in total twenty-nine made it. Celee, the spacer, made only a tolerable adjustment, but he's got all his senses, so he's been shunted to shuttle piloting. I don't think that goes against his grain, anyway."

"And Shillawn? Does he mind?" Killashandra knew her voice was sharp, and Rimbol's face clouded until she hugged him. He was going to have to learn not to care so much about people now. "I really think Shillawn will be happier in research than cutting. Celee was already a pilot, so he's lost nothing . . . Antona told me Carigana wouldn't surrender to the spore."

Rimbol frowned, his body stiffening so that she released him.

"She rebelled against everything, Rimbol. Didn't you ask Antona?"

"No." Rimbol ducked his head, a silly grin on his face. "I was afraid to while others were going through transition."

"Now it's all over. And you're installed on Singer level." She saw the wrist-band and showed him hers. "Where're you bound for now?"

"To be fitted with my cutter." His green eyes brightened with enthusiasm.

"Then we can go together. I'm to collect mine."

They had entered the lift, and Rimbol half turned in surprise.

"Collect it?"

"They did tell you how long you've been ill, didn't they?" Killashandra knew her quick question was to give herself time. Rimbol's eyes mirrored surprise and then perplexity. "Oh, I lucked out. I had what Antona calls a Milekey transition, so they pushed me out of the infirmary to make room for someone else and put me into training to keep me out of mischief. Here we are, and don't mind the technician's manner. He hates to be kept from his fishing."

They had come to the cutter office and found Jezerey, Mistra, and two others.

"Killashandra! You made it!"

Killashandra thought there was a note of unwelcome surprise in Jezerey's voice. The girl looked gaunt and had lost her prettiness.

"Quiet out here," the Fisher said, his voice cutting through Killashandra's attempt at reply. He had a cutter in his hand, patently new.

"You. Killashandra," and he beckoned her brusquely to the counter as the others stepped back.

Killashandra was uncomfortably aware of the attention focused on her as she accepted the device. Then she curled her fingers around the power grip, the right hand on the guide, and forgot embarrassment in the thrill of being one step closer to the Crystal Ranges. She gave a little gasp as she saw that her name had been incised in neat letters on the plas housing that covered the infrasonic blade.

"Bring that back to be serviced after every trip, d'you hear? Otherwise, don't fault me when it doesn't cut proper. Understand?"

Killashandra would have thanked him, but he had turned to the others, beckoning to Borton. Cutter in hand, Killashandra turned and saw the indignation in Jezerey's eyes, the hurt, surprise, and betrayal in Rimbol's.

"Antona tossed me out of the infirmary," she said, more to Rimbol than the others, but they all seemed to accuse her. "So the Guild put me to work."

Holding her head high, she gave them all a polite smile and left the office.

As she marched down the hall to the lift shafts, she was perversely angry with herself, with their ignorance, and with the Guild for thrusting her ahead of the others. She remembered similar scenes in the Music Center when she had achieved a role or an instrumental solo after unremitting practice and knew that the majority of her peers had favored another. Then she had been responsible. Now, though she had done nothing, consciously, to provoke her fellow recruits, she was being faulted because she'd had a bit of luck, just as she'd been blamed at the Music Center for hard work. What was the use!

"Watch that fardling cutter!" A savage tone interrupted her mortified self-pity, and someone shoved her to the right with unnecessary force. "I said, watch it!"

The man backed hastily away from her, for Killashandra had instinctively raised the cutter at the aggressive voice. Her confusion was further complicated by the knowledge that she had been careless and now was acting the fool. To be brought to task did not improve her temper.

"It's not on."

"It's bloody dangerous, on or off. Haven't you had the proper guidance with that?" The tall man glaring at her was Borella's companion from the shuttle.

"Then complain to Borella! She instructed us."

"Borella?" The Singer stared at her with a perplexed frown. "What has she to do with you?"

"I was one of her recent 'catch,' I believe was her word."

His frown increased as his eyes flicked over her, pausing at the wristband.

"Just received your cutter, my dear?" He smiled now with supercilious condescension. "I'll forget any charge of discourtesy." With a slight bow and a sardonic grin, he strode on to the workshop.

She stared after the man, aware again of the strange magnetism of the Crystal Singer. She'd been furious with him, and yet her anger had been partially fed by his diffidence and her wish to impress him. Had Carrik once been like that, too? And she too green to know?

She continued to the lift and entered. The encounter with the Singer had restored some perspective to her. Whatever else, she was a Crystal Singer: more of one than the rest of her class by a physical anomaly and a time factor that were no connivance of hers.

As she entered training room 47, she received another surprise. Trag was there, leaning against a heavy plastic table, arms folded across his chest, obviously awaiting her.

"I'm not late?" she asked, and experienced a second jolt of confusion, for the tones of her question seemed to echo sourly in the room. Then she saw the unmistakable plasfoam cartons on the table behind Trag. "Oh, how curious?"

"Soured crystal," he said, his deeper voice resounding as hers had. Then he extended his hand for her cutter.

She released it to him, somewhat reluctantly since it was so recent an acquisition. He inspected every part of the device, even unsheathing the infrasonic blade, which he gave the keenest scrutiny. He moved to her left side, proffering the cutter and watching as she took it by the grips. He checked her hand position and nodded.

"You are familiar with the controls?" he asked, although he must have known that the Fisher had carefully explained them. "And the process of tuning?" She nodded again, impatient with the catechism.

Now with a disregard for its contents that made her catch her breath, he dumped onto the plastic table a crystal carton. Trag grinned.

"This is soured crystal. Sent to us from some of the nearer systems which never bother to employ tuners. These will teach you how to learn that weapon you carry."

For one horrified second, Killashandra wondered if Trag had been a witness to her encounter with the other Singer. She glanced down at the device which, she realized, could be used as a weapon.

From the carton, Trag took five octagons of rose crystal. With a hammer similar to the one Enthor had used, he tapped each in turn. The third crystal was sour, off significantly.

"Now the five must be retuned to match. I suggest you sing them a full note below this"—and he tapped the faulty octagon—"and shave the top of this until it rings pure against the infrasonic cutter." He placed the soured crystal in an adjustable standing vise. He tightened the braces and tugged to be sure the crystal was secure. "When this sings properly, you merely recut the others in scale."

"How did it go sour?"

"Bracket flaw. Common enough in rose quartz."

"Dominant or minor?"

"Minor will be acceptable."

He nodded at her control grip, and she turned on the cutter, remembering to brace her body against the power that would surge through the handle. Trag tapped the sour crystal with his hammer, and she sang the minor note below, twirling the tuner with her thumb until the sound of the cutter matched her pitch.

The crystal screamed as she laid the blade against it. It took every ounce of self-control she had not to pull away.

"Slice it evenly," Trag commanded, his abrupt order steadying her.

The rose scream blended into a purer tone as the infrasonic cutter completed its surgery. Trag signaled her to turn off the cutter, ignoring her trembling hold. He tapped the crystal, and it sang a pure A minor. He tapped the crystal next in line. A major.

"Go to the G minor," he said, fastening the second octagon in place.

Killashandra found it took an effort to erase the echo of the major note from her mind. Turning on the cutter, setting the tuner to G minor, this time she was ready for the power surge and the cry of crystal. It was not as shrill, but the rose octagon seemed to resist the change in note as she drew the blade across it. Trag tapped the recut G minor and nodded approval, setting the third in the vise.

When Killashandra had recut the five, she felt drained and, in a bizarre fashion, elated. She had actually cut crystal. She leaned against the table, watching Trag repack them and make appropriate notations on the carton. Then he reached for a second container. Bracket rub again, and Trag made a few derogatory comments on technicians who did not recognize that proper bracketing prolonged the life of crystal.

"How would beginners like me learn if someone didn't make such mistakes?" she asked. "You surely don't use fresh crystal from the ranges."

"Those octagons were relatively new. They ought not need tuning yet. I object to carelessness in any form."

Killashandra rather thought he would and determined to give him no cause to complain about her.

She recut the contents of nine boxes, twelve sets of crystal, blue, yellow, and rose. She had earnestly hoped that one of the boxes might reveal black crystal, and as the last box was unpacked to expose two squat blue dodecahedrons, one with a vertical split, she asked if black never had to be recut.

"Not within my service," Trag said, glancing at her keenly. "That is partly because the segments are separated and partly because their installation is handled by technicians of impeccable training and standard. Black does not suffer from bracket erosion or mishandling. Black crystal is too valuable." He put the damaged blue into the brace, split side exposed. "This will require a slightly different technique with your blade. If you slice off the damaged portion entirely, you will have destroyed the symmetry of the form. Therefore, the entire piece must be reshaped, scaled down in the dodecahedron. Ordinarily, one goes from major to minor, minor to major down the scale. This time, you must drop at least a sixth to achieve a pure note. As blues are nearly as common as rose, error presents no great loss. Relax. Proceed."

Killashandra had felt unequal to such an exercise, but Trag's inference that she could err with impunity stiffened her resolve. She heard the sixth below the moment she tapped the blue, set her cutter, and was slicing before he had time to step out of her way. She made the next two cuts without hesitation, listening to the change of pitch in the crystal. Curtly, she nodded for him to turn the dodecahedron in the vise and did three more passes. Only when she had completed the recutting did she turn off her device. Then she stared challengingly at Trag. Blandly, he placed the second crystal in the grips, tapped it and then the recut dodecahedron. They were in tune with each other.

"That is sufficient for one day, Trag."

At the unexpected voice behind her, Killashandra whirled, the cutter again rising in automatic defense, as Lanzecki finished speaking. With the slightest movement of his lips, he eyed the blade turned broadside to him. Instantly, she lowered it and her eyes, embarrassed and agitated by her reaction, and utterly wearied by the morning's intense concentration.

"I'd always heard that Fuerte was a pacific planet," Lanzecki said. "Nevertheless, you take to cutting well, Killashandra Ree."

"Does that mean I can get into the ranges soon?"

She heard Trag's snort at her presumption, but Lanzecki did not reflect his chief assistant's attitude. The brown eyes held hers. Meeting that appraising stare, she wondered why Lanzecki was not a Crystal Singer: he seemed much more, so much more than Carrik or Borella or any of the other Crystal Singers she had met or seen.

"Soon enough not to jeopardize a promising career. Soon enough. Meanwhile, practice makes perfect. This exercise"—and Lanzecki gestured to the boxes of tuned crystal—"is but one of several in which you must excel before you challenge the ranges."

He was gone in one of those fluid movements that was swift enough to make Killashandra wonder if Lanzecki had actually made his visit. Yet his brief appearance was undeniable by the effect he had on her and Trag.

The assistant Guild Master was regarding her with covert interest.

"Take a radiant bath when you reach your quarters," Trag said. "You are scheduled for sled simulator practice this afternoon." He turned away in dismissal.

The training pattern held until the next rest day, though she wished the two elements could have been reversed, with the sled simulation in the morning when her reflexes were fresher and the cutting in the afternoon so she could collapse. There proved to be a reason for that apparently irrational schedule. As she would invariably be flying the sled after she had cut crystal, she must learn to judge blunted reactions.

The radiant baths, the viscous liquid a gentle pressure on her tired body, its thick whirling like the most delicate of massages, did freshen after a morning's intense cutting drill. She checked with the computer and discovered that she was being paid a tuner's wage for her morning work but charged for the flight officer's instruction in the afternoon.

After six days of such an exhausting routine, she looked forward to a day of relaxation. A low-pressure ridge was moving in from the White Sea, so rest day might be cloudy with rain. She had begun to develop the Ballybraners' preoccupation with meteorology, encouraged by Trag's invariable questions about weather conditions at the start of each training session.

Her flight instructor also pressed heavily on weatherwise

acumen. His insistence made more sense than Trag's since a good deal of her simulation drill involved coping with turbulence of varying degrees and types. She began to distinguish among the tonal differences of the warning equipment with which the simulator was equipped. Sound could tell her as clearly as the met display the kind and scope of the gale her practice flights trained her to survive.

Privately, Killashandra decided the warnings were an overkill situation; after being banged at, rung out, and buzzed, your mind would turn off most of the noise. The nerve tingler, last of the series of cautionary devices, couldn't be ignored.

Meanwhile, her practice performance developed from merely adequate to perfect automatic reaction as she simulated flights over every sector of Ballybran, land, sea, and arctic ice. She learned to identify, within seconds of their being displayed on her plan board, the major air and sea currents everywhere on the planet.

As she practiced, so she learned confidence in her vehicle. The sled was highly maneuverable with VTOL capabilities and a variety of assists to the basic crystalline drive, which had been highly refined for Ballybran's unusual conditions.

Killashandra had had only glimpses of the other members of Class 895. Rimbol had waved cheerfully at her from a distance, and she saw Jezerey scooting across the hangar floor once, but Killashandra wouldn't count on her tolerance unless the girl's temper had markedly improved since the last time they'd met. Jezerey might be more amenable now that she and the others were in full training.

She saw Borton first as she wandered into the Commons hall of the Singers' level. It was an evening when most of the Guild's full members could relax. No storms were expected despite the low-pressure ridge, and Passover—the ominous conjunction of the three moons that produced the fiercest storms—was nine weeks away. Borton didn't see Killashandra, for he and the others in the lounge with him were on the far side. Augmented vision had advantages: see first; plan ahead.

She ordered Yarran beer, a beaker for herself and a

pitcher for the group. She was annoyed with herself for anticipating a need for subtle bribery, but an offer made in good faith was unlikely to be refused. Especially of Yarran beer.

Borton saw her coming when she was about twenty meters away. His expression was of mild surprise, and he beckoned to her, speaking to someone hidden from view by the high back of the seating unit. A stir, exclamations, and Rimbol emerged, meeting her with a wide grin. The sense of relief she felt caused the pitcher to wobble.

"Don't waste a drop of good Yarran," he admonished, rescuing it. "Not everyone's down. Some are flaked out in radiant tanks. Shillawn has been transferred to the North Helton continent. That's where they do most of the pure research. Would you believe it, Killa? He doesn't stammer anymore."

"No!"

"Antona said the symbiosis must have corrected the fault in his palate." Rimbol was being determinedly affable, Killashandra thought as she took a place on the wide seating unit. Jezerey, seated in a corner of the unit, acknowledged Killashandra's arrival with a tight smile, Mistra nodded, and Celee and two other men whose names she couldn't call to mind greeted her. All of them looked tired.

"Well, I can't really say I'm sorry Shillawn didn't make it as a Singer because he certainly won't be wasted in research," Killashandra said, raising her beaker in a circular toast to him.

"You mean, you haven't cut crystal yet?" Jezerey asked, a strident note in her voice as she pointed to the wristband evident as Killashandra made her toast.

"Me? Bloody no!" The disgust and frustration in her tone made Rimbol laugh, head thrown back.

"I told you she hadn't got that far," he said to Jezerey. "She only collected the cutter the day we met her."

Killashandra overtly eased the band on her wrist, aware now that it constituted her passport to friendship as well as to Singer levels.

"Furthermore, Jezerey," she went on, letting resentment sharpen her words, "I'll be spending weeks more tuning crystal and simulating gale flights before I'm so much as allowed to put my nose past skimmer chart range. And by then there'll be Passover storms!"

"Oh, yes." Jezerey's attitude brightened, and her smile was complacent. "We'll all be storm bound then."

Killashandra was sensitive to the perceptible change of the atmosphere around her and decided to secure the advantage.

"I may be a little ahead of you in training—you do know that injured Singers take it on only for the bonuses? Good. Well, once you've got those wretched cutters, you'll know what 'tired' means. Cut in the morning, then they send you on simulator flights, and when you're not doing either of those, it's drill; regs, rules, claims, fines—" Groans rose from her listeners. "Ah, I see you're getting the drills."

"So what other jollies are we to get?" Rimbol asked, his eyes sparkling with an almost malicious delight.

Most of those present were interested in any details she'd give concerning the retuning of crystal. She explained as best she could, truthfully if not fully, for she said nothing about Lanzecki's flattering appearances, her empathy with black crystal, and the rapid progress she seemed to be making in cutting difficult forms. She found it took an effort to be discreet, for she had never practiced tact in the Music Center. She'd be spending the rest of a very long life with these people, had nearly lost their friendship once through circumstances beyond her control, and she wasn't knowingly going to jeopardize it again.

Sufficient beer and other intoxicants were consumed by the recruits to make it a convivial evening. Killashandra found herself ready to be on old terms with Rimbol, and many of the tensions that had built over the past few weeks were dissolved in that most harmonious of activities.

When they woke, rested, they continued, although Killashandra was a trifle surprised to find that they had ended up in Rimbol's quarters. Location made little difference, as the apartments were in every respect similar. He had done little to furbish his rooms and solicited Killashandra's assistance. In this way, they passed agreeable hours and virtuously ended with a game reviewing rules and regulations from the clue of a phrase. In the glow of utter relaxation, Killashandra came very close to mentioning Keborgen's black crystal to Rimbol, rationalizing her evasion later by her desire not to burden her friend with unnecessary detail.

The next week, she suggested to Concera that she join the others in their classes rather than hold Concera up. The Singer's two fingers were complete except for nails.

"You're not holding me up," Concera replied, her eyes sliding past Killashandra's, her mouth pursing with angry frustration. "Those others evidently have priority over a Singer of my long standing. Besides, I only accepted you as a favor, I much prefer single teaching to group learning. Now let's go on to claims and counterclaims."

"I know those paragraphs sideways, frontwise, and backward."

"Then let's start in the middle of one," Concera said with unexpected levity.

As Killashandra really could rehearse claims and counterclaims as well as she boasted, she could also let her mind deal with her biggest problems: how to get her sled, how to get Lanzecki's attention and obtain clearance to cut crystal rather than chant about it. With the prodigious Passover storms looming only nine weeks off, she had to speed up. Research in the data banks about post-Passover problems indicated that it would be weeks before a new Singer would be permitted to claim hunt in ranges made more dangerous than ever by the ravages of Passover. Keborgen's claim could be so altered that her sensitivity to his black crystal might be nullified. Mach storms could damage or substantially alter an exposed crystal face, flawing deep into the vein and rendering it useless. She *had* to get out soon.

Lanzecki had been in the habit, over the preceding two weeks, of appearing as if teleported, generally when Killashandra was retuning crystal under Trag's scrutiny. Once Lanzecki had sat in the observer's seat of the sled simulator while she flew a particularly hazardous course. Instead of making her nervous, his presence had made her fly with heightened perception. Lanzecki also roamed through the Commons in the evenings, stopping for a word with this or that group, sorter, or technician. Now, when she very much wished him to materialize, he wasn't anywhere to be seen.

The fourth day, she casually asked Concera if she'd encountered the Guild Master and was told that Trag would know better where to find him. Trag was not the easiest person to question or converse with at all except in the handling of cutter or about incisions into crystal. Gathering all her self-assurance, Killashandra resorted to stratagem on the sixth day.

Trag had her shaving cones: she had ruined three the day before and quite expected to spend the morning's lesson avoiding future failures. After she had made a cut, she would look behind her. The fourth time, Trag frowned.

"Your attention span has been longer. What's the matter?"

"I keep thinking the Guild Master will appear. He does, you know, when I least expect it."

"He's on Shankill. Attend to your business."

She did, with less enthusiasm than ever, deeply grateful that the morrow was a rest day. She had half promised to spend that evening and the next day with Rimbol: half promised because her urgency to reach the ranges was in no way shared by the young Scartine. Trag released her at the end of the gruelingly precise session, his impassive face giving her no indication that she had learned to cut cones properly, though she felt in every muscle of her aching hands that she had achieved some proficiency.

She considered a radiant bath before the afternoon's flight practice. Instead, she put in a call for Rimbol: his company would be a soothing anodyne for her increasing frustration. Waiting for his answer, she had a quick hot shower. She paced her apartment, wondering where in hell's planets Rimbol had got to. Her mealtime was nearly gone, and she hadn't eaten. She ordered a quick meal from the catering unit, bolting the hot food, adding a seared mouth to her catalog of grievances before she went to the hangar level.

She was now one of many using the sled simulator so she had to be on time. She knew the flight was only an hour long, but this one, a complicated wind and night problem that kept her preternaturally alert and made her wish she'd taken the radiant bath instead of the shower, seemed endless. She was very pleased to avoid several crashes and emerge unscathed from the simulator. She waved impudently at the flight training officer in his booth above the sled and passed the next student, Jezerey, on her way.

"He's either crash happy or he hates me," Killashandra commented to Jezerey.

"Him? He's crazy. He killed me three times yesterday."

"Kill or cure?"

"That's the Guild's motto, isn't it?" Jezerey replied sourly.

Killashandra watched the girl enter the simulator, wondering. She hadn't been killed yet. She thought of going to the ready room and watching Jezerey's flight. No one else was in the ready room, so she dialed a carbohydrate drink to give her blood sugar level a boost. She was watching Jezerey take off when she became conscious of someone in the doorway. She turned and saw the Guild Master.

"I understand you've been looking for me," he said to compound her astonishment.

"You're on Shankill. Trag told me so this morning."

"I was. I am here now. You have finished your afternoon's exercises?"

"I think they've about finished me."

He stood aside to indicate she should precede him.

"The severity of the drills may seem excessive, but the reality of a mach storm is far more violent than anything we can simulate in the trainers," he said, moving toward the lift while touching her elbow to guide her. "We must prepare you for the very worst that can occur. A mach storm won't give you a second chance. We try to insure that you have at least one."

"I seem to hear that axiom a lot."

"Remember it."

Killashandra expected the lift to plummet to the Singers' level. Instead, it rose and, tired as she was, she swayed uncertainly. Lanzecki steadied her, hand cupped under her elbow.

"The next bad storm is Passover, isn't it?" She was making conversation because Lanzecki's touch had sent ripples along her arm. His appearance in the ready room had already unnerved her. She glanced sideways at him as unobtrusively as possible, but his face was in profile. His lips were relaxed, giving no hint of his thoughts.

"Yes, eight weeks from now is your first Passover."

The lift stopped, and the panels retracted. Killashandra stepped with him out into the small reception area. No sooner had he turned to the right than the third door opened. The large room they entered was an office, with one wall covered by a complex data retrieval system. Printout charts hung neatly from the adjacent wall. Before it, a formidable console printed out fax sheets that neatly folded into a bin. Several comfortable chairs occupied the center of the room, one centered at the nine screens that displayed the meteorology transmissions from the planet's main weather installations and the three moons.

"Yes, eight weeks away," Killashandra said, taking a deep breath, "and if I don't get out to the ranges before it comes, it will be weeks, according to every report I've scanned—"

Lanzecki's laugh interrupted her.

"Sit." He pushed two chairs together and pointed a commanding finger to one.

Amazed that the Master of the Heptite Guild laughed and infuriated because she had not been able to state her case, she dropped without much grace into the appointed chair, her self-confidence pricked and drained. Presently, she heard the familiar clink of beakers. She looked up as he handed one to her.

"I like Yarran beer myself, having originated on that planet. I'm obliged to the Scartine for reminding me of it."

Killashandra masked her confusion by drinking deeply. Lanzecki knew a great deal about Class 895. He raised his glass to her.

"Yes, we must get you out to the ranges. If anyone can find Keborgen's claim, it's likely to be you."

Feeling the beaker slip through fingers made nerveless by shock, she was grateful when he took the glass and put it on the table he swung before her.

"Conceit in a Singer—voice or crystal—can be a virtue, Killashandra Ree. Do not let such single-mindedness blind you to the fact that others can reach the same conclusions from the same data."

"I don't. That's why I've got to get out into the ranges as soon as possible." Then she frowned. "How did *you* know? No one followed me that night. Only you and Enthor knew I'd reacted to Keborgen's crystals."

Lanzecki gave her a long look that she decided must be pity, and she dropped her gaze, jamming her fingers together. She wanted to pound him or stamp her feet violently or indulge in some release from the humiliation she was experiencing.

Lanzecki, sitting opposite her, began to unlock her fingers one by one.

"You played the pianoforte as well as the lute," he said, his finger tips gently examining the thick muscle on the heel of her hand, the lack of webbing between her fingers, their flexible joints and callused tips. If this hadn't been her Guild Master, Killashandra would have enjoyed the semicaress. "Didn't you?"

She mumbled an affirmative, unable to remain quite silent. She was relieved, taking a deeply needed breath as he leaned back and took up his drink, sipping it slowly.

"No one did follow you. And only Enthor and I knew of your sensitivity to Keborgen's black crystal. Very few people know the significance of a Milekey transition beyond the fact that you somehow escaped the discomforts they had to endure. What they will never appreciate is the totality of the symbiotic adjustment."

"Is that why Antona wished me luck?"

Lanzecki smiled as he nodded.

"Does that have something to do with my identifying black crystal so easily? Did Keborgen have a Milekey, too?"

"Yes, to both questions."

"That totality didn't save his life, did it?"

"Not that time," he said mildly, ignoring her angry, impudent question. Lanzecki voice-cued a display screen, and the guild's chronological roster appeared. Keborgen's name was in the early third. "As I told you that evening, the symbiont ages too, and is then limited in the help it can give an ancient and abused body."

"Why Keborgen must have been two hundred years old! He didn't look it!" Killashandra was aghast. She'd had only one glimpse of the injured Crystal Singer's face, but she never would have credited twenty decades to his age. Suddenly, the pressure of hundreds of years of life seemed as depressing to Killashandra as her inability to get into the ranges.

"Happily, one doesn't realize the passage of time in our profession until some event displays a forcible comparison."

"You had a Milekey transition." She shot her guess at him as if it were undeniable.

He nodded affirmation.

"But you don't sing crystal?"

"I have."

"Then . . . why . . ." and she gestured around the office and then at him.

"Guild Masters are chosen early and trained rigorously in all aspects of the operation."

"Keborgen was . . . but he sang crystal. And you have, too." She sprang to her feet, unable to assimilate the impact of Lanzecki's quiet words. "You don't mean . . . I have to train to be . . . You're raving!"

"No, you are raving," Lanzecki replied, a slight smile playing on his face as he gestured her to her seat and pointed at her beer. "Steady your nerves. My only purpose in having a private talk with you is to reassure you that you will go out into the ranges as soon as I can arrange a shepherd for you."

"Shepherd?"

Killashandra was generally quick enough of wit to absorb the unexpected without floundering, but Lanzecki's singular interest in her, his awareness of intentions that she had kept utterly private, and his disclosures of the past few minutes had left her bewildered.

"Oh? Concera neglected to mention this facet of training?"

"Yes, a shepherd, Killashandra Ree, a seasoned Singer who will permit you to accompany him or her to a worked face, probably the least valuable of his claims, to demonstrate in practice what, to that point, has been theory."

"I've had theory up to my eyeballs."

"Above and behind them is better, my dear, which is where your brain is located, where theory must become reflex. On such reflexive knowledge may lie your survival. A successful Crystal Singer must have transcended the need for the *conscious* performance of his art."

"I've an eidetic memory. I can recite—"

"If you couldn't, you wouldn't be here." Lanzecki's tone reminded Killashandra of her companion's rank and the importance of the matter under consideration. He took a sip of his beer. "How often has Concera told you these past few weeks that an eidetic memory is generally associated with perfect pitch? And how often that memory distortion is one of the cruel facets of crystal singing? Sensory overload, as you ought to know, is altogether too frequent an occurrence in the ranges. I am not concerned with your ability to remember: I am concerned with how much memory distortion you will suffer. To prevent distortion, you have been subjected to weeks of drill and will continue to be. I am also vitally concerned in a recruit who has made a Milekey transition, retunes crystal well enough that Trag cannot fault her, who drives a sled so cleverly that the flight officer has given her patterns *he* wouldn't dare fly, and a person who had the wit to try to outsmart as old a hand at claim-hiding as Keborgen."

Lanzecki's compliments, though delivered as dry fact, disconcerted Killashandra more than any other of the afternoon's disclosures. She concentrated on the fact that Lanzecki actually wanted her to go after Keborgen's claim.

"Do you know where I should look?"

Lanzecki smiled, altering the uncompromising planes of his craggy face. He crossed one arm on his chest, supporting the elbow of the other, sipping at his beer.

"You've been doing the probability programming. Why don't you retrieve the data you've been accumulating?"

"How do you know what I've been doing? I thought my private voice code was unbreakable!"

"So it is." The sardonic look on Lanzecki's face reproved

her for doubting. "But your use of data retrieval for weather, sled performance, and the time you have recently spent programming was notable. In a general way, what recruits or newly convalesced Singers do is unregarded. However, when the person in question is not only sensitive to black crystal but signs out a skimmer to track the crash of a sled known to have transported black crystal, a quiet surveillance and a performance check are justified. Don't you agree? My dear girl, you are a very slow drinker. Finish it up and call up your program on Keborgen." He stood and indicated that she was to sit at the big console. "I'll get more beer for us and something to munch." He sauntered off to the catering unit.

Killashandra quickly took her place at the console, voice-coding the program. Though she might have doubted before now, Lanzecki's reproof reassured her. Nor did she doubt that he wanted more black crystal from Keborgen's claim, and if she offered the Guild the best chance of retrieving the loss, he would support her.

"Did you know Keborgen?" she asked, then realized that this must sound a stupid query to his Guild Master.

"As well as any man or woman here did."

"Part of my theory"—and Killashandra spoke quickly, tapping for the parameters she had stored on sled speed, warning time, and storm winds' velocity based on Keborgen's crash line—"is that Keborgen flew out direct."

Lanzecki put a fresh beaker on the ledge of the console, a tray of steaming morsels beside it, and smiled indulgently at her.

"No consideration, even his own safety, would have weighed more with Keborgen than protecting that claim."

"If that was what was expected of him, mightn't he once, in his desperate situation, choose the straight course?"

Lanzecki considered this, leaning against the console edge.

"Remember, he'd left escape to the last minute, judging by his arrival," Killashandra added earnestly. "The sled was not malfunctioning: the medical report postulated that he was suffering from sensory overload. But when he set out, he would have known from the met that the storm

would be short. He would have known that everyone
else would have cleared out of the ranges so a direct route
wouldn't be observed. And he hadn't cut that claim in nine
years. Would that be important?'"

"Not especially. Not for someone who had sung as long
as Keborgen." Lanzecki tapped his forehead significantly
and then looked down at the display where her parameters
overlaid the chart of the area. "The others are searching
west of your proposed site."

"Others?" Killashandra felt her mouth go dry.

"It's a valuable claim, my dear Killashandra; of course, I
have to permit search. Don't be overly anxious," he added,
resting one hand lightly on her shoulder. "They've never
sung black."

"Does being sensitive to it give an advantage?"

"In your case, quite likely. You were the first other
person to touch the crystal after Keborgen cut it. That
seems to key a perceptive person to the face. *Seems*, I
emphasize, not does. Much of what we should like to know
about cutting crystal is locked within paranoid brains; silence is their defense against detection and their eventual
destruction. However, one day, we shall know how to de-
fend them against themselves." He was standing behind her
now, cupping her shoulders with his hands. The contact
was distracting to Killashandra, though she fancied he
meant to be reassuring. Or supportive, because his next
words were pessimistic. "Your greatest disadvantage, my
dear Killashandra, is that you are a total novice when it
comes to finding or cutting crystal. Where"—and his blunt
forefinger pointed to the rough triangle on the map—
"would your projected flight place his claim?"

"Here!" Killashandra pointed without hesitation to the
spot, equidistant from the northern tip of the triangle and
the sides defined.

He gave her shoulders a brief squeeze and moved off,
walking slowly across the thick carpeting, hands behind his
back. He tilted his head up, as if the blank ceiling might
give him back a clue to the tortured reasoning of a dying
Crystal Singer.

"Part of the Milekey transition is a weather affinity. A

spore always knows storm, though its human host may choose to trust instrumentation rather than instinct. Keborgen was old, he'd begun to distrust everything, including his sled. He would have been inclined to rely on his affinity rather than the warning devices." Lanzecki's bland expression cautioned her against such ignorance. "As I told you, the symbiosis loses its capabilities as the host ages. What you haven't accounted for in your program is Keborgen's desperate need to get off-planet during Passover—and he hadn't quite enough credit to do so. A cut of black crystal, any size, would have insured it. Those shards would have been sufficient. My opinion is that, having cleared them, he found he had a flawless cut. He ignored both the sled's warnings and his symbiont and finished the cut. He lost time."

He paused behind Killashandra again, put both hands on her shoulders, leaning slightly against her as he peered at the overlay.

"I think you're nearer right on the position than the others, Killashandra Ree." His chuckle was vibrant, and the sound seemed to travel through his fingers and down her shoulders. "A fresh viewpoint, unsullied as yet by the devious exigencies of decades spent outwitting everyone, including self." Then, releasing her when she did not wish him to, he continued in a completely different tone of voice. "Did Carrik interest you in the Guild?"

"No." She swung the console chair about and caught a very curious and unreadable movement of Lanzecki's mouth. His face and eyes were expressionless, but he was waiting for her to elaborate. "No, he told me the last thing I wanted to be was a Crystal Singer. He wasn't the only one to warn me off."

Lanzecki raised his eyebrows.

"Everyone I knew on Fuerte was against my leaving with a Crystal Singer in spite of the fact that he had saved many lives there." She was bitter about that, more bitter than she had supposed. While she knew it had not been Maestro Valdi's fault, if he hadn't initiated the hold on her, Carrik and she would have been well away from Fuerte and that shuttle crash; Carrik might still be well. But would she have become a Singer?

"Despite all that is rumored about Crystal Singers, Killashandra, we have our human moments."

She stared at Lanzecki, wondering if he meant Carrik's saving lives or warning her against singing.

"Now," and Lanzecki walked to the console and touched a key. Suddenly, the triangle of F42NW down to F43NW in which Killashandra hoped to search was magnified on the big display across the room. "Yes, there's plenty of range totally unmarked."

At that magnification, Killashandra could also discern five paint splashes. Within the five-klick circle centering on the paint splash, the tumbled gorges and hills were under claim. A Singer could renounce his claim by listing the geographical coordinates, but Concera had told Killashandra that such an occurrence was rare.

"You could search an entire ravine and still miss the hoard inside the face," Lanzecki said, staring at the target area. "Or come a cropper with the claim's rightful owner." He reversed the magnification, and slowly the area was reduced until it faded into the rocky wrinkles surrounding the bay.

"Monday you will go out. Moksoon is not willing. He never is. But he's trying to get off-planet; with a decent cut and the bonus for shepherding, he could make it this time.

"Killashandra?"

"Yes, I go out on Monday. Moksoon is not willing but for the bonus—"

"Killashandra, you will find the black crystal!" Lanzecki's eyes took on an uncanny intensity, reinforcing his message and the strength of his conviction that Killashandra Ree was an agent he could command.

"Only if I'm bloody lucky." She laughed, recovering her equilibrium as she gestured to the vast area she'd have to comb.

Lanzecki's eyes did not leave hers. She was reminded of an ancient piece of drama history: a man had hypnotized a girl, a musical idiot, into vocal performances without peer. She couldn't recall the name, but to think of Lanzecki, Resident Master of one of the most prestigious Guilds in the Federated Sentient Planets, attempting to . . . ah . . . Svengali her into locating the nardy precious black crystal was ludicrous. Only she couldn't suggest that to Lanzecki, not when he was regarding her in so disconcerting a fashion.

Suddenly, he threw up his head and started to laugh. He abandoned his whole body to the exercise, his chest caving in, his ribs arching, his hands spread on his thighs as he bent forward. If anyone had told her five minutes before that Guild Master Lanzecki was capable of humor at all, she'd have thought them mad. He collapsed into a seating unit, his head lolling against its back as he roared.

His laughter had an oddly infectious quality, and she grinned in response. Then laughed, too, to see the Guild Master so reduced in dignity by mirth.

"Killashandra . . ." He gasped her name as the laughter subsided. "I do apologize, but the look on your face . . . I've thrown the reputation of the entire Guild into jeopardy, have I not?" He wiped moisture from the corners of his eyes and straightened up. "I haven't laughed in a very long time."

A wistful quality in that last remark made Killashandra change her reply.

"They used to say at Fuerte that I'd have been a good comic singer if I hadn't been so hipped on leads."

"I find nothing comic about you, Killashandra," he said, his eyes sparkling as he held out his hand.

"Dramatic?"

"Unexpected."

He took the hand she had unconsciously extended, caressing the palm with the ball of his thumb before turning her hand over and dropping a kiss in it.

She caught her breath at the spread of sensation from her palm through her body to the nipples on her breasts. She wanted to snatch her hand from his but saw the tender smile on his lips as he raised his head. Lanzecki had his eyes and face under control; his mouth betrayed him.

The pressure he exerted on her hand to draw her to him was as inexorable as it was gently and deftly done. With her across his thighs, her body against his, and her head in the crook of his arm, he brought her hand again to his mouth, and she closed her eyes at the sensuality of that delicate kiss. Her hand was placed palm down against warm skin, and she felt him stroke her hair, letting one curl wrap round his finger before he dropped his hand to her breast, lightly and with skill.

"Killashandra Ree?" His low whisper asked a question that had nothing to do with her name but everything that pertained to who she was.

"Lanzecki!"

His mouth covered hers in so light a caress that she was at first unaware of being kissed. It was so with the rest of her first experience with the Guild Master, a loving and sharing that paled into insignificance any other encounter.

CHAPTER 8

When she gradually awakened the next morning, she found his fingers lightly clasping her upturned hand. Her slight movement of surprise caused his fingers to tighten, then caress. Opening her eyes, she turned her head toward him, to meet his eyes, sleepily narrow. They were lying, she on her back, he on his stomach, stretched out, the only point of contact the two hands, yet Killashandra felt that her every muscle and nerve was in tune to him and his to her. She blinked and sighed. Lanzecki smiled, his lips relaxed and full. His smile deepened, as if he knew of her fascination with his mouth. He rolled to his back, still holding her right hand, now pulling it up to kiss the palm. She closed her eyes against the incredible sensation the lightest touch of his lips created within her.

Then she noticed the fine white lines across his bare arm and chest, parallel in some places, criss-crossed in others.

"I believe I mentioned that I sang crystal," he said.

"Cut crystal would be nearer the truth from the look of you," she said, raising her upper body to see the rest of his well-muscled torso. Then she frowned. "How do you know so accurately what I'm thinking? No one mentioned a telepathic adaptation to the spore."

194

"There is none, dearling. I have merely become adept at reading expressions and body language over the decades."

"Is that why you're Guild Master instead of Singer?" She had heard, and savored, the endearment.

"There must be a Guild Master."

"Trag would never make it."

"Now who is telepathic?"

"Well, you'd better watch your mouth."

"My mouth said nothing about Trag's future."

"It didn't have to. So, are recruits deliberately selected?"

His mouth gave nothing away to her. "Where did you get that idea, Killashandra Ree?" His eyes were laughing, denying her remembrance of Borella's conversation to the other Singer on the shuttle from Shankill.

"The notion had occurred to me from the pounds of prevention FSP applies to keep people from joining the Guild."

"The FSP"—and Lanzecki's mouth drew into a thinner line—"is also the largest purchaser of crystal. Especially black crystal." He rolled back to her, his eyes on her mouth. "This is my rest day, too. I earnestly desire to relax in your good company." He was indeed as earnest as she could have wished and exceedingly obliging. While they paused to eat, she asked him how they had moved from his office suite to his apartment on the Singer level.

"Private lift." He gave a careless shrug of his cicatriced shoulders as he sought morsels of food in the rich spicy sauce. "One of my perquisites."

"Is *that* how you do your appearing act?"

Lanzecki grinned at her, delighted in an unexpectedly boyish way—*that* put her guiltily in mind of Rimbol—that he had disconcerted her.

"I often have need to 'appear' unexpectedly."

"Why?"

"In your case?" His smile altered slightly, his lips taking a bitter twist. "Serendipity. I liked your misplaced loyalty to Carrik. I wished you well away from the Scoria system. Once you passed the entrance requirements, you became my responsibility."

"Isn't everyone in the Guild?"

"More or less. But you, Killashandra Ree, had a Milekey transition."

"You do this every time? . . ." She was piqued by his candor and gestured with all the contempt of an outraged opera heroine around the bedroom.

"Of course not," he said with a burst of laughter. He caught her hand and kissed her palm with the usual effect, despite her indignation. "This is not one of my perks, dearling. It is a privilege you have granted me. I did—and have no doubts on that score for the duration of your memory —want to know you before you went into the ranges."

"Before?" She caught that subtle emphasis.

He made an untidy pile of their dishes and shoved them into the disposal slot.

"Before singing crystal has stung your blood."

He turned back, and she could see the sadness in the droop of his mouth.

"But you've sung crystal?"

He put both hands on her shoulders, looking down at her. There was no expression in his eyes; the planes of his face were still, the line of his mouth uncompromising.

"Do you mean that after I have sung, I won't be any good. Or any more good to you?" She flung the options at him.

Instead of repudiating either, he caught her resisting body up in his arms, laughing as he swung her around and around, tight against him.

"My darling, I shall make love to you until tomorrow morning when I shall . . . shepherd . . . you to your sled and to Moksoon. You shall endeavor your best, once Moksoon has demonstrated the Cutter's art on an actual face, to find Keborgen's claim. When you return from your first trip"—and he gave an enigmatic laugh—"I shall still be Guild Master. But you"—and here he kissed her—"will be truly a Crystal Singer."

He did not let her speak then; nor did they return to the subject of their occupations.

The following morning, Lanzecki was completely the Guild Master when she met him and the petulant Moksoon in the flight officer's ready room. She had been out in the hangar checking *her* sled, putting her cutter in its brackets with a loving snap, aware of the acrid, chemical tang of new plastic and metal from the run-in of the drive.

Moksoon was not Killashandra's notion of a shepherd for her first trip into the dangerous Milekeys. That he was as dubious about her was unmistakable in the sidelong glances he gave her. A slightly built man who had probably always had a wizened appearance to his face, he looked old, odd enough in a Crystal Singer. He also looked thoroughly annoyed, for the maintenance officer was suavely explaining why it had taken so long to repair his sled. Since Lanzecki had explained to her that Moksoon's most important qualification as her guide was that he was known to be cutting in the Bay area, Killashandra knew that the delay had been contrived.

"Remember, of course, Moksoon, that the bonus alone sees you safely off-planet," Lanzecki said, deftly entering the conversation. "This is Killashandra Ree. Master recorder on! Moksoon, this will be on continuous replay in your cabin. You are shepherding Killashandra Ree in accordance with Section 53, Paragraphs one through five. She is cognizant of the fact that she is entitled to nothing that she may cut under your direction at your claim. She is entitled to stay with you two working days when she will depart to seek a claim of her own. She will never make any attempt to return to your claim under Section 49, Paragraphs 7, 9, and 14. Killashandra Ree, do you . . ." And Killashandra found herself repeating, affirming, avowing, under the strict penalties imposed by the Heptite Guild that she would obey the strictures of the two sections and the paragraphs cited. Moksoon was also required to repeat his willingness, which was forced, above and beyond the bonus offered, to instruct her in the cutting of crystal for the two-day period as allowed by Guild rules and regulations.

Moksoon's repetition was so marred by lapses into silence and prompts from Lanzecki and the flight officer that Killashandra had half a mind to revoke her contract. Lanzecki caught her eye, and her rebellion ended.

The official recording made, replicas were patched into the communications units of both sleds. The flight officer escorted Moksoon to his vehicle, slightly canted to the left and battered in spite of fresh paint that attempted to blend

the most recent repairs into the older dings. Lanzecki
strode beside Killashandra to her brand new sled.

"Use the replay whenever he falters. Your switch is
rigged to activate his."

"Are you sure that Moksoon is the right—"

"For your purpose, Killashandra, the only one." Lanzecki's tone allowed no argument. "Just don't trust him
about anything. He's cut crystal too long and sung too long
alone."

"Then why—" Now Killashandra was totally exasperated.

Lanzecki cupped her elbow and half lifted her into her
sled.

"His hands will automatically do what you need to see.
Watch how he cuts, what he does, not what he says. Heed
your inner warnings. Watch your met report as often as
you think of it. Fortunately, you'll think of it often enough
the first trip out. Passover's in seven weeks. Storms *can*
blow up days before the actual conjunction. Yes, I know
you know all this, but it bears repeating. He's in and belted.
No time now. Follow him. The charts of the Bay area
have been put on instant review. Be sure to pack crystal as
soon as you have cut, Killashandra!"

He had smoothly engineered her departure, Killashandra
thought, giving her no time for regrets and none for personal farewell. Yesterday, she reminded herself, he had
been Lanzecki the man. Today he was Guild Master. Fair
enough.

Moksoon took off just as she switched on her sled's
drive. His craft canted even in the air, a distinctive sil-
houette, like that of a person with one shoulder higher
than the other. Despite her severe doubts about Moksoon,
Killashandra experienced a rush of elation as she drifted
her sled from the hangar. She was going to cut crystal at
last. At last? She was first out of Class 895. She thought of
Rimbol and grimaced. She ought at least to have left a
call for him, explaining her absence. Then she remembered
that she had placed a call to him that hadn't been answered. That could suffice!

Bollux, but that fool Moksoon was running like a scared
mushman! She increased the speed of her sled, closing to a

proper following distance. In a peculiar change of direction, Moksoon now headed due north and dropped to a lower altitude, skimming the first folds of the Milekey Range. As she was above him, she caught his second, easterly shift, and then he disappeared over a high fold. She decelerated to a near hover, scanning both ends of the drop as she approached it. He was hovering on the north end of the fault. She caught the merest glint of sunlight on the orange of his sled, then flew on to the next ravine as if she hadn't spotted him and mimicked his tactics until he showed at the southern edge, just as she'd expected.

"Twithead's forgotten I'm supposed to follow him," she said, and slapped on the replay. The one in his sled would project its messsage. She sighed deeply, resigned to a long and difficult day, but suddenly his sled popped up into sight, and Moksoon made no immediate attempt to evade her.

She checked his new heading, south at four, which was an honest direction for Moksoon's eventual destination. She wondered how long she could trust the reinforcement of the replay. A direct flight would get them to the Bay area in two hours at the reasonable speed Moksoon was maintaining. She might not know where he was leading her, but she had the advantage over him in a new sled capable of speed and maneuverability.

Even on a direct course, Moksoon was an erratic flyer. There shouldn't have been thermals or violent air currents at his level, but his sled bounced and lolled. Was she trying to make her air sick following?

Why had Lanzecki chosen this man? Because of his faulty memory? Because, once Moksoon had achieved his desired trip off-planet, he would not, in the fashion of Crystal Singers of long service, remember that he had shepherded one Killashandra Ree into the Bay's range. Well, that was logical of Lanzecki, provided she could also find Keborgen's claim. Before the others who were looking for it. Patently, Lanzecki was backing her.

"Once a Singer has cut a certain face, she only needs to be in its general area and she'll feel the pull of the sound," Concera had said. "Your augmented vision will assist in distinguishing the color of crystal beneath storm film, base rock, and flaw. Catch the sun at the right angle and crystal cuttings are blindingly clear."

Phrases and advice flooded through Killashandra's mind, but as she looked down at the undulating folds of the Milekey Ranges, she entertained serious doubts that she would ever find anything in such a homogeneous land. Kilometers in all directions flowed in similar patterns of fold, ridge, valley, gorge.

A sudden stab of piercing light made her clutch the yoke of the sled to steady herself. She peered down and saw an orange slice of sled top, half hidden by an overhang and deep in the ravine, only its luminescent paint and her altitude disclosing it. On the highest of the surrounding ridges was the splash of paint indicating a claim.

That crystal flash, as unlikely as everything else that had been happening to her recently, confirmed that some of the other improbables might also be true on Ballybran.

Fardles! Where had Moksoon got to? During her brief inattention, the old Singer's orange sled had slipped from view. She speeded up and caught a glimpse of the orange stern winding through a deep ravine. Without changing altitude, she matched pace with his cautious forward movement, her viewscreen on magnify. Since she had his sled well in view, she did not reactivate the tape. He might just as easily slam into one of the odd stone buttresses that lined the canyon if she startled him.

She checked the heading; Moksoon had gone north by 11. Suddenly, he oozed up and over a ridge, down into a deeper, shadowed valley. She dove, noting quickly that the deep went south. Unless he flipped over the intervening fold, Moksoon would have to follow the southerly course. That gorge continued in its erratic fashion stubbornly south by 4. She couldn't see Moksoon in the shadows, but there was no place else he could be.

The long winding of the gorge ended in a blockage of debris, the erosion of a higher anticline. There was no sign of Moksoon. He had to be in the gorge, hiding in shadow. Then she saw the faded claim blaze on a ridge. Even in Ballybran's climate, the stuff was supposed to take decades to deteriorate so much. A released claim always had the piss-green countermark—not that she'd seen any of those during her pursuit of Moksoon.

Cautiously, she guided her sled down the rock slide and into the gorge. In some places, the sides nearly met; in others, she had a view of ranges folding beyond. Something glinted in the little sunlight that penetrated. She increased the magnification and was surprised to see a thin stream meandering the base of the gorge. There had been no lake at the blocked point, so she assumed that the little stream went underground in its search for an outlet to the Bay.

She was beginning to feel anxious when an oxbend revealed a wider valley; the orange sled was parked on the right, on a shadowed ledge that would have been invisible from all except a direct search of this particular canyon.

She keyed the replay and turned up the volume so that Lanzecki's voice was echoing off the rock walls as Moksoon slipped and slid toward her; the crystal cutter held safely above his head.

"Claim jumper! Claim jumper!" he shrieked, stumbling to the ledge on which she had rested her sled. He turned on the cutter, held it well in front of him, as he approached her sled door.

"In accordance with Section 53, Paragraphs 1 through 5 . . ." the replay roared.

"Lanzecki? He's with you?" Moksoon glanced wildly around and above him, searching for another sled.

"Playback," Killashandra yelled through Lanzecki's amplified words. "I'm *not* claim jumping. You're *shepherding* me. You get a *bonus*." She used her voice training to shoot her message through the pauses in the recording.

"That's me!" Moksoon pointed accusingly at her sled from which his own hesitant voice emanated.

"Yes, you made the tape this morning. You *promised* to *shepherd* me for the *bonus*."

"Bonus!" Moksoon lowered the cutter, though Killashandra adroitly maneuvered herself farther from its point.

"Yes, *bonus*, according to Section 53, Paragraphs 1 through 5. Remember?"

"Yes, I do." Moksoon didn't sound all that certain. "That's you speaking now."

"Yes, promising to abide by Section 49, Paragraphs 7, 9 and 14. I'm to stay with you two days only, to watch an expert cut crystal. Lanzecki recommended you so highly. One of the best."

"That Lanzecki! All he wants is cut crystal." Moksoon snorted in sulky condemnation.

"This time you'll have a bonus to get you off-world."

The cutter pointed down now, the fingers of the tired old man so slack on the grip, Killashandra hoped he wouldn't drop it. She'd been told often enough how easily the wretchedly expensive things damaged.

"I gotta get off Ballybran. I gotta. That's why I said I'd shepherd." Head bent, Moksoon was talking to himself now, ignoring the replayed affirmations.

Suddenly, he swung the tip of his cutter up and advanced towards her menacingly. Killashandra scooted back as far as she could on the ledge.

"How do I know you won't pop right back in here when I'm off-world and cut my claim?"

"I couldn't find the bloody place again," she said, exploding, discretion no advantage in dealing with the fanatic. "I haven't a clue where I am. I had to keep my eyes on you, zipping here and dropping there. Have you forgotten how to pilot a sled? You sure have forgotten a perfectly valid agreement you made only five hours ago!"

Moksoon, his eyes little slits of suspicion, lowered the cutter fractionally. "You know where you are."

"South at four is all I bloody know, and for all the twists and turns in this ruddy gorge, we could be north at ten. What in damnation does it matter? Show me how to cut crystal and I'll leave in an hour."

"You can't cut crystal in an hour. Not properly." Moksoon was scathingly contemptuous. "You don't know the first thing about cutting crystal."

"You're quite right. I don't. And you'll get a huge bonus for showing me. Show me, Moksoon."

With a combination of cajolery, outrageous flattery, constant repetition of words like "bonus," "Lanzecki expects," "off-world," and "brilliant Cutter," she pacified Moksoon. She suggested that he eat something before showing her how to cut and let him think she was fooled into offering from her own supplies. For a slight man, he had a very hearty appetite.

Well fed, rested, and having filled her with what she knew must be a lot of nonsense about angles of the sun, dawn, and sunset excursions down dark ravines to hear crystal wake or go to sleep, Moksoon showed no inclination to pick up his cutter and get on with his end of the bargain. She was trying to think of a tactful way of suggesting it when he suddenly jumped to his feet, throwing both arms up to greet a shaft of sunlight that had angled down the ravine to strike their side just beyond the bow of his sled.

A peculiar tone vibrated through the rock on which Killashandra was sitting. Moksoon grabbed up his cutter and scrambled, emitting a joyous cackle that turned into a fine, clear ringing A sharp below middle C. Moksoon sang in the tenor ranges.

And part of the ravine answered!

By the time she had reached him, he was already slicing at the pink quartz face his sled had obscured. Why the old—

Then she heard crystal crying. For all his other failings, Moksoon had an astonishing lung capacity for so old a man. He held the accurate note even after his pitched cutter was excising a pentagon from the uneven extrusion of quartz, which flashed from different facets as the sunlight shifted. The dissonance that began as he got deeper into the face was an agony so basic that it shook Killashandra to her teeth. It was much worse than retuning crystal. She froze at the unexpected pain, instinctively letting loose with a cry of masking sound. The agony turned into two notes, pure and clear.

"Sing on!" Moksoon cried. "Hold that note!" He reset his infrasonic cutter and made a second slice, cropped it, sang again, tuned the cutter, and dug the blade in six neat slashes downward. His thin body shook, but his hands were amazingly steady as he cut and cut until he reached the edge. With an exultant note, he jumped to a new position and made the bottom cut for the four matched crystals. "My beauties. My beauties!" he crooned and, laying the cutter carefully down, dashed off to his sled, reemerging seconds later with a carton. He was still crooning as he packed the pieces. There was a curious ambivalence in his motions, of haste and reluctance, for his fingers caressed the sides of the octagons as he put them away.

Killashandra hadn't moved, as stunned by the experience of crystal as she was by his agile performance. When she did sigh to release her tensions, he gave an inarticulate shout and reached for his cutter. He might have sliced her arm off, but he tripped over the carton, giving her a head start as she raced back to his sled, stumbled into it, and hit the replay button before she slid the door closed. It caught the tip of the cutter.

And Lanzecki had suggested she go with this raving maniac? Lanzecki's voice rolled out, reverberated back, and made a section of the rock face above the sled resonate.

"I'm sorry, Killashandra Ree," Moksoon said, a truly repentant note in his voice. "Don't break my cutter. Don't close that door."

"How can I trust you, Moksoon? You've nearly killed me twice today."

"I forget. I forget." Moksoon's tone was a sob. "Just remind me when I'm cutting. It's crystal makes me forget. It sings, and I forget."

Killashandra closed her eyes and tried to catch her breath. The man was so pitiful.

"I'll show you how to cut. Truly I will."

Moksoon's recorded voice was duly affirming his willingness to shepherd her, Section 53. She could break his cutter with one more centimeter of leverage on the door. Her own voice dinned into her ears, affirming and averring to abide by section and paragraph.

"You'd better be able to show me something about cutting crystal that I couldn't learn at the Complex."

"I'll show you. I'll show you how to find song in the cliffs. I'll show you how to find crystal. Any fool can cut it. You've got to find it first. Just don't close that door!"

"How do I keep you from trying to kill me?"

"Just talk to me. Keep that replay on. Just talk to me as I'm cutting. Give me back my cutter!"

"I'm talking to you, Moksoon, and I'm opening the door. I haven't damaged the cutter." The first thing he did when she eased up the pressure was examine the tip. "Now, Moksoon, show me how to find song in the cliffs."

"This way, this way." He scrabbled to the outcropping. "See . . ." and his finger traced the faultline, barely discernible. "And here." Now a glint of crystal shone clearly through the covering dirt. He rubbed at it, and sunlight sparkled from the crystal. "Mostly sunlight tells you where, but you gotta *see*. Look and see! Crystal lies in planes, this way, that way, sometimes the way the fold goes, sometimes at right angles. You sure you can't find your way back here?" He shot her a nervous glance.

"Positive!"

"Rose always drops south. Depend on it." He ran his finger tips lightly down the precipice. "I hadn't seen this before. Why didn't I see this before?"

"You didn't look, did you, Moksoon?"

He ignored her. At first, Killashandra thought a breeze had sprung up, highly unlikely though that was in this deep gorge. Then she heard the faint echo and realized that Moksoon was humming. He had one ear to the rock wall.

"Ah, here. I can cut here!"

He did so. This time, the crystal cry was expected and not as searing an experience. She also kept herself in Moksoon's view, especially when he had completed his cuts. She got a carton for him, carried it back and stored it, all the time talking or making him talk to her. He did know how to cut crystal. He did know how to find it. The gorge was layered in southerly strips of rose quartz. Moksoon could probably cut his claim for the rest of his Guild life.

When the sun dropped beyond the eastern lip of the gorge, he abruptly stopped work and said he was hungry. Killashandra fed him and listened as he rambled on about flaw lines and cuts and intruders, by which he meant noncrystal rock that generally shattered the crystal vein.

Since she recalled Enthor's poor opinion of rose quartz, she asked Moksoon if he cut other colors. It was an unwise question, for Moksoon had a tantrum, announcing that he'd cut rose quartz all his working life, which was far longer than she'd drawn breath, or her parents, or her grandparents for that matter, and she was to mind her own business. He stalked off to his sled.

Taking the precaution of locking her door panel, she made herself comfortable. She wasn't sure that she could endure, or survive, another day with the paranoid Moksoon. She didn't doubt for a moment that the uneasy rapport she had finally achieved would fade overnight in his crystallized brain pan.

In the cool darkness of the gorge, where night made the rocks crack and tzing, she thought of Lanzecki. He had wished to know her, he said, before she sang crystal. Now that phrase had both an overtone of benediction and a decided implication of curse. Would just one trip to the Crystal Ranges alter her so much? Or had their nights and day together occurred to form some bond between them? If so, Lanzecki was going to be very busy over the next few weeks, cementing links between Jezerey, Rimbol—and then Killashandra's sense of humor overruled vile whimsies. Lanzecki might be devious but not that damned devious!

Besides, none of the others had made Milekey transitions or appeared sensitive to black crystal. It was a concatenation of circumstances. And he had said that he liked her company. He, Lanzecki, liked her company. But Lanzecki the Guild Master had sent her out with crazed Moksoon.

Killashandra set her waking buzz for sunrise so that she'd be out of the gorge before Moksoon woke.

CHAPTER 9

She woke to darkness and a curious pinging. Cautiously, she put her head out the sled door, checking first in Moksoon's direction. Not a sign of life there. She looked upward, between the steep walls of the gorge, to a lightening sky. After her hide-and-seek with Moksoon the day before, she appreciated the navigational hazards of semidark. She also didn't wish to be around when the old Crystal Singer roused.

She checked that all her lockers were closed and secure, an automatic action learned during her simulated-flight instruction. Fortunately, she had made "dark" landings and takeoffs in imaginary shallow canyons and deep valleys, though she wished she'd paid more attention to the terrain just beyond Moksoon's claim. She couldn't risk retracing yesterday's circuit to the avalanche.

She strapped into her seat, turned the drive to minimum power, easing up half a meter by the vertical and out ten horizontal, then activated the top scanner to be sure of her clearances.

The sky was light enough for her purposes but not as yet touched with the rising sun. She lifted slowly, carefully, her eyes on the scanner to be sure she didn't bounce off an unexpected outcropping.

Abruptly, she was above the gorge and hovered, quickly

207

switching the scan to under-hull and magnify. Her departure had not aroused Moksoon. With luck, he would have forgotten that she'd been there until he received his bonus. And how *she* had worked for that!

The notion that one day she might be as Moksoon now was crossed her mind, but that, she firmly assured herself, was a long time in the future. She'd make it as future as possible.

She proceeded with fair haste to the F42NW–43NW where five old paint splashes made an irregular pattern on Lanzecki's aerial map. The sun was rising, an awesome sight at any time, but as it gilded the western folds and heights of the Milekey Range, it was truly magnificent. She settled the sled on a flattened, eroded syncline to enjoy the spectacle of morning breaking as she ate breakfast. It was a lovely clear morning, the light breeze tainted with sea, for the Bay was not far. She checked meteorology, which indicated that the clear, dry weather was confirmed for the next six hours.

She would come in over F42NW at altitude and proceed to F43NW, just to get an overall picture. If her hunch was right, and Lanzecki's privileged information had only confirmed it, one of those five claims had to be Keborgen's black crystal.

From height, the area looked desolate—valleys and ravines, blind canyons, few with water, and not so much as a glint of crystal shine in the morning sun. Furthermore, one of the painted claim marks was newer than the others. The sun reflected off the mark. Had one of the other Singers actually found Keborgen's claim? She reminded herself sternly that none of the others had come this far north. One new claim mark among five. But Lanzecki's original aerial scan had displayed five old marks.

Killashandra caught her breath. Keborgen had not been to this claim in nine years. Because he couldn't remember where it was? He had garnered useful shards and splinters and a triad, worth a fortune of credit. Might he not have used up his margin of time between storm warning and escape to repaint his claim so he could find it more easily after the storm?

Killashandra searched her mind about claims and claim-jumping. Nothing prevented her from checking the circumscribed area. Lifting or cutting crystal was the felony.

She reduced her altitude and swept round the claim in a circle roughly five kicks in diameter from the brightly painted ridge mark. She could see no other sled, though she hovered over several shadowed ledges and overhanging cliffs to be sure. She also noted no spark or glint of sunstruck crystal. After the initial survey, she landed on the ridge. The paint was new, only scored here and there by the last storm. She could see edges of the old where the new had been applied in haste. Then she found the paint container, wedged in some rocks where it had been thrown or wind-swept. She hefted it, smiling in exultation. Yes, Keborgen didn't want to forget *this* claim. He'd wasted time to preserve it.

She looked out across the ridges and nearest gullies and wondered where. From this vantage point, she could see the five klicks in every direction.

Since Keborgen had obviously cleared the crystal shards from his site, there'd be none to indicate where he'd worked. But he would have had to hide his sled from aerial observation, as Moksoon had done.

So Killashandra spent the rest of the morning flying search patterns over the circle. She found five locations; two partial hides in the south on 7 quadrant, an undercut in west 10, a very narrow blind valley in 4, and two shadowed gorges in north 2. On her master chart, she noted each location by some distinguishing contour or rock and the angle at which she had been flying to discern it.

She had no further support from the weather, for a drizzle began midafternoon. There'd be no sunset flashes to lead her, no sun-warmed crystal to speak. She saw no advantage in sitting on the claim ridge, either. There were other Singers looking for Keborgen's claim. No sense being so visible.

"Eena, meena, pitsa teena," she chanted, pointing at one site on each syllable. "Avoo bumbarina, isha gosha, bumbarosha, nineteen hunded and one!"

"One" was the west 4 undercut.

As she approached from the south, she noticed that the ridge was curiously slanted. Since it was protected on all sides by higher folds, the erosion had not been caused by wind. She landed the sled as well as she could on uneven ground beside the overhang. She would inspect first. As she pulled on wet-weather gear, she noticed that debris had showered on either side of the ledge, which was, in fact, just the right length for a sled.

Much heartened, she went out and prowled around. The rock falls were of long residence, well chinked with grit and dirt. The ledge was solid, but at one end heterogeneous rocks had been tamped in for critical reinforcement. A little scrape of orange paint along the inside wall was her final reassurance. A sled had parked there. She parked hers with a sense of accomplishment.

She was not so happy after she had climbed to the highest point above the blind valley. She stared about her in the mizzling gloom. The valley was in the form of a blunted crescent, any part of which was an easy hike from the undercut. Crystal Singers exerted themselves only to cut crystal, not heft it any distance. Keborgen's claim had to be somewhere in the valley.

She slithered down the rocky side, adding more rubble to what was scattered about. When she returned to her sled, she checked the met report. Cloud cover ending midday, unless the cold front moving up from the southern pole picked up speed. She'd probably have a clear afternoon and sun on the southern tip of the valley. Rain or not, she told herself, she'd be out at first light. Keborgen had made two obvious mistakes: fresh claim and old sled paint.

Keborgen's cutting eluded her the entire damp gray morning as she searched the crescent for any signs of cutting, rubbed her hands and fingers raw scraping at stone. The valley's walls varied in height, on the longer curve up to 10 meters, sloping down to a dip almost directly across from the undercut. From the bottom of the valley, she couldn't see any signs, even accounting for the fact that Keborgen had taken crystal rubble with him.

She clambered back to her sled for something to eat, totally discouraged. She might just as well have braved Moksoon another day for all she had accomplished on her own.

A sudden gleam of light attracted her attention to the

window. Clouds were scuttering across the sky to the
north, and she saw patches of bright sky. As she left her
sled, a light breeze blew directly into her face. Suddenly,
sunlight shafted from the clouds, blinding after almost two
days of dismal gray.

With sun, she might just be lucky enough to catch crystal flash—if she was turned in the right direction at the
exact moment. Keborgen's cut could not have built much
dirt cover after the short storm.

The sun was more west than east. She'd have a better
chance if she was facing the west. She scrambled up the
valley side to the ridge, turning to her right and stopped.
With the sun shining, she could discern what the rain
had hidden the day before, a clear if uneven and winding
path of packed dirt, suitable for an agile pair of feet. The
path had been worn by a long-legged man, and as she
eagerly followed it, she occasionally had to hop or stretch.
She was so much occupied with her footing that she would
have tripped into the fault if she had not first noticed the
tamped-down flat space 2 meters from the edge. Just where
someone could leave crystal cartons. It could have been
excitement at first, but Killashandra felt a prickling along
her legs. Then she heard the soft sighing, more noise than
so light a breeze should make. It was as if someone distant
were humming softly, and the sound floated to her on the
breeze. Only this sound emanated ahead of her.

Trembling, she took the last two steps and looked down
into a trench, a V shape, slanting down toward the valley
floor, some 10 meters below the lowest arm of the V.
Muddy water oozed off the V point. Water had collected in
a too obviously geometric puddle halfway down the uneven
side. Uneven because Keborgen had left foot rests for easy
access to the heart of his claim. As she descended, she
could feel black crystal surrounding her. When she reached
the bottom, she knelt by the symmetrical pool, a fingertip
deep, and felt its sides. Smooth. Her fingers tingled.

Rising, she looked around. Roughly 6 meters long, carefully cut to maintain that rough, natural look, the V
opened to a width of 4 meters on the ravine side. Reverently now, she took a waste-cloth and brushed mud away.
The dull shine of cold black crystal was revealed. Using the

cloth, she mopped away the water. Keborgen's triad had been cut true, but to themselves, not to the angle of the vein, leaving this little wedge to accumulate water. No, this little piece was flawed, storm damage, more than likely. She caressed it, feeling the roughness of the flaw. Then she began excitedly to clean the ledge, to find out where the flaw stopped, where was the good black crystal. Ah, here, at the side, just where Keborgen had stopped cutting when the storm arrived.

How big, how deep, how wide was this crystal vein? This treasure store? Killashandra's elation overwhelmed her initial caution; laughing, she scrubbed at first this spot in the opposite wall, then along the slanty arms of the V, mopping the disguising grit and mud from the crystal and giggling softly to herself. Her titter echoed back to her, and she began to laugh, the louder sound reverberating.

She was surrounded by crystal. It was singing to her! She slid to the floor, oblivious of the mud, stroking the crystal face on either side of her, trying not to giggle, trying to *realize*, get it through her dazed brain, that she, Killashandra Ree, had actually found Keborgen's black crystal claim. And it was hers, section and paragraph.

Killashandra was unaware of the passage of time. She must have spent hours looking around the claim, seeing where Keborgen had cleared flawed crystal from the outside. He had undoubtedly expected to return once the storm had blown out. He was cutting from a shelf a meter above the higher arm of the V. He was an astute Cutter, for he hadn't ravaged crystal but worked for flawless cuts, the triads, and quartets, the larger groupings that would command the highest price from the greedy FSP who were eager to set up the crystal links between all inhabited planets. Keborgen had kept a natural-fault look to his claim, allowing the foot of the V to gather mud and dirt that wind and water would spill naturally across the lower part. By comparison, Moksoon was a very lazy Cutter, but then he had only rose quartz.

The crystal around her began to crackle and tzing, soft reassuring noises. As if, Killashandra thought fancifully, it had accepted the transfer of ownership. Enchanted, she listened to the soft sounds, waiting almost breathless for the next series until she also became aware of chill, that she sat in true dark, not shadow.

Reluctantly and still bemused by the crystalline chorus, she hoisted herself from the claim, retracing the rough path to her sled.

Relative sanity returned to her in the clean newness of her vehicle. She sat down and made a drawing of the claim, testing her recall of the dimensions, jotting down her assumptions on Keborgen's work routine.

She'd get an early start in the morning, she thought, looking at her cutter. She'd have several clear days now.

"I'll have several clear days?" The certainty of her thought on that score astonished her. She snapped on the met forecast. Tomorrow would be fair, with a likelihood of several more to come.

What had Lanzecki said about a weather affinity in the Milekey transition? That she could trust her symbiont? Distrust of the mechanical had brought about Keborgen's belated start to safety. Ah, but if he'd stopped to repaint his claim mark, he *had* listened to some warning.

Killashandra hugged her arms tightly to her. In theory, the symbiotic spore was now part of her cellular construction, certainly no part of her conscious mind nor a restless visitor in her body. At least until she called upon its healing powers. Or resisted its need to return to Ballybran.

She made a voice-coded note on the recorder about her instinctive knowledge of the weather. She could keep a check on that.

She remembered to eat before she lay down, for the excitements of the day had fatigued her. She set her buzz alarm for twenty minutes before sunrise. Breakfasted, and refreshed by her sleep, she was on the summit path as the sun's first rays found their way over the top of the far range, cutter slung over her shoulder, carton swinging from her free hand.

She left the carton where Keborgen had left his—how long would echoes of the dead accompany her in this site? —and stepped down into the claim. Sun had not yet reached even the higher point of the V. It would be easier to cut now, she thought, before the crystal started its morning song. She wiped clean the protuberance she meant to cut, roughly 50 centimeters long by 25 centimeters high and varying between 10 and 15 centimeters wide. She had to follow the ridges left by Keborgen's last cuts. Why ever didn't he just make straight lines? Flaws? She ran her hands across the surface, as if apologizing for what she was about to do. The crystal whispered under her touch.

Enough of this, she told herself severely. She imagined that both Trag and Lanzecki were watching, then struck the shelf with the tone wedge. Sound poured over her like tsunami. Every bone and joint reverberated the note. Her skull seemed to part at its seams, her blood pulsed like a metronome in time with the vibrations. Echoes were thrown back to her from the other side of the claim and, oddly soured, from crescent valley.

"Cut! You're supposed to tune your cutter to the note and cut!" Killashandra shouted at herself, and the echo shouted back.

Nothing as devastating as this had occurred when Moksoon had sung for note. Was it because she was sensitive to the black, not pink, nor attuned to his claim? He had also not been standing in the center of his claim but on granite. Nor was this experience like the scream of retuned crystal: there was no agony, no resentment in that glorious resonance, overpowering as it was.

She did not have to strike the crystal again. The A was locked in her head and ears. She hesitated just once more as she steadied the infrasonic blade to make the first incision. As well, for only an unconscious resolve, an obstinacy that she had never had to invoke, kept her cutting. Sound enveloped her, an A in chords and octaves, a ringing that made every nerve end in her body vibrate in a state that wasn't painful, was oddly pleasurable but curiously distracting. She felt the blade sound darken and pulled it out. She made the second vertical cut just before Keborgen's mark. This block would be shorter than the others and narrower. It couldn't be helped. She gritted her teeth against the coursing shock as blade met crystal and sound met nerve. Her hands seemed to respond to the endless hours of drill under Trag's direction, but she didn't consciously tell herself to stop the second vertical cut. Some practiced connection between hand and eye stopped her. She let that instinct assist her in making the horizontal slice that would sever the crystal from the vein. Its cry was not as fierce.

Carefully, she put the cutter down, awed by the thread-thin separation she had caused. With hands still shaking from the effort of guiding the cutter, she tipped the rectangle out and held it up. Sun caught and darkened the oblong, showing to her wondering eyes the slight deviation from a true angle. She couldn't have cared less and wept with joy as the song of sun-warmed black crystal, now truly matte black in response to heat, seeped through her skin to intoxicate her senses.

How long she stood in awed thrall, holding the rectangle into the sun like an ancient priestess, she would never know. A cloud, one of the few that day, briefly obscured the light and broke the song. Killashandra was conscious then of the ache in her shoulders from holding weight aloft and a numbness in fingers, feet, and legs. She was strangely unwilling to release the crystal. "Pack crystal as soon as you have cut." The echo of Lanzecki's advice came to her. Moksoon, too, had packed as soon as he had cut. She remembered how reluctant the crazed old Singer had seemed to release the rose into the carton. Now she appreciated both advice and example.

Only when she had snuggled the crystal block into its plastic cocoon did she realize her debilitation. She leaned, drained of strength, against the crystal wall and sank slowly to the floor, marginally aware of the murmuring crystal against which she rested.

"This will never do," she told herself, ignoring the faint, chimed echo of her voice. She took a food packet from her thigh pouch and mechanically chewed and drank. The terrible lethargy began to ease.

She glanced at the sky and realized that the sun was dropping to the west. She must have spent half a good clear day admiring her handiwork.

"Ridiculous!"

The scoffing "d" sound spat back at her.

"I wouldn't mock if I were you, my friend," she told the

claim as she eyed the cuts for the second block. She'd want to get this one squarer or she'd end up with a suspiciously symmetrical puddle as Keborgen had done.

She didn't need to tap for pitch: the A was seared into her mind. She turned on and adjusted the cutter, nerving herself for the crystalline response. She was almost overset by the pure, unprotesting note given back. Immensely relieved, she made the two vertical cuts, watching to keep the cutter blade straight. She made the third, horizontal slice and cursed herself for unconsciously following the pattern of her first, uneven cut. Sensation palpably oozed off the cut black, but this time she knew crystal tricks and quickly buried it beside its mate in the carton.

The third crystal ought to have been the easiest. She made the first cut deftly, pleased with her expertise. But the vertical incision to sever the rectangle from the face went off the true pitch. She halted, peered in at the grayish, pale-brown mass, touched it and felt, not tactilely, but through the nerves in her finger tips that she was cutting on flaw. If she moved a half centimeter out . . . The block would not match the other two but the crystal cried clear. She turned it over and over in her hands, her back carefully to the sun, inspecting the block for any other sign of flaw. This was, she told herself sternly, an excuse to caress it with fingers that delighted in the smooth, soapy texture, the whisper of sound, the sensations that reached her nerves as delicate as . . . as Lanzecki's kiss in her palm?

Killashandra chuckled, her laughter tinkling back from all sides. Lanzecki, or recollections of him, would seem to constitute an anchor in this exotic arena of sound and sensation. Would he appreciate that role? And when, or if, she returned to Lanzecki's arms, would she remember crystal in them?

Thoughts of him effectively blotted the lure of the third rectangle that she packed away. She was then aware of a coolness, a light breeze, where before the air had been warm and still. Looking westward, she realized that she had once more been crystal-tricked. The day was almost over, and she'd only three black crystals to show for sixteen hours' work—or mental aberration. There was a whole side to be cut.

Obviously there was much about the cutting of crystal
that could not be explained, programmed, or theorized. It
had to be experienced. She hadn't acquired enough tips or
tricks or insights from watching Moksoon. She had learned
a good deal from observing Keborgen's cutting. Intuition
suggested that she would never learn all there was to the
cutting of crystal. That ought to make a long life as a
Singer more eventful. If she could just handle the frustration of losing hours in contemplation of her handiwork!

The three crystals were quiescent in their packing case,
but her hands lingered on it as she fixed the stowage webbing. She assembled a large hot meal for herself and a
beaker of Yarran beer. Taking food and drink outside, she
strode to the dip and seated herself on a convenient
boulder.

She watched the sun set on her claim and the moons
rise. The cooling crystal cried across the blind valley that
separated them.

"You had your way—" and Killashandra stopped her
mocking sentence as her first word was echoed back from
the newly exposed crystal. "You who—" And the vowel
came back to her, in harmony. Amused by the phenomenon, she pitched a second "you who" a third lower and
heard it chime in with the faint reverberations of the first.
She laughed at her whimsy. Crystal laughed back. And the
first stirrings of the night breeze as great Shankill moon
rose brought counter harmonies to her solo.

She sang. She sang to the crystal; the wind learned the
tune, though gradually the crystal chorus died as the last
sun warmth left it, and only the wind softly repeated her
lyric line.

Shilmore rose and the night air brought a chill that
roused her from a trance of the kind that Maestro Valdi
must have meant. He was right, she thought. Crystal song
could be addictive and was utterly exhausting. She staggered back to the sled. Without shedding her coverall, Killashandra drew the thermal sheet over her as she turned her
shoulder into the mattress. And slept.

A faint sound roused her. Not the buzzer, for she hadn't
remembered to set an alarm. Groggily, she raised her head,
staring in accusation at the console, but there was no warn-

ing light and certainly no buzz. However, *something* had
awakened her.

Outside, the sled the sun was shining. She pushed herself
off the bed and dialed a strong stimulant. The time display
read midmorning. She'd missed five hours of cutting light!
She'd a cramp in one shoulder, and her knees ached. The
heat of the drink flowed through her, dispersing the slug-
gishness of her mind and easing her muscles. She drank as
quickly as she could, dialed a second cup, shoved protein
bars into her coverall pockets. Unbracketing her cutter, she
slung it across her back, got another carton, a handlight,
and was on her way to the claim ten minutes after waking.
The sound that woke her had been the crack of raw black
crystal feeling the touch of sun.

First she had to clear splinters that had fallen from the
end of her cut, the result of the night's chill and the morning's sun. Stolidly, she set her mind and collected the small
pieces, dropping them into the packing case. With the handlight, she could now see where another flaw crazed the
crystal quartz on the hillside. Using the inner edge of the
previous day's shelf, however, she could make an interlocking group, four medium—or five smaller—rectangles.
She'd cut these now, let the chill crack off flaw. A little
expeditious trimming on the ravine side and the temperature would remove the blemishes. Tomorrow she'd have a
rare day's cutting.

Killashandra set her nerves for the first incision of the
infrasonic cutter and was relieved to endure less shock.
Relieved and dismayed. Was the claim admitting her right
to it by lack of protest? Or did one day attune her body to
the resonance? She had half wished to experience that pleasurable, nerve-caressing distraction, as if a highly skilled
lover were inside her body.

She did not remember, due to those reflections no doubt,
to pack away as soon as she'd turned off the blade. She did
remember to shield the rectangle from the sun as she
stroked it, totally in rapport with her creation. She admired
the clever angle she had contrived to make an old cut—

And suddenly realized that she had been communing
with the violated crystal. She resolutely packed it away,
and the next four were stowed as soon as she laid the

cutter down. She had to teach herself the automatic sequence. "Habit," Concera had endlessly and rightly said, "is all that saves a Singer."

Killashandra set herself to clearing the ravine face, but the sun's reflection off the quartz pained her eyes. She'd wasted too much time in sleep and in crystal thrall.

She woke in the night suddenly, an odd apprehension driving sleep from her mind. Uneasily, she checked the stored cartons, wondering if something had caused them to resonate. Outside the night was clear, the moons had set, and the range was deep asleep. She glanced at the console and the storm alarms. She cursed under her breath. She hadn't had a met reading. The printout showed clouds moving in from the White Sea, some turbulence, but at an altitude that might reach the dominant easterly air current and dissipate. A pattern to watch, to be sure.

She slept uneasily until the first crack of light. Apprehensively she dialed a met printout. The picture wasn't alarming, though cloud cover had increased in depth and speed. A high-pressure area was coming south, but no storm warning was issued for the Bay area. If a storm were making, she'd've had a satellite warning by now.

The continual awareness of something out of kilter made cutting easier. She completed a cut of four large five-sided blacks, had stored all the debris, when the pressure of her subjective anxiety became too intense to continue. Operating on an intuition too powerful to be refused, she slung the cutter over her shoulder, grabbed a carton in each hand, and started back to the sled. Halfway there she heard the hooter and nearly tripped for looking up at the still-cloudless sky above her.

She tapped out an update for the weather. The hooter was only the first warner: a watch-the-weather-picture caution. Everything inside her head was far more alarmed than the Guild's signal. The met displayed a brewing turbulence that could flow either north or south, depending on the low pressure ridge.

She stared at the display, not at all reassured. She did her own calculations. If the very worst occurred, the storm could boil across the tip of the main continent and run across her position in four or five hours, building speed at a tremendous rate once it acquired the impetus of the advancing ridge.

"I thought you were supposed to warn us!" she shouted at the other silent storm-alerts. The hooter had automatically ceased blaring when she had programmed the weather picture. "Four, five hours. That doesn't give me time to cut anything more. Just sit here and stew until you lot wake up to the danger. Isn't anyone analyzing the met patterns? Why all this rigmarole about distant early warnings and weather sensors if they don't bloody work?"

As she vented her tension in a one-sided tirade, she was also rigging her ship for storm-running. The four precious cartons of black crystal were securely webbed in front of the mocking empties. She changed her coverall and realized from the grime on her wrists and ankles that she hadn't bathed since coming to the ranges. She wanted to reappear at the complex looking presentable. A quick wash was refreshing, and she ate a light meal as she did some computations of deviation courses that would disguise the direction from which she came and confuse other Singers called in by the storm. She had just completed what would be a most elaborate break-out when the first of the dead-earnest storm warnings came on.

"About bloody time! I came to that conclusion an hour ago."

Airborne, she skimmed ridge and hollow, heading north at 11 for half an hour. She turned on a western leg for twenty minutes and was starting a southern track when she flipped over a gorge that looked familiar. A blur of orange in the shadows brought to mind Moksoon and his wretched pink crystals. The storm readings were insistent now. She made another pass up the gorge and saw Moksoon bent over his outcrop, two cartons beside him. He ought to have been heading out, not calmly cutting as if he had all day and a mach storm wasn't bowling down.

She came in as quietly as she could, but the grating of her sled runners on the loose rock at the valley bottom warned Moksoon. He charged down the slope, cutter held aggressively. She slapped on the playback, turned up the volume, but he was caterwauling so loudly about Section 49 that he couldn't have heard it.

The wind however had picked up and made it difficult for him to swing and keep his balance, though Killashandra doubted that the infrasonic blade would do her sled much harm. Break his cutter.

"Storm, you addled pink tenor!" She roared out the open window.

Despite the wind scream, she could hear the hooter-buzzer-bell systems of his sled.

"Mach storm on the way. You've got to leave!"

"Leave?" Panic replaced wrath on Moksoon's face. He now heard her ship's klaxons as well as his own. "I can't leave!" The wind was tearing the sound from his mouth, but Killashandra could read his lips. "I've struck a pure vein. I've—" He clamped his mouth shut with caution and had to lean into a particularly strong gust to keep from being knocked over. "I've got to cut just one more. Just one more." He raced up the slope to his site.

Unbelievingly, Killashandra watched him raise his cutter, to tune it in the teeth of a gale. Cursing, Killashandra grabbed up her handlight. Not as sturdy a weapon as she'd've liked, considering the probable denseness of Moksoon's skull, but used with the necessary force in the right spot, it ought to suffice.

As she left her sled, she experienced a taste of what it would be like to be caught in a mach storm in the crystal ranges. Sound, waves of dissonance and harmony, streamed through her head. She covered her ears, but the sound maintained contact through the rock under her feet. The keening wails masked her slithering approach, and Moksoon was too preoccupied with cutting to see anything but the octagon he was excising. Just as she had braced herself to slug him, he laid the cutter down but caught a glimpse of her descending hand and flung himself to the side. She grabbed up his cutter and pelted for his sled, nearer than hers. He'd follow her for that cutter, she was positive. She bounced into his sled, plastered herself against the wall, the brackets digging into her shoulders, wincing against the shrill obligato of Moksoon's unheeded warning devices.

He was wilier than she'd credited him. Suddenly, a strong hand grabbed her left ankle and hauled her leg sideways, a rock coming down to crush her kneecap. But for the fact she still held his cutter, she would have been crippled. She brought the cutter handle up, deflecting the rock, bruising Moksoon's fingers. She pivoted on her captured foot and delivered a second blow to the old man's jaw. He hovered a moment until she thought she'd have to club him again, but it was the wind that supported him, then let him crumple.

Automatically, Killashandra bracketed his cutter. She tapped for a weather printout, which silenced three of the mind-boggling alarms. Glancing to the rear of the sled, she saw that Moksoon had not bothered to web his packed cartons. She did so, ignoring the filth and discarded food that littered the living section. Then she remembered that there were several cartons by his claim.

Luckily, she hadn't any rocky height to negotiate from Moksoon's sled to his claim or she wouldn't have made it back with the heavy cartons. Moksoon showed no signs of reviving. She lugged him into the sled, then deposited him on the couch. He didn't so much as groan. He was alive, though she was revolted by the grease on his neck as she felt for a pulse.

It was then she realized her dilemma. Two ships and one conscious pilot. She tried to rouse Moksoon, but he was completely oblivious, and she couldn't find the medaid kit that contained stimulant sprays.

The alarms attained a new height of distress, and she recognized that time was running out. She couldn't transport all of Moksoon's cargo to her sled. She had four cartons more precious than all of his. There *must* be something in Guild rules about rescue and salvage. She'd got two vouchers for escorting Carrik, so she decided the wind had gotten her wits. She made a battered dash to her own sled, slung her cutter over her shoulder and grabbed two cartons. The warnings in Moksoon's sled had climbed several deafening decibels toward the supersonic, but there was no way she could diminish them until she had taken off.

She staggered back to her sled, which was bouncing now from the gusting wind. She wondered if she could secure her craft, somehow keep it from being flung about the gorge, and decided against wasting the time.

She grabbed her remaining cartons and was glad of the weight to anchor her feet to the ground. She was gasping for breath as she finally closed the door of Moksoon's sled. He still lolled on the couch. She webbed her four cartons and secured her cutter among his empties. She strapped Moksoon tightly to the couch and then took her place at the console.

All sleds had similar control panels, though Moksoon's was much the worse for wear.

Moksoon's claim was a dangerously enclosed area from which to ascend into a wild storm. She fought to keep the vertical, fought again to increase the horizontal to clear the ridge top, then let the wind take the sled, hauling as hard as she could on the yoke toward the west.

The mach-tuned dissonances were worse in the air, and she made a grab for Moksoon's buffer helmet. It was stiff, dusty, and too small, but it blocked the worst of the wind-shriek. She'd not got it on a moment too soon, for the sled behaved like a crazed beast, plunging and diving wildly then sliding sideways. Killashandra learned appreciation of the simulation drills sooner than she would have liked.

It was as well she'd strapped Moksoon down, for he regained consciousness before they'd quite cleared the Milekeys and started raving about pain. She felt quite enough jabbing at her nerve ends through the ear pads.

Moksoon regained unconsciousness after throwing his head against the duralloy wall, so the last hour into the Guild Complex gave her sufficient quiet to ease her own aggravated nerves.

She had reason to be proud as she brought Moksoon's canting sled up over the wind baffles at the complex and landed it conveniently close to the racks. She signaled for medics, and as she pointed them toward Moksoon, one of the hangar personnel grabbed her arm and gestured urgently toward the hangar office. The information that Lanzecki awaited her was reinforced by that message on the green display, blinking imperatively.

Cargo personnel had opened the sled's storage, and now

Killashandra moved to collect her precious cutter and to point out the four cartons which held her blacks.

"Enthor!" she roared at the handlers. "Take these immediately to Enthor!"

Despite their obliging grins and nods, she wasn't sure they understood her urgency. She followed them, but halfway there, someone matched pace with her, tugging angrily at her arm.

"Report to Lanzecki," the hangar officer yelled, pushing her away from Storage. The look in his eyes was not reassuring. "You might at least have saved the *new* sled!"

She jerked her arm free and, leaving the man astonished at her imprudence, ran after her cartons. She saw the first handler just plop his burden down on the stack. She grabbed it and roared at the others to follow her into Sorting.

"Killashandra? Is it you?" a familiar voice asked. Without checking her determined forward march, she saw Rimbol following her, one of her cartons held carefully against his body.

Two absurdities impinged on her thoughts as she rushed into Sorting: Rimbol was unaware of the fortune of black crystal he carried, and he had trouble identifying her.

"Yes, it's me. What's the matter?"

"You haven't looked in a mirror lately, have you?" was Rimbol's reply. He seemed amused as well as surprised. "Don't scowl. You're terrifying, you—you crystal, you!"

"Be careful of that carton," she said, more commanding than she should be of a friend, and Rimbol's welcoming smile faded. "Sorry, Rimbol. I had one helluva time getting in. That bollux Moksoon wouldn't believe a storm was coming and him having trouble standing straight against the gusts."

"You brought another Singer out of the ranges?" Rimbol's eyes widened with incredulity, but whatever he had been about to add was cut off as Killashandra spied Enthor and called his name.

"Yes?" Enthor's query was surprised. He blinked at her uncertainly.

"I'm Killashandra Ree," she said, trying to keep the

irritation out of her voice. She couldn't have changed that much since she'd last seen Enthor. "I've black crystal!"

"Black?"

"Yes, yes. Black! Here!"

"And how were so you fortunate as to find that which eludes so many?" an implacable voice demanded.

Killashandra was setting her carton down on Enthor's table, but the cold, ominous tone paralyzed her. Her throat went dry and her mind numb because no consideration was excuse enough for her to have ignored the Guild Master's summons, to make him seek her out.

"Well, it doesn't surprise *me* that you have," Enthor said, taking the box from her.

Lanzecki's eyes never left hers as he advanced. She let the sorting table support her shaking body and clutched its edge with nerveless fingers. Regulations and restrictions that could be levied against a disobedient member by the Guild Master sprang to her mind far more vividly than the elusive ones about rescue and salvage. His lips were set in a thin, hard line. The slight flare of his nostrils and the quick lift of his chest under the subtle gleam of his shirt confirmed that he had appeared through effort, not magic.

"You could improve on your acute angles," Enthor was saying as he unpacked her triad. "However, the credit is good." Enthor blinked before he peered approvingly at Killashandra. He noticed her immobility, looked around, not unsurprised to see the Guild Master, and back to Killashandra, aware now of the reason for her tension.

"Which is as well for Killashandra Ree," Lanzecki said with deep sarcasm, "since she has not returned in her new sled."

"Moksoon is all right?" Killashandra asked, anything to be able to speak in the face of Lanzecki's fury.

"His head will heal, and he will doubtless cut more rose quartz!"

That Lanzecki's tone was not derisory did not signify. Killashandra understood what was implied. Nor could she break from his piercing stare.

"I couldn't very well *leave* him," she said, the solace of indignation replacing fear. After all, Lanzecki had arranged for Moksoon to shepherd her.

"Why not? He would have shown no compunction in leaving you had the circumstances been reversed."

"But . . . but he was cutting. All the storm warnings were on in his sled. He wouldn't listen. He tried to slice me with his cutter. I had to knock him out before he . . ."

"You could be subject to claim-jumping, Section 49, Paragraph 14," Lanzecki went on irreconcilably.

"What about the section dealing with rescue and salvage?"

Lanzecki's eyelids dropped slightly, but it was Enthor who answered her in a startled voice.

"There are none, my dear. Salvage is always done by the Guild, not a Singer. I would have thought you'd been taught to know what exactly *is* in rules and regs. Ah, now these . . . these are very good indeed. Two a trifle on the thin side."

Enthor had unpacked the quintet. For the first time, Lanzecki's attention was diverted. He shifted his body slightly so that he could see the weighplate. He lifted one eyebrow in surprise, but his lips did not soften with appeasement.

"You may come out of this affair better than you deserve to, Killashandra Ree," Lanzecki said. His eyes still glinted with anger. "Unless, of course, you left behind your cutter."

"I could carry that, and these," she retorted, stung more by his amusement than his anger.

"Let us hope then that Moksoon can be persuaded not to charge you with claim-jumping since you preserved his wreck of a ship, his skin, and his crystal. Gratitude is dependent on memory, Killashandra Ree, a function of the mind that deteriorates on Ballybran. Learn that lesson now!"

Lanzecki swept away from Enthor's table and walked down the long room to the farthest exit, thus emphasizing that he had come on discipline.

CHAPTER 10

Killashandra stayed with Enthor while he tallied her four cartons, though she was hardly aware of what the old Sorter was saying to her. She kept glancing toward the far door where Lanzecki had made his dramatic exit, aware of the surreptitious looks in her direction from other Sorters, aware of an emotion more intense than hatred, emptier than fear.

"Now *that'll* buy you your two sleds." Enthor's words penetrated her self-absorption.

"What?"

"Those black crystals brought you a total of twenty-three thousand credits."

"How much?" Killashandra stared incredulously at the displayed figures, blinking green. "But a sled only costs eight thousand."

"There's the tithe, my dear. Thirty percent does eat a hole in the total. Actually, you have to pay for two sleds, the one you lost and the replacement. Still, 16,100 clear does help."

"Yes, it does." Killashandra tried to sound grateful.

Enthor patted her arm. "You'd best take a good long radiant bath, m'dear. Always helps. And eat." Then he began to package her beautiful black crystal.

She turned away, unexpectedly feeling the separation

from her first experience of crystal. The weight of the cutter made her sag as she slung it to her back. She would take it to be checked in the morning. She estimated she had just enough strength left to get her body back to her quarters and into the radiant bath. She took the nearest door out of the Sorting room, aware marginally that people were still rushing cartons in to Storage, that the howl of the wind was loud at this level even inside the complex. She should be grateful! She was too weary to laugh or snort at her inappropriate choice of word. She got into the lift and its descent, though smooth, made her sink toward the floor. She was able to prevent complete collapse only by hanging on to the support rail.

She wobbled to her room, oblivious to the gaze of those in the Commons. As she walked, the drag of the cutter pulled her to the right, and once she caromed numbly from a doorway.

When she finally raised her hand to her own doorplate, she realized that she still wore the ident wristband. She wouldn't need that anymore, but she hadn't the strength to remove it. As she passed a chair, she dropped her right shoulder, and the cutter slid onto the cushioning. She continued to the tankroom where she stared in dazed surprise at the filling tank. Did her entry into the room trigger the thing? No, it was almost full. Someone must have programmed it. Enthor? Rimbol? Her mind refused to work. She tore at her coverall, then her sweatliner, pulling her boots off with the legs of her coverall, and crawled up the three steps to the platform around the tank. She slid gratefully—that word again—into the viscous liquid, right up to her throat, her weight supported by the radiant fluid. Fatigue and the ache of crystal drained from her body and nerves. In that suspension, she remained, her mind withdrawn, her body buoyed.

Sometime later, the room announced a visitor, and she roused sufficiently to deny entrance. She didn't want to see Rimbol. But the intrusion and the necessity of making a decision aroused her from her passivity. The fluid had provided the necessary anodyne, and she was acutely aware of hunger. She had pulled herself from the tank, the radiant liquid dripping from her body, and was reaching for a wrap when a hand extended the garment to her.

Lanzecki stood there.

"I will not be denied twice!" he said, "though I will allow you couldn't know that it was I at your door."

Surprised at his presence, Killashandra wavered on the edge of the tank, and he immediately held out a steadying hand.

"You can fill tanks and open doors?"

"One can be programmed, and the other was not locked."

"It is now?"

"It is," he said smoothly; his mouth, she quickly noticed, was amused. "But that can be changed."

For a picosecond, she wanted to call his bluff. Then she remembered that he had said she might be luckier than she deserved as Enthor tallied her cut. He had implied she had enough credit not only to buy a new sled but pay off what she already owed the Guild. Lanzecki had remembered the vouchers she still held. With those, she would have just enough. What mattered was that Lanzecki had remembered that margin at a time when he was rightfully infuriated by her disregard of her Guild Master's summons.

"I'm much too tired to change anything." She gathered the toweling about her and extended her hand to him, palm up, summoning a weary smile.

He looked from her smile to her palm, and his lips curved upward. Now he took a step forward. Placing both hands on her slender waist, he swung her down from the tank platform. She expected to be set on her feet. Instead, Lanzecki carried her into the lounge. The spicy aroma of a freshly cooked meal was heady, and she exclaimed with pleasure at the steaming dishes on the table.

"I expected you might be hungry."

Killashandra laughed as Lanzecki deposited her in the chair, and she gestured with the overblown gentility of an opera heroine for him to assume the other seat.

Not that evening or ever did Lanzecki ask her if she had found Keborgen's black crystal, though he had occasions later to refer to her claim. Neither did he ask her any

details of her first trip to the Milekey Ranges. Nor was she
disposed to volunteer any comment. Except one.

Having teased her adroitly, Lanzecki finally gave her the
caress she had been anticipating so long, and the sensation
was almost unbearable.

"Crystal touches that way, too," she said when she could
talk.

"I know," he murmured, his voice oddly rough, and as if
to forestall her reply, he began to kiss her in a fashion that
excluded opportunity.

She awoke alone, as she had expected, and much later
than she had planned, for the time was late evening. She
yawned prodigiously, stretched, and wondered if another
radiant bath would further her restoration. Then her belly
rumbled, and she decided food was the more immediate
concern. No sooner had she dialed for a hot drink than a
message was displayed on her screen for her to contact the
Guild Master when convenient.

She did so promptly before she considered convenience,
expedience, or opportunity.

Her reply was cleared immediately, and her screen produced a visual contact with the Guild Master. He was
surrounded by printout sheets and looked tired.

"Have you rested?" Lanzecki asked. Belatedly, Killashandra activated her own screen. "Yes, you look considerably improved."

"Improved?"

A slight smile tugged at his lips. "From the stress and
fatigue of your dramatic return." Then his expression
changed, and Lanzecki became Guild Master. "Will you
please come to my office to discuss an extraplanetary assignment?"

"Will," not "would," Killashandra thought, sensitive to
key words.

"I'll be there as soon as I've eaten and gotten dressed."
He nodded and broke contact.

As she sipped the last of the drink, she took a long look
at herself in the mirrors of the tankroom. She'd never been
vain about her appearance. She had good strong face
bones, wide cheeks, a high forehead, and thick, well-arched
eyebrows, which she had not narrowed, as the natural em-

phasis made a good stage effect. Her jaw was strong, and she was losing the jowl muscles formed by singing. She slapped at the sides of her chin. No flab. Whatever produced the gaunt aspect of her face was reflected in her body. She noticed how prominent her collarbones were. If her appearance was now an improvement, according to Lanzecki, whatever had she looked like the previous day? Right now, she wouldn't have needed face paint to play Space Hag or Warp Widow.

She found something loose and filmy to wear, with ends that tied about her neck and wrists and a long full skirt. She stood back from the mirrors and did a half turn, startled by her full-length reflection. Something had changed. Just what she couldn't puzzle out; she had to see the Guild Master.

She was almost to the lift shaft when a group emerged from the Commons.

"Killashandra?"

"Rimbol?" Killashandra mocked his surprised query with a light laugh. "You ought to know me!"

Rimbol gave her an odd grin that relaxed into his usual ingenuous smile. Jezerey, Mistra, and Borton were with him.

"Well, you're more like yourself this evening than you were yesterday," Rimbol replied. He scratched his head in embarrassment, grinning ruefully at the others. "I didn't believe Concera when she kept saying singing crystals makes a big change, but now I do."

"I don't think I've changed," Killashandra replied stiffly, annoyed that Rimbol and, by their expressions, the others could perceive what eluded her.

Rimbol laughed. "Well, you've used your mirror"—and he indicated her careful grooming—"but you haven't *seen*."

"No, I haven't."

Rimbol made a grimace of apology for her sharp tone.

"Singers are notorious for their irritability," Jezerey said with an uncordial look.

"Oh, pack that in, Jez," Rimbol said. "Killa *is* just in off the ranges. Is it as bad as it's made out, Killa?" He couched that question in a quiet tone.

"I would have been fine if I hadn't had to deal with Moksoon."

"Or the Guild Master." Rimbol was sympathetic.

"Oh, you stayed on?" Killashandra decided to brazen through that episode. "He was quite right, of course. And I pass on that hard-learned lesson. Save your own sled and skin in the ranges. Will you be around later, Rimbol? I've got to see Lanzecki now." She allowed her voice to drop, expressing dread and looking for sympathy in their expressions. "I'd like to join you later if you're in the lounge."

"Good luck!" Rimbol said, and he meant it. The others waved encouragingly as she entered the lift.

She had much to think about during the short drop, and none of it about her interview with Lanzecki. How could she have changed so much in the past few days just by cutting crystal? Jezerey had never been overly friendly, but she had never been antagonistic. She was annoyed with herself, too, for that offhanded reassurance to Rimbol. "I would have been fine without Moksoon." Yet how could she possibly have explained the experience that had annealed her, confirmed her as a Crystal Singer? Maybe, alone with Rimbol, she would try to explain, forewarn him that once past the curious unpainful agony of the initial cut, there was an elevation to a totally bizarre ecstasy that could only be savored briefly or it overwhelmed mind, nerve, and senses.

She sighed, standing before the door to the Guild Master's office. In the second between the announcement of her presence and the panel's smooth retraction, she remembered how hard Concera had tried to explain some facets of crystal singing. She recalled the odd harsh tone in which Lanzecki had admitted knowledge of the tactile feel of crystal.

"Killashandra Ree." Lanzecki's voice came from the corner of his large office, and she saw him bent over a spotlighted work surface, layers of printout in front of him. He did not look up from his research until she reached him. "Did you have enough to eat?" he asked with more than ordinary courtesy and a close scrutiny of her face.

"I had a high-protein and glucose cereal—" she began

because, as soon as he mentioned eating, she felt hungry again.

"Hmmm. A bowl was all you had time for, I'm sure. You've slept sixteen hours, so you've missed considerable nourishment already."

"I did eat in the ranges. Really I did," she protested as he took her hand and led her to the catering console.

"You've still wit enough to feed yourself, but you can't know how immensely important it is to replenish reserves at this point."

"I won't be able to eat all that." She was appalled at the number and variety of dishes he was dialing.

"I get peckish myself, you know," he said, grinning.

"What happens that I need to eat myself gross?" she asked, but she helped him clear the catering slot of its first deposit, sniffing appreciatively at the enticing mixture of aromas from the platters.

"You'll never see a plump Singer," he assured her. "In your particular case, the symbiont is only just settled into cell tissue. A Milekey transition may be easier on the host, but the spore still requires time to multiply, differentiate, and become systemically absorbed. Here, start with this soup. Weather and other considerations compelled me to direct you into the ranges prematurely as far as the process of your adaptation is concerned." He gave her a sardonic glance. "You may one day be grateful that you had only two days on your claim."

"Actually three. I didn't spend two with that twithead Moksoon. He's utterly paranoid!"

"He's alive," Lanzecki replied succinctly, with sufficient undertone to make the statement both accusation and indictment. "Three days! In ordinary training, you would not have gone out into the ranges until the others were also prepared."

"They won't make it out before the Passover storms now." Killashandra was dismayed. If she had had to wait that long . . .

"Precisely. You were trained, eager and clever enough to precipitate the event."

"And you wanted that black crystal."

"So, my dearling, did you."

The caterer chimed urgently to remind them to clear the slot for additional selections. Lanzecki slapped a hold on the remainder of the programmed order.

"Even with your help, I'll never eat all this," Killashandra said after they had filled the small table and three more dishes remained in the slot.

"Listen to me while you eat. The symbiont will be attenuated after intense cutting. I could see that in your face. Don't talk. Eat! I had to be sure you ate last night, once the radiant fluid had eased your nerves. Your metabolism must be efficient. I would have thought you'd been awakened by hunger a good four hours ago."

"I was eating when I got your message."

He grinned as he inserted a steaming, seeded appetizer into his mouth. He licked his fingers as he chewed, then said, "My message was programmed the moment your caterer was used." He stuffed another piece of appetizer into her mouth. "Don't talk. Eat."

Whatever it was he fed her was exceedingly tasty. She speared another.

"Now, several unexpected elements are in display. One"—and he ate a spoonful of small brilliant green spheres— "you brought in five medium black crystals for which we have received an urgent request." He waved his empty spoon at the printout layers on his desk. "Two, you have no sled, nor can Manufacturing produce a replacement before the Passover storms. Which, by the way, were heralded by that unpredicted blow in the Bay area. Short, hard, but destructive. Even though conjunction occurs over the seas north and east of this continent, Passover is going to be particularly nasty, as it coincides with spring solstice. Weather is generally cyclical on Ballybran, and the pattern which has been emerging coincides with '63 . . . 2863GY, that is—eat, don't gawk. Surely you have wandered through data retrieval, Killashandra, and discovered how long I've been a member. Fuerte cannot have eradicated human curiosity, or you wouldn't be here."

She swallowed as the significance of his qualifying the century occurred to her.

"But not how long you've been Guild Master."

He chuckled at her quick reply, passing a dish of stewed orange-and-green milsi stalks to her. "Excellent for trace minerals. The Passover turbulence will be phenomenal even in terms of Ballybran's meteorological history. Which, I might ' add, goes back further than I do. Don't choke now!" he rose to give her a deft thump between her shoulder blades. "Even the Infirmary level will shake. You, so recently exposed to crystal for the first time, will be severely affected by the stress. I can, as Guild Master, order you off Ballybran," and his face fell into harsh immobile lines, impersonal and implacable. But his mouth softened when he saw her determined expression. "However, I would prefer that you cooperate. The five blacks you brought in are currently, if you'll forgive the pun, being tuned and should be ready for shipment. I would *like* to assign you to take them to the Trundimoux System and install them."

"This duty will provide me with the margin of credit for my future foolishness?"

Lanzecki chuckled appreciatively.

"Think about the assignment while you eat some fried steakbean."

"It is, then, a suggestion?" she asked around a large mouthful of tasty legume.

"It is—now—a suggestion." His face, mouth, and tone were bland. "The storms will soon be hammering the ranges and forcing Singers in. Others would undertake the assignment happily, especially those who haven't cut enough crystal to get off-world at Passover."

"I thought Passover was an incredible spectacle."

"It is. Raw natural forces at their most destructive." A lift to his shoulders suggested that it was a spectacle to which he was inured and yet . . .

"Do *you* leave during Passover?"

He gave her a keen glance, his dark eyes reflecting the spotlights over his work desk.

"The Guild Master is always accessible during Passover." He offered her some lemon-yellow cubes. "A sharpish cheese, but it complements the steakbean."

"Hmmm. Yes, it does."

"Help yourself." He rose and took the next dishes from the catering slot, which had been maintaining them at the appropriate heat. "Will you have something to drink?"

"Yarran beer, please." She had a sudden craving for the taste of hops.

"Good choice. I'll join you."

She glanced at him, arrested by some slight alteration of tone, but his back was to her.

"Rimbol's from Scartine, isn't he?" Lanzecki asked, returning with a pitcher and two beakers. He poured with a proper respect for the head of foam. "He should cut well in the darker shades. Perhaps black, if he can find a vein."

"How could you tell?"

"A question of resonance, also of the degree of adaptation. Jezerey will do lighter blues, pinks, paler greens. Borton will also tend to cut well in the darker. I hope they team up."

"Do you know who will cut what?"

"I am not in a position to imply anything, merely venture an informed guess. After all, the Guild has been operating for over four hundred years galactic, all that time collecting and collating information on its members. It would show a scandalous want of probity not to attempt more than merely a determination of probability of adjustment to Ballybran spore symbiosis."

"You sound like Borella's come-all-ye pitch," Killashandra replied.

Lanzecki's lips twitched in an amusement that was echoed by the sparkle in his brilliant eyes. "I do believe I'm quoting—but whom, I've forgotten. How about some pepper fruit? Goes with the beer. I've ordered some ices to clear the palate. A very old and civilized course but not one taken with beer." As he passed her the plate, the tangy scent of the long, thin furry fingers did tempt her to try one. "As I was saying, by the time candidates are through the Shankill checkpoint, as many variables as can be resolved have been." He began to pile empty plates and dishes into one untidy stack, and she realized that while he had sampled everything, she had eaten far more. Yet she didn't feel uncomfortably full. "You ought to have been shown the probability graph," he said, frowning as he rose. He tossed the discards deftly into the waste chute before pausing yet again at the catering slot.

"We were." She nibbled at another pepper fruit while wondering why his face showed no trace of aging. He wasn't singing crystal anymore, but that was the ostensible reason for the specious youthfulness. "We were told nothing about individual capabilities or forecasts."

"Why should you be? That would create all sorts of unnecessary problems." He set two dishes of varicolor sherbets, two wine glasses, and a frosty bottle on the table.

"I couldn't eat another thing."

"No? Try a spoonful of the green. Very settling to the stomach and clears the mouth." He seated himself and poured the wine. "The one critical point is still adaptation. The psychological attitude, Antona feels, rather than the physical. That space worker, Carigana, should not have died." Lanzecki's expression was one of impersonal regret. "We can generally gauge the severity of transition and are prepared for contingencies."

Killashandra thought of the smooth disappearances of Rimbol and Mistra during the night, of meditechs collecting Jezerey before she had fallen to the plascrete. She also recalled her indignation over "condition satisfactory."

"How do you like the wine?"

"Does it have to be so mechanical?"

"The wine?"

"The whole process."

"Every care is taken, my dear Killashandra," and Lanzecki's tone reminded her incontrovertibly that he was Guild Master and that the procedure she wished to protest was probably of his institution.

"The wine's fine."

"I thought you'd appreciate it." His response was as dry as the wine. "Not much is left to chance in recruiting. Tukolom may be a prosy bore, but he has a curious sensitivity to illness which makes him especially effective in his role as tutor."

"Then it was known that I—"

"You were not predicted." He used the slightest pause

between each word for emphasis, and raising his glass to her, took a sip.

"And . . ." It was not coquetry in Killashandra that caused her to prompt him but the strongest feeling that he had been about to add a rider to that surprise comment.

"And certainly not a Milekey, nor resonant to black crystal. Perhaps"—and his quick reply did, she was positive, mask thoughts unspoken—"we should initiate handling crystal with recruits as soon as possible. But"—and he shrugged—"we can't program convenient storms which require all-member participation."

"Rimbol said you couldn't have planned that storm."

"Perceptive of him. How did those ices go down?"

"They went." She was surprised to find dish, bottle, and wine glasses empty.

"Fine. Than we can start on more."

"More?" But already a pungent spicy odor emanating from the caterer had sharpened her appetite. "I'll bloat."

"Very unlikely. Had you gone out with your class, this is exactly what would have been served on your return from the ranges. Yarran beer, since you have cultivated a taste for it, would be appropriate to wash down the spicefish." He dialed for more. "Beer has also, for millennia, had another normal effect on the alimentary system."

His comment, delivered in a slightly pompous tone, made her laugh. So she ate the spicefish, drank the beer, responded to certain natural effects of it, and, at one point, realized that Lanzecki had coaxed, diverted, bullied her into continuously consuming food for nearly three hours. By then, her satiation was such that when Lanzecki casually repeated his suggestion that she install the black crystal, she agreed to consider it.

"Is *that* why you've stuffed and drunken me?" she demanded, sitting erect to feign indignation.

"Not entirely. I have given you sufficient food to restore your symbiont and enough drink to relax you." He smiled away her defective grammar and any accusation of coercion. "I do not wish you to endure Passover's mach storms. You might be ten levels underground, buffered by plascrete a meter thick, but the resonances cannot be"—he paused, averted his face, searching for the precise word—

"escaped." He turned back to her, and his eyes, dark and subtly pained, held hers, his petition heightened by the uncharacteristic difficulty in expressing his concern.

"Do you ever . . . escape?"

The delicate bond of perception between them lasted some time, and then, leaning across the table, he kissed her question away.

He escorted her back to her quarters, made certain she was comfortable in the bedroom, and suggested that in the morning she take her cutter down to be checked and stored, that if she was interested in weather history, she could review other phenomenal Passover storms in the met control the next day at eleven and see something of Storm Control tactics.

The next morning, she reflected during her shower and notably hearty breakfast on Lanzecki's extraordinary attentions to her, sensual as well as Guild. She could see why Lanzecki, as Guild Master, would exploit her eagerness to get into the ranges and secure Keborgen's priceless claim. She'd succeeded. Now, in an inexplicable reverse, Lanzecki wanted her off-planet. Well, she could decide this morning when she watched the weather history, whether that was the man or the Guild Master talking. She rather hoped it was the former, for she did like Lanzecki the man and admired the Guild Master more than any man she had so far encountered.

What had he meant when he said she was unpredicted? Had that been flattery? The Guild Master indulging a whimsy? Not *after* he had assisted her in getting out into the ranges; not *after* she had successfully cut black crystal? Especially, not after Lanzecki had very forcefully defined to her in the Sorting Room the difference between the man and the Guild Master.

She winced at the memory. She had deserved that reprimand. She could also accept his solicitousness for her health and well-being. He wanted more black crystal—if that was his motive. All right, Killashandra Ree, she told herself firmly, no section or paragraph of the Charter of the Heptite Guild requires the Master to explain himself to a member. Her ten years at Fuerte Music Center had taught Killashandra that no one ever does a favor without expecting a return. Lanzecki had also underscored self-preservation and self-interest with every object lesson that was presented.

She didn't really want to leave Ballybran, though it was probably true that she could use the credit margin of an off-world assignment. She looked up the payment scale; the credit offered was substantial. Perhaps it would be better to take the assignment. But that would mean leaving Lanzecki, too. She stared grimly at her reflection in the mirror as she dressed. Departing for that reason might also be wise. Only she'd better mend her fences with Rimbol.

Grateful that she would not have the additional expense of replacing the cutter or facing the Fisher with that request, she brought the device up to Engineering and Training. As she entered the small outer office, she saw two familiar figures.

"I'm not going to be caught here again during Passover," Borella was saying to the Singer Killashandra remembered from the shuttle.

"Doing your bit again on recruits, Borella?" the man asked, negligently shoving his cutter across the counter and ignoring the technician's sour exclamation.

"Recruits?" Borella stared blankly.

"Remember, dear"—and the man's voice rippled with mockery—"occasionally, you pass the time briefing the young hopefuls at Shankill station."

"Of course, I remember," Borella said irritably. "I can do better than that this time, Olin," she went on smugly. "I cut greens in octave groups. Five of them. Enough for an Optherian organ. Small one, of course, but you know that *that* addiction will last a while."

"I'm rather well off, too, as it happens." Olin spoke over her last sentence.

Borella murmured something reassuring to him as she handed over her cutter to the technician, but showed a shade more concern for the device. Then she linked her arm through Olin's. As they turned to leave, Killashandra nodded politely to Borella, but the woman, giving Killashandra's cutter a hard stare, walked past with no more sign of recognition than tightening her clasp on Olin's forearm.

"Of course, there are those unfortunate enough to have to stay here." Her drawl insinuated that Killashandra would be of that number. "Have you seen Lanzecki lately, Olin?" she asked as they left the room.

For a moment, Killashandra was stunned by the double insult, though *how* Borella would have known where the Guild Master spent his time was unclear. She resisted the insane urge to demand satisfaction from Borella.

"Are you turning that cutter in or wearing it?" A sour voice broke through her resentment.

"Turning it in." She handed the cutter to the Fisher carefully, wishing she didn't have to encounter him as well.

"Killashandra Ree? Right?" He wasn't looking at her but inspecting the cutter. "You can't have used this much," and he peered suspiciously at handle and blade casing. "Where'd you damage it?"

"I didn't. I'm turning it in."

The Fisher was more daunting than Borella and her rudeness.

"You could have left it in your sled, you know," he said, his tone not quite so acerbic now that he had assured himself that one of his newest cutters had not been misused. "No one else can use it, you know," he added, obviously making allowance for her ignorance.

She was not about to admit to anyone that she had lost the sled.

"I'm going off-planet for Passover," she said and belatedly realized that he had no such option.

"Go while you can, when you can," he said gruffly but not unkindly. Then he turned and disappeared into his workroom.

As she made her way back to the lift, Killashandra supposed she ought to be relieved that someone remembered her. Possibly the Fisher was able to associate her with a device he had so recently crafted. Or perhaps it was common knowledge through the Guild that Lanzecki had berated a new Singer.

She shouldn't let the encounter with Borella rankle her. The woman had inadvertently confirmed Lanzecki's advice. Furthermore, if Moksoon could not remember Killashandra from moment to moment, how could she fault Borella?

How long did it take for a Singer's memory to disintegrate? Killashandra must learn to overcome habits and values acquired on Fuerte in the Music Center. There one sought to put people under obligation so they could be called in as support for this role or that rehearsal room, to form a trio or quartet, throw a party on limited credit, all the myriad arrangements that require cooperation, good will, and . . . memory of favors past. As Lanzecki had pointed out, "Gratitude depends on memory." The corollary being "memory lasts a finite time with a Singer." The only common bond for Crystal Singers was the Guild Charter and its regulations, rules, and restrictions—and the desire to get off Ballybran whenever one could afford that privilege.

Carigana shouldn't have died? Now why did that come to mind, Killashandra wondered as she stepped out of the lift at Meteorology. According to the ceiling-border message panel, the viewing was already in progress in the theater. As she hesitated, another lift, this one full of people, opened its door, and she accompanied the group to their mutual destination.

The theater was semidark and crowded, people standing along the walls when all seating was occupied. On the wide-angle screen, cloud patterns formed and reformed with incredible speed. At one point, Killashandra saw Rimbol's face illumined; beside him were Borton and Jezerey. She recognized other members of Class 895 and the weather man who had taken them to the sensor station. The turbulence of the storm was not audible. Instead a commentator droned on about pressure, mach-wind velocities, damage, rain fall, snow, sleet, dust density, and previous Passover tempests while a print display under the screen kept pace with his monologue. Killashandra managed to find space against the far wall and looked over the engrossed audience for Lanzecki's face. She hoped he hadn't made his offer of the off-planet trip to anyone else. If he was being magnanimous, surely he would also give her first refusal.

Then she became caught up in the storm visuals, thinking at first they must have been accelerated—until she compared wind velocities and decibel readings. She was aghast at the fury of the storm.

"The major Passover storm of 2898," voice and print

informed viewers, "while not as severe or as damaging as that of 2863, also formed in the northeast, during spring solstice, and when Shilmore was over the Great Ocean in advance of Shanganagh and Shankill. The inauspicious opposition of the two nearest planets will emphasize the violence of this year's storm. Seeding, improved emulsions, and the new wave disruptor off the coasts of Buland and Hoyland should prevent the tsunami drive across the ocean which caused such widespread havoc on the South Durian continent."

The screen switched frequently from satellite pictures to planetary weather stations where the wind shifts were marked by waves of debris flung in vertical sheets. Killashandra fell into that mesmerized state that can befuddle the mind, and for one hideous second she almost heard windshriek. A particularly frenzied cross-current of detritus shattered the trance by inducing motion nausea. She hastily left the theater, looking for a toilet. The moment she reached the soundproof stability of the quiet corridor, her nausea waned, only to be replaced by the gnawing of severe hunger.

"I had breakfast," she said through clenched teeth. "I had plenty of breakfast."

She entered a lift, wondering just how long the postrange appetite remained critical. She punched for the infirmary level and swung into the same anteroom she had entered barely four weeks before.

No one was on duty.

"Is anyone here?" she demanded acidly.

"Yes," the verbal address system responded.

"I don't want you. I'd like to see—"

"Killashandra Ree?" Antona walked through the right-hand door panel, an expression of surprise on her face. "You can't have been injured?" The chief medic took a small diagnostic unit from her thigh pocket and advanced toward Killashandra.

"No, but I'm starving of the hunger."

Antona laughed, slipping the instrument back into her pocket. "Oh, I do apologize, Killashandra. It's not the least bit funny! For you." She tried to compose her face into a more severe expression. "But you put it aptly. You're "starving of the hunger" for several reasons. While the others were convalescing from the fever, we could administer nutritional assists. You had no fever, and then you were sent out to cut. The appalling hunger, you realize, is quite normal. No, I see you don't, and you look hungry. I'm just about to have a morning snack. The lounge will be deserted, as everyone's peering at last year's storms. Join me? I can think of nothing more boring than to be compelled to eat mountains and gulp them down in solitary confinement. You did remember, of course"—and by this time Antona had guided her back to the lift and, at their destination, down the length of the lounge to a catering area as she talked—"that the symbiont takes twenty weeks to establish itself thoroughly. We have never managed to find out the average spore intake per diem since so much depends on the individual's metabolism. Now, let's see . . ." Antona pressed menu review. "You don't mind if I order for you? I know exactly how to reduce that hunger and restore the symbiont." Antona waited for Killashandra's agreement and then toured the catering area, dialing several selections at each post before signaling Killashandra to take a tray and start collecting the items delivered.

Food enough for the entire final year student complement of the Music Center presently covered two large tables, and Killashandra ravenously started to eat.

"If it's any encouragement, your appetite will slack off, especially after the symbiont has prepared for Passover." She smiled at Killashandra's groan. "Don't worry. You'll have no appetite at all during the height of Passover—the spore buries itself in crevices." Antona smiled. "In the Life lab, we have rock crabs and burrow worms over four hundred years old." Antona's grin became wry. "I don't suppose that aspect of Ballybran's ecology figured in your orientation. There isn't much life on this mudball, but what there is lives in symbiotic relation to the spore. That's how it keeps itself alive, by increasing the survival mechanisms of whatever host it finds. It behooves us, the new dominant life form, to study the indigenous."

As she ate, Killashandra found Antona's ramblings more interesting than Tukolom's lectures. It did cross her mind that Antona might just be indulging in the luxury of a captive audience. Antona was not lazy with fork and spoon, so her "morning snack" must have answered a real need if not as urgent as Killashandra's.

"I keep trying"—and Antona emphasized that word—"to correlate some factor, or factors, which would once and for all allow us to recruit without anxiety." She paused and looked with unfocused eyes to one corner of the dining area. "I mean, I knew what I was to do before I came here, but if I had made the complete adjustment, I'd've been required to sing crystal." Antona made a grimace of dislike, then smiled radiantly. "The prospect of having all the time in the world to delve into a life form and carry through a research program was such a gift—"

"You didn't want to be a Crystal Singer?"

"Shards and shades, girl, of course not. There's more to life here than that."

"I had the impression, that crystal singing was the function of this planet."

"Oh, it is," and Antona's agreement rippled with laughter. "But the Crystal Singers could scarcely function without support personnel. More of us than you, you know. Takes five and three-quarters support staff to keep a Singer in the ranges. Furthermore, the Guild doesn't have the time or the facilities to train up members in every skill needed. There are plenty of people from the Federated Sentient Planets quite willing to risk adaptation and the possibility of having to sing crystal to come here in other capacities."

"I'm a little confused . . ."

"I shouldn't wonder, Killashandra. You do come from Fuerte, and that conservative government had off notions about self-determination. I did wonder how you came to be recruited, though you are one of our nicer surprises." Antona patted Killashandra's arm reassuringly. "The Fuertans we've had in previous decades also made good hosts." Suddenly, Antona frowned, eying Killashandra speculatively. "I really must run your scans again. I've developed five separate evaluation tests, two at the primary level, which, if I say so myself"—and Antona smiled modestly—"have increased the probability figures by 35%."

"I didn't think the Guild was permitted active recruiting," Killashandra said, doggedly returning to that blithe comment.

Antona looked startled. "Oh, nothing *active*. Certainly less blatant than service programs. The FSP definitely frowns on any sort of conditioning or coercion due to the specific adaptation, you see. That's a direct contradiction of the freedom of movement in the FSP Charter. Of course, when FSP recruits, no one dares complain but it's common knowledge what Service people do." She emitted a sort of giggle. "Freedom of movement, indeed. Most good citizens of the FSP never leave or want to leave their home worlds, but they have to be *able* to do so according to FSP, and that forces us to use the Shankill clearing point."

"Don't you mind being restricted to this planet?"

"Why should I?" Antona did not appear to be resigned.

"Singers seem very keen to get off Ballybran," Killashandra said, but her mind was chaotic, remembering Carigana's intransigence, the farce of the Shankill Moon Recruitment, Rimbol's passing his "preliminaries," Carigana and her "trap," the way Killashandra found herself reacting to the suspicion that Antona had confirmed.

"Singers *should* leave Ballybran whenever possible," she said, completely sincere and much at her ease. "It's a tense, demanding profession, and one should be able to . . . escape . . . from one's work to completely different surroundings."

"Escape." That was the verb Lanzecki had used. "Do you escape *your* work Antona?"

"Me? Of course. My work is in the Infirmary and the labs. I have the whole planet to roam and the moons if I wish a change of view."

"Even at Passover?"

Antona chuckled indulgently at Killashandra's jibe. "Well, everyone holes up during Passover. Or gets off the planet if possible." She leaned over to touch Killashandra's arm. "For your own sake, I wish you hadn't cut so near to Passover, but you can be sure I'll help you all I can."

"Why should I need help?" Killashandra had no trouble affecting innocent surprise. "I've only cut once."

"The most dangerous cut of them all. I'm really surprised that Lanzecki permitted it. He's *so* careful about his new Singers. I *had* to pass you over to training, my dear. No point at all in keeping you with sick people. But this Passover is the most inconvenient one, and it *will* be ages before the weather settles and damage can be cleared. I suppose Lanzecki wanted to get as much crystal cut as possible when he could. Of course, repair won't concern you as a Singer. You'll be sent out as soon as possible to check your claims for storm alteration."

"What will happen because I have cut crystal once?"

"Oh, dear." Antona inhaled deeply and then exhaled on a short, exasperated breath. "I will blather on. Very well, then, I'd have to tell you soon, anyhow. It's only I don't like to alarm people unnecessarily."

"You have unless you come to the point."

"You've been told that storms in the Crystal Ranges are lethal because the winds whip resonance out of the mountains that produce sensory overload. During Passover, the entire place, right down to its core, I sometimes feel, quivers—a noise, a vibration, multiple sonics are formed and transmitted which cannot be"—Antona gave another shrug of helplessness—"escaped. We'll sedate you, and you can be harnessed safely in a radiant tub in the infirmary, which has special shielding. Every possible care will be taken."

"I see."

"No, you'll hear. That's worse. Now eat. Actually, at your stage, a surfeit of food is the best cushion I could prescribe. Think of the sedation as hibernation; the food is protection."

Killashandra applied herself to the untouched dishes, while Antona silently and slowly finished her last portion.

"Do the others go through this, too?" Killashandra flicked her hand at the array of plates.

"Oh, we all start eating quantities now."

"Will the others have to be sedated and—"

"They'll be uncomfortable, but so will anyone with hearing—and quite a number who are in other respects clinically deaf hear storm resonance. We provide maskers. The white noise relieves the temporary tinnitus caused by turbulence. We really do try to help."

"I'm sure you do."

"Small comfort, you may think, but all things are relative. Just read the early history of the Guild and the members' comments. Oh, dear, I don't want to be caught here." Antona's hasty rising caused Killashandra to look around. People were streaming in from the lifts. "I'll just slip out the back. You finish your meal!" She pointed imperatively at the remaining dishes and then retreated into a dimmer area of the Commons.

Killashandra finished the milsi stalks and regarded the final dish of nut-covered cubes. People were lining up at the catering areas, the first serving themselves with generous trays. So she wasn't the only hungry one.

"*Here* she is!" Rimbol's delighted cry startled her. She twisted in the chair and saw the Scartine. Mistra, Jezerey, Borton, and Celee were close behind him. "I told you I saw her at the storm scan. You get hungry or something?" His eyes bright with mischief, Rimbol began to count the empty plates.

"You must have cut a lot of crystal to afford all that," Jezerey commented. Her eyes were unfriendly.

"Antona's orders. I didn't have a convalescence like you lot, so I'm eating for two now."

"Yes, but you got out into the ranges, and we're stuck here!" Jezerey was almost savage. Borton shook her arm.

"Cut that, Jez. Killa didn't do it to spite you, you know." Borton looked across to Killa, his eyes entreating.

"Yes, you did get out into the ranges," Mistra said in her soft voice, "and I'd very much appreciate it, Killashandra, if you'd tell us what actually does happen when you cut. I've got the awfullest notion that they don't tell us all, for all they do tell."

"Here, get rid of the debris"—Rimbol was shoveling dishes and plates together—"and someone order beer and things. Then Killashandra can divulge trade secrets." ·

Killashandra was not in a confessional mood, but the mute appeal in Mistra's brown eyes, the wary concern in Rimbol's, and Borton's stiff, blank expression could not be denied by a classmate, no matter what doctrine of self-preservation Lanzecki was preaching. Jezerey would find her own level; that was certain. Rimbol, Mistra, and Borton were a different matter.

Celee returned then with pitchers and beakers. "Look, since singing isn't my trade, why don't I just shuttle food for you?" he asked good-naturedly. He winked at Killashandra to emphasize his indifference to the outcome of his adaptation.

Orders were given him, and as he left, complaining that his back would be broken, the others settled at the table and looked expectantly at Killashandra.

"Most of what happens is explained," Killashandra began, not knowing precisely how to describe the phenomenon.

"Theory is one thing. Where does it differ from practice?" Mistra asked gently.

"She doesn't say much but she gets to the point," Rimbol noted while raising his eyes in comic dismay.

Killashandra smiled gratefully at Mistra.

"Those storm simulation flights—the real thing can be worse. I didn't cut squarely for all the practice I had retuning soured crystal. I suppose your hands get stronger, but don't be surprised if your first block has a reptilian outline." She was rewarded with a chuckle from Rimbol, who clowned with an exaggerated wriggle of his torso. "You know you've got to be shepherded into the ranges by some experienced Singer? Well, keep one fact perfectly clear: he or she is liable to forget from moment to moment that you are legally supposed to be with him. Mine damned near sliced my leg off. Just keep the tape playing on repeat so he can't forget it. Talk to him all the time, keep yourself in his sight, especially after he's just cut crystal . . ."

"Yes, yes, we've been told that. But when you find crystal . . ." Jezerey interrupted abruptly.

Killashandra looked at her coolly. "When" the girl said. "It's if, not when—"

"But you found crystal. Black crystal," Jezerey began indignantly.

"Shut up, Jez." Borton pressed his fingers warningly into her shoulder, but she shrugged off his hold.

"The unexpected starts when you cut your own crystal. You tap for the note on the face and then tune the cutter and then . . ." Killashandra was back in the fault, the first black segment, uneven cut line and all, weighing in her palms, dazzling her with its slow change in sunlight from transparency to the black matte of the thermally responsive crystal, losing herself in the memory of that shimmering resonance, feeling the incredible music in her blood and bones . . .

An insistent tugging on her sleeve finally broke her trance.

"Killa, are you all right? Shall I get Antona? Killa?" Rimbol's urgent and anxious questions brought her to dazed awareness of her present position. "You've been away for—"

"Six minutes, four seconds," Borton added, tipping his wrist to see the display.

"What?"

"What? she says"—Rimbol turned to the others with a teasing manner—"when she's been visiting her claim on the sly. Look, friends, no visible means of contact and yet our fair lady— Does it truly take that kind of a hold on you, Killa?" He dropped his antic pose and touched her gently on the arm, his face concerned.

"Well, I didn't think it could get me sitting here with my friends, but this advice I will freely give you, having just demonstrated. Cut, and pack! If you don't, you may stand there like I just was and commune with your crystal until the storm breaks over you."

"Communing with crystal!" Jezerey was impatient, skeptical.

"Well, it might not happen to you." Killashandra tried to speak mildly, but Jezerey aggravated her. "Got your sled yet?" she asked Rimbol.

"Yes . . ." Rimbol said.

"But we're not allowed to use them," Jezerey finished, glaring at Killashandra.

"Which might be just as well, considering your performance on the simulator," Borton said.

"So crystal singing is really addictive? How fast is the habit formed?" Rimbol was off in a seriocomic vein to lighten the tension that was developing. "Can it be broken? Is it profitable?"

"Yes, fast, no, and yes," Killashandra responded. "Don't let me inhibit your enjoyment of your meal." She rose quickly, keeping Rimbol from rising by a restraining hand on his shoulder. "See you tonight here?"

She hardly waited for his answer, for she had seen a figure entering the Commons at the far end, moving with Lanzecki's unmistakable stride. She walked to intercept him.

He was Guild Master, she realized, as he scanned the faces in the lounge. He barely paused as she reached him.

"I'd like that assignment."

"I thought you would."

No more than that and they had passed each other, he for the catering area and she for the lifts.

CHAPTER 11

It was a relief to be back in her quarters. Somehow the absurdity of the bizarre, triatmospheric wall-screen restored to her a sense of the absurd. Her attempt to verbalize her experience of crystal cutting to her friends and its aftermath disturbed her. How could memory, even of such an ecstatic moment, dominate mind and body so? She had broken that first communion with the crystal block by packing it. Or had she? And whom could she ask? Was addiction why it was so easy for a Singer to lose the data retrieval function of the mind?

Had she hesitated over Lanzecki's offer because she actually didn't want to be far from the ranges? She remembered then the longing in Borella's voice to return to the ranges when her wound had healed. On the other hand, Borella could now not wait to get off the planet.

The ambivalence, Killashandra decided, could be explained. Oddly enough, it was analogous to having the starring role in a large company. The applause could be the crystal singing in your hand, fresh from the vein, stimulating, ecstatic. The same emotional high every time you cut, until body and mind were exhausted by the clamor, the concentration. The thrall of crystal confounded by the urgent need of rest and relief.

She had seated herself by the computer keyboard, motivated to record some of her reflections. The automatic
time display winked the change of hour. Even thinking
about crystal took enormous hunks of time. She'd been
back in her room more than two hours.

Briskly sitting upright, she keyed for the original entry
she had made and listened dispassionately to her voice
rehearsing the few facts she had entered. Then she tapped
the record tab.

"I found an abandoned black crystal vein and cut with
success. The trick with crystal is to pack it away before the
song gets to you in the sun. I lost my sled trying to save old
Moksoon. A waste of a good sled. Lanzecki is generous,
and I shall be installing the five interlocking segments I cut
in the Trundimoux System. That way I avoid Passover
storms which are expected to be unusually violent."

She played back the terse synopsis of her last two weeks.
Would the bones of experience remind her of the degree
and emotional heights at some later time? She sniggered at
her own pretentiousness. Well, she never had considered
herself any sort of a playwright.

As she leaned back in the console chair, she became
aware of rumbling in her belly.

"Not again!"

To deny the stimulus of hunger, she determinedly dialed
a furniture catalog though she had nothing to put on
tables or shelves since she had hung her lute on the wall.
She thought of playing the instrument which she hadn't
done in a long time, but the E string broke the moment she
turned the pin. Very carefully, she replaced the lute. Then,
clenching her teeth, she made for the caterer in angry
strides to assuage her unacceptable appetite.

She was dialing vigorously when the communit buzzed.

"Lanzecki here."

"Are you linked to my catering dial?"

"It is not coincidence. Guild Masters are allowed to eat
when their daily duties permit. May I join you?"

"Yes, of course." She sounded as genuinely welcoming
as she could after her facetious greeting.

Lanzecki was, she supposed, as much a victim to pre-

Passover appetite as anyone else. Nor did she suppose him
to be exploiting her by conveniently dispatching her off-
world. Or . . . taking the cup of protein broth she had
dialed as Lanzecki's call came through, she went to the
console and checked with Marketing. The display confirmed that the Trundimoux order for a five-place communications system utilizing black-crystal components had
been received five days before. The order was priority rated
by the FSP sector chief. She returned to the caterer and
dialed enticing food for a tired, hungry man.

And it was Lanzecki the man who entered her apartments as she was vainly trying to squeeze plates, platters,
and pitchers onto the limited surface of her table. She really
ought to have got in more furniture.

"I started," she said, waving her soup. "I didn't think
you'd mind." She handed him a steaming cup.

"Nor do I." As he smiled, the tension lines around his
eyes and mouth eased.

"I had a morning snack with Antona after hunger overcame me during the storm scan," she said as he seated
himself, stretching out his legs.

"She undoubtedly reassured you that we're all eating
heartily at this moment."

"She ate a lot, too."

Lanzecki laughed. "Don't worry. You'll have no appetite
during Passover."

"But I won't be here."

"The instinct operates independently of your physical
whereabouts. Especially, I regret to inform you, when your
transition was so recent."

"So long as I'm not gorging like this while I'm installing
the crystals." Some planets, particularly new ones like the
Trundimoux system with limited food supplies, might consider a hearty appetite unbecoming.

"No, more likely you'll be sleeping it all off." He finished
his soup and seemed more interested in picking out his
next item. "Tomorrow, Trag will instruct you in installation procedures. We had a secondary communication from
the Trundimoux giving us the disposition of the five units.
I understand that the kindly call them Trundies; the informed style them the Moux."

"The what?" Killashandra demanded on a laugh, for she couldn't see herself using either nickname.

"Two crystals will be installed on mobile mining stations. Trundimoux has three asteroid belts. That's how they can afford black crystal." Lanzecki snorted. "They've fortunes in ore whirling about, waiting to be grappled. The third unit is to be on the one habitable planet and one each on the large satellites of the gas and the ice planets. Trundimoux mining operations have been seriously hampered by lack of real-time communications, so they mortgaged half a belt and, I expect, will discharge that indebtedness in short order. Originally, the system was exploited merely for the asteroid ores, with several multi-hulks hauling the metal to the nearest manufacturing system—Balisdel, I think it is. The Balisdelians got greedy, Trundimoux miners rebelled, settled the better planet and one of the outer moons. In less than seventy-five years, they're a going concern."

"With money enough for black-crystal communications."

"They'd already a linkage with Balisdel and two other systems, but this will be their own internal link. Yarran beer?" Lanzecki rose to dial the order.

Killashandra laughed. "Who drank Yarran beer before Rimbol got here? Besides you."

"The discovery was by no means original with me, either. Yarran beer is as close to addictive as anything can be for us."

There was a heaviness about Lanzecki this evening, Killashandra thought. It wasn't fatigue, for he moved as easily as ever for a man of his build.

"I'd forgotten how pleasant the taste is," he went on, returning with a pitcher and two beakers.

"Is this Passover going to be that bad?" she asked.

Lanzecki took a long draught of the beer before he answered, but his eyes were twinkling, and his mouth fell into an easier line.

"We always plan for the worst and generally are not disappointed. The challenge thus presented by each new Passover configuration is irresistible, forces that are changeless and changing, as unpredictable as such natural phenomena are."

Killashandra was startled by his unexpected philosophizing and wondered if she had been wrong about his mood.

"You actually enjoy this!"

"Hmmm. No—'enjoy' is not the appropriate word. Stimulated, I think, would be more accurate." He was teasing her. His lips told her that. Teasing, but something more, something deeper, the element that caused the heaviness about him. "Stop thinking and eat. I've ordered up a particular delicacy which I hope you'll enjoy, too. Catering goes to great pains at this time of Ballybran's cycle, and we must respond."

Tonight, his appetite equaled hers as they sampled the marvels of taste and texture that had been conjured from the cuisines of all the elegant and exotic worlds in the Federation. Lanzecki knew a great deal about food and promised her that one day he would personally prepare a meal for her from raw produce to finished dish.

"When eating is not a necessity, as it is now, but can be enjoyed," and his eyes twinkled at the repetition of that word "in complete *leisure*."

"We're not at leisure now?"

"Not completely. As soon as I have satisfied my symbiotic self, I must meet with the storm technicians again."

She suppressed an irrational disappointment that their dinner was not a prelude to another loving night.

"Thank you, dear heart," he said.

"Thank me? For what?"

"For being . . . aware."

She stared at Lanzecki for a long moment.

"You're certain telepathy is not in the symbiotic . . ."

"Absolutely not!" Lanzecki's assurance was solemn, but she wasn't sure about his mouth.

Killashandra rapidly catalogued some of her responses to him and sighed.

"Well, I am sorry you're not staying!"

Lanzecki laughed as he reached for her hand and kissed it lightly. Not light enough so that she didn't respond to his touch.

"I have never intended to invade your privacy, Killashandra, by watching the shift and flow of your thoughts and emotions. I enjoy them. I enjoy you. Now" —and he rose purposefully—"if it were anything but storm tactics . . ." He kissed her palm again and then strode swiftly from the room.

She let her hand fall back to her lap, Lanzecki's graceful compliment echoing through her mind. Quite one of the nicest she had ever been paid.

Oddly enough, that he had been invading a Fuertan's treasured privacy, once her most defended possession, did not distress Killashandra. If Lanzecki continued to "enjoy" what he saw. She took a long swallow of beer. How much she had changed since that aimless, aching ride on the pedestrian way to Fuerte's spaceport! How much of the change was due to her "symbiotic self?" That, too, had been an invasion of privacy to which she had, before officialdom of the FSP, agreed.

Now that she had held crystal, vibrant in the palm of her hand, light and sound coruscating off the sun-warmed quartz, she felt no regrets for loss of privacy, no regrets for an invasion that had been entrance into a new dimension of experience.

She laughed softly at her whimsy. She finished the beer. She was sleepy and satiated, and tomorrow would be a wearying day. She hoped that Trag did not get reports from Enthor on the raggedness of her first cuttings.

The next morning, after a sturdy breakfast, she reported to Trag in the cutting room. Other members of Class 895 were already busy under the supervision of Concera and another Guild member. Killashandra greeted Concera and smiled at the others.

Trag jerked his head to a side door, and she followed him. She experienced a double shock, for there on the work table amid installation brackets and pads were five black crystals. And she didn't respond to their presence at all!

"Don't worry!" Trag picked up the nearest one and tossed it negligently at her.

She opened her mouth to scald him with an oath when

the object reached her hands and she knew it wasn't black crystal.

"Don't you ever frighten me that way again!" Fury was acid in her belly and throat.

"Surely you didn't think we'd risk the black in practice." Trag had enjoyed startling her.

"I'm too new at this game to know what is risked," she replied, getting her anger under control. She hefted the block in her hand, wanting more than anything else to loft it right back at Trag.

"Easy now, Killashandra," he said, raising a protective hand. "You knew it wasn't black crystal the moment you walked into the room!"

The coolness in Trag's voice reminded her that he was a senior Guild member.

"I've had enough surprises in the ranges without having to encounter them here, too, Trag." As she controlled panic and rage, she also reminded herself that Trag had always been impersonal! Her relations with Lanzecki were clouding other judgments.

"Coping with the unexpected must become automatic for a Singer. Some people never learn how." Trag's eyes shifted slightly to indicate the room behind them. "You proved just now that your instinct for the blacks is reliable. Now"—and he reached out to take the block from her hand—"let us to the purpose for which these were simulated." He put the block among its mates.

Only then did she realize that the five mock crystals had been cast in the image of those she had cut, wiggles, improper angles and size.

"This substance has the same tensile strength and expansion ratio as black crystal but no other of its properties. You must learn today to install crystal properly in its bracketing with enough pressure to secure it against vibration but not enough to interfere with intermolecular flow." He showed her a printed diagram. "This will be the order and the configuration of the Trundimoux link." He tapped the corresponding block as he pointed out its position, repeating what Lanzecki had rattled through. "Number one and two, the smallest, will be on mining stations, number three on the gas planet satellite, number four on the ice planet satellite, and number five, the largest crystal, will be installed on the habitable planet. You and you alone will handle the crystals."

"Is that Guild policy?" How much more did she have to learn about this complex profession.

"Among other considerations, no one in the Trundimoux System is technically capable." Trag's voice was heavy with disapproval.

Killashandra wondered if he considered them "Trundies" or "Moux."

"I would have thought Marketing would handle installation."

"Generally." His stiff tone warned her off further questions.

"Well, I don't suppose I'd've been saddled with the job if I hadn't lost my sled and if Passover weren't so near."

She got no visible reaction from her rueful comment.

"Remember that," Trag advised, and added with an unexpected wryness, "if you can."

Installing crystal in padded clamps was not as simple as it had sounded, but then, as Killashandra was learning, nothing in the Heptite Guild was as simple as it sounded. Nevertheless, by evening, with arm, neck, and back muscles tense and hands that trembled from the effort of small, strong movements, eyes hot from concentration on surface tension readings, she believed she understood the process.

She was philosophical when Trag said they would repeat the day's exercise on the morrow, for she knew she must be motion perfect during the actual installations. Guild members had a reputation to maintain, and she would be up to Trag's standard of performance even if this was the only installation she ever made. Since her notion tallied with Trag's, she was undaunted by his perfectionism.

Lanzecki joined her again for her evening "gorge," but he excused himself as soon as he'd finished. She didn't mind so much that night because she was very tired.

By mealtime the following day, she had secured Trag's grudging approval for a deft, quick, and competent installation within a time limit he had arbitrarily set.

"Why not take more time?" she'd asked reasonably. "Installing a link between people ought to be an occasion."

"You won't *have* time," Trag said. "You'll be on an inbound gravity deflection course. There'll be no *time* to spare."

He gave her no chance to query his emphasis on time. With a curt nod, he left the room. Maybe Lanzecki would be in an expansive mood. If, she qualified to herself, he joined her for dinner.

Dinner? She was starving for her midday meal. As she passed through the main training room, Rimbol had just finished making a diagonal cut under Concera's tutelage.

"Are you eating soon?" she asked Rimbol and the Older Singer.

"I'm always eating!" Rimbol's reply was half groan, half belch, and Concera laughed.

"Finish the last cut," Concera told him.

"Go save us a table." Rimbol shooed her off, then turned his attention to his cutting.

Killashandra went directly to the Commons and found the dining area well occupied, tables stacked with a variety of dishes that bore witness to the problem of symbiotic instinct. She was about to order something to sustain her during the search for a free table when a large group vacated one of the booths. She ordered hastily, dialing for beer in a pitcher and beaker and setting them about the table to prevent occupation. She had retrieved her first order and was already eating as Rimbol, Concera, and two others of Class 895 joined her.

The meal became a convivial occasion, and all made suggestions of this or that favored delicacy they'd discovered during what Concera styled "the hunger."

"It's so good to have new members," she said in a giddy voice, waving her beaker of beer, "to remind us of things we've forgotten. I can't think, of course, who it was the last time, but Yarran beer is so satisfying."

Rimbol rose, bowed to the entire table. "Be upstanding all. Let us toast to the brewers of Yarran beer. May they always be remembered—by somebody!"

As the company hastily stood, the table was knocked

askew, and before the toast could be made, the surface had to be mopped and more beer dialed.

Killashandra was suffused by a sense of comaraderie that she had often observed in the Music Center but had never been part of. She supposed it was Rimbol's special gift that, given half a chance, he could make an occasion of any gathering. She said little, smiled much, and ate with a heartier appetite for such good company.

As she sat facing the dispensing area, she found herself identifying high-ranking Guild members as well as Singers obviously just in from the ranges, some of whom were gaunt, nervous, and confused by the throng of diners. Others, despite the same noise-pollution discomfiture, appeared in very good spirits. The nervous ones hadn't cut enough crystal to get off-planet, Killashandra thought, and the relaxed ones had. Certainly, when Borella entered with Olin and another pair of Singers, they were a vivacious group. Obstreperously so, Killashandra thought, for they would whisper among themselves, then burst into laughter as they looked with mock surreptitiousness at silent diners.

Though Rimbol was joking with Concera and Celee, he had noticed Borella's table.

"D'you know?" he said in an undertone to Killashandra, "she doesn't remember any of us."

"I know. She has been out in the ranges since we were recruited." Killashandra knew she wasn't excusing Borella, and she didn't need to explain to Rimbol.

"I know, I know, but that was only a few months ago." Rimbol's blue eyes were clouded with worry. "Do we lose our memories that quickly?"

"Borella's sung a long time, Rimbol." Killashandra could not reassure herself, either. "Have you started your personal file? Good. That's the way to remember what's important."

"I wonder what she considers important." Rimbol looked at Borella with narrowed eyes.

"Getting off this planet during Passover!" Even to herself, Killashandra sounded sharp. Rimbol threw her a startled look, and then he laughed. "I only know because I heard her talking to that tall fellow, Olin." Killashandra added in an easier manner. "Say, have you been in contact with Shillawn at all?"

"Sure have. In fact, we're meeting here tomorrow. Join us?"

Killashandra met Rimbol's mildly challenging stare.

"If I'm free. I'm scheduled to take some crystals to the Trundimoux system. Evidently, having cut crystal, I'd be particularly susceptible to Passover, so they're whipping me off the planet."

"Once I thought I'd have no trouble keeping up with you, Killa." Rimbol's expression was rueful.

"What d'you mean by that?" Killashandra was aware of a flurry of unexpected feelings: anxiety, surprise, irritation, and a sense of loss. She didn't want to lose her friendship with Rimbol. She put her hand on his arm. "We're friends, remember. Class 895."

"*If* we remember."

"What is the matter with you, Rimbol? I've been having such a good time." Killashandra gestured at the others laughing and chatting, and the evidences of a hearty meal. "I haven't had a chance to see much of anyone because of that wretched Milekey transition and being shepherded out by that sonic-shorted Moksoon—"

"Not to mention finding black crystal."

She took a deep breath against her seething reaction to Rimbol's implicit accusation.

"When"—she began slowly and in a taut voice—"you have been in the ranges looking for crystal, then you will know what I cannot possibly explain to you now." She rose, the tenuous sensation of comradeship abruptly severed. "Give my regards to Shillawn if you'd be so good as to remember."

She excused herself and stalked past a startled Concera, who tried to protest Killashandra's exit.

"Let her go, Concera. She has matters of great importance to attend."

Striding quickly into the main aisle, Killashandra nearly ran into Trag just entering the dining area.

"Killashandra? Don't you ever watch the call display?" Trag pointed to the moving line above the catering area, and she saw her name flashing. Trag took her arm and hurried her toward the lifts. "The Trundimoux ship is at Shankill. We've been holding the shuttle for you."

"The Trundimoux ship? Leave?" Killashandra glanced back at the table she had so hurriedly left. Only Concera was looking in her direction. She gave Killashandra a little wave for reassurance.

"They made time around their last sun and are here ahead of schedule and cannot hold at slow much longer or they'll lose momentum."

"I'll only need a few things . . ."

Trag shook his head impatiently and pushed her into a waiting lift.

"A Carisak is being prepared for you on the Base. Anything else you require, your accommodations and expenses are to be met by the Trundimoux. There's no time to lose now!"

Killashandra's protests waned. Her initial confusion turned quickly to resentment. Not only was she leaving without a chance to vindicate herself in Rimbol's opinion, she wasn't to see Lanzecki either. Or perhaps he had planned so hasty a departure to prevent her from embarrassing him? Soured as she was by Rimbol's accusations, it was easy to include Lanzecki.

That Milekey transition might have appeared to be a blessing, but that bit of "luck" had alienated her from the few friends she had ever made and left her vulnerable to speculations and subtly accused of harsh and indefensible suspicions.

"We were not expecting the Trundimoux to arrive so soon," Trag said, "but that may be fortuitous with Passover not long away." He thrust a sheaf of printout at her as she was puzzling that cryptic remark. "Antona said you were to read this. Medical advice on symbiotic adjustment and replenishment, so examine it carefully. The crystals are already on board the shuttle and locked in the supercargo's security hold. This is your Guild identification"—he offered her a slim folder like the one Carrik had carried— "and the Guild band," which he clasped around her right wrist. "With these, you have access to planetary governing organizations, including the Session of the Federated Sentient Planets. Though they're a boring lot, and I cannot see this assignment leading to a meeting, it's wise to be prepared for all contingencies."

Access to the Session of the Federated Sentient Planets? Killashandra did not think Trag would joke about such a privilege. The stimulation of such prestige and surprise lifted her depression.

They had reached the hangar level, and Trag's hand under her arm propelled her forward at a good pace toward the waiting shuttle. At the ramp, the boarding officer was gesturing them urgently to hurry. Trag increased his pace, and every inch of Killashandra wanted to resist as she glanced around the immense hangar area for one glimpse of Lanzecki.

"C'mon! C'mon!" the boarding officer exhorted. "Stragglers can be left for tomorrow's shuttle!"

"Quiet!" Trag turned Killashandra just as she put her foot on the ramp. "The Guild Master has considerable confidence in your abilities. I do not think it is misplaced. Lanzecki wishes you a good voyage and a safe return! Remember!"

With that, Trag whirled, leaving Killashandra staring after him, his last words echoing in her mind.

"I canNOT close the ramp if you are standing on it," the boarding officer exclaimed petulantly.

Obedient in her confusion, Killashandra hastened into the shuttle. The ramp retracted, and the shuttle's door slid with a ponderous whoosh and hiss across the aperture.

"Don't just stand there. Get a seat." The boarding officer gave Killashandra a little push toward the rear of the shuttle craft.

She strapped herself into a seat without thinking, holding her identification folder and Antona's instructions with both hands resting on her thighs. She let her body relax to the motion of the shuttle as it lifted on air cushions and glided from the hangar. Having no viewport, she endured what seemed hours before she felt the power surge as the crystal drive was engaged. She was thrust back into the cushioning of her seat as the shuttle took off. The pressure was welcome as a source of minor discomfort. She wished that the gravity drag pushing flesh and muscles against resisting bone might squeeze unwelcome thoughts from her head.

Then the shuttle was free of Ballybran's pull, and the relief of weightlessness was accompanied by the return of common sense to Killashandra's tumultuous thoughts. She had built into a personal tragedy two totally unrelated incidents: Rimbol's curiously aggressive attitude during an otherwise convivial occasion when she had felt particularly relaxed, and Lanzecki's apparent dismissal. She'd muddled these about with her tendency to dramatize and a subconscious guilt about her easy transition, the Keborgen incident, Lanzecki's unexpected friendship, her first overcharged trip into the ranges, and pre-Passover sensitivity.

So. Deep breath and rationalize. Rimbol was also feeling pre-Passover sensitivity. Not only had Trag personally escorted her to the shuttle, but he had given her three different messages: the Guild Master had confidence in her. So, unexpectedly, had Trag, whom Killashandra knew to be harder to please than any other instructor she had ever studied with. And Lanzecki wished her a good voyage and a safe return.

Killashandra smiled to herself and began to relax. With the unstated import as reassurance, she ceased to regard the precipitous departure as more than coincidence. Still, she'd been on the handy end of coincidence rather much recently. From the moment the sorters recruited her class to help with crystal and Enthor had chosen her; her sensitivity to black crystal; a Milekey transition that, according to Antona, no one could predict. Chance had been on Killashandra's side when she'd gone with the rescue team to Keborgen. True, an application of deduction and fact had helped her determine Keborgen's flight path. Her premature introduction to the ranges had occurred at Lanzecki's direction, governed by the Guild's necessity to keep Keborgen's claim operative. She might not have found it, might have been deterred by the fresh claimer paint. She wondered about the effect of Passover storms on paint.

Then she remembered Antona's message, and shoving

the Guild ident into a hip pocket, she unfolded the print sheet.

Antona had researched the foods available in the Trundimoux system and listed the best for Killashandra's needs. The list was ominously short. Antona reminded the new Singer that her hunger would slacken but that she might also encounter considerable drowsiness as Passover point was reached. This effect most frequently occurred when symbiont and host were adjusting. Antona advised her to complete the installations as quickly as possible and gave her a mild stimulant to overcome lethargy. Antona ended by advising Killashandra not to return to Ballybran's surface until Passover was completed, and the farther away from the system she stayed, the better.

The message, typed by voice-printer, sounded like Antona in a cheerful way, and Killashandra was extremely grateful for the thoughtfulness that prompted it. Her uncertainties allayed, she mentally reviewed the installation procedures in which Trag had drilled her. Both he and Lanzecki had confidence in her. So be it.

The retrodrive and the swaying, dropping motion of the shuttle indicated it was maneuvering to the base docks. She felt the impact as the maneuver was successful.

"Clumsy!" a familiar voice commented several rows up from Killashandra.

"No doubt, one of your recruits showing off," the drawling voice of Olin replied.

She must really have been in a daze when she boarded the shuttle, Killashandra thought, if she hadn't noticed Borella and her companion. Killashandra had just unstrapped when she was surprised to hear her own name in Borella's unmistakably scornful voice.

"Killashandra Ree? Now how should I know whether she's on board or not. I don't know her."

The calculated indifference to what must have been a courteous query infuriated Killashandra. No wonder Crystal Singers had such bad reputations.

She made her way to the shuttle door, coming to an abrupt halt as her augmented vision was assaulted by the garishly uniformed pair standing to one side of the dock port. On the chests of each man, emblazoned in vivid, iridescent, and unharmonious colors, was a stylized symbol, a planet, two moons ringed by three whirling asteroid belts. The movement, Killashandra decided as she closed her eyes for a moment, must be due to the men's normal breathing and some special quality of the material.

"I'm Killashandra Ree," she said politely, but she could almost understand Borella's curt arrogance. To the more sensitive eyes of an altered human, the Trundimoux uniform was visually unbearable.

"Star Captain Francu of the Trundimoux Navy, at your service, Guild Member Ree." A stiff gesture introduced his companion. "Senior Lieutenant Engineer Tallaf."

By narrowing her eyes, Killashandra could filter out the appalling color and appreciate that these were very attractive men, lean as most spacers were, and equally obvious, uncomfortable. Nervous?

The shuttle pilot, his casual coverall a complete contrast to the Trundimoux officers', emerged from the lock.

"You're from the Trundy ship? Cargo's unloaded on the lower deck."

Killashandra noted Captain Francu's wince at the nickname and thought that the lieutenant was amused.

"Senior Lieutenant Supercargo Pendel is attending to that matter, Captain . . ."

"Senior Captain Amon, Francu. Pendel has been thoroughly briefed on the crystal?"

Francu stiffened.

"Where's your ship docked?" Amon continued, looking at his wrist-unit.

"Our cruiser"—and Francu emphasized the type of vessel in such a pompous tone that Killashandra had a presentiment that her voyage companions might be very dull —"is in hyperbolic."

"Oh, your system did get the 78 then." Amon replied with such genial condescension that Killashandra nearly laughed aloud. The two officers exchanged startled glances. "Well, you'd hardly have got here so fast in any of your old 59s. Quite a compliment to you, Killa, for them to send their newest."

To her knowledge, Killashandra had never met Amon, but she didn't miss the slight wink that accompanied the abbreviated form of her name.

"I don't think the compliment is to me, Amon"—and she smiled understandingly at the officers—"but rather to the black crystals."

"You Trundies are lucky to get the quintet," Amon went on; he, too, had caught Francu's disapproval of the nickname.

"After all, there is an FSP priority for the Trundimoux system," Killashandra interjected diplomatically. Amon might be getting some pleasure out of antagonizing Francu, but she was the one who had to travel with the man.

"True," Amon replied, and smiled affably. "Now, Killa, there are a few details . . ." and he began to shepherd her toward the Guild exit.

"Captain Amon, we were assured that there would be no delays as soon as the Guild—" Francu's wrist-unit blurted a noise. "Yes? They are? Secured? We'll be in the cutter—"

"Not until Killashandra has cleared Shankill authority, Captain. If you'll just wait at—which port is your cutter at?"

"Level 4, port 18." Francu yielded the information with a look compounded of anger and apprehension. "We *are* hyperbolic."

"This won't take long."

Amon hustled her through the Guild door, and she smiled back reassuringly at the startled officers.

"What's all this nonsense about?" she demanded, breaking Amon's grip as the panel slid behind them. "If they're on hyperbolic, we've only so much time to catch up with their cruiser."

"Over here!" He grabbed her hand again and pulled her into a side room. The odors of food that assailed her aroused an instant appetite. She groaned.

"Eat!" Amon exhorted her. "You've got to cram as much as you can into your belly." He shoved some pepper fingers into her mouth. "You won't get a chance to eat while that cruiser is on interplanetary drive. Those 78s don't carry luxuries like catering devices, and the mess will be closed while they build speed. You'd starve. I got the ship to fix up a necessaries kit for you. I know the Trundies have females on board, but it isn't right for a Singer to wear their uniforms. Your eyes'd bleed. There're lenses in this kit to filter the color intensities to the bearable level." Amon rattled through the inventory as he checked the items in the small bag. "Not much variety in clothing but good quality. I'll put in some of this food, too. We really have to hop if they're on hyperbolic. Bells and bollux, they must be separating some expensive rocks in their asteroid belts if they could buy a 78." He whistled. "I saw the length of the drone string they brought. However, if they traded with the Guild, I know who came out best. Here, try these nut meats. Heard you liked Yarran beer. Have a gulp to wash the meats down. Good. Now, another word of advice. Play Crystal Singer to the hilt with those belt knockers. That captain's a bad print, and I've seen enough to know. Eat! I can't hold you up much longer." He was covering the remaining uneaten dishes and stowing them in the kit. His wrist-unit bleepéd. "Yes? Yes, I know. Mere formalities? Fardles, she was starving to death, shafthead. It is rising Passover and you know cruisers. We'll be off in a pico." Amon slung her kit bag over her shoulder, thrust a bowl of small crispy fried squares in one hand, took up another dish and her beer in the other. "You can eat as we go, but Francu's cutting up stiff with Authority about the delay. Bells and bollux! Did anyone remember to warn you about the sleepies?" Amon was guiding her down the corridor to the peripheral lifts.

"Antona mentioned them. I've instructions and a stimulant."

"I put a strip of pink tablets in your stuff. Bollux! And you've only just been in the ranges. It just isn't fair on you, you know."

"Trag trained me on installations."

"*Trag?* Oh, Lanzecki's shadow," and Amon appeared impressed. "It's not so much what you have to do as where and with what. The Trundies being a prime example of Problem. Here we go. Take a deep breath, girl, and you're on stage as Heptite Guild Member from now on. Good luck!"

Amon whipped the dish from her hand as she faced the

door panel, motioned for her to wipe her mouth, and then the door slid apart.

Killashandra blinked as the raucous colors on the stiffly attentive escort of six men half blinded her. The haste with which she was then propelled into the cutter was indicative of the tension she sensed in the atmosphere. She barely had time to mumble thanks to Amon before the cutter airlock closed. Killashandra nearly fell over the crystal container, cross-tied in the center of the narrow aisle. She noticed the familiar Heptite dodecahedron and the rather astonishing large Trundimoux symbol. Even the stamp radiated offensive color. The captain indicated the seat she should take, and the lieutenant tested her seat webbing.

Rather to her surprise, the captain took the control seat, Tallaf sitting second in the traditional left-hand place. The release formalities were completed with Shankill Authority, and the lock coupling to the cutter was released.

Francu was a competent driver, but Killashandra had the distinct notion that cruiser captains rarely lifted lowly cutters from moon bases. Or was this a Trundie tradition? She must NOT fall into the habit of their nickname.

The cutter was equipped with external video cameras, so Killashandra rather enjoyed the spectacular views of Bally-bran, little Shilmore, and the dazzling array of small and large merchant craft attached to the locks of the base or in synchronous orbit. Probably everyone was getting in for what crystal was available before Passover. She wondered if Andurs's ship was in a berth. As the cutter wended its way through the orbiting traffic, she didn't see *Rag Delta Blue Swan*.

The cruiser became visible early in the short trip. It was planet lit on its long axis, which made it seem larger. She had half expected it to be decorated in wild patterns, but the hull was the usual space orange. The drones tethered to it were much patched and dented. As the cutter was matching speed for contact, she could not judge the cruiser's forward motion, but it had that inevitable, inexorable, *military* look—"I am going in this direction, and nothing is stopping me." Which, Killashandra mused, was fair enough since the vessel was traveling on a hyperbolic trajectory utilizing the gravitational pull of whatever suns or planets that deflected it.

The captain made a clean insertion into the cruiser's dock, and a moment later the airlock bumped gently against the hull. The crewmen jumped to their feet. The captain, with Tallaf a half step behind, stopped abruptly at Killashandra's seat. Hastily, she unbuckled her webbing, realizing that she was holding up the landing drill.

With a hiss, the hatch swung open, and an incredibly high pitched whine pierced her skull. The noise stopped as quickly as it had started. Outside, two rows of stiffly attentive men formed an aisle from the cutter to a larger hatch. There, more officers, including two whose outlines were female, awaited her.

A snap and scuff behind her, and from the corner of her eye, Killashandra saw crewmen lifting the crystal container. She felt another twinge of apprehension about this assignment. Even if getting off-planet during Passover was vital to her, was this fuss and formality the right environment?

She took a deep breath and moved forward, head high, and stepped on to the cruiser's deck with the dignity of a reigning queen of ancient times.

The two female subordinate officers, Tic and Tac, for she never could get them to repeat their proper names above a mumble, escorted her to quarters, which made her student's cubicle at the Music Center seem spacious. However, she told herself firmly as she was shown the ingenious disposition of the tiny cabin's conveniences, that Ballybran had given her delusions of grandeur. The cramped accommodation would deflate her sense of self-importance to a manageable level. Tic and Tac demonstrated how the bunk could be converted to a table, where the jug of water—one per cabin—was stored, the panel behind which the tri-d was located and the ship's library code; they reminded her five times about water rationing. A toilet facility was cleverly tucked away but easily located by the chemical odor.

The hum of crystal through the deck plates gave Killashandra a chance to suggest that they must have flight duties. She wanted to place the lenses in her aching eyes to tone down the revolting color around her. Also, in the close confines of the room, the odors of her unfinished meal were apparent to her, if not to them, and she wasn't about to share. The few mouthfuls she'd been able to bolt on Shankill had only sharpened her appetite.

Tic and Tac did respond to another ear-piercing sound, promising to return to satisfy her smallest wish, once full drive had been established.

Closing the cabin door with one hand and kicking down the bunk were simultaneously possible in her new accommodations. As Killashandra stoked her symbiont's craving, she read the instructions on the lenses, pausing long enough in her eating to slip them over her irises. The demonic shades of the cabin settled into a bland wash. Ballybran had looked so dull to her at first! She finished the food Amon had packed, then tried to calculate how long it would be before her next meal.

She felt the drive taking hold, but the crystals were well tuned and caused her no twinges. She could do nothing more at this stage of the cruiser's journey, so she made herself as comfortable as possible on the narrow bunk and fell asleep.

Another ear-shattering whine brought her bolt upright on the bunk and very wide awake. Would there be any way for her to block that dreadful noise in her quarters?

"Journey speed achieved. Cruising drill is effective as of—now! All officers to the mess. Will Guild Member Killashandra Ree do us the honor of joining the assembly?"

She would also have to do something about receiving such ship-wide announcements.

"Guild Member Ree? Are you in hearing?"

"Yes, yes, of course," the Guild Member replied, hastily depressing the toggle so quaintly placed at eye level by her bunk. "Honored to join the officers' mess."

She emptied the carisak on the bed, sorted through the tunics and caftans, found the "sleepy" pills Amon had mentioned, and secured them in the arm pocket of her coverall. Then she changed into the more elaborately decorated caftan and was wondering where the officers' mess would be located on a 78 when a brief rap on her door was followed by its being opened by Tic or Tac.

"Privacy, sub, privacy. Never open my door until I have acknowledged."

"Aye, aye, ma'am, sorry, ma'am, I mean—" The girl had recoiled at Killashandra's severity.

"Isn't there a Privacy light on this cabin?" Killashandra could not contemplate easy access to her quarters with any equanimity either as a Fuertan or a Guild Member.

"No light, ma'am. This is an official vessel." The subordinate officer regarded her with anxious trepidation.

"Yes, of the Trundimoux system. But I am of the Heptite Guild and expect the courtesy of Privacy wherever I am."

"I'll pass the word, ma'am. None of us will forget."

Killashandra did not doubt that, but she must contrive the same respect from the officers. Francu would be no threat, but Tallaf . . . As Killashandra followed Tic to the officers' mess, she decided that she would retrieve a deck plan from the library as soon as she had the opportunity. The cruiser was obviously being refitted to Trundimoux requirements en route, for work parties were busy at various corridors and levels, all pausing to inspect her as she passed.

The officers' mess might have been a pleasant room but was poorly furnished, its walls hung with diagrams and hard copy, suggesting that it served a dual purpose. Francu formally introduced her to the numerous officers, some of whom immediately excused themselves to take up their watch duties. Those who remained were served a tiny cup of an inferior wine that the captain enjoined them to take to the mess table.

In Killashandra's estimation, the occasion rapidly deteriorated into a very bad comic opera in which no one had studied lines or recognized cues. Francu and his executive officer would never have advanced past preliminary auditions. The other flight deck officers seemed to take turns asking her conventionally stupid questions to which, piqued, she gave outrageous and contradictory answers. Only Tallaf, seated at the other end of the table, appeared to have a sense of humor. The supercargo, also placed at an inconvenient distance from her, was the only extraplanetarian. Since he seemed as bored as she was, she made a note to cultivate him as soon as possible.

The food served was dreadful, although from the appetites of the younger officers, it was evidently a feast. Killashandra could find nothing on the table that matched the items on Antona's list and, with great difficulty, chewed and swallowed the unappealing stodge.

Dinner ended with everyone's jumping to their feet and dedicating themselves to the further ambitions of Trundimoux System, against all natural obstacles and phenomena.

Killashandra managed to keep her expression composed during this unexpected outburst, especially when she realized that the younger subs were emotionally involved in their statement. When Killashandra considered that the system had managed to purchase a 78 as well as five black crystals, there might be some merit to unswerving dedication. The Guild inspired its members, too, but toward selfish rather than selfless aims. Well, the Trundimoux system's results were very good, but it was from the Guild that they made their most prestigious purchases.

The table was cleared efficiently by the mess crew, and Killashandra watched them, there being nothing else to do. She could think of nothing to say in the silence and dreaded the prospect of more evenings like this.

"Would you care for a drink, Guild Member?" the supercargo asked as he appeared at her side.

"Why, yes, a Yarran beer would top off that meal," she said with considerable irony, for beer would more likely bring the stodge back up.

To her utter amazement, the super gave her a bright smile.

"*You*"—and his emphasis implied that she should have been the last person in the galaxy to have such tastes— "like Yarran beer?"

"Yes, it's my favorite beverage. Have you heard of it?"

"Of course, I've heard of it," and the man's good-humored chuckle included those standing nearby. "I'm Yarran. Pendel's the name, ma'am. You shall have a beaker from my own keg!" He signaled to one of the mess crew, mimed the careful pouring of beer into a beaker, and held up two fingers.

"Guild Member," the captain said, stepping in, "we have wines—"

"Actually, Captain Francu, the Heptite Guild is partial to Yarran beer," she said, knowing that she was irritating the man, yet unable to resist. "If I'm not depriving you, super—"

"Depriving me?" Lieutenant Supercargo Pendel was enormously amused by the suggestion. Nor did Killashandra miss his quick glance at Francu or Francu's displeasure. "Not at all. My pleasure, I assure you. I keep telling 'em how satisfying a good Yarran brew is, far and above the ordinary since Terran malt and hops adapted well to our soil, but to each his own, I always say."

The beakers were served, and Francu's disapproval grew as Killashandra sipped with overt delight, though the beer was slightly flat, and she wondered how long it had been in Pendel's keg. Perhaps the Guild brewmasters excelled Yarra's own.

Pendel chattered away to her about different brews from different planets. Killashandra was relieved to find at least one traveled person among the Trundie belt-knockers. As long as they could stay on the subject of food and drink, Killashandra could give Pendel the impression of being widely-traveled herself.

"Do you remember much about Yarra?" he asked, as he signaled for another round of beer.

The phrasing of that question startled Killashandra, though she wasn't certain why, since Pendel's manner posed no threat.

"Of all the planets I have visited, it has the best brew and the most affable population. I wonder if the two are related? Have you been long away?"

"Too long and not long enough," the Yarran replied, his jolly face lengthening into sadness. He sighed heavily, taking the fresh beaker and sipping at it slowly. How the man could become homesick on one glass of flat beer, Killashandra wasn't certain. "However, it was of my choosing, and we Yarrans make the best of everything, and everything of the best."

Unexpectedly the harsh buzzer that announced watch

changes penetrated the room. Killashandra took that op-. portunity to excuse herself from the mess.

Tac, for she'd seen Tic go off with the duty crew, guided Killashandra through the maze of companionways to her cell. As she slipped out of her caftan, she wondered how she was going to endure six days of this. And how was she going to replenish her symbiont on the *gundge* that was served? She was thinking that flat Yarran beer had a more soporific effect than the proper stuff as she fell asleep.

The next morning, it abruptly occurred to her that if Pendel had Yarran beer in his private supplies, he might have other delicacies, so she asked Tic, then on duty, to lead her to the supercargo's office.

She felt crystal as she passed a sealed and barred hatch, grinning over the useless precautions. For who could steal crystal in space? Or were the Trundies afraid of crystal's ensnaring the unwary? She experienced a start of amazement as Tic, after merely rapping on the panel, pulled it aside and entered. Presumably, Yarrans did not object to casual invasions of their pirvacy. Pendel was on his feet and full of genial welcomes in a cabin only slighter larger than hers. All three. had to stand in close proximity to fit beside the bunk table. There were, however, a basket of fruit and a half-finished beaker of Yarran beer on the shelf.

"How may I serve you?" Pendel asked, smiling at Tic as he waved her out and closed the panel behind her.

Killashandra explained, giving him the list of Antona's suggested diet.

"Ah, I can supply you with these and more. What they choose to eat"—and he waved his hand in the general direction of the control section amidships—"is well enough if one is not used to better. But you, Guild Member—"

"Killashandra, please . . ."

"Yes? Well, thank you, Killashandra. You have been accustomed to the very best that the galaxy has to offer—"

"So long as my immediate dietary requirements are met" —and Killashandra pointed to Antona's list—"I will have no complaint." She could not help eying the fruit basket wistfully.

"Haven't you eaten yet this morning?" Appalled, Pendel deposited the basket in her hands, turning past her to haul back the panel and roaring at Tic, standing on guard. "Breakfast, immediately, and none of the glop." He glanced at the list. "Rations twenty-three and forty-eight and a second issue of fruit."

Consternation at having to relay such an order warred with fear in Tic's face.

"Go on, girl. Go on. I've given the order!" Pendel assured her.

"And I have seconded it!" Killashandra added firmly. Then she bit into a red fruit to ease the gnawing in her belly.

Pendel slid the panel closed and smiled with anticipatory glee. "Of course, we'll have Chasurt down in a pico . . ." The super rubbed his hands together. "Those rations are his. He's the medic," Pendel grimaced as he added, "with far more experience in space-freeze and laser burn. The rations contain just what your list specifies, high in trace minerals, potassium, calcium and such like."

The food and the medic arrived at the same time. But for Pendel's smooth intervention, Killashandra's breakfast would have been confiscated from Tic's nerveless hands by the irate Chasurt.

"Who gave orders to release *my* rations?" Chasurt, a stolidly built, blank-faced man of the late middle decades, reminded Killashandra of Maestro Valdi in his outraged indignation.

"I did!" said Pendel and Killashandra in chorus. Pendel took the tray from Tic's shaking hands and smoothly transferred it to Killashandra, who, moving herself and Chasurt's rations to the farthest corner of the cabin, left Pendel to impede Chasurt's effort at retrieval.

Eating with a speed not entirely generated by hunger, Killashandra consumed the hot cereal and nutmeat compound. Pendel was trying to get Chasurt to examine Antona's list, and Chasurt was demanding to know what he was to do if a real emergency were to occur, one in which sick people would need the rations that this—this—obviously healthy woman was devouring. The medic did not

approve of Killashandra's haste. That Pendel had the right
to order such rations seemed to infuriate Chasurt even
more, and by the time Killashandra had finished the second
dish, she felt obliged to interfere.

"Lieutenant Chasurt—"

"Captain! Guild Member," and, puce with the added
insult, the man pointed to the rank emblem at his neck.

"All right, Captain." Killashandra accorded him an apol-
ogetic inclination of her head, "Pendel is acting on my
behalf, obeying my instructions, which were firmly impressed on me by Chief Medical Research Officer Antona
of the Heptite Guild Ballybran. It was understood by my
Guild Master and myself that my requirements would be
met on this voyage. If I am physically unfit to complete the
installations, all your efforts will have been an expensive
waste, and your system still incommunicado. I am given to
understand that the journey to your system is not a long
one, so I cannot think that my modest dietary needs will
seriously deplete the resources of a newly commissioned
78. Will they?"

Chasurt's face had reflected several emotions as she
spoke, and Killashandra, though not as adept as Lanzecki
in reading body language, received the impression that
Chasurt would have preferred the system to lose the interplanetary link. But that was an irrational premise, and she
decided that Chasurt must be one of those officious people
who must constantly be deferred to and flattered. She remembered Amon's advice and realized its merit with this
sort of personality.

"Not wishing to remind you, Captain Chasurt, that in
the Federated Sentient Planets' hierarchy, as a Guild
Member traveling on Heptite Guild business, I outrank
everyone on this ship, including Captain Francu, I will
suggest that you check your data retrieval under Crystal
Singers and be thus reassured in your dealings with me on
this journey. Now, just pass me the fruit."

Chasurt had intercepted that basket, delivered during
Killashandra's reply.

"Trace minerals are especially important for us," she
said, smoothly reaching out to take the basket. She had to

secure it with a bit of a jerk. Chasurt was livid. Killashandra nodded pleasantly at Tic and dimissed her before closing the panel on Chasurt's fury.

Pendel raised his Yarran beer in salute to Killashandra as he leaned against the wall.

"We'll have the captain next, you know."

"You seem to manage them rather well," Killashandra said between bites of the tangy redfruit.

"They can't get rid of me." Pendel chuckled, pressing the side of his nose and winking at her. "I'm employed by the Mining Consortium, not the Trundie Council. The MC is still keying the priorities. Oh, they're not bad sorts for parochial chaps with metal on the mind. They'll change. They'll change now for sure." Pendel swept his beaker from her to the sealed cabin where the crystal was secured.

"Do I have the suspicion that not all concerned wish to change?"

Pendel gave a laugh. "And when has that been news?"

A peculiar squawk was emitted by the communit, and Pendel winked at Killashandra.

"Captain here, super. What's this about special rations being issued without consultation?"

"Captain Francu"—Pendel's tone was a drawl, just short of insult—"I believe the orders read that Guild Member Ree's requirements are to be met by the—"

"They told me she didn't require anything special."

"Guild Member Ree doesn't require anything *special*, but as I've been telling you, the mess served on this ship isn't universally nourishing or satisfying. Chasurt has more than enough in stores. I should know. *I* buy for him."

There wasn't an audible click at the end of the exchange, but the captain's complaint had been dismissed. Killashandra regarded Pendel with more respect.

"Hard worker, that Francu. Runs a tight ship. Never lost a person. Just the sort of man to trust the newest ship to." Pendel rubbed the side of his nose, his broad grin implying all the negative facets of Captain Francu that he did not voice.

"I appreciate your cooperation and support, Pendel, almost as much as the beer. One more favor, if it's possible.

Do I have to listen to all the ship's business?" Another
harsh buzz punctuated her request.

"Just leave it with me, Killashandra," Pendel said comfortably. "I'll send round some handy rations for you in
the meantime." He gestured apologetically at the plates and
chips piled on the printouts on his desk, and she took the
hint. She also took the second bowl of fruit, winking at
Pendel as she left.

The man contrived well and shortly after Tic led her
back to her dinky cabin, the unnerving sounds of command were muted.

Tic arrived, tapping politely and waiting for Killashandra's acknowledgment, with parcels of plain plastic in both
hands. One was a variety of the special rations, the other
an array of food. Tic kept her eyes averted from that
luxury, but Killashandra perceived that any generosity
from her would be ill advised. She thanked Tic and dismissed her until evening mess. Killashandra knew that she
had to put in at least one appearance a day and sighed at
the thought of such boredom. While she munched on
Chasurt's prized packages, she occupied herself by studying
the deck plan of the 78. Even as she watched, certain
sections were updated and changed for purposes that escaped her. Was this to be a cargo ship, a passenger liner, or
a training vessel? Its specifications meant nothing to her,
but the length of the numericals was impressive.

She was duly escorted to the officers' mess, Chasurt and
Francu mercifully absent, so she chatted with Tallaf, an
agreeable enough young man without his captain's presence
to inhibit him, though when he got flustered, his neck had
the tendency to puff out. He admitted to being planet-bred,
educated for his duties as executive in theoretics rather
than the practical. Most of the other officers and crew
members were space or station born. His tone was a shade
wistful, as if he regretted the difference between himself
and his shipmates.

"I understand that your system has been isolated due to
poor communications," Killashandra said conversationally.

Tallaf looked anxiously around him.

"I also understand that a step forward is not generally
popular."

Tallaf regarded her with awe.

"Oh, come now, Tallaf," Killashandra said in a teasing voice, "that's been obvious to me since I boarded. I assure you, it's not an unusual phenomenon."

"Crystal Singers get to go everywhere, don't they?" An ingenuous envy flickered across his face.

"Not necessarily. This is an unusual assignment for an unusual world and unusual circumstances." Tallaf preened a little at the implied compliment to his system. "Quite an achievement for an emergent political unit"—Killashandra was a little awed by her own eloquence—"to purchase a 78 and black crystals."

She watched Tallaf keenly as she spoke and decided that the young engineer was evidently *for* instant interstellar communications. She wondered briefly how the split of support went—spacers against planetaries or parochials against galactics. She sighed, wishing someone had given her more data on the Trundies. Perhaps there just wasn't much in the galactography.

Pendel arrived, smiling pleasantly to the small groups of officers standing around. It was then that Killashandra realized that she and Tallaf had formed a solitary pair. She smiled more graciously at Tallaf for his fortitude as a crewman appeared from the galley with two beakers of Yarran ale. Tallaf drifted away discreetly, and Killashandra toasted Pendel, whose jolly self evidently masked considerable prestige.

Pendel chuckled. "Good boy, that Tallaf."

"He's *for* crystal?"

"Oh, yes, indeed. That's why he's exec this trip. His first." Pendel's affable smile was truly in place as he glanced around the messroom. Killashandra was certain he knew exactly who should be there and who wasn't. "Not bad at all for a shakedown crew." Killashandra wondered what the deficiencies were. "A man looks for certain goals at certain times of his life," and his eyes caught hers over the rim of the Yarran beer glass. "Adventure brought me to this system two and a half decades ago. My timing was right. They urgently needed an experienced supercargo. They were being done out of their sockets on cargo rates." Pendel's tone was laden with remembered indignation.

Then he smiled. "Can't do business properly without proper communication."

"Which is why crystal and this 78 are so important!" She tilted her glass toward him as if Pendel had single-handedly accomplished all. "You Yarrans are known for your perspicacity. Quite a few from your system have become Crystal Singers . . ." She was subtly aware of Pendel's reaction. "Oh, come now, Pendel," she continued smoothly, for if she couldn't have this man's support, she might well be left in Chasurt's hands, and that wouldn't suit. "Surely you don't believe the spaceflot about Crystal Singers?" She contrived a very amused gurgle of laughter.

"Of course not," and Pendel shrugged negligently, though his smile was not quite as assured.

"Especially now you've met and talked with me and discovered a Crystal Singer is as human as anyone on board this ship. Or"—and Killashandra glanced about the mess-room and its subdued occupants—"perhaps a bit more so."

Pendel surveyed his fellow officers and grimaced.

"At least I can appreciate a proper brew," Killashandra continued, inwardly suppressing both apprehension and amusement. Pendel was nowhere near as cosmopolitan as he liked to appear, though in contrast to the other Trundies, he was tolerably informed about the galaxy. Somehow Killashandra must contrive to keep a friendly distance from him. "I do give them credit," and she glanced around her with an air of compliment.

"So evidently does the Heptite Guild." Pendel had recovered his basic optimism. "But none of us expected a Crystal Singer would install the things."

"The Federated Sentient Planets have their own schedule of priorities. Ours not to reason why." Killashandra couldn't remember where that line came from, but it seemed to apply.

Fortunately, the steaming platters and trays of their evening meal arrived, and Killashandra noted that only she and Pendel were served the one appetizing selection.

Without the repressive presence of Captain Francu and Chasurt, Killashandra managed to draw into conversation most of the older officers. Though the youngsters were far too shy to speak, she could sense that they were listening very closely and storing every word exchanged. The subs were still malleable, and if she could influence them favorably and maintain Pendel's good will by judicious flattery, she'd have done more than she'd been contracted to do. And the Trundies would need more crystal.

That night, as she stretched out on the appallingly hard bunk, she reviewed her extravagant performance of that evening. "Crystalline cuckoo" and "silicate spider," Maestro Valdi had called Crystal Singers. She thought she knew why now: the survival instincts of the symbiont. And judging from Pendel's subconscious reaction to her, she knew why the symbiont remained a trade secret. There were, she decided, more invidious threats than giving space and survival to a species that paid good value with the rent.

CHAPTER 12

Killashandra made good use of her next five days, having Tic or Tac lead her on exercise walks about the cruiser, dropping hints about the exacting nature of her work and how she had to keep fit. The silicate spider preparing its web for a Passover sleep. She had a few uncomplimentary thoughts about the Guild, mainly Lanzecki, for sending her among the uninformed without a hint that the Trundimoux were so parochial.

She did a great deal of listening to the subordinates when they relaxed enough to talk in her presence and to the general conversations, mostly good-natured slagging among work teams. She learned a great deal about the short and awesome history of the Trundimoux system and stopped referring to them as Trundies in the privacy of her thoughts.

As it had Pendel, the system had attracted many restless and adventurous people, a percentage of them either physically or temperamentally unsuited to the hazards. The survivors bred quickly and hugely, and natural selection again discarded the weaknesses and the weaker, some of whom could usefully work in the relative safety of the larger mining units. The second generation, who survived the rigors of knocking likely chunks of the suburanic metals out of orbit and jockeying their payloads into long drone strings, those hardy souls perpetuated their genes and became yet another variant of human. This system was, in its own way, as unique as Ballybran's, its entrance requirements as stringent and its workers as rigorously trained.

One night while juggling those elements in her mind—the dangers of space as opposed to the physical tests on Shankill—Killashandra waxed philosophical. The galaxy was not merely physical satellites circling flaming primaries but overlapping and intertwining metaphysical ones. She was currently the bridge between two such star systems and two totally opposite mental attitudes. She'd use the charm of one to survive in the other.

The Trundimoux had already developed some strong traditions, the evening's solemn dedication of the officers to their system's survival, the worship of water, a callousness toward death, a curious distrust of out-system manufactured equipment. This, Killashandra thought, was why they were so assiduously altering the 78's interior. Then, after she'd seen some tri-di's of the mining stations and the space-built edifices themselves, she understood. In a spatial sense, the Trundimoux were adapting constantly to the needs of their hostile environment. In another, they were refusing to admit that any other system, hers included, had something worthwhile to offer them that couldn't be improved on.

Killashandra listened, too, to subtler opinions on the wisdom of instant interstellar communications. Some were skeptical that the crystals would work, due, it was claimed, to some peculiarity of the Trundimoux system that was designed to keep them isolated. Others thought it a shocking waste of time, effort, and precious metal-credit. The division of thought split age groups, first- and second-generation representatives, and even contracted extraplanetaries on local assignment.

Meanwhile, the cruiser was fast closing with its home system on its hyperbolic trajectory. Killashandra's appetite had leveled off, a relief to herself as well as to Pendel's dwindling supply of her requirements. Passover was occurring over Ballybran, and conjunction was as imminent as her first installation. She judiciously kept the stimulant tabs on her person.

The change in the crystal drive tone heralded her first

unexpected nap. Tic's insistent tapping on her door panel roused her.

"Captain Francu's compliments, Killashandra Ree, and would you follow me to the bridge?"

Tic was suddenly very formal, not so much as a shy answering smile to Killashandra's acknowledgment. She followed the sub, much refreshed by her sleep, but she felt for the stimutabs in her sash pocket.

The bridge, a misnamed cavern midship, was busy and full. Tic found the captain among those circled about the dimension tank, caught his attention, presented Killashandra, and retreated.

"If you will observe the tank, Guild Member," the captain began at his most overbearing.

"I would if I could," Killashandra said, and smiling sweetly, inserted her hip between two male bodies and with a deft twist pushed the men sideways so that she occupied their previous vantage point. She left one officer between her and Francu, consoling the startled man with a soothing glance. "Ah, yes, fascinating." She *was* fascinated, though she wanted to give the distinct impression that this was scarcely the first time she had been on a bridge or gazed at a dimension tank. The cruiser was a very tiny blip, coasting inward, past the orbit of the outermost planet, toward the primary. Blinking lights indicated major mining stations in the asteroid belts; two tiny solid lights, the two moon bases. The bright planet, fourth from the primary, exuded a supercilious superiority despite being the last to be settled in the hard-working system.

"We are coasting now, Guild Member, if you haven't noticed the change of the drive—"

"A Crystal Singer is unusually sensitive to crystal drive, Captain—an occupational skill."

Francu set his jaw, unused to being interrupted for any reason.

"We are traveling on a hyperbolic course that will intersect the orbit of the two mining stations, which have deviated from their courses to meet us—"

"Sometimes progress can be awkward—"

Francu glared at her. "The moon bases provide no problem on their relative planes, though Terris will require a longer shuttle flight—"

"You will have a far more difficult maneuver in catching up with your planet, won't you?" and Killashandra pointed.

"Not at all," and it was Francu's turn to be scornful. "Merely a question of braking, using the planetary attraction, pick up the sun's gravitic pull marginally, deflect away and on to our next destination."

"How very clever of you." Killashandra winced inwardly, wondering why the man's simplest explanation evoked the worst side of her nature.

"You must realize, Guild Member, how tight the schedule is. I was informed that mounting the crystal takes no more than six minutes. We shall need every spare second available to get you to and away from these installation points—particularly at the planet. You do understand the spatial considerations?"

"It has always seemed essentially simple when expertly and efficiently handled, Captain Francu. I'm sure there'll be no problem." Six minutes. That gave her quite a safety margin, or had Trag in mind the lethargy that would soon overcome her? She gazed at the dimensional tank, smiling diffidently. Problem was, if she took less than six minutes installing at one point, it still wouldn't affect her arrival at the next one. "Thank you, Captain. May I have updated printout as we near each installation point?"

"Certainly. You will be given eighteen minutes warning before each shuttle run."

"As much as that?" Again, Killashandra was reacting to Francu's grating manner.

"Ah, yes, I have to take the crystal from the super's locked room."

"Really, Captain, no one will steal it in Trundimoux space and, until all the elements are installed, they are quite harmless. The container can be webbed in at the shuttle lock for easier access now and give you that much more time to spare."

Captain Francu's anxiety about crystal itself warred with his time factors. He accorded her a stiff bow and turned resolutely back to contemplation of his dimensional tank.

"Close to first objective and give me a deviation check."

"How long before the first objective, Captain?"

"Five hours, six minutes, and thirty-six seconds, Guild Member."

Killashandra moved away from the tank, her place quickly taken by those she had ousted. She nodded to Tic, and the subbie, with an air of intense relief, hurried to guide her away from the bridge.

She would have liked to stay and watch the cruiser angle toward the first mining station, a delicate and tedious affair since four dimensions—five, really, if one considered the captain's obsession with the time factor—were involved.

Six minutes in which to cement or change the attitudes of an entire system, six minutes five times gave her exactly one-half hour prime time. Killashandra smiled to herself. The Trundimoux system had traditions already. She'd add to them an extrastellar treat. She'd alter Francu's plan merely to slip in and slip out to a significant occasion that should be one of the greatest rejoicing for the Trundimoux—they could talk with each other: surely a moment for ceremony rather than secrecy. Six minutes wasn't much time. She would see to it that it was enough, and a whole new mass of rumor about Crystal Singers would circulate.

Trundimoux clothing was wildly colored, and bits of metal were woven into the fabric to refract whatever light was available. Even the life-support units blazed with color, shocking oranges and vibrant pinks. Offensive as such hues were to Killashandra, they served a purpose for the Trundimoux space-bred population.

While the cruiser jockeyed toward its first destination, the mining station named Copper, she created her costume. Black for the crystal she would carry: black and flowing to stand out against the gaudy Trundimoux in their tight-fitting garb. She wished for some of the cosmetics she had abandoned in her student cubicle at Fuerte, but she was tall enough to stand out, in black, her hair loose to her shoulder blades, unusual enough in a society of space-goers with shaved or clipped hair.

Six minutes! That time bothered her even though she

had mounted the mock crystals in far less. Then she re-membered. *Crystal* was what she would be handling. She could get lost in touching crystal. She might, at that, be grateful to Francu and his neat slots of time. She could count on him to break a crystal trance. But she mustn't fall into one. *That* would spoil the image she wished to create.

She worried about that problem until Tallaf arrived to escort her.

"Cutter's ready and waiting, ma'am," he said, alertly poised and very formal.

"And the crystal?"

Tallaf cleared his throat; his eyes avoided hers, although she rather thought that the young man was amused.

"Supercargo Pendel has conveyed the container to the lock, awaiting your arrival. All webbed and secure."

Indeed the carton was, with a double row of alert guards standing as far from the crystal as they could in the con-fines of the lock. The sides and bottom of the carton were webbed securely to the deck, but the top had been un-sealed. One of the guards carried a seal-gun on his belt.

Killashandra strode forward, remembering to keep her full skirts clear of her toes.

"Open it," she said to no one in particular. There was a brief hesitation, then Pendel performed that office, winking at her surreptitiously.

To her intense relief, the five crystals had been cocooned before shipment. She did not need to handle raw crystal until she reached the actual installation point. She picked up the small package, feeling the mild shock with a double sense of relief. Crystal knew she was there and responded but bided its time. And this was real crystal. She'd had a sudden horrid thought that, in a crazy set of errors, the mock shafts had been sent instead.

She held the package straight-armed before her as she walked to the cutter's entrance. No sooner was she seated than everyone seemed to move at double speed, webbing her in, taking their own places as the hatch was sealed. She was forced back into her cushions by the acceleration away from the cruiser.

"Are we running behind time, Tallaf?" she asked.

"No, ma'am, precisely *on* time."

"How far from the station lock to the communications room?"

"Exactly five minutes and twenty seconds."

"In free-fall?" Free-fall in this gown would be ridiculous. She wished she'd thought of that aspect before.

Tallaf looked surprised.

"All but the very small detector units have gravity, ma'am."

The cutter fired retrorockets, again pushing her into the cushions.

"I thought we were on time."

"We are, ma'am, but we're correcting to match velocities."

A second spate of jockeying occurred, but the actual docking was no more than a cousinly kiss. The deck crew was again working double time, and infected by their pace, she rose and entered the first of the mining stations. The five minutes and twenty seconds of travel time within Copper was spent twisting down corridors and jumping over security frames. She prided herself on managing all the awkward bits without stumbling or losing her balance, the cocoon of crystal held before her so that all could see. And many people were gathered at intersections wanting a glimpse of the momentous occasion.

It is a shame, Killashandra thought as she was ushered into the communications nerve center of the Copper Station, that this was not the linkage point. Nothing really exciting would happen here or on the other stations until the final shaft was fitted and their bonding would produce the instantaneous link.

Still, she was conscious of stares, hostile and thoughtful, as she was directed to the installation point. It was on the raised outer level of the huge room, an excellent vantage.

Killashandra mounted the shallow steps, her quick glance checking the brackets to be sure they were correct, and then turned to the center of the area. She stripped the plastic from the cocoon and held up the dull, muddy shaft. She heard the gasps as the assembled saw for the first time what they had mortgaged their system to buy. Even as she heard their mumble, the crystal warmed in her hands, turning the matte black, which gave it its name. It vibrated against her hands, and before she could fall in trance, she whirled and laid the crystal in its place. The pressure arms moved silkily at her light touch. She brought the upper brackets to bear and, one finger on the still darkening crystal, increased the pressure on each side carefully. The crystal began to resonate along her finger, making her throat ache. She fought the desire to caress the crystal and made her hands complete the installation. As if burned, she snatched her hands back from the beautiful crystal mass. She took the small hammer and tapped the mounted crystal. Its pure note sang through the room's sudden hush.

Head high, she strode from the chamber, Tallaf running to get ahead of her, to lead her back to the cutter through the station's twists and turns.

Each step took her farther from the crystal, and she twisted with the pain of that separation. Another small matter no one had explained to her before: that it would be so difficult to leave crystal she had herself cut.

The brief ride to the cruiser did ease that pain. And so did the lethargy that slowly overcame her. It couldn't, she decided, be fatigue from that little bit of dramatization. It must be the sleepies that she'd been warned about. Conjunction was very near. Fortunately, she managed to stay awake until she reached her quarters.

"Tic, if I am disturbed for any reason whatsoever before the next station, I'll dismember the person! Understood? And pass that on to Pendel just to make sure."

"Yes, ma'am." Tic was trustworthy, and Pendel had authority.

Killashandra slid sideways onto the hard bunk, pulled the thin cover over her, and slept.

It seemed no time at all before a thumping and Tac's anxious voice called her politely but insistently.

"I'm coming. The next station has been reached?" She swallowed the stimulant, forced her eyes wide in an attempt to appear alert as she opened the door.

Tallaf was there with a tray of food, which she imperiously waved away.

"You'll need some refreshment, Killashandra," the young officer said, concern overcoming his previous formality.

"Are we at the next station?"

"I thought you'd need something to eat first."

She reached for the Yarran beer, trying not to exhibit the revulsion she felt at the smell of what once would have been a tempting meal. Even the beer tasted wrong.

"I'll just take this in my room," she said, closing the door panel and wondering if the nausea was due to the pill, the beer, her symbiont, or nerves. She made illicit use of drinking water and splattered her face. The effect was salutary. Without a qualm, she poured the Yarran beer down the waste disposal. Pendel would never know.

Tallaf rapped at her door panel again. This time, Killashandra was alert; the stimulant had taken effect. She swept forward, secure in the false energy and aware that more of the cruiser's crew were in evidence as she made her way to the lock.

Pendel was unlashing the top of the crystal carton, stepping back to give her space to extract the next crystal. Holding it at arm's length in front of her, Killashandra was congratulating herself on her smooth routine when she tripped getting over the cutter's hatch. She'd best raise the skirt a trifle in front before the first moon installation. However, no one had noticed her slight gracelessness, and she settled down for the ride.

Station Iron was larger than Station Copper but as haphazardly contrived as far as companionways, hatches, and corridors were concerned.

"This is more than five minutes twenty seconds, Tallaf," she said in a stern voice of complaint, wondering how long the stimutab lasted.

"Just in here, now."

Communications obviously rated more unfragmented space than any other of the stations' functions. And the larger station was reflected in the larger crowd that crammed into the area. Killashandra stripped the cocoon from the black crystal, held it up for all to see, and deposited it deftly in its position before it could woo her from her duties. Or maybe the stimulant helped counteract crystal's effect. Nonetheless, Killashandra still experienced the pain of leaving behind her forever the shaft of darkening crystal.

The stimulant kept her functioning on the slightly longer swing to catch up with the cruiser. She graciously accepted Pendel's offer of Yarran beer but, once alone, poured it down the drain. She squandered a day's water ration to quench her thirst and reached her bunk before sleep again overtook her.

It was harder for her to wake up when Tic roused her at the first moon. One stimulant kept her awake on the outbound trip, a second got her through the installation, but Tallaf had to wake her to disembark at the cruiser. Pendel insisted she eat something, though she could barely keep her eyes open. She did have soup and some succulent fruit since her mouth was dry and her skin felt parched. She ached for the crystal she had consigned forever to an airless moon.

Three stimulants roused her sufficiently for the fourth installation, and she had to sneak one into her mouth as she set the crystal in its brackets. She was doing her high priestess routine by reflex, only peripherally aware of the blur of faces that followed her every movement and the thrilled sigh as the crystal's pure note sounded in the communications room.

One thing she could say for the Trundimoux, when they found an efficient structure, they kept repeating it. All the communications rooms were of the same design. Blind, she could have found her way to the crystal mounting. Walking back, she kept tripping on the skirt hem she'd not had time to alter. Then Tallaf put one arm under hers. She concentrated on smiling serenely at the assembled until she had reached the cutter. She collapsed with relief into her seat.

"You're all right, Killashandra?" Tallaf was asking.

"Just tired. You've no idea how difficult it is to surrender crystal you've cut yourself. They cry when you leave them. Let me sleep."

But for that chance remark to Tallaf, Killashandra might have been forced to endure the ministrations of Chasurt, for her alternate periods of intense vivacity and somnolence had not gone unremarked. Nor were the opponents of the crystal communications purchase impressed by small unscintillating blocks received in exchange for massive drone loads of high-quality metals.

The moment he had seen Killashandra safely to her cabin, Tallaf had a word with Pendel. Pendel spoke quickly to others, and Chasurt was summoned to deal with a minor epidemic of food poisoning, investigate two other illnesses that required lengthy tests, and then was required to consult, at ordinary space-message exchange pauses, on a serious space-burn casualty.

Killashandra was roused for the longer shuttle flight to the planet's surface for the final installation. The extended sleep had been beneficial, and although she ran nervous fingers over the short length of stimulant tabs remaining, Killashandra thought she could defer their use. She accepted the fruit and glucose drink Pendel offered her, though she would dearly have loved water, even the stale recycled water the cruiser supplied.

She felt equal to this final scene until she saw the crystal container. Abruptly, she realized that this largest piece would be the hardest to surrender. She didn't dare have it on her lap all during the journey to the planet's surface.

"Bring the container on board. The king crystal will be safer that way," she said, curtly gesturing. She entered the shuttle before anyone could countermand her instruction.

Pendel and Tallaf hastily motioned the guard to comply, and the container was already aboard the shuttle, webbed tight, before Captain Francu arrived. He stopped abruptly, stared with rage and shock at the carton, then at Killashandra who smiled pleasantly at him.

"You carried the other crystals, Guild Member—"

"Ah, but this is a longer journey, captain, and unless that crystal is *safely* installed in your main communications room, all the others are useless and this voyage of your cruiser an exercise in futility."

"Captain, the time factors—" Tallaf stepped forward, his expression one of cautious concern.

Francu set his jaw, edged past the crystal to the stern of the cutter. She could hear the crack of metal tabs as he webbed himself in. She supposed that she was lucky that, in his current frame of mind, Francu wasn't the pilot.

The shuttle disengaged itself from the cruiser, seemed to hang suspended as the cruiser moved obliquely away from it. Actually, before the view ports were closed, Killashandra realized that the shuttle had done all the moving: the cruiser was inexorably set in its direction, and nothing would deter it.

She had meant to stay awake, but the scream and heat of entry into the planet's atmosphere roused her from another irresistible snooze. She stared about, momentarily startled by the unfamiliar surroundings. Hastily, she swallowed two stimutabs, smiling serenely around as if she had only been conserving her energy.

The shuttle had been brought to a complete halt before the medicine took effect, and she debated taking a third as the hatch was being opened.

A landing platform appeared at once, and from her seat, she could see the vast crowd assembled on both sides of a wide aisle leading to the huge communications building with its roof clusters of dish antennas, tilted like caps to the sky, caps raised to salute their own obsolescence.

"The crystal, Guild Member!" Francu's acid voice reminded her, too, of this final surrender.

She flipped open the carton and removed the king crystal, took a deep breath, and walked down the landing ramp, holding the crystal before her. She always played best to a full house, she reminded herself. The other installations were only rehearsals for this one.

The fresh air of the planet was naturally scented and crisp. She breathed in deeply and would not be hurried in this ceremonial walk.

Francu appeared at one side, Tallaf at her other, both muttering about walking faster.

"It's so good to breathe uncontaminated air. My lungs have been stifled. I must breathe."

"You must walk faster," Francu said, a smile jiggling his cheeks as he responded nervously to the presence of a large crowd of people in an open space greater than his huge new cruiser.

"If you can, Killashandra. We've a time boggle," said Tallaf, his voice anxious.

"They're all here to see the crystal," Killashandra noted, but she lengthened her stride, holding the cocoon above her head, hearing the surprise wave of exclamations, seeing the nearest drawing back. Was the crowd here to see crystal succeed, she wondered, or fail? This was not a receptive audience! She'd faced enough to sense the animosity and fear.

She strode on to the building's entrance, slightly outdistancing the two spacemen.

"We will have to hurry this, Guild Member," a man said, taking her arm as she passed the doorway.

"Yes, we will, or we can't be responsible for your safety."

She heard heavy metal doors thud shut behind her and a muffled noise emanating from outside and becoming louder.

"I've been given to understand that this project is not universally favored, gentlemen. But one message sent and received will disperse that . . ." and she indicated the crowd which had pressed in about the building.

"This way, Guild Member."

They were all almost running now, and she was annoyed that the urgency of the situation was going to ruin her performance. Ridiculous! How absurd to be put in such a position! Especially when she was possessed of an overwhelming desire to go to sleep again. She shoved the crystal into the crook of one arm—there was no one to impress with her theatrics in this hurry—and managed to stuff two more tabs into her mouth.

Then she was whirled into the main chamber of the immense building, where nervous technicians were more interested in the outward-facing security scanners than the printouts and displays common to their business.

"Do hurry with this one, Killashandra," Tallaf urged as she took the last few steps to the raised level and the empty niche where the king crystal would be mounted.

She stripped the plastic away with nervous fingers and suddenly found serenity and surcease as the bared crystal caressed her skin.

"Hurry!" Francu exhorted her. "If that thing won't give us a message from Copper—"

Killashandra withered him with a glance, but her dislike of him broke the tenuous enchantment she had been hoping to enjoy. Now she heard the noise of the crowd, the increasing pitch of its excitement and frustration. She dare not delay the mounting. Nor did she want to relinquish her black crystal to this system of ignorant savages, this society of metal-mongerers, this—

The black crystal was mounted, turning matte black as it responded to the heat of the room.

"Hurry!" "Has something gone wrong?" "It won't work!"

"Of course, crystal will sing," said Killashandra, raising the little hammer and striking the king block.

The rich full A of the king crystal rang through the large room, silencing the irreverent babble. Killashandra was transfixed. The A became the louder note of the five-crystal chord, the two F and two E crystals singing back to her through the king. The human voice cannot produce chords. With the pitch of the A dominant in her head, that was the note that burst from Killashandra as the shock of establishing the link between the five crystals enveloped her. Sound like a shock wave, herself the sound and the sounding board, vision over vision, a fire in her bones, thunder in her veins, a heart-contracting experience of pain and pleasure so intense and so total that every nerve in her body and every convolution of her brain echoed. The chord held Killashandra in a thrall more absolute than her first experience of crystal. Sustaining the note despite the agony of the physical mechanics of breath, Killashandra was simultaneously in the communications rooms of the two mining stations and the two moons. She splintered in sound from one crystal block to the next, apart and indissoluble, a fragment of the first message sent and instantly received and forever divorced from it.

"Copper to home. Copper to home base!" She knew the message, for it passed through her as well as the crystal. She heard the exultant reply and the incredulous response to its simultaneity. She had cut the crystals for this purpose, she had borne them to their various sites, and she had condemned them to sing for others. No one had told her they would cause her to sing through them in a space-crossing chord!

"Killashandra?" Someone touched her, and she cried out. Flesh upon flesh broke her awesome communion with the crystal link. She fell to her knees, too bereft to cry, too stunned to resist.

"Killashandra!" Someone raised her to her feet.

She could feel crystal power singing behind her through the king block, but she was forever excluded from its thrall.

"Get her back to the shuttle."

"Is it *safe*?"

"Of course, it's safe. The link works! The whole system knows that now!"

"Through this door, lieutenant. You'll have to detour. The crowd is blocking your way to the shuttle."

"We don't have time to detour."

"We'll break through the crowd. Carry her first. That'll make them give way!"

"They can't be afraid of a woman!"

"She's not a woman. She's a Crystal Singer!"

Killashandra was aware of being carried through a dense crowd. She heard a rapid clattering, and loud but jubilant cries and, somewhere in the section of her brain that recorded impressions, she correlated sound and cheers with applause. So many people in such proximity was an unexpected torture.

"Get me out of here," she whispered hoarsely, clutching the man who carried her with desperate hands.

He said nothing but quickened his pace, his breathing ragged with effort. He could barely disentangle himself from her when a second man came to his assistance.

"This delay may abort the whole intercept."

"Captain, we'd no idea how feelings ran here. No warning that there'd be such a crowd. We're almost there now."

"If we've lost the window—"

"We'll have a frigate standing by ready to catch up—"

"Do shut up and let me sleep. Stop joggling me so."

"Sleep?" The indignation in Francu's voice roused her briefly from her torpor. "Sleep she wants when—"

"Just settle yourself in this seat, Killashandra. I'll do the webbing."

"Drink. Need a drink. Anything. Water."

"Not now. Not now."

"Yes, now! I thirst."

"Captain, you fly. Here's water, Killashandra."

She drank deeply, aware that the substance was water, real water, crisp, clear, cool water, used only this once, for her consumption. Some of it spilled when she was jolted about, and she protested the loss, licking it from her hands. She was shoved away from the water by a tremendous force and pleaded to be given more to drink.

She was soothed, and then finally the weight was lifted, and she was given as much as she wanted to drink.

"Are you all right now, Killashandra?" She rather thought it was Tallaf asking.

"Yes. Now all I need is sleep. Just let me sleep until I wake."

CHAPTER 13

Waking up was a gradual and remarkably languorous process. Killashandra felt that she was unfolding in sections, starting with her mind, which sent out sleepy messages to her extremities that movement was possible again. She went through a long series of stretchings and yawnings, interspersed with rather wild and vivid flashes. At first, she thought them pico-dreams but then realized that all were from one viewpoint: hers! And she was overwhelmed by faces and applause and light flashing from the blackening crystal. An orgasmic sensation in her loins completed her unfolding and brought her to sharp consciousness and regret. Those half dreams had been lovely echoes of the linkage with black crystal.

Crystal! She sat up in bed and nearly caught her head on the bedside shelf. She was on the wretched cruiser! She glanced at her wrist-unit, confirming it with the cabin time display.

"Three days! I've been asleep three days!" Antona had warned her.

Killashandra lay back, easing shoulder and tightening back muscles. She must have slept all three days in one position to have such cramps.

A soft scratching at her door panel caught her attention.

"Yes?"

"Are you awake, Guild Member?"

There were several answers she would have given if she hadn't recognized Chasurt's voice.

"You may enter."

"Are you awake?"

"I certainly wouldn't be answering you in my sleep. Come in!" As the door panel slid open, she added, "And would you ask Pendel if he can supply me with something decent to eat?"

"I will ascertain if food is advisable," the man said, holding in her direction a diagnostic tool similar to Antona's.

"Not the stodge that's served in the cruiser's mess but liquid and fruit—"

"If you'll just be cooperative—"

"I am!" Killashandra felt that attitude rapidly changing. "This sort of sleep phase is perfectly normal—"

"We haven't been able to contact Ballybran for specific instructions—"

"For what?"

"Proper treatment of your prolonged coma—"

"I wasn't *in* a coma. Did you not check the printout in your own medical library? I want something to drink. And eat."

"I am the cruiser's meditech—"

"Who has never met a Crystal Singer before and knows nothing of *my* occupational hazards." Killashandra had pulled on the nearest piece of clothing, her Guild coverall. Now she swung herself off the bunk and lurched past Chasurt, who made a vain attempt to grab her. "Pendel!" Killashandra started down the corridor. She surprised herself that she could maneuver so readily after the exhaustion that had overtaken her. The symbiont might take, but it also gave.

"Guild Member!" Chasurt was in pursuit, but she had the head start and longer legs.

She turned again, into the super's corridor, and saw Tic at Pendel's door, and then his head was visible.

"Pendel? I'm perishing for a glass of Yarran beer! Please say you have some fruit left? And possibly a cup of that excellent soup you served me some time a hundred years ago?"

By the time she reached his door, Pendel handed her a half-empty glass of Yarran beer for one hand and a fruit for the other. She squeezed past him and Tic, leaving them to block Chasurt.

"There you are, Killashandra," Pendel said, standing across the doorway so that Chasurt could not barge in. Tic moved staunchly in front of Killashandra as the second line of defense. "More fruit within hand. Now, Chasurt, don't get yourself knotted. Come with me, and you can add whatever nutrients and restoratives you feel are required to the soup I'm getting Killashandra. Put those stupid sprays back into your pockets. Crystal Singers don't ordinarily require any medication. Don't you know anything beyond space-freeze and laser burn?"

Pendel hurried Chasurt away, signaling Tic to close the door and stand guard. Killashandra had finished the beer and started on the fruit. She closed her eyes with relief as juice and pulp soothed her parched mouth. She ate slowly, an instinct imposed on her by the symbiont, which knew very well what it required after fasting. With distaste, she remembered the mad hungers of pre-Passover and was grateful that the affliction had waned.

"Ma'am? . . ."

Killashandra only heard the soft whisper because there was no other sound in the cabin but her chewing.

"Tic?" It was the first time the girl had addressed her.

"Ma'am—thank you for the crystal!" Tic blurted her words. "Comofficer let me speak with my mother on Copper. Right away. No waiting. No worrying that something's gone wrong and I wouldn't hear . . . Comoff says with crystals I can call Copper any time I want!" Tic's eyes were round and liquid.

"I'm happy for you, Tic. I'm happy for you." Killashandra thought that response a little graceless on her part, but Tic's awed response embarrassed her.

The panel was suddenly whipped aside, and Tic tried not to fall into Killashandra's lap as Captain Francu, radiating fury, stood in the opening.

"My medic tells me that you have refused his assistance."
The cubicle was too small for his oppressive manner.

"I do not need his assistance. I am a Crystal Singer—"

"While you are on board my vessel, you are under my orders—"

Killashandra rose, pushing Tic into the seat she had vacated, facing the captain with a wrath far more profound than his. From her thigh pouch, she produced the Guild ident and shoved it at the captain.

"Even you must recognize this authority!"

Pendel arrived at that moment, carrying a laden tray.

"Federated Sentient Planet Sessions authority!" Pendel gasped as he read, and the tray wavered in his grasp. "I've only seen one other."

"You are clearly suffering from aberrant behavior following a period of deprivation—" the captain began.

"Nonsense. Hand me that tray, Pendel. Thank you."

"Guild Member, attend me!"

"I am, but I'm also eating, as my body needs sustenance after my long rest."

"You were in coma—"

"I was doing what all Crystal Singers do, resting after a difficult and exhausting assignment. And that is all I wish to say until I've eaten."

"You are mentally affected, shoving an FSP authority at me to obtain food." Captain Francu was sputtering now.

"That authority will be invoked as soon as I find out the nearest transfer station—"

"You are to remain on this cruiser until the Five Systems' Satellite—"

"I will remain on this cruiser only as long as it takes me to call up a shuttle or cutter or gig from the next system. And my authority permits me to do so. Right?"

"Right," Pendel affirmed.

The captain glared at him and stared for a moment longer at Killashandra, speechless with suppressed anger. Then he turned on one heel and stamped down the corridor.

Tic was regarding Killashandra in white-faced perturbation.

"That's all right, now, girl," Pendel said to her soothingly. "You will, of course, discuss this with no one no matter how you are pressed. I don't think Captain Francu will care to remember the incident."

"How soon can I get off this ship? No offense to you and Tic, of course."

Pendel edged himself in front of his keyboard and tapped a code. It took longer than usual for the display to start rippling across the screen, and there were only four lines.

"I wouldn't suggest that one. Drone tanker and primitive food supplies." Pendel tapped again. The printout was denser. "Ah. We can arrange a transfer to a small but adequate changeover station for a Selkite direct to Scoria. Ordinarily, I wouldn't recommend Selkites for any reason, but you'd be the only passenger in their oxygen life-support section."

"Grand! I'll take it."

"Means another three days aboard us."

"I'll sleep a good deal of the time. Light meals when I need 'em."

"There's just one thing," and Pendel cleared his throat, ducking his head from her glance. "The Selkite reaches Ballybran just toward the end of the Passover storms. The original E.T.A. would land you well after they'd completed."

"Oh, you've been doing some retrieving, have you?" Killashandra grinned.

Pendel winked, laying his finger along his nose. "I did feel some objective information a wise precaution."

"So Chasurt decided the storms produced my mental aberrations?"

"Some such conclusion."

"No fool goes out in Passover storms. We leave the planet if at all possible. If not, sleep through it!"

"I had heard the rumor that Crystal Singers hibernated."

"Something of the sort."

"Well, well. Have another Yarran beer, Killashandra?"

Whatever caused Pendel such satisfaction, he preferred to keep to himself, but they enjoyed several glasses until

drowsiness overcame her again. Pendel escorted her back
to her cabin where Tac stood very much on duty. Small
light meals were arranged, and Killashandra lay down to
sleep, fervently blessing the forethought that had provided
her with the FSP authority. And what had Francu intended to do with her if he had managed to overrule her?
Give her to Chasurt to find out why Crystal Singers are
different?

She wasn't well pleased to have to spend a few more
days on the cruiser, but she could sleep and relax, now that
the pressures of installation were behind her. And she had
completed those well. Trag would be pleased with her.
Even if some percentage of the Trundimoux were not. Pity
about that!

Still, they'd given her a big hand. She'd knocked herself
out to give them a new tradition. Her performance at the
planet installation had turned an angry mob into a jubilant
throng. Yes, she'd done well as a Crystal Singer.

Would she ever again be able to experience that incredible surge of contact as black crystal segments linked? That
all-enveloping surge as if she were aligned with every black
crystal in the galaxy?

She shuddered with the aching desire. She turned from
that thought. There would be other such times; of that she
was now certain. Meanwhile, once the storms of Ballybran
were over, she could sing crystal.

Sing crystal? Sing?

Killashandra began to laugh, recalling herself as she
strode into the planetary communications building, stage
center with a near riot occurring around her. She, playing
the high priestess, completing the ritual that linked the
isolated elements of the Trundimoux! A solo performance
if ever there was one. And she had played before an audience of an entire system. What an opening note she had
struck with crystal! What an ovation! Echoes from distant
satellites. She had done exactly as she had once boasted
she'd do, had arrogantly proclaimed to her peers in Fuerte
that she would do. She had been the first Singer in this
system and possibly the only Crystal Singer ever to appear
in Trundimoux.

Killashandra laughed at the twisted irony of circumstance. She laughed and then cried because there was no one to know except herself that she had achieved an ambition.

Killashandra Ree was a Singer, right enough. Truly a Crystal Singer!

Reprise

"**W**hat are you doing back now?" the lock attendant demanded as she entered. "Wough? What sort of transport were you on? You reek."

"Selkite," Killashandra said grimly. She had become used to her own fragrance within the Selkite's O-breather quarters.

"There's some ships no one will travel on. Pity you weren't warned." He was pinching his nostrils closed.

"I'll remember, I assure you."

She started for the Guild's transient quarters.

"Hey, there's vo vacancies. Passover storms aren't over yet, you know."

"I know, but getting here was more important than waiting the storms out."

"Not if you had to travel Selkite. But there's plenty of space in the regular quarters," and the man thumbed the archway that she had entered so naively a few months before. "No travelers here yet. Doesn't make any difference with your credit where you stay, you know."

Killashandra thanked him and walked on through the blue-irised entrance toward the hostel, trying to remember the girl she'd been at that point and unable to credit how much had occurred since then. Including the simultaneous realization of two ambitions.

The aroma she exuded alerted Ford, still at his reception counter.

"But you're a Singer. You oughtn't to be here." His nose wrinkled, and he shuddered, licking his lips. "Singers have their own quarters."

"Full up. Just give me a room and let me fumigate myself."

Killashandra advanced to the counter to put her wrist unit to the plate.

"No, no, that won't be necessary!" Ford handed her the key, his arm stretching out to keep as much distance from her as possible.

"I know I'm bad, but am I that bad?"

Ford tried to stammer an apology, but Killashandra let the key guide her to her quarters.

"I've given you the biggest we have." Ford's voice followed her through the hallway.

The room was down a level, and assuming that the lock attendant had been correct—that there were no visitors at that time—Killashandra began ripping off her stinking clothes. The key warmed at the appropriate room, and she shoved through the panel, shutting it and leaning against the door to shuck off her pants and footwear. She looked at the carisak and decided there was no point in fumigating those things. She stuffed everything into the disposal unit with a tremendous sense of relief.

The Shankill accommodation had only shower facilities but a decent array of herb and fragrance washes. She stood under the jets, as hot as the spray would come, then laved herself until her skin was raw. She stepped out of the shower enclosure, smelling her hands and her shoulders, bending to sniff her knees, and decided that she was possibly close to decontaminated.

It was only drying her hair that she realized she didn't have any fresh clothes to put on. She dialed the commissary and ordered the first coverall that appeared on the fax, then keyed for perfumes and ordered a large bottle of something spicy. She needed some spice in her life after the Selkite vessel. Well, Pendel had tried to warn her. Come to consider, even the Selkites were better than remaining in the vicinity of Francu or that bonehead Chasurt.

Then she remembered to take out her lenses and sighed with relief as color, decent soothing color, sprang up around the room.

She ordered a Yarran beer and wondered how Lanzecki had weathered Passover. Immured by herself in the Selkite ship, she had come to terms with lingering feelings of resentment for the Guild Master and wanted very much to continue in friendship with the man. Solitude was a great leveler: stinking solitude made one grateful for remembered favors and kindness. She owed Lanzecki more of those than accusations.

The beer was so good! She lifted her beaker in a toast to Pendel. She hoped that for every Francu she met, there would be at least one Pendel to be grateful for.

The door chime sounded. She wrapped a dry towel around her, wondering why her order was being delivered instead of sent by tube. She released the door lock and was about to slide the panel back when it was moved from without.

"What are you doing back here?" Lanzecki stepped into the room, looming angrily above her in the narrow confines. He closed the panel behind him and lobbed a parcel in the direction of the bed.

"What are you doing on Shankill?" She tried to tighten the towel above her breasts.

He brought both hands to his belt and stared at her, his eyes glittering, his face set in the most uncompromising lines, his mouth still.

"Shankill affords the most strategic point from which to assess the storm flows."

"Then you do escape from the storms," she said with intense relief.

"As I wanted you to escape them, but you're back here days early!" He swept an angry gesture with one arm as if he wanted to strike her.

"Why not?" Killashandra had to stand her ground before him. "I'd finished the wretched installations. Were the storms as bad as predicted? I've heard nothing."

"You were scheduled to return on a comfortable passenger frigate seven days from now." He scrutinized her closely. "The damage could have been worse," he added grudgingly. She wasn't sure whether he referred to her or the storms.

"I took the Selkite freighter."

"I'm aware of that." His nostrils flared with distaste.

"I've tried to decontaminate. It was awful. Why wasn't I told about Selkites? No, I was, but I wouldn't listen because I couldn't stay one more moment on that fardling Trundie cruiser." The towel was coming loose as she remembered Francu. "Why didn't you at least warn me about the Trundies?"

Lanzecki shrugged. "We didn't have much on them, but you at least had no preconceptions or the residue of partial memories of other isolated systems to prejudice your actions."

"They may never deal with another Crystal Singer."

"They'll deal with the Guild." Lanzecki was smiling, his body relaxing, his eyes warming.

"More important, Lanzecki"—and she tried to step back, away from him until she'd aired her grievances— "why didn't you tell me about link-shock? I sang the king crystal, link and all, and they brought me to my knees."

"Link-shock's about the only thing that would." He put his warm hands on her shoulders and held her firmly, his eyes examining her face. "No one can describe link-shock. It's experienced on different levels by different personalities. To warn is to inhibit."

"I can certainly appreciate that!"

He chuckled at her sarcastic comment and began to draw her to him, his embrace as much of an apology as he was ever likely to give her.

"Some people feel nothing at all."

"I'm sorry for them." She was not sarcastic now.

"For you, Killashandra, to link a set of crystals you yourself cut binds you closer to black crystal." He spoke slowly, again with the hidden pain that she had once before heard in his voice. She let herself be drawn against his strong body, realizing how keenly she had missed him even as she had damned him, grateful now to give and receive comfort. "The Guild needs black-crystal Singers."

"Is that why you've personally guided my career, Lanzecki?" She reached her hand to his lips, feeling them curve in amusement.

"My professional life is dedicated to the Guild, Killashandra. Never forget that. My personal life is another matter, entirely private." His lips moved sensuously across her fingers as he spoke.

"I like you, Lanzecki—damn your mouth." She bubbled with laughter and the joy of being with him again.

He took her hand and kissed the palm, the contact sending chills through her body.

"In the decades ahead of us, Killashandra, *try* to keep that in mind?"

ABOUT THE AUTHOR

Born on April 1, Anne McCaffrey has tried to live up to such an auspicious natal day. Her first novel was created in Latin class and might have brought her instant fame, as well as an A, had she attempted to write in the language. Much chastened, she turned to the stage and became a character actress, appearing in the first successful summer music circus at Lambertsville, New Jersey. She studied voice for nine years and, during that time, became intensely interested in the stage direction of opera and operetta, ending this phase of her life with the stage direction of the American premiere of Carl Orff's *Ludus De Nato Infante Mirificus*, in which she also played a witch.

By the time the three children of her marriage were comfortably at school most of the day, she had already achieved enough success with short stories to devote full time to writing.

Between appearances at conventions around the world, Ms. McCaffrey lives at Dragonhold, in the hills of Wicklow County, Ireland, with three cats, two dogs, and assorted horses. Of herself, Ms. McCaffrey says, "I have green eyes, silver hair, and freckles: the rest changes without notice."

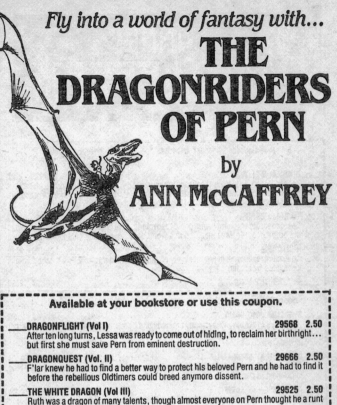